High Praise for Carolyn Brown

HOME OF THE HEART

CAROLYN BROWN

FOREVER
New York Boston

Copyright © 2015 by Carolyn Brown
Buttercup Farms copyright © 2022 by Carolyn Brown

Cover design by Sarah Congdon. Cover photography © Shutterstock. Cover copyright ©2022 by Hachette Book Group, Inc.

Forever
Hachette Book Group
1290 Avenue of the Americas New York, NY 10104
read-forever.com
twitter.com/readforeverpub

Home of the Heart was originally published in 2015 as a Forever mass market called *Wild Cowboy Ways*

First trade paperback edition: December 2022

Forever is an imprint of Grand Central Publishing. The Forever name and logo are trademarks of Hachette Book Group, Inc.

The publisher is not responsible for websites (or their content) that are not owned by the publisher.

The Hachette Speakers Bureau provides a wide range of authors for speaking events. To find out more, go to www.hachettespeakersbureau.com or call (866) 376-6591.

Library of Congress Control Number: 2022944387

ISBN: 978-1-5387-2402-6 (trade paperback)

Printed in the United States of America

LSC-C

Printing 1, 2022

To Leah Hultenschmidt
Behind every author is a brilliant editor.
Thank you for everything.

Acknowledgments

I'm so excited to have the opportunity to revise and update *Wild Cowboy Ways*. I hope you enjoy this new version, *Home of the Heart*.

A big thank-you to all my readers who continue to support me by reading my books—both new and revised—by telling your neighbors about them, for writing reviews, for sharing them with your friends, and everything else that you do. Without readers, there would be no need for authors, so y'all really are the wind beneath my wings.

Until next time, may love surround you and your life be filled with happy-ever-afters!

Carolyn Brown

HOME OF THE HEART

CHAPTER ONE

The Lucky Penny had never lived up to its name, and everyone in Texas knew it. Owners had come and gone so often in the past hundred years that if the deeds were stacked up, they'd put the old Sears catalog to shame. Maybe the two sections of land should have been called Bad Luck Ranch instead of the Lucky Penny, but Blake Dawson couldn't complain—not for the price he, his brother, and his cousin had paid for the place.

A cold north wind cut through Blake's fleece-lined denim jacket that January morning as he hammered the bottom porch step into place. The wind was a bitch, but then it was winter, the first Monday in January to be exact. And that robin out there pecking around in the dead grass sure didn't mean spring was on the way. No, sir, there would be a couple of months of cold weather. If they were lucky, they wouldn't have to deal with snow and ice. But Blake wouldn't hold his breath wishing for that. After all, when had anything in this place been lucky? Besides, in this part of Texas, weather could change from sunny and seventy to blustery and brutal with a foot of snow within twenty-four hours.

He finished hammering down the last nail, stood up straight, and stretched. Done. It was the first job of too many to count, but he sure didn't need someone falling through that rotted step and getting hurt. His dog, Shooter, had watched from the top of the four steps, his eyes blinking with every stroke of the hammer.

Shooter's ears shot straight up, and he growled down deep in his throat. Blake looked around for a pesky squirrel taunting him, but there was nothing but the north wind rattling through the dormant tree branches. Blake gathered his tools and headed back into the house for another cup of hot coffee before he started his first day of dozing mesquite from the ranch.

Clear the land. Plow it. Rake it. Plant it and hope for a good crop of hay so they wouldn't have to buy feed all winter. His brother Toby would bring in the first round of cattle in early June. Blake had promised to have pastures ready and fences tightened up by then. Meanwhile, Toby would be finishing his contract for a big rancher. His cousin, Jud, would be joining them, too. But he was committed to an oil company out in the panhandle until Thanksgiving. So it was up to Blake to get the groundwork laid for their dream cattle ranch.

He shucked out of his coat, hung it on the rack inside the front door, and went straight to the kitchen. Sitting at the table, he wrapped his big hands around the warm mug. He was deep in thought about clearing acres and acres of mesquite when he heard the rusty hinge squeak as the front door eased open. He pushed back the chair, making enough noise to let anyone know that the house was no longer empty, when he heard the shrill, muffled giggle.

Surely folks in Dry Creek knocked before they plowed right

into a person's home. Maybe it was a prank, kind of like an initiation into the town, or a bunch of wild kids who had no idea that the ranch had been sold. Whatever was going on, either his instincts had failed him or else his neck was still too cold to get that prickly feeling when someone was close by.

Shooter, who had been lying under the table at his feet, now stood erect and staring at the doorway. Blake would give the joker one more chance before he let him know he was messing with the wrong cowboy.

"Who's there?" he called out.

"Don't play games with me, Walter." The voice was thin and tinny and definitely not a teenager.

"And who are you?" he asked.

"Don't be silly. You know who I am, Walter." The voice got closer and closer.

What was going on?

Back in the summer when the Lucky Penny went on the market, Blake, Toby, and Jud decided that they didn't believe in all that folderol about bad luck. The Lucky Penny's previous owners clearly just hadn't put enough blood, sweat, and tears into the land, or it would have been a productive ranch. They hadn't understood what it took to get a place that size up and running and/or didn't have the patience and perseverance to stick it out until there was a profit. But now Blake was beginning to question whether the bad luck had something to do with the supernatural.

He scooted his chair back and stood, Shooter close at his side, hackles up and his head lowered. Blake laid a hand on the dog's head. "Sit, boy, and don't move unless I give you the command." Shooter obeyed, but he quivered with anticipation.

"Walter, darlin', where is she?" If it wasn't a ghost, then

whatever mortal it was with that voice should audition for a part in a zombie movie.

Before Blake could call out a response, a gray-haired woman shuffled into the kitchen. The lady had to be flesh and blood because no self-respecting ghost or apparition would be caught anywhere looking like that. She wore a long, hot-pink chenille robe belted at the waist with a wide leather belt, yellow rubber boots printed with hot pink flamingos, and her thin hair looked like she'd stuck her finger in an electrical outlet. The wild look in her eyes gave testimony that her hair wasn't the only thing that got fried when she tested the electricity that morning. He felt a sneeze coming on as the scent of her heavy perfume filled the room.

"Aaaaachoo." He grabbed a paper napkin from the middle of the table in time to cover his mouth, when it burst from him like a bomb.

"I hope you're not getting sick, Walter," she said as she marched across the room, grabbed his cheeks with her cold hands, and pulled his face down to kiss him on the cheek. "Katy's wedding is coming up, and I don't want a red nose and puffy eyes."

"Of course not. Just a tickle in my nose, that's all." Best thing he could think to do was play along until he was able to find who the woman was talking about.

The woman hung her cane on the edge of the table and plopped into a chair. When she sat down, the tail of her robe fell back to show that she was wearing jeans underneath it. She must have escaped from an institution, but Blake couldn't remember anything resembling a nursing home closer than Throckmorton or Wichita Falls, and the old gal would have frozen to death if she'd walked that far.

She laid an icy hand on his forearm. "Is she out feeding the chickens? Are we safe?"

"I'm not sure." Blake eyed her closely as he sat back down.

She squeezed his arm pretty tight for such bony fingers. "Aren't you even going to offer me coffee? I walked the whole way over here to see you, Walter, and it is cold as a witch's tit out there."

Holy smoke! Would the real Walter please stand up and do it in a hurry?

Blake opened his mouth to tell her that he was not Walter but then clamped it shut. If he made her mad, he'd never find out her name and without that, he wouldn't be able to get her back where she belonged. He could call the police, but Dry Creek depended on the sheriff's department out of Throckmorton for emergencies, and he didn't have that number.

"Yes, let's get you warmed up. You take cream and sugar, sweetheart?" he drawled.

"Oh, sweetheart now, is it? You know very well I take it black, Walter."

"Should I call you baby? Sugar bun? Hot lips?"

"Irene will do just fine," she harrumphed, but Blake could see a smile tilting her lips.

He patted her hand as he pulled his arm away and got up from the table to retrieve a second coffee mug. "How about a toaster pastry to go with that?" he asked. Maybe if he got some food in her, she'd snap out of it and figure out he wasn't Walter.

"What is a toaster pastry? Your mama usually makes gravy and biscuits." The smile faded and her eyes darted around the room.

"Not this morning, darlin'." So the woman who put even

more craziness in the old gal's eyes wasn't Walter's wife but his mother.

"I keep telling you to move out on your own," Irene continued as he placed a steaming mug of coffee in front of her. She wrapped her hands around it like a lifeline. "If you had your own place, I'd leave my husband and we could be together all the time." She pursed her mouth so tight that her long, thin face had hollows below the high cheekbones. "A man who's almost forty years old has no business living with his mother, especially one who won't make you a decent breakfast."

"But what if she can't get along without me to help her?" Blake asked.

She shook her fist at him. "You've got four brothers. Let them take a turn. It's time for you to own up to the fact that this ranch is bad luck—always has been, always will be. You aren't going to make it here, but we could do good out in California. We'll both get a job pickin' fruit and get us a little house in town. I always wanted to live in town." She took his hand, hope shining in her eyes. The old girl just about broke Blake's heart.

"Let me make a call and see what I can do," he said gently.

The only phone number he had for anyone in Dry Creek was right there in bold print on the bottom of a 1999 feed store calendar hanging on the wall beside the refrigerator. Strange but January 4 was on a Monday that year, too. Blake wouldn't even need to get a new calendar.

Maybe the folks from the feed store would know who to call. He hoped that phone number hadn't changed in the past seventeen years.

"Well, what are you waiting for?" she yelled, all the anger coming back in a hurry. "Call one of them. Call them all. I don't really care, but it's time for you to cut the apron strings and get on with your life, Walter." She picked up the coffee and sipped it. "And put that dog outside where he belongs."

"Yes, ma'am," he said.

The wild look in her eyes got even worse. "Don't you ma'am me! I'm not an old lady. I'm a woman in her prime, and don't you ever ma'am me again."

He had to bite his cheek to keep from laughing out loud. Whoever this woman was, she wasn't about to let anyone steamroll her.

"And after you've called and we've had our coffee, we can fool around until *she* gets back in the house." Irene smiled up at him.

As if Shooter understood he wasn't welcome, he circled the table, keeping a wary eye on the newcomer until he got to the back door, where he whined. Glad to have an excuse to leave the table, Blake went to open the door and let the old boy out, wishing the whole time that he could escape with him.

Just exactly what did she mean by "fool around"? Did it mean the same in her demented mind that it did in today's world? If so, he'd have to make that cup of coffee last until someone could come get this woman or else learn a whole new level of talking his way out of a messy ordeal.

He eased the cell phone out of his pocket and poked in the numbers from the calendar. Irene seemed very content to sip her coffee and mumble about a dog being in the kitchen where womenfolk made food. Dog hairs, according to her, were covered with deadly diseases that could kill a person if they got into their fried potatoes.

"Dry Creek Feed and Seed. May I help you?" a feminine voice answered on the third ring.

"Ma'am, I'm the new owner of the Lucky Penny, and

an elderly woman named Irene showed up at my door this morning. It's starting to rain and..." He didn't get another word out.

"Oh, no! Just hang on to her, and I'll send someone for her in the next few minutes. Don't let her leave," the woman said, and the call ended.

CHAPTER TWO

Allie hated two things: cleaning and cooking. But every third week it was her turn to clean the big two-story house known as Audrey's Place.

Back during the Depression, Audrey's had been a rather notorious not-exactly-legal brothel. Miz Audrey, the lady who owned the place, had seen an opportunity where everyone else around Dry Creek saw defeat. She'd hired six girls at a time when everyone needed jobs. She was one of the few folks who hung on to her land, her business, and came out on the other side of the Depression with more money than she knew what to do with. Her girls, too. The hundred-year-old house had withstood tornadoes, winds, and all the other weird weather that Texas could throw at it.

But Allie wasn't appreciating her family home's rich history as she trudged through each of the six bedrooms on the second floor to vacuum, dust, and tidy up. She would far rather be the one creating mess. Give her the glorious smells of wood shavings, plaster dust, or varnish during a home remodel and she'd be much happier than breathing in pine-scented cleaners.

She paused on the bottom step, making sure that Granny was arguing with the characters of *Golden Girls* on the television in the living room before she toted the bucket of cleaning supplies up the stairs. Allie had put in the new railing the previous spring and still liked to run her hand over the new wood, taking a moment to admire the intricate spindles she'd turned on her lathe. Her father had given her the tools, the knowledge, and the love for carpentry. Some days she missed him even more than others, like when she opened the bathroom door and there was the lovely vanity they'd worked on together the year before he died.

She was about to return downstairs when her phone buzzed in the side pocket of her cargo pants. She pulled it out, and without even checking the caller ID, she answered. "Hello."

"Alora Raine Logan," her mother said.

"Why are you double-naming me? I couldn't possibly get into trouble while cleaning the house!"

"You let your grandmother get away from you." Katy's voice was so shrill it hurt Allie's ears.

"Impossible, Mama. The doors are locked with those new baby guards that she can't open. Besides, not fifteen minutes ago, I checked on her. She was sitting on the sofa watching *Golden Girls*."

Granny had shaken her fist at the television with a string of cuss words. Even in her moments of confusion, she never lost her spirit.

"Well, she's at the Lucky Penny now," Katy said.

A gust of cold wind hit her in the face when Allie reached the foyer. The door was thrown wide open, and Lizzy's yellow boots were gone from the lineup beside the hall tree.

"You're right. She's gone! But why the Lucky Penny?" Allie was already cramming her feet into a pair of boots.

"She must've heard us talking about a new cowboy buying that place. I can't leave the store, so you'll have to go get her," Katy said. "It's going to rain, so take a vehicle. I hope she at least put on a jacket or else she'll catch pneumonia, frail as she is."

"Lizzy's rubber boots are missing from the foyer, and I dressed her in jeans and a sweatshirt this morning." Allie stuck her free arm into a stained mustard-colored work coat.

"Thank goodness she's at least got something on her feet. Last time she went over there, she was wearing nothing but a nightgown when I went to get her. There she sat on the porch flirting with someone in her head because the only living thing on the whole ranch was an old gray tomcat," Katy said.

Allie picked up her van keys from the foyer table and headed out the door. "I'm on the way, Mama. She's probably sitting on the porch like last time. I don't think anyone has moved in yet."

"Lizzy said that Herman Hudson came in for a load of feed this morning and that at least one cowboy moved in on Saturday," Katy said.

"How'd you find out where she is?" Allie asked.

"The cowboy who bought the place called the feed store. The number was on the bottom of one of those calendars we used to give out at Christmas. Lizzy answered and then called me."

"I'll call you when I've got her back in the house." Allie jogged out to her work van and hopped inside. She shivered as she shoved the key into the ignition. They'd had a mild winter up until now, but January was going to make up for it for sure if this was a taste of what was to come. She didn't give the engine time to warm up but shoved the truck into gear, hit the gas, and headed down the lane toward the road, where she made a right-hand turn. The steering wheel was as cold as icicles, but in her hurry she'd left her gloves on the foyer table. Half a mile farther, she made another right and whipped into the winding lane at the Lucky Penny.

Had she gone by foot, Allie would have walked a few hundred yards, crawled over or under a broken-down barbed-wire fence, and gone another hundred yards to the old house. That was most likely the way that Granny had gone, and it took less than ten minutes to get there. Allie came to a screeching halt outside the house and with a carpenter's eye saw how much more dilapidated it had gotten since she was last on the ranch.

How long had it been? At least eight years because she'd been divorced more than seven, and the last time she'd been there was back when she and Riley, like all the other kids in that day and age, parked there to make out. Looking back, the smartest thing she'd done when she and Riley split ways was take her maiden name back.

A big yellow dog met her halfway across the yard. His head was down and his tail wagging, which meant he wasn't going to take a chunk out of her butt. But the sight of him did slow her down.

She held out a hand. "Hey, feller, what's your name?"

The dog nosed her hand in a friendly gesture, so she rubbed his ears. "You got my granny in that house, or is she hiding in one of the barns this time?"

The first big raindrop hit her on the cheek and rolled down her neck. It was as cold as ice water, and more quickly followed before she made it to the porch. Shivers chased down her spine as the water hit her bra and kept moving to the waistband of her underpants.

She knocked on the door and waited.

"Walter, don't open that door," her granny called out loud and clear.

"Are you Walter?" she asked the dog, who'd followed her to the porch, just as the front door swung open.

"No, he's Shooter. Are you Katy?"

Allie looked up into the greenest eyes she'd ever seen, rimmed by dark lashes. Her gaze traveled to his wide shoulders, the Henley shirt stretched over bulging abs, and the big belt buckle with a bull rider on it. She had to force herself to look back up, only to find him smiling, his arms now crossed over his chest.

Lord, have mercy! Crazy cowboys who bought a bad luck ranch were definitely not supposed to be that sexy.

She wanted to crawl under her work van because there she stood wearing cargo pants, a faded thermal knit shirt frayed out at the wrists, black rubber boots, and the old coat she wore on the job site. She smelled like pine oil and ammonia and didn't have even a smidgen of makeup on her face.

Granny shuffled across the floor. "Don't be silly, Walter. This is Katy, my daughter. You've seen her lots of times at church for the past six months. Don't you have enough sense to get in out of the rain, girl? Why haven't you invited her inside, Walter? Where are your manners?"

"Granny, I am not Katy. I'm Allie, your granddaughter. You know better than to sneak out of the house like this. You scared all of us," Allie fussed.

"Maybe we can sort this out inside, where it's warm and dry," Blake offered. He stuck out his hand. "I'm Blake Dawson. C'mon in." His eyes were so green that she would have sworn he was wearing colored contact lenses.

She put her hand in his. "I'm Allie Logan, your neighbor. I'm so sorry about this."

Her hand tingled, and the feeling lingered as she followed him into the house and through to the kitchen, tugging Granny after her. Maybe it was the weather, or the fact that he was one sexy piece of baggage. Most likely it was the fact that she hadn't had sex in so long that she might have to get out the how-to booklet to even remember what body part went where.

"I'm ready to go home now." Irene's head tilted to one side, and she shoved her hands into the pockets of the chenille robe. "I came over here to welcome this young man to Dry Creek. You should have come with me."

"You live nearby?" Blake asked.

"Yeah, the big house called Audrey's Place. It's just past your east field and over the fence."

"Audrey's Place? Is this Audrey? She told me her name was Irene." Blake shoved his thumbs into his hip pockets.

Irene's face went into that mode that reminded Allie of a dried apple doll: all wrinkles with deep-set eyes and a puckered-up mouth, hollowed cheeks, and a sharp little chin. She poked Blake in the chest with a bony finger and raised her voice as high as it would go. "Hell, no! Audrey was a whore. I'm a fine, upstanding, churchgoin' woman. I'm not a hooker like my great-great-grandma. I am Irene Miller, young man, and don't you forget it." She held her hand up to catch a drop of water when it fell from the ceiling. "Don't know why we're wasting our time with makin' casseroles to welcome him. He won't be here more'n a year. The good-lookin' ones never stay. Couple of ugly ones made it two years, but the cold winter will put this one on the run."

"Granny!" Allie said as soon as she could get a word in edgewise.

Irene shrugged. "Better get a pan and put it under that leak, young man, or you're going to be mopping all day. Now take me home, Allie."

"Granny, you're being rude."

Blake chuckled. "She does manage to keep things lively."

"You have no idea." Allie glanced at the drip coming from the ceiling. "It's been leaking awhile from the size of that brown ring. You're lucky someone put down linoleum flooring because it could ruin carpet or hardwood."

Blake nodded. "I hoped that the water marks on the ceiling were from a long time ago and the leak had been fixed. I'll just have to add it to the list of the million other repairs."

"Allie's great at repairs," Irene piped in. "We have a construction business, and we're very good at what we do."

"Really?" Blake's eyes lit up. "Could I hire you to put on a new roof?"

Allie threw an arm around her grandmother, wishing she had a muzzle. "We'll have to check our workload and get back to you."

"You was complainin' last week that you needed a job and things were slower," Irene fussed. "But I'm not doing one thing to help anyone on this ranch after the way Walter acted. You didn't know him like I did, Allie. What in the hell are we doing here anyway? Take me home right now."

"Let me get your things, Miz Miller," Blake said.

Allie's eyes followed him as he walked away with a swagger. Good Lord, she had to get a grip.

"Who's Walter?" Allie asked.

Irene's lips tightened and she shook her head. "You just stay away from this ranch. It don't bring nothing but heartache and pain to anyone who comes around it because no one ever stays. It should be called Hard Luck, not Lucky Penny."

Allie folded Irene's hand in hers. "Tell me more about Walter and his family. When did they live on this ranch?"

Before Allie could get any more information, Blake came back with Irene's flamingo boots and her cane, plus an empty trash can to put under the leak. "So, can you ask the carpenter in your family if he'd be interested in a job?"

Irene waggled a finger at him. "No and that is final. We ain't interested in your leaky roof, and I'm not talking about Walter even if you put me in my room and give me nothing but bread and water for a month." She pulled free from Allie's hand and stormed out of the house into the rain.

Allie watched as she marched straight to the van, stomping right through the mud puddles. The bottom of her robe was soaked by the time she slung the passenger door open and crawled inside.

Blake chuckled. "And to think thirty minutes ago she was trying to talk me into running away to California with her to pick fruit. Someone named Walter must have lived on this ranch, and she loved him at one time."

"Sorry that you had to be Walter, whoever he is, today," Allie said.

"I wasn't going to argue with her. Besides, I got to meet you. Like Mama says, dark clouds can have silver linings." He shot her a wicked grin that zinged right through her. "You will check that calendar and have your carpenter give me a call. I'll get you my number." He hurried over to the sofa, wrote the number on the bottom edge of a magazine page, and handed it to her.

His fingertips grazed hers, and there was definitely a tingle. Sweet Jesus! She had to remind herself that this was the Lucky Penny. Folks came and went on it, and no one ever lasted, especially not any sexy cowboys. She straightened herself and put some steel in her spine.

"I'll call when I check the calendar. And I'll keep a better eye on Granny. Thanks for calling the feed store."

"You could call about other things, too…if you wanted," he drawled.

The glint in his eyes promised some temptation beyond imagining, and the gravel in his voice had an underlying tone of making all her dreams come true. She came close to promising to build him a brand-new house for free from the ground up. Lord, have mercy! He was flirting. Flirting with Allie when she was wearing her work clothes and had her hair up in a messy ponytail. He was a player for sure, one of those wicked, wild cowboys who got what they wanted with a slow drawl and a sexy strut. He flirted, not because he was interested in Allie, but because it was a way to get a roof on his house.

"I should be going. She's going to be a handful the rest of the day. Her mind is like a dozen jigsaw puzzles in one box. Who knows what pieces go with what time frame? It's all a muddle. Thanks again for taking care of her." Allie opened the screen door and took a step out onto the porch.

Blake leaned against the doorjamb, his arms crossed—the

perfect pose to show off those long legs and broad shoulders. Just the sight had her almost forgetting about her grandmother altogether.

"Well, you're both welcome here anytime. Pleased to meet you, Allie," he said.

"Goodbye, Blake." She jogged through the rain to the van, but she could feel the heat of his eyes on her back the whole way.

CHAPTER THREE

Shooter gave Blake a wistful look with his big brown eyes and wagged his tail.

"What?" Blake said. "She has pretty brown eyes, and I need a roof on the house."

Shooter yipped as if arguing with him.

His mama said that good looks and hard work would get a cowboy far in life, but charm would get him anything he wanted. So far, she'd been one hundred percent right. Hopefully, the charm would work one more time, and then he'd settle down to being a stable rancher.

Shooter growled and gazed at the window.

"What is it, boy? That poor old lady back to yell at me some more?" Blake rushed to the window to memorize the phone number on the side of the van. The first six numbers were the same as the one on the calendar, which meant Logan Construction was a local company. The last four were 2200. His birthday plus two zeros. He went straight to the kitchen and wrote it on the bottom of the old calendar right below the feed store number. He wasn't going to take any chances on not being able to reach Allie again.

His phone rang, and he grabbed it from the cabinet beside the sink, checked the ID, and said, "Hey, Toby."

"How are things going down there? Are you getting unpacked?" his brother asked.

"It's raining and there's a leak in the living room ceiling, but I've got a trash can under it. Just found out there's a carpenter next door, so if he's not busy..." Blake went on to tell his brother what had happened that morning, conveniently leaving out any mention of the old lady's offer to fool around.

"What a welcoming committee!" Toby laughed. "I wish I'd been there to see that. You say she even put old Shooter out?"

"I opened the door, but he didn't waste any time scootin' his butt outside. At the time, I wished I could follow him. Even that cold wind and rain would've been better than having coffee with our neighbor."

"Good you're getting to know the neighbors—even if they are crazy. Most small towns are alike. Friendly folks who make newcomers pretty welcome. I saw a church when we moved you down there. Did you go yesterday?"

"No, I was too busy just trying to make the place habitable. It's a mess, bro. And now we need a whole new roof on top of everything else." Blake leaned his head back and stared at the rusty rings on the ceiling. "I've cleared land, plowed land, worked with cattle, even ridden a few bulls in the rodeo, but redoing a whole roof by myself is beyond me. I just hope that the neighbor has a slot on the calendar with enough time to fix it."

"Oh, come on, now," Toby said seriously. "Surely you can sweet-talk that woman into getting her family to work for you."

"It's against my rules to play in a sandbox that close to home. It'll get you in trouble every time. And I'm trying to leave that player reputation behind me and start a new life here," Blake said.

"I'll believe it when I see it," Toby said. "I'll drive up in a week or so for the weekend to see what I can do to help out—even if it's sweet-talking the neighbor myself."

Blake tensed at the thought of his brother trying to charm Allie. He practically had to restrain the growl that rose in his throat. "I'll take care of it," he said curtly, rolling his neck to get the kinks out.

Toby just laughed. "I'll see you either this weekend or the next. Soon as I can get away."

"From what? Your ranch or the bars?" Blake asked.

"Both. Got to get these new folks comfortable with the place before I leave them with it, and I'll get my time at the bars while I can, especially since the Lucky Penny is in a dry county."

"Yeah, you keep playing while I do all the dirty work," Blake grumbled.

"Just remember the end game," Toby said. "I'll be there in the spring and Jud before the end of the year. In five years we'll have the Lucky Penny solidly established, maybe even with a decent barn built to have our own cattle sale if we work hard at it. Suck it up, brother. This is only the first week."

Blake inhaled deeply and let it out slowly. "Think you and Jud will be able to survive with no bars in the whole county?"

"If you can, I can. I'm tougher than you, and now I've got to go." The call ended before Blake could reply.

He went to the kitchen, poured another cup of coffee,

and stared at all those boxes stacked everywhere. Saturday seemed like years ago. The excitement of finally moving onto the ranch had been replaced with doubts as big as Longhorn bulls' horns.

"My first challenge after getting this roof fixed is to work my way into the community." He looked up again at the dripping ceiling. "Look on the bright side, Shooter. At least it's dripping in the hallway and not right on top of my bed or on your lazy old hide. And I can't let Toby and Jud think I can't manage my end of this bargain."

The dog answered with a couple of tail thumps, but he didn't open his eyes.

Blake picked up a notepad from the end table where he'd started a grocery list and carried it with him through the house. Roof first, and then, if there was money left in the repair budget for the house, he'd see how far he could stretch it. He started in the living room, checking everything and writing down what needed to be fixed, putting a star beside the things that were most important in each room. Two hallways split off from the living room. The one to the north led to three bedrooms with a bathroom at the end. A huge country kitchen and a dining room opened up from the southern hall. The small table with four chairs around it looked even tinier in the kitchen, surrounded on three sides with cabinet space. An archway on the other end led into the dining room, which was every bit as big as the kitchen but empty except for boxes.

Whoever built the house either had or intended to have a big family. Lots of space in the living room for children to play, in the dining room where lots of people could be seated, and in the kitchen for family to gather around at mealtimes. He shut his eyes and imagined a day in the future when there would be laughter as well as arguments in the old ramshackle house. It would look different then because it would be a home filled with love, not a house where one lonesome, wild cowboy lived with his dog.

As he went from one room to the next, writing down what it would take to restore the house to some kind of livable condition, his mood sank. The place hadn't seemed nearly so dilapidated back when they came to Dry Creek and looked at the ranch. But then, back in the summer, they'd been a whole lot more interested in the ranching part of the deal and not the house.

"I will make this work," he mumbled.

Shooter's tail thumped against the worn leather sofa.

Blake gulped down the last of the coffee and set the cup on the coffee table. "Are you agreeing with me or telling me I'm an idiot?"

Shooter's eyes snapped shut and he snored.

Since it was raining and he couldn't do any outside work, Blake decided to tackle everything his mama had marked "kitchen" when she helped pack boxes. He ripped the tape from a box and started the job. Dishes in the upper cabinets. Food in the pantry right off the utility room. Pots and pans in the lower cabinets. During the whole process, he thought about Allie.

She was a pretty girl, and he could sink into her dark brown eyes and drown—not exactly his usual type, but there was something about her he couldn't get out of his head. He and Toby tended to go for the tall, willowy blondes with blue eyes. It was Jud who liked petite brunettes. Blake didn't like the thought of befriending Allie just to have Jud swoop in and steal her heart.

When the rain finally stopped, he carried an armload of flattened boxes out to his truck and threw them into the back. Later, when he figured out where his burn pile would be, he'd take care of them. He heard a vehicle coming down the lane and parking in the front yard and hoped that Allie had returned to tell him that the Logan Construction Company would fix the roof. He jogged through the kitchen and dining room and threw open the door the minute she knocked.

A tall, blond woman holding a casserole dish smiled at him from the other side of the screen door. "Welcome to Dry Creek. I'm Sharlene Tucker." She batted long lashes and tilted her head to one side.

He picked up on all the take-me-home-tonight signs and instinctively moved in to close the deal. "Come right in, darlin'. It's shapin' up to be a fine day when a pretty woman brings food to my door."

A brighter smile and a definite extra wiggle under those skintight pants said that she was there for more than food and talk.

He lowered his voice an octave and whispered softly. "Let me take that for you, and then I'll help you with your coat."

"I'll just come in and put this in the refrigerator for you and be on my way. I work at the bank in Olney and I'm already a little late, but thank you for the offer. Maybe I'll take a rain check." That deliberate brush of her breasts across his chest as she walked by said that she'd be glad to come back anytime.

"The church ladies will be coming around in a day or two with food, but I wanted to welcome you personally, Mr. Dawson." She bent over to put the casserole on the bottom shelf of the fridge, giving him a perfect view of a rounded butt stretching the seams of her black pants.

She straightened, turned around, and tipped her head up, moistening her lips seductively. "Don't you tell that I came a little early." She tapped a manicured nail against his chin. "This is just to hold you over until they get here. Got to run. Call me if you need anything, Mr. Dawson." A pen appeared out of her jacket pocket, and she wrote her name and number on the outdated calendar. "We'll have to see about getting you a new calendar. Bye now, and enjoy the casserole."

He followed her to the door and opened it for her. "Thank you so much for the food, and I'm Blake, not Mr. Dawson."

"Right nice to meet you, Blake. I'll be waiting for you to call."

* * *

Katy Logan popped her hands on her hips. That gesture usually brought her three girls to attention, but since Fiona was in Houston, only Lizzy and Allie sat up straighter in their chairs. "I heard the new cowboy next door is mighty handsome. Sure you're not planning to do any more than fix his roof?"

Allie took down four plates from the cabinet, put the silverware on the top one, and started setting the table for breakfast. "For goodness' sake, Mama. I'm not going to marry the man. I'm going to put a roof on his house and that's it."

Katy pushed her dark hair, with streaks of white starting to show, behind her ears. "Your grandmother said he looked at you like he could eat you up when you were over there."

"Good grief, Mama. Granny was so busy talking about Walter that she didn't know who she was or where she was. And I smelled like pine oil and ammonia. I don't think he wanted to bite into that. He just wanted to get me to say yes to helping him out. His kind isn't interested in women like me."

Her youngest sister, Lizzy, whipped her dishwater-blond hair up into a ponytail and went to the pantry to get several bottles of syrup. "This new guy sounds like a player. Why can't you find a good, decent man like my Mitch? He wouldn't have to be a preacher, but he needs to be a godly man."

Allie rolled her eyes. "Yes, we all know Mitch is a paragon of men. But I had a man. A husband! I gave him my heart, and he broke it. So no, thank you, not just to godly men but to any man. I'm going to the Lucky Penny to put a roof on the house, not have a fling," Allie said.

Lizzy plopped the syrup on the table and went to the refrigerator for the butter dish. "If you go over to the Lucky Penny, you can bet you'll be in the gossip spotlight even worse than when you left Riley. Besides, every unmarried woman in Throckmorton County probably is layin' out plans to get to know Brian. I heard that Sharlene was making a Mexican casserole to take to him. You know what that means."

Allie popped Lizzy on the arm. "His name is Blake, and I did not leave Riley. He left me, and that was seven years ago. And yes, I know that Sharlene expects something hot in return for her hot Mexican casserole."

"Mama, she hit me," Lizzy said.

"I barely touched you," Allie protested. Sisters might grow up in body, but in spirit they stayed children. Some habits weren't breakable, like Allie's instinct to slap Lizzy for being a smartass.

"Don't get all hateful with me," Lizzy said. "I'm trying to make you see that this is a bad idea. You can't stop gossip, and it's been a long dry spell in town for good rumors."

Allie brought out butter and a bowl of fruit. "A roofing job will only last a week. What can happen in a week?"

"Stop your bickering. You know it upsets your grandmother." Katy piled the pancakes on a platter, slathering each layer with the butter she had melted earlier. "Who did you say she kept calling the new guy? Walter? I remember some folks who lived there years ago and tried to make a go of that place. An elderly woman and her son. I think his name was Walter, but that was about the time I married your father, so I didn't pay a lot of attention in those days."

"Maybe she knew him but was married to Grandpa at that time. I can't see her falling in love with a man when she'd been married more than twenty years," Allie said.

"She's got it all mixed up. I bet she liked some guy from over there back when she was a young girl, and her mama refused to let her get mixed up with him because she knew no one ever lasted over there," Lizzy said.

Allie peeled paper towels off the roll to use for napkins. "I'm going to take this job. I don't care what people say. We're lucky that the weather is going to be decent the next few days."

"You'll call Deke?" Katy sighed. "Promise me you'll call Deke. At least you'll have a chaperone as well as someone to help you. Maybe folks won't talk so much that way."

"I don't need a chaperone, Mama. But I called Deke this morning, and he's free the rest of this week." Allie nodded. "One of you will have to take Granny to work with you today so I can make a trip to Wichita Falls for supplies. If the weather holds, we can get started today and have the job done by Friday."

Lizzy pushed a strand of wayward hair behind her ears. "Mitch is supposed to come by today. You know how Granny hates him, so you'd best take her today, Mama, and I'll babysit tomorrow."

"I still don't like it," Katy said. "That new man didn't even come to church on Sunday. If he wanted to fit in with the community, he'd come to church."

"He was settling in on Sunday, Mama, and his name is Blake," Allie said.

"I hear Granny rustlin' up the hallway. Best stop talkin' about the Lucky Penny. Seems like that sets her off into a tizz." Lizzy put a finger to her lips. "And, Allie, there ain't no need to remember his name anyway. He won't be here past spring. Besides, Brian could have come to church for one hour just to show the community that he is a God-fearin' man."

"Blake as in Blake Shelton, your favorite country singer," Allie said.

"Okay, okay! I'll remember. Why is it so damn important to you anyway? You said you weren't going to marry him. Is he handsome?" Lizzy slapped a hand over her mouth. "He is, isn't he? Mama, he's sexy, and she's going to make a fool out of herself again."

"You cussed! Not very fitting for the future wife of a preacher. Mama, did you hear that?"

Katy gave her daughter a hard stare and sighed. "Really? What are you girls, five years old again?"

Lizzy shrugged. "Quit trying to change the subject and just answer my question. Is he sexy?"

Allie took a step closer to her sister. "You answer mine first. Why should he come to church?"

"Because that's the first thing a respectable person should do when he moves to a new town. For all we know, he's going to run a brothel over there," Lizzy answered.

Laughter exploded out of Allie. It bounced off the walls and echoed all the way through the two-story house. "That's the pot calling the kettle black for sure. And, darlin', he is so sexy that my underpants crawled all the way to my ankles."

Lizzy pulled out a chair and loaded her plate with pancakes. "Mama, she's takin' up for him and talkin' dirty, too."

"Don't you worry none about Allie," Katy said. "She's learned her lesson."

Lizzy smiled smugly. "At least I've got more sense than that. My Mitch is a man of God."

"Well, bless your little heart," Allie smarted off. "I'm happy for you, but even men of God have faults."

"Not my Mitch," Lizzy declared.

Irene poked her head around the corner and giggled. "I've been eavesdropping for a long time. In my opinion, it's a bad idea for Allie to go to the Lucky Penny. That man is plumb deadly to women, and she can't afford another broken heart. And, Lizzy, crawl down off that high horse. The Good Book is full of men who couldn't keep it in their pants. Even David, the man after God's own heart, had a problem along those lines." She crossed the room and pulled out the fourth chair. "Pancakes. I do love pancakes."

CHAPTER FOUR

Blake's and Shooter's breathing fogged up the cab window of the bulldozer that morning before the heater finally kicked in. The machinery was far from new, and the heater worked sporadically, running awhile and then shutting down until it was good and ready to start up again.

Shooter sat straight and tall in the passenger seat and listened to the music coming from the radio. At least the speakers worked better than the heater.

Blake hummed along to a Josh Turner song.

Shooter kept his eyes straight ahead, watching every mesquite tree that the dozer blade ripped out of the cold ground by the roots.

"You lookin' for rabbits or squirrels to come out from those thickets?"

Shooter's ears shot straight up.

Blake's phone vibrated against his chest, and he unzipped his coveralls enough to reach inside and fetch it. He glanced down and took a deep breath. This was it. Either Allie was calling to tell him that Logan Construction was taking the job or else he would have to learn how to shingle a roof.

He touched the screen and put the phone to his ear. "Hello."

"Mr. Dawson, this is Allie Logan. We have decided that we can fix your roof. We're going for supplies this morning after we run by and measure it. And we will probably start removing the old shingles this afternoon. Do you have a preference of shingle color? White is what you've got on there, but before we agree on a price, you have to understand that if I'm needed at home to take care of my grandmother, then I'll have to work around that."

"Whew! Slow down, Miz Logan! That pretty little mouth of yours was made for something other than talking too fast."

"Flattery won't get you anywhere with me. Do you still want me to fix that roof?"

"Yes, I do," he said. "And I was stating a fact, not flattering you. Your lips are perfect and made for kissing."

"I want to get supplies today and get to work so it can be done by the time the bad weather rolls in that the weatherman is calling for."

He chuckled. "Thank you for that."

"Now, shingles or metal roof?"

"Which is cheaper? I'm on a budget." She was a tough nut to crack for sure. Usually those lines had a woman in his pocket for at least a night and maybe a whole weekend.

"Shingles." One word. Her tone said business.

"Then that's the route to take, and I'm not particular about color. What would you suggest?" Blake asked.

"Are you going to repaint the outside in the spring when it's warm enough?" she asked.

"Of course. The way the paint is peeling, it's a wonder

some of the boards aren't rotted out," Blake answered. "Thank goodness the lower half of the place is fieldstone."

"What color?" Allie asked.

"The color of your eyes when the sun makes them sparkle."

"Get serious, Blake Dawson!"

"Okay then. Light gray with white porch railings and trim work." He wasn't sure where the idea came from, maybe from that big two-story house painted gray with white trim he noticed as he drove through Throckmorton on his way to Dry Creek. "How do you see it?"

"That would be beautiful. How about a charcoal-gray roof?" Allie asked.

Blake turned down the volume on the radio. "Sounds good to me."

"Do you want to see samples? I could send pictures by phone."

"Couldn't you bring them by? We could decide together over a cup of coffee or a bowl of ice cream." His voice went into its most seductive mode.

"Maybe you need to consult with your girlfriend?"

She was all business. Nothing was working. Did the bad luck on this ranch turn his good luck with women upside down?

"That's not necessary. Don't have a girlfriend and don't imagine my two partners care what color the house is. Just pick out what you think would look good with light gray and bring it back with you. Do you need a check before you send your men after the supplies?"

"No, but I will want half this afternoon when we get there and the other half when the job is done, maybe by Friday evening, definitely by Saturday," she answered.

"That sounds great." Blake gave Shooter the thumbs-up sign.

"I'll be over there by noon, and we'll get started removing those old white shingles and seeing how much damage control we need to do to the decking. Goodbye, Mr. Dawson," Allie said stiffly.

He caught his smile in the rearview mirror. "Call me Blake. We are neighbors."

"Thank you. You can call me Allie, and is it convenient for me to drop by in an hour to do some measuring? You don't have to be there. It's all outside work," Allie said.

"Whatever you need to do is fine, and the back door is unlocked if you need to go inside the house." Blake tucked the phone inside his denim jacket pocket and whistled through his teeth.

* * *

By noon there were two enormous piles of mesquite in the pasture ready to be cut up into firewood and/or burned. Blake felt like his butt had calluses on it from bouncing around in the dozer seat all morning. When he stepped down onto steady ground, he did several stretches to get the kinks out of his back.

Shooter raced past him, put his nose to the ground, and flushed three rabbits before Blake could take two steps away from the machinery. Then the old dog was off and running, barking happily until the rabbits took refuge in a pile of dead mesquite. Shooter couldn't figure out a way to get inside the tangled brush to go after them.

Blake caught up and scratched the old boy's ears. "Don't worry. They'll have to come out sometime. Would you look at all that beautiful firewood? We'll bring the chain saw out here real soon and tear up their hiding places."

The wind had gotten colder since he'd started work that morning. It was so cold that it burned his lungs when he took a breath, so he pulled his coat collar up over his mouth and nose. Shooter backed his ears and took off for the house at a dead run. Blake did a fast trot right behind him, cleared the steps, and landed on the porch. He did not envy Allie and whoever she had working with her one bit. Working on a roof with that cold wind whipping around them would be a real task.

He hadn't even hung up his coat when someone knocked on the door. He turned around, opened the door, and there on the other side was a curvy brunette with streaks of blue in her shoulder-length hair. It looked like someone had cut it with a chain saw. Maybe that's what happened, and it had terrified her so badly that it turned part of her hair blue.

"You must be Blake Dawson. I'm Mary Jo Clark, and I brought over some chili and a chocolate pie to welcome you to Dry Creek," she said in a gravelly voice that matched her skinny jeans and formfitting sweater.

"Well, thank you, Mary Jo Clark. I was about to fix myself a sandwich, but chili does sound so much better," he drawled in his most seductive voice.

"If you'll bring those big strong arms and help me carry it in from the van, I would appreciate it." She batted her eyes at him like a seasoned bar bunny.

He followed her to the van, and she raised the back hatch. "You carry that slow cooker, darlin', and I'll get this box. My phone number is right here." She pointed to the end of the cardboard box, and there it was, written in three-inch numbers. "If you need anything at all, honey, you just give me a call and I'll be here in five minutes."

"You want to stick around and eat some of this with me?" he asked.

"Oh, darlin', I would love to, but I've got to be in Wichita Falls by one thirty. I work at the hair salon in Walmart, and I've got the late shift today. But maybe on my next day off we can plan something."

Yep, a seasoned bar bunny. He could spot one from a hundred yards and reel them in like a catfish out of the river. Mary Jo was proof that he hadn't lost all his luck with women. It was Allie Logan who couldn't be swayed by his pickup lines, not the whole female population of Throckmorton County.

He wiped his brow and then remembered that he really wanted to leave the wild cowboy ways behind him. *Get thee behind me, Lucifer! You are not going to make this change in my life easy, are you? Already you're throwing up temptations that are pretty danged hard to avoid.*

When they'd unloaded the food on the kitchen cabinet, he followed her back out to the porch. That was the polite thing to do. After all, she'd brought enough chili to last until spring thaw, a chocolate meringue pie, and that sure enough looked like jalapeño cornbread in the box with the pie.

When they reached the yard gate, he stuck out his hand and said, "Thank you again, Mary Jo. That was real sweet of you to welcome me to Dry Creek."

She bypassed the hand, ran her hands up under his jacket, and pressed her body close to his. She rolled up slightly on her toes and kissed him on the chin. "Put that hand away, Blake. I believe in hugs to welcome a person, not a handshake. And the second time I see you, I'll expect a hug and a real kiss."

He didn't even hear the truck coming up the driveway until it stopped beside her van, and there was Allie staring right at him from the passenger window. Mary Jo winked at Allie and hugged Blake one more time.

The window of the truck rolled down slowly. "Didn't take you long to find a girlfriend."

Blake propped one forearm over the other against the truck, his face only a few inches from Allie's. "Just met her ten minutes ago. Don't think we've got far enough to call it a relationship."

"Hello." A big man reached across Allie with an open hand. "I'm Deke, and I'll be helping Allie put a roof on your house."

Blake's arm grazed Allie's shoulder when he stuck his hand through the window. He blamed the sparks on the cold weather and a little static electricity.

Deke had a firm handshake and a friendly smile, but it was too cold to stand outside and talk when a warm fire and a pot of chili waited in the house.

"Let's take this conversation inside," he said.

Deke nodded.

Blake was careful not to touch Allie again as he pulled his hand back and then jogged to the house. The second the door was open, Shooter raced inside and curled up in front of the fireplace on a worn rug. Blake laid a couple of logs on the embers, and the old dog sighed.

He went to the kitchen and lifted the lid from the slow cooker. The spicy aroma of chili filled the whole room. He'd be eating it for a week or else divvying it up into plastic containers and freezing it. The crunch of tires pulling the trailer around back filtered through the kitchen window, but it wasn't until someone knocked on the back door that Shooter's head popped up.

Blake slung the door open, and Deke, taller than Blake's six feet by at least four inches, stood behind Allie. He had curly brown hair that covered his ears and poked out around a well-worn cowboy hat. His hazel eyes studied Blake like he was a bug under a microscope. Allie's husband, maybe? He couldn't help the twinge that ran through him at the thought.

"Come in." Blake motioned them out of the cold weather. "I put a couple of logs on the fire, so it's getting nice and warm in here."

Allie handed him a bill. "This is for the total job. Gray shingles were on sale this week, so I got a little better deal than we talked about on the phone. It's five hundred less than the estimate I gave you. You can pay half now and half when the job is done or pay all now."

Deke sniffed the air. "Is that chili? Don't mind Allie's rudeness. She's worried about this bad weather, and she wants to get this roof done before it hits. And she talks too much when she's nervous."

"I was not being rude," Allie countered with a shove to the tall man.

"Yes, you were," Deke said. "You didn't even say hello before you threw that bill on the counter. That's rude. Loosen up, woman. We'll get the job done."

"Sorry if I was rude," she said. "I'll start all over. Hello, Blake. How are you today? Can we talk about this bill now? How do you want to pay?"

Blake glanced at the bill and reached for the checkbook on the top of the refrigerator. "Might as well pay up now. Glad that y'all could get to work on the job for me this quick. Y'all want to have dinner with me? Mary Jo brought enough chili to feed an army."

"I love Mary Jo's chili. Got dessert?" Deke asked.

"Talk about rude," Allie said.

"Well, I've got a sweet tooth that will not be denied," Deke admitted.

Blake made out the check and handed it to Allie. "Man's got to speak his mind, and if he's got a sweet tooth, then he doesn't just want dessert, he needs it."

His gaze went from Allie's work boots, past those luscious curves, to her eyes. That line should have worked on anyone, but her eyes said that he bored her.

"That's right, and I will eat with you. Besides, I see a chocolate pie and jalapeño cornbread in that box over there on the counter." Deke removed his coat and hung it over the back of a kitchen chair. "Where's the bowls? I'll get them down. I got a six-pack of beer in the truck I can contribute."

"Deke!" Allie hissed.

"Hey, it's a hot meal with dessert in a good warm house. I ain't turnin' it down for a bologna and cheese sandwich in a cold truck." He opened the cabinet door that Blake pointed toward. "You stayin' with us or goin' out to the truck?"

"I've got my dinner in the truck. This is a job, not a social visit," she said.

"It can just be a meal, not a social visit. You can eat without talking and then leave without even cleaning up," Blake said.

Her hesitation said that she considered it, but then she shook her head. "No, thank you."

"Good! That leaves more for me. I can't believe you are turnin' down a good bowl of chili when I know for a fact it's your favorite. Are you sick, or have you started getting that stuff that your granny has?" Deke asked.

"Hush. I'll meet you on the roof in thirty minutes." She marched out the back door, back straight and chin up.

So Allie wasn't married. She wasn't afraid of hard work. She liked chili better than anything in the world, and she had a temper to boot. His kind of woman if she'd been tall, blond, and had clear blue eyes.

"I've never been in this house. Looks like it needs more than a roof job," Deke said.

Blake removed a block of cheese from the refrigerator, along with a jar of hot dill pickles. "Yes, it does. You reckon you and Allie could do some patch jobs in here to get us through until we can start showing a profit on the ranch? It needs new drywall on the ceiling and maybe some paint on the walls. Don't want to spend a lot until we start making money, but that shouldn't make me have to take out a mortgage on the place."

"If Allie's got time to do some work for you, I reckon I could help her. But come spring, I'll be busy with my own place and the rodeo rounds," Deke answered.

"We don't need three bowls, Deke. My dog, Shooter, he doesn't like chili."

Deke chuckled. "Allie will be back. She don't turn down chili for nothing."

And they called the cowboys who bought the Lucky Penny foolish? Hadn't Deke seen the look on Allie's face when she marched out of the house?

"How long has it been since a real family lived here?" Blake kept an eye on the door and an ear tuned to the sound of boots on the wooden porch.

"Maybe four years. Last bunch didn't last a month. Moved in, came to church one time, and left. Guess they took one look at all that mesquite and cactus and threw up their hands in defeat before they even got started. Before that they came and went so fast the folks in Dry Creek didn't even get a chance to get to know them. Do you really think you can make this work?" Deke asked.

"Hope so," Blake said. "My brother and cousin and I've sunk a lot of money into the place. I was just wondering if the place had gone empty for seventeen years since the calendar on the wall is that old."

"Looks that way. Guess someone liked that picture of a barn on it," Deke said.

* * *

Allie bit into a cold bologna and cheese sandwich and got madder each time she chewed. Chili—really fine chili—Mary Jo's chili, which was the best in the whole county, was in that house. What was wrong with this picture? She took her phone from her coat pocket and called her sister.

"I hope you are happy. Blake and Deke are eating chili, and I'm sitting in a cold truck eating a soggy, cold sandwich because I'm proving to you and Mama that this is just a job," she blurted out before Lizzy could even answer.

"You get one star in your eternal crown for such a sacrifice," Lizzy said sarcastically.

"I deserve two diamond stars because it's my favorite food and Mary Jo made it and it smelled so good."

"It's not a social call," Lizzy smarted off. "Eat your sandwich and do the job and forget about the chili. Folks are already gossiping. I'll be glad to report to the next one that comes in the store that you didn't succumb to the devil's wiles because he offered you chili. Got customers. See you later this evening," Lizzy said.

"Somebody's Knockin'" started playing on the radio, and Allie groaned.

She remembered the lyrics so well that said someone was knockin' and she wondered if she should let him in; that she'd heard about the devil, but who would have thought he'd be wearing blue jeans and have blue eyes when he came knocking on her door.

Allie squeezed the sandwich so hard that her fingers went through it. She wanted a bowl of that chili so bad she could taste it. And she was meaner than the devil, and one bowl of chili did not mean it was a social call. It was food that would provide warmth for her to work on the roof in the bitter cold all afternoon.

Lizzy could fuss at her later that night, but she was going back into that house and eating chili at a table and maybe even a piece of chocolate pie afterward. Besides, Deke loved Mary Jo's chili even more than she did, and he'd tease her all afternoon about how good it was if she didn't eat with them.

The house smelled scrumptious when she knocked on the back door and entered without waiting for an invitation. "I changed my mind, and I don't want to hear any sass from you, Deke Sullivan."

"I ain't sayin' nothing. I was about to walk on back to my ranch if you hadn't come on back in here," Deke said.

"Why did you change your mind?" Blake asked.

"Because the day she turns down chili, then I figure she's gettin' that stuff that her granny has, and I ain't workin' with a woman who's holdin' a nail gun if her mind ain't right. Why are you in a bad mood today anyway?" Deke asked.

Allie scowled at him. "I'm not in a bad mood. Where are the bowls?"

Blake pointed. "There's a bowl beside the slow cooker. Help yourself."

She removed her coat and hung it over the back of a chair.

Blake's eyes caught with hers and sparks flew. "Well, whatever the reason, I'm glad you changed your mind. A dinner table is always nicer with a lovely woman sitting at it."

Deke pushed back his chair, and in a couple of long strides, he was beside Allie. "You best not skimp on your helping because I'm having seconds. Mary Jo hasn't made chili for me in more than a year."

Allie filled her bowl to the brim and carried it carefully to the table. She sat down and dipped her spoon deep into the chili, keeping her eyes on the food instead of looking at either Deke or Blake. "Mmm. Mary Jo's chili is the best in the world."

Deke set his second bowl on the table. "If you hadn't come back, I really was going to give you a hard time about it."

Blake pushed back his chair and went to refill his bowl. "Sometime I'll make a pot of chili and let y'all be the judge if it's this good. My mama had four old ornery boys, and she said that we had to learn our way around the kitchen. So every fourth day, one of us had kitchen duty. We hated it, but I can make a pretty good pot of chili and I know how to grill a steak. And sharing it with a pretty lady and a friend makes everything better."

"Allie still hates the kitchen. Only thing she hates worse than cooking is cleaning. She's pretty good at both, but that don't mean she enjoys it," Deke said between bites.

"I'm sitting right here," Allie said bluntly. "You aren't supposed to talk about me when I'm close enough to smack you." Allie reached for a piece of cheese and then cut it up in cubes on top of her chili. "I'm surprised you didn't buy this place, Deke."

"I started to. Went to the bank and asked for a loan and then changed my mind. It's not what I really want."

"And that would be?" Blake asked.

One of Deke's shoulders rose a couple of inches in a shrug. "I want the place my cousin has across the road from mine. He'll get tired of his bitchin' city wife within the year and put it up for sale. Besides, this place ain't nothing but mesquite and cow tongue cactus. Only thing it's got going for it is those three spring-fed ponds so you don't have to carry water to the cattle in the hot summertime."

"Mesquite can be removed right along with cactus, and the ranch was cheap." Blake changed the subject. "Got a wife and kids, Deke?"

Deke slapped his forehead. "I forgot the beer. Not that this sweet tea isn't good, but I said I'd contribute the beer to our dinner. Sorry about that."

"He doesn't have a wife or kids." Allie answered the question for him.

"And you, Allie? Got a husband or kids?" Blake asked.

"No." Her answer was tight and left no room for discussion.

Deke went on. "I got a little spread of about three hundred acres, and I run some cattle, grow some hay, and do odd jobs with Allie when she needs a tough cowboy. It butts up to your place on the west side. Other than that, I'm a rodeo junkie. I ride a few bulls and broncs and even play at rodeo clown when they need me. No wife, no kids, and I ain't interested in neither one right now."

"That's because no sane woman could live with you. He's so set in his ways that you'd think he was eighty-five rather than twenty-five." Allie pushed back her chair and took her bowl to the cabinet for a refill. Lizzy would scream that she'd sold her soul, but the chili was worth every bit of her sister's bitching.

When she returned, she reached for a piece of cornbread at the same time Blake did, and a shiver ran from her fingers to her gut. Dammit! She was not giving in to her hormones. She had to keep things in perspective.

"You look like you are getting in that mood again," Deke said.

"She might be fighting with the voices in her head. My brother gets that look on his face when he is doing that," Blake said. "Most of the time it involves which woman he's taking home from a bar. You thinkin' about a fellow, Allie?"

"That's the last thing on my mind. Do you ever fight with yourself, Blake?" Allie asked.

One of Blake's shoulders hitched up a few inches. "I do it all the time."

Deke made circles with his forefinger up next to his ear. "I swear she'll be loony by the time she's thirty. Maybe I should leave the beer in the truck. She can't hold her liquor."

"What are you talkin' about? Just because you are big and mean and tough don't mean I can't drink you under the table," she protested.

Deke held up a finger and swallowed. "They say that liquor kills brain cells, and you've been talking to the voices in your head. I rest my case."

Allie shook her fist at Deke. "Enough. Eat your dinner and stop being a clown. We've got to get at least half the shingles kicked off today and new felt put down if there's not rotting boards."

"Y'all get in a bind, holler at me. I can leave what I'm doing and help any way I can," Blake said.

"We might do just that if it starts to get dark. Days don't last nearly as long in January as they do in July." Deke polished off the last of his chili. "Is it all right if I get the chocolate pie out and slice it up?"

Blake refilled his glass with sweet tea. "Help yourself to the pie. There's a Mexican casserole in the refrigerator and lots of leftover chili. Y'all might as well join me at noon while you're workin' on the roof. I hate to see good food go to waste."

Deke said, "Count me in. Is that Sharlene's Mexican casserole?"

Blake nodded.

"Thanks for the offer, but you don't have to feed us every day." Allie met Blake's steely gaze down the length of the table.

"It's no problem. The food is already here. We just have to heat it up, and I sure like to have someone other than Shooter to talk to while I eat." He smiled and went back to eating.

Deke reached under the table and squeezed her knee. She jumped like she'd been hit with a stun gun and shifted her gaze to him. He was warning her that he could and would go home before the first shingle was removed if she didn't agree to Blake's offer.

"Okay, then," Allie said. "Thank you. It's very generous of you to invite us."

* * *

An hour later, Deke had unloaded shingles from the trailer onto a couple of pallets and had repositioned the trailer to catch the old shingles as they threw them off the roof. The sound of the dozer tearing trees up by the roots could be heard in the distance as Deke set up a boom box on the roof and put in a Conway Twitty CD.

"I'm a pretty good judge of bulls, broncs, and cowboys," Deke said, climbing back down the ladder and then toting two shingle remover tools up to the roof.

"So?" Allie scrambled up the ladder right behind him.

"So Blake Dawson is a good man."

"And?" Allie picked up one of the bright orange tools with a long handle and slid it under the shingles at the peak of the roof.

Deke started on the next row, sending shingles sliding down the roof to land on the trailer.

"He won't be our neighbor long. And besides, I did my homework on this one."

Deke's eyes widened. "You investigated him?"

"Gossip works more than one way. I can find out things pretty easy, especially if it happened only a little more than a hundred miles from here. There are four Dawson boys. The older two are married and settled, but the younger ones have quite a reputation," she said.

"For ranchin'?" Deke asked. "Or with the ladies?"

She expertly popped off a shingle and moved down to the next one. "Both. Rumor has it that they're both crackerjack ranchers, and their cousin Jud, who's buying the Lucky Penny with them, is not only good with ranching but he can smell an oil well. How are you going to feel if they strike oil on the Lucky Penny and we've got all those trucks running through Dry Creek night and day?"

"That might be the kick start that Dry Creek needs to grow, and maybe some of us other ranchers can talk Jud into sniffin' around our land. Now, tell me the part about him being a wild cowboy."

Shingles started sliding down the slope of the roof and landing on the empty trailer. "Why? You afraid of the competition?"

"No way! I'm the most eligible bachelor in the whole county. I can share. Come on, Allie. Tell me."

"They call Blake the wild Dawson and his brother Toby the hot cowboy. They say that they can talk women out of their underpants in less than two hours once they meet them."

Deke threw back his head and laughed. "So that is the reason you wouldn't look at him at the dinner table. Don't worry, darlin', you can superglue your under britches to your butt so you'll be safe."

Allie moved on down the roofline. "Maybe I want him to sweet-talk me."

"What did you say?" Deke yelled.

"Nothing," Allie replied from the other end of the roof.

CHAPTER FIVE

The squeaky sounds of rusty hinges told Blake that he had to start keeping his doors locked. If Irene had arrived five minutes earlier, she would have walked in on him strip-stark naked standing in front of the fireplace. Thank goodness when she eased the door open, he was wearing flannel pajama pants and a long-sleeved thermal knit shirt. Before the door closed, he grabbed his phone from the end table and hit the numbers to call Allie.

While he waited, he picked up the remote control, put the television on mute, sighed, and threw back the blanket he'd tossed over his legs. Shooter's ears popped up and he growled, but he didn't move a muscle.

"Gettin' kind of slow there, old boy. I heard the hinges squeak before you did. And we thought that we were moving to a quiet place. Boy, were we wrong," Blake said.

"Walter, darlin'." Irene stopped and glared at Shooter. "When did you get a dog, and what is it doing in the house? They have fur to keep them warm outside. They don't belong in the house." Irene crossed her thin arms across her chest.

That night she wore purple sweatpants and cowboy boots that didn't match on the wrong feet. Sprigs of gray hair poked out around her hot-pink stocking hat. The stained work coat was three sizes too big, and her bright-red lipstick had sunk into all the wrinkles around her mouth.

"Shhh! You'll hurt my dog's feelings, Miz Irene. Have a seat. I'm making a phone call," he said.

"I didn't come over here for you to shush me, Walter. Do you think it's easy getting out of that house? Well, it's not. Besides, it's cold out there. If it don't snow before the end of the week, it's going to miss a good chance."

Allie answered on the fifth ring. "Hello."

"Hi there. This is Walter," Blake said.

"I'm on my way as soon as I can get my boots and coat on," she said.

He returned the phone to the end table, flipped the lever on the side of his worn brown leather recliner, got to his feet, and dragged a wooden rocker up close to the fire. "Here, darlin', you must be freezing. Sit right here and warm your hands while I make you a cup of hot chocolate. Can I take your coat?"

She must have loved Walter a lot, not only to trudge through the snow, but also to wear a coat that weighed half as much as she did. It's a wonder that the thing didn't fracture her frail shoulders.

"Yes, you can, and I like my hot chocolate with lots of extra cream, but you know that. Why aren't you wearing your glasses tonight? You know you can't see anything without them."

"I got those newfangled contact lenses, remember?" he said.

Irene squinted up at him. "Those what?"

"Little tiny lenses that go right in my eyes," he said. "I don't have to wear glasses all the time now."

"That's impossible, Walter. I bet they were expensive, if there is such a thing, and your mama paid for them to make you feel guilty about wanting to move her in with your brothers, didn't she?" Irene eased down into the rocking chair and held her hands out to the blazing fire. "When did you get that fancy chair? Did she buy that for you, too? I'm not surprised since she let you bring that mangy mutt in the house. She'll do anything to guilt you into keeping her with you forever."

Once she was settled, he went to the kitchen to make her hot chocolate.

"Did you put in the extra cream?" Irene asked when he brought out the steaming mug.

He set the hot chocolate on the coffee table. "Of course I did, ma'am. Be careful now. The mug is hot."

"Don't you ma'am me. I'm not your mother or an old lady." She picked up the mug and wrapped her hands around it. "Ahh, nice and warm." She closed her eyes in bliss, then snapped them open again as a car crunched on the gravel driveway. "Who would be coming around this late? Don't folks have any manners at all? You don't go visiting after dark. It's not proper."

"I guess we'll find out soon enough," he said.

Irene nodded and sipped her hot chocolate while she rocked back and forth in front of the fire. A gentle knock on the door brought the rocking chair to a stop, and Irene's expression changed. Blake turned on the porch light, opened the door, and motioned Allie inside.

Irene's eyes narrowed into little more than slits. "What are you doing here? You're supposed to be having a good time with your girlfriends because this is the last night before you get married tomorrow."

"Granny, I am your granddaughter, Allie, not your daughter, Katy, and it's time for us to go home."

Irene's face went blank as she looked around the room. "Why did you bring me to this place? I told you to stay away from here. It don't bring nothing but heartache, and yet here you are, flirting with this cowboy. It's a good thing I saw you sneaking out of the house and followed you. I'll have to watch you closer or else you'll ruin your life like your mama almost did."

"You want a cup of hot chocolate or coffee?" Blake asked.

Allie shook her head. "What's this about Mama ruining her life?"

Irene popped up out of the rocking chair and pointed her finger at Allie. "I don't want to talk about that, Alora Raine Logan. I told Katy that she'd have to get over it and she did, so we're not discussing it no more. Let's go home, and I swear, if I catch you over here one more time, you're going to be in big trouble."

"Let me help you with your coat," Allie said.

"I'm a grown woman. I don't need any help," Irene protested.

Allie stood aside and let her grandmother get the heavy coat up on her shoulders, then watched as Irene slammed the screen door and stomped out to the van. "Thanks for calling. We thought she was asleep in her room. She crawled out a window. Guess I'll have to put locks on them so she can't get out."

"She must've loved Walter a lot," he said.

"I don't even know who Walter is. He might be a boyfriend she had in the fourth grade and she's got him mixed up with someone who lived over here at some time in her life. Who knows what triggers her these days." Allie sighed.

Shooter whined, yipped, and then opened his eyes wide. He jumped up and raced across the floor like he'd been poked with a red-hot brand. Blake barely had time to sling open the screen door before the yellow blur sped past him and Allie. Then, as if in slow motion, Allie was tumbling forward, grasping at nothing more than air to break her fall.

Blake quickly wrapped his big arms around her and pulled her to his chest. Her heart pounded against his as he tightened his arms around her and her arms snaked up around his neck.

"I am so sorry," she gasped, but she didn't push away from him.

"It's all right. I've got you," he whispered. "Sorry about Shooter. I've never seen him act like that, and I've had him since the day he was born."

Her arms fell to her sides and her face turned scarlet. "I had visions of a broken arm and not being able to work."

Blake didn't know that women blushed in today's world, especially those who were tough enough to put a roof on a house and run a construction business.

Without thinking of anything other than comforting her, Blake kissed her on the forehead. "So did I, and all I could think was that the roof wasn't nearly finished."

She stiffened and took a step back. "I should be going. Thanks for not letting me fall."

In seconds she was outside, and Blake wondered what just happened. It was a simple kiss, nothing passionate or demanding, and yet there was no denying that fear in her eyes. Was it just him, or was she afraid of all men? And why?

* * *

With a racing pulse and feeling more than a little like a teenage girl who'd just gotten her first kiss, Allie crawled into the driver's seat of the van. She touched her forehead and was surprised to find that it was cold as ice and not on fire.

Granny had crossed her arms over her chest, which wasn't a good sign.

Allie started the engine and turned to face her grandmother. "Granny, you could have hurt yourself crawling out the window like that. Promise me right now that you won't do that again." She backed the van around to her left so she could straighten it up and drive down the lane. "You are going to fall and hurt yourself one of these days, and then the doctor will make us put you in a nursing home."

"I did not crawl out a window. I drove over here to get you. Don't you be making me out to be the one who did wrong. It was you, and I'm tellin' your mother what you've done. I told you to stay away from this place. I'm getting tired of having to get out in the cold to come get you," Irene said.

"Okay." Allie reached the end of the lane and turned left. "Who is Walter?"

Irene stuck her bottom lip out in a pout. "I don't know why you keep asking me that. I don't know anyone by that name, but your mama fell in love with a boy from over there, and he was bad news. The apple never falls far from the tree, and you are going to fall for that sexy cowboy who wants to get into your pants."

"Was Walter the man Mama fell in love with?" Allie asked.

Irene stomped her foot against the floorboard. "We're not talking about Walter. We're talking about you and that cowboy. You need to stay away from him. Nobody ever stays long on this place, and you'll get your heart broken."

Allie parked in front of the house, but before she could get her seat belt unfastened, Irene was out of the van and marching toward the porch with purpose. When Allie reached the foyer and shut the door, her grandmother was tattling, pointing at Allie, and her old eyes were flashing anger.

Dementia was a demon disease, and nothing could explain the way it worked other than what the doctor told them about the jigsaw puzzles. It must have been frightening to grab a piece from this part of her past and a piece from that one, and try to create a world that made sense when she was losing control of everything.

Allie could not imagine living in such a constant state of turmoil and hoped that someday only one puzzle remained and her grandmother would have a few days of lucid peace before everything was completely gone.

"Alora Raine won't do what I say and she's got a boyfriend and you know those men at the Lucky Penny are drifters who never stay in one place. I'm going to get a cookie and go to my room," Irene said tersely.

Katy winked at Allie. "I'll see to it that she's punished real good. You get your cookie and go on to bed."

Allie hung her coat on the hall tree and kicked off her boots. "Mama, who is Walter? She keeps going over there and flirting with Blake because she thinks he's Walter. And tonight she talked about you being in love with a boy from the Lucky Penny."

Katy looped her arm through Allie's and led her to the kitchen. "I've got a pot of hot spiced tea made."

Allie poured two cups of tea. "Granny said that you got mixed up with some no-good man from the Lucky Penny, too. Is that true, or just another one of her wild stories?"

"She's remembering Ray Jones. He was about eighteen when his mama and daddy bought the ranch. I was seventeen that year, and we rode the school bus together." Katy busied herself cleaning an already spotless countertop.

"And did you love him?" Allie asked.

"It was a long time ago." Katy disappeared into the utility room and returned with half a basket of kitchen towels and washcloths. She set it on the counter and started folding them. "And yes, I loved him very much, but Mama threw a hissy fit because he was wild. He was really good-lookin' with that hair combed back in a duck's tail and those pretty blue eyes and Lord, have mercy, but he could kiss good. But trouble followed him around like a little puppy, and he liked taking risks."

"What kinds of risks?"

Katy's mouth twisted up in a grin. "Like throwing stones at my window at midnight and talking me into sitting on the front porch and making out with him. Mama caught us one night, and she almost sent me to a convent over it."

"We're not Catholic," Allie said.

"She would have kissed the pope's ring if it kept me away from that boy. But then he was really pressuring me to do things I didn't want to do, so I listened to her."

"You broke up with him?"

Katy sighed. "Yes, I did, and then I fell in love with your father and figured out what real, mature love was." Her hands shook as she folded the last towel in the basket.

Allie picked up a towel and folded it neatly. "Do I hear a *but*?"

Katy finished the last tea towel and sat down at the table. "There are always buts with every story, but that's all I'm saying tonight about Ray."

"Then who is Walter?" Allie sipped her lukewarm tea.

Katy opened the cookie jar in the middle of the table and removed a chocolate one with a chocolate cream center. "He and his mother moved in after Ray's family moved out west. They were only there a year, and it was when I was all tied up with my engagement to your dad and planning my wedding. I was eighteen, but I do remember that Walter was a tall man with dark hair. But Daddy was still alive, so I can't imagine Mama being in love with him. Want a cookie?"

Allie shook her head. "I think she was in love with Walter, and Blake has brought that memory to the surface."

"Surely not! She'd been married to Daddy nineteen or twenty years that summer when I got married. I can't imagine her having an affair."

"Maybe they were only flirting," Allie said.

"Well, even flirting can be dangerous sometimes," she replied as she flashed Allie a warning look.

Allie laid a hand on her mother's arm. "You don't have to worry about me, Mama. I'm not so sure there's a man out there I could trust with my heart. I loved Riley with my whole heart and look what happened. If it hadn't been for hard work, I would have lost my mind that first year. I couldn't eat or sleep, and my brain kept running in circles trying to figure out what I could have done to prevent it. I don't think I can ever take a chance on hurting like that again. I might never be all put back together enough to trust someone else."

Katy stood up and carried a stack of tea towels to the cabinet. "You deserve something better than a pocketful of bad luck if you ever do fall in love again. And like you've already heard dozens of times, no one stays at the Lucky Penny very long."

"Thank you, Mama, but you don't have anything to worry about."

Katy sighed. "It's late and we've got a full day ahead of us tomorrow. When you finish your day's work at the ranch, you need to figure out a way to lock those windows. It's a wonder Mama didn't break a hip or an arm crawling out."

"I'll get new locks put on the windows tomorrow and be sure they're the kind she can't work." Allie dropped a kiss on her mother's head as she passed by her and went straight to her room.

She eased down into an overstuffed rocking chair in the corner and looked up at the moon hanging in the top half of her bedroom window. Only a quarter of a mile across the pasture, Blake could be looking at that same moon.

Shaking her head did not erase the picture of him in those pajama pants and that tight knit shirt. And that kiss! His soft lips on her forehead, the heat it had fired up in her heart, the way it had made her knees go so weak that she had to stiffen her whole body—all of it combined to awaken emotions she thought she'd finally buried.

She'd known Riley her whole life. He'd loved her and they'd had a marriage and he'd broken her heart. Blake Dawson was a stranger and as wild as a class-five tornado, from everything she'd heard, and Allie did not need that in her life.

But need and want were two different things altogether, and Allie's heart was daring her to test the waters in a river that she had no business putting her toes into.

* * *

Blake was amazed at how much work Deke and Allie had gotten done in only half a day. The front part of the roof was without shingles and covered with black tar paper. Deke had said that tomorrow they'd put on the new gray shingles, and on Thursday they would repeat the process on the back side of the roof. With that in mind, they'd be done Friday, so Blake only had three more days to enjoy having someone to talk to at noon.

Suddenly the loneliness of living so far from his family and friends hit him. He'd thought it would be easy because he'd work hard all day and be ready for bed come nightfall, but he hadn't figured in the fact that dark came so early in January. It wasn't even eight o'clock and he was bored out of his mind. It was five months until Toby would move to Dry Creek. That meant lots of lonely nights on his own if he didn't make friends.

Make friends, the voice in his head said loudly. *Go to church. Drop in the feed store and make friends with the lady who answered the phone. Go to the convenience store to buy a Coke. Talk to Allie. You can ask about her grandmother.*

He started to poke the telephone numbers into the phone and made it to the last number before he stopped. That was the lamest excuse to call a woman that he'd ever used, and besides, after that impromptu kiss on her forehead, she might not even finish the roof. He could be up there trying to figure out how to get the final half of the roof done by himself come daylight.

He tried to watch a movie, but it couldn't hold his attention. Then he picked up a book and read ten pages without comprehending a single thing. He could call Toby, but he'd only get a hat full of sarcasm out of him.

Yes, Blake had volunteered to live on the ranch alone for the first stretch, to get enough land cleared, to get enough fences repaired or built to hold a small herd by summertime. Then Toby would join him and then the house wouldn't seem so empty. Then, in the fall, Jud would move in with them, and he'd be wishing he had some peace and quiet.

Blake paced the floor, went to the kitchen, and opened the refrigerator. Nothing looked good. He took a cookie from the jar, but it didn't have any taste and he gave the last half to Shooter. He went to the window and pulled up the ratty blinds. The moon hung out there with a whole sky full of stars around it. They looked cold up there in the sky, as if they were aware that in a few days they'd be blotted out from sight.

What was wrong with him? He had called many women with less reason than to ask about her grandmother. Had this place robbed him of all his wild ways? No, sir! Nothing could tame a wild Dawson cowboy! And if Allie didn't want to talk, he could call Sharlene or Mary Jo.

He poked in the numbers again without pausing.

"Hi, Blake. Please don't tell me Granny is back over there," Allie answered.

He paced the floor again as he talked, moving from the living room to the kitchen, around the table, and back to the living room. "No, I wanted to be sure you got her home all right, though."

"She's fine," Allie said.

"You got time to talk?"

"About what?"

He hesitated, looking for something, anything, to keep her on the phone other than the job. "Did you figure out who Walter is or was?"

"Mama says he moved in over there more than thirty years ago."

"I wonder what it is that she remembers in bits and pieces." He could listen to her read the dictionary with that soft Southern twang in her voice.

"Mama said it was the year she was planning her wedding, and she got married when she was eighteen. I think Granny had her when she was about nineteen because Mama is fifty-one."

Shooter looked up from the end of the sofa, and Blake stopped to scratch his ears. "And you are how old?"

"Twenty-nine in the spring, and you do know it's not polite to ask a woman how old she is or how much she weighs?" Allie said.

"Let me guess: one hundred twenty-five pounds, but that's with your boots on." Did that slight lilt in her voice mean that she was enjoying talking to him?

A long pause made him check the phone to see if she was still there. Then Shooter went to the door and looked up at the doorknob.

"Just a minute, old boy," he whispered. The dog could cross his legs for a few minutes. Blake was just starting to get Allie to open up, and he wasn't about to lose the opportunity to talk to her some more.

"What did you call me? Did you really say *old boy* to me? And I'm going to shoot Deke for telling you my weight," Allie said.

"Deke didn't tell me. I caught you when you fell, and I'm a pretty good judge of how much dead weight I can hold." Blake started for the door to let Shooter out, but the dog changed his mind and returned to his rug by the fire.

"So, how old are you?" she asked.

"Twenty-nine last November, and I weigh two hundred pounds without my boots." He searched his mind for something else to talk about so she wouldn't make an excuse to end the call. Church! He planned to go on Sunday to get to know more people in the area. That was a safe topic. "Do you go to that church down the road from the feed store?"

"It's the only church left in Dry Creek, so yes, that's where my family goes on Sunday."

She surely must not be nervous because she wasn't talking too fast or spitting out too many details like Deke said. Was she only being nice to him because for the next few days he was her employer?

Shooter went back to the door, and he headed in that direction. "Do they make newcomers walk through hot coals?"

"We tend to welcome them, not punish them. But we might kill a chicken and use the blood for war paint on your cheeks." She giggled.

He shivered at the visual that reply produced. "Is that initiation, or do you get your cheeks painted, too, since you invited me?"

"I didn't invite you. I just said that we have church and we welcome newcomers," she argued.

He opened the door, but Shooter barely stuck his nose out. "So, if I show up in my best jeans and polished boots, they might not tar and feather me?"

"No, but they might make you eat the raw chicken, feathers and all, to prove you are tough enough to live in our part of Texas." She laughed.

Her laughter was like tinkling bells on a belly dancer's costume. Matter of fact, the only time he saw a real belly dancer, she had dark brown hair and brown eyes. Could Allie have secrets hiding somewhere in the pockets of those cargo pants?

"Sounds like I'd better sneak in late and sit on the back pew so I can make an escape if I hear clucking."

"You might as well sit on the front pew. Where's the fun in not taking risks?" she answered.

She was warming up. He could hear it in her voice. He closed his eyes and imagined her doing a seductive dance for him in a flowing costume with little bells sewn into the fabric around the hips. His breath caught in his chest and he gasped.

"So you don't take risks?" she asked.

"Shooter can't make up his mind whether to go out or stay in. Cold wind about took my breath away. And, honey, I do take risks. I bought the Lucky Penny, remember?" He closed the door, but Shooter didn't go back to the rug.

"Point taken," she said. "Don't bother polishing your boots or they might take you for a city boy. We're pretty casual here in Dry Creek."

"Do you polish your boots?" he asked.

"Mama says that on Sunday I have to wear shoes and a dress. It's painful, but I do it for her."

Blake sat down in his recliner. "Where do the strangers sit?"

"Anywhere there's an empty pew."

He would have liked it a lot more if she'd said that he could sit with her family, but that could prove disastrous if Granny decided he was Walter halfway through the service.

"So, are you thinkin' about coming to services on Sunday morning, then?" she asked.

Shooter came over to his side, and Blake scratched the top of the dog's head. "Thought I might. You want to drive over to Olney and get a hamburger with me afterward?"

"Already got plans for Sunday dinner, but thank you all the same," she said.

"Another time?"

"We'll see," she said. "I hear Shooter whining. Sounds like he's ready to brave the cold. Thanks for checking on Granny."

"I feel sorry for her, trying so hard to get things in order. Poor old girl doesn't need to be traipsing through the cold. See you tomorrow at noon. Hey, would you know anyone who'd like to have some firewood? I'll give away all the mesquite wood that anyone wants to haul off. It's already piled up, so they can bring their chain saws and help themselves."

"You could put up a sign in the feed store and Mama's place. Lots of folks around here use wood in the winter, and mesquite burns really well," she said.

"Good idea. Thanks, Allie. And thanks for visitin' with me. See you tomorrow."

"Good night, Blake," she said softly.

He hummed all the way to the door to let the dog out one more time that night and decided as he waited for Shooter to water a nearby bush that he didn't want to talk to Sharlene or to Mary Jo. Maybe he was making progress after all.

CHAPTER SIX

A blast of warm air and the familiar smell of a feed store hit Blake square in the face when he opened the door to the Dry Creek Feed and Supply store that cold Wednesday morning. He removed his sunglasses and tucked them into his coat pocket while he took stock of the store. Not too different from the one he and his folks used in Muenster but quite a bit smaller. Shelves of supplies to his right along with a small assortment of tools, three or four round racks of clothing to the left, with a few sacks of feed piled up at the back of the store. Most likely that door at the back led into a warehouse, where folks who bought large quantities of feed backed their trucks up to load them.

"Can I help you?" A lady made her way to the front.

"I need to place an order for about three hundred steel fence posts, five feet tall should do it, and maybe ten rolls of barbed wire," he said. "I'm Blake Dawson. I'm new in town."

"I know who you are." She was pretty danged cute in those tight-fitting jeans and chambray shirt tucked in behind a cowgirl belt that cinched up to show off a small waistline.

"But I don't know you." He smiled.

She smiled back. "I'm Lizzy, Allie's sister. Welcome to Dry Creek."

"I'm pleased to meet you, Lizzy," he said.

"I have what you need in the warehouse. It's twenty dollars extra to deliver it unless you spend five hundred dollars, and I can get it there tomorrow." She circled around behind the cash register and hit several buttons, then looked up and said, "Cash or credit card?"

"Credit card, and I reckon that order mounts up to a lot more than five hundred dollars, so I'd appreciate it if you'd deliver it to the Lucky Penny. Tomorrow is fine. You mind if I put a flyer up there on your bulletin board with those others?"

"What are you selling? Surely you're not already leaving the ranch." Her dishwater-blond hair was pulled up in a ponytail, and those light brown eyes had more questions behind them than whether he was leaving Dry Creek before he'd even unpacked.

Blake headed toward the front of the store. "I'm giving away mesquite wood to anyone who wants to come get it. Folks are welcome to cut down however much they want for free." He used four thumbtacks stuck on the outside of the corkboard to attach the flyer he'd made the night before on his computer. "How long have you been in business?" He handed her his business credit card.

"My whole life." She pulled it free from his fingers and ran it through the machine, then handed it back, waited a second for the tape to roll out of the cash register, and laid it in front of him. "Sign right there."

He scrawled his name on the bottom. "Are you the person I talked to when Irene showed up on my doorstep?"

She gave him his copy. "Yes, I am. Are you going to be home by eleven today? I hear the church ladies are bringing more food."

"Yes, ma'am, I will definitely be there. How long have you worked here?" he asked.

"I own this place," she said.

She'd been coolly friendly, but she hadn't flirted with him. Was he losing his touch? What if he was never able to entice a woman into his bed again?

Then he saw the engagement ring on her left hand and he could breathe again. "When are you getting married?"

She held up the ring and looked at it as if seeing it for the first time. A bright smile lit up her face. "In March. If you are still here, you are invited to the wedding. It will be held at the church, with the reception in the fellowship hall."

"Thank you. I'll be there for sure because, Miz Lizzy, I will definitely still be around." He stopped at the door, settled his cowboy hat on his head, and turned around before he opened the door. "You own the store down the block, too?"

"No, that's still Mama's business, but she won't mind if you put up a flyer," Lizzy answered. "Don't forget. Eleven o'clock. And act surprised. Don't tell them I told you. Don't want them to be disappointed if you weren't home. They've probably been cooking for two days."

He gave her the thumbs-up sign and stepped out into the harsh January wind. Oklahoma had its own song about the wind coming swooping down the plains, but they couldn't hold a candle that day to the Texas wind blowing dead leaves and dirt down the sidewalk between the feed store and the service station–slash–convenience store on the other corner of the block.

Four empty buildings with either dirty windows or newspaper covering the windows separated the feed store on one corner of the block and the convenience store on the other end. The faded signs said at one time there had been a beauty and barbershop combination, a clothing store, a café, and a bakery in Dry Creek. He glanced across the street at the empty places on that side with windows so dirty that he couldn't even see what kind of signs might have been written on them in past days.

He bypassed two gas pumps and crossed a wooden porch into the store that was set back from the rest of the empty buildings. The windows were sparkling clean, and the inside of the store was neatly put together. He was met with the rich aroma of breakfast food, maybe sausage gravy and hot biscuits.

"Hello, what can I help you with?" It was easy to see that this was Allie's mother. They had the same brown eyes, and although her hair had a few gray streaks, it was still mostly dark brown. Katy was taller than Allie by a couple of inches and a few pounds heavier. Crow's-feet around her eyes said that she'd enjoyed life and laughed a lot.

The store was set up with the cashier's counter to the right inside the door and shelves of staples lined up neatly to the left with restroom signs in that corner. Tables were back there with chairs pushed up around them, and a meat counter with a stove behind it took up the room beside the counter.

He removed his cowboy hat. "I'm Blake Dawson, and I'd like to put up a flyer to give away mesquite wood. So, this is a gas station, a convenience store, and a café all combined?" he asked.

"Not a real café. Since we don't have a place for folks to

grab a bite of lunch on the run, I put in a small deli counter and I make one thing at noon. Something simple like chili or soup or maybe tacos."

"Beer, bait, and ammo," he said with a smile.

"Something like that, only it's gas, Cokes, and tacos." She grinned back at him.

"Walter! What are you doing here this time of morning?" Irene pushed back a chair from one of the three old tables covered with yellow Formica with mismatched chairs around them. "You moved away and said you'd never come back to Dry Creek."

"Miz Irene, look at me closely. I'm Blake Dawson, not Walter," he said gently.

"That's right. You're that scoundrel who's trying to get Alora Raine into bed with you. Well, it won't work. I'll protect her." Irene stuck her nose in the air and disappeared behind a curtain separating the front of the store from the back.

"Sorry about that," Katy said.

"It's all right. If I tell her often enough that I'm not Walter, then maybe she'll forget about him. So, I can run in at noon if I don't want to cook?"

"Or in the morning." She pointed to the chalkboard above the counter.

He took his gloves off and shoved them into the pockets of his coat. "Breakfast and dinner, both. I'll have to remember that."

"Breakfast is the same every morning. Sausage gravy and biscuits. Dinner is take it or leave it, but I've got a lot of folks who are willing to take it. I do make deli sandwiches out of the meat market back there." She nodded toward the display of pork chops, steak, and lunch meats.

"And I thought this was only a convenience store," he said.

Katy handed him a roll of tape. "Go on and put your flyer in the window. But you might get more folks on your ranch than you want. Mesquite makes for some good hot fire."

He laid two packages of chocolate chip cookies and a bag of chips on the counter. "I'd also like two pounds of bologna sliced thick and a pound of ham sliced real thin. My dog, Shooter, likes a piece of bologna every night before bedtime."

She headed for the back of the store. "And the ham?"

"That's for me," he said.

"I'll take care of it. Blake, you do know what they say about the Lucky Penny?"

"I'm hoping to change that," he said.

* * *

Allie was sitting on the roof, waiting for Deke to bring up another roll of tar paper, when her phone rang. "Hey, Lizzy. Please tell me Granny hasn't run off again."

"Nope. But I did just meet your hot cowboy. No wonder you keep going over there every chance you get."

Allie wanted to chew up shingles and spit out bricks. "You're right, darlin'. I might seduce him soon as I crawl down off this ladder," she said, her voice laden with sarcasm.

"Alora Raine!" Lizzy gasped.

"For the last time, I'm only here to put on his roof. Now, Deke has the paper ready to roll so we can get this job done. Was there something you needed, or were you just calling to annoy the crap out of me?" Icicles dripped from Allie's words.

"Well, for your information," Lizzy huffed, "Mitch's cousin Grady is coming for his tux fitting, and we've planned a dinner for the four of us in Wichita Falls on Friday night. He sounds really eager to see you again. Play your cards right, and I bet he could make you forget all about your cowboy."

Allie came close to dropping the nail gun at the thought. The way Grady looked at her made her skin crawl. "Good grief, Lizzy! I'm perfectly capable of taking care of my own love life, and I'm absolutely not going to dinner with Grady."

"Yes, you are. Be ready at seven, and that means good jeans or a dress and makeup, too," Lizzy said.

"You'd better have a backup plan in your hip pocket because I'm not going," she said.

The phone went silent, and she looked at it. Sure enough, her sister had hung up on her. Deke had barely gotten the tar paper unrolled across the length of the roof, when her phone rang again. She fished it out of her pocket, hoping that it was Lizzy so she could give her a piece of her mind.

"I know you are busy, so I won't talk but a minute," her mother said. "I really think you should go with Mitch and Lizzy on Friday night. You will be standing up there with her, and he's the best man. It's not a date but an evening to discuss wedding plans."

"That tattletale! What makes you take her side in this? Why would you want me tangled up with Grady? He's even worse than Riley was," Allie fumed.

"She's your sister and she's worried about you, and frankly so am I. Blake came in here today, and the way he looks, he's got heartbreaker written all over him. Come on, Allie, listen to the voice of experience when it talks to you," Katy said tersely.

Allie took a deep breath and let it out slowly. "I'm not going to dinner with them." Allie heard Deke huffing and puffing as he climbed the ladder with a heavy roll of black roofing paper on his shoulder.

"Okay, then I'll invite them to Sunday dinner, and you can discuss wedding plans then," Katy said.

Allie had never wanted to hit something so badly in her life. "Mama!"

"Friday or Sunday. Your choice."

She thought about it a second. "I'm not going Friday."

"Then Sunday it is," Katy said. "Blake bought a few things and put up a flyer to give away mesquite for firewood. And, Allie, the church ladies are coming at eleven this morning to welcome him to Dry Creek. You might want to be on the roof working instead of in the house with him. Even if y'all are only talking business, it wouldn't look good."

Allie motioned for Deke to drop the roll of black paper beside her. "Good way for Blake to get to know the people, ain't it? Give them something for free? And, Mama, stop worryin' about me."

"I'm a mother. It's my job to worry. Men that good-lookin' are out for a good time, and all they leave in their wake are tears. Grady is a good man. Youth minister at the church up around Gainesville," Katy said.

"Whoopee for him. I've got to get to work. Deke is ready for me to start nailing. See you at supper." Allie pushed the END button.

"Who's giving away what for free?" Deke asked.

Blake poked his head up over the edge of the roof. "I am. News travels fast around here, don't it? I'm giving away all the mesquite for firewood."

"You care if we sell it once we take it off your place?" Deke asked.

Blake chuckled. "You can boil it and make mesquite pie with it for all I care. I want it gone."

"You've got a fireplace." Allie looked up from her nail gun. "Why don't you use it?"

His gaze locked with hers, the heat melting the cold all around her. She'd never had a man look at her and create such an intense reaction. One part of her, the emotional side, wanted to dive into those green eyes and see what lay beneath that flirting nature—down deeper than his wild cowboy ways and into the very man. The other side, the sensible side, told her to run from him as fast as she could.

"I'm going to cut up as much as I can this afternoon and stack it up behind the house. I can probably save enough on my heating bill to pay for the ceiling and the paint that way," he said.

She looked down at her nail gun and snapped another shingle in place. "Price of fuel these days, you just might."

"Thought I'd check on the progress before I take the chain saw out to the brush pile. This roof is lookin' really good. I guess you really will get it done by the weekend." He took a step back down the ladder.

Allie looked up from the nail gun and nodded. "If the weather holds for us, we will. I told you in the beginning I thought we could get it done by quittin' time on Friday."

Now that her mother and sister kept going on about how sexy Blake was, it was all she could think about as she pulled the trigger on the gun and moved down the roof to the next spot.

Blake nodded. "See y'all at noon. I'll be in a little early today. Allie, you want me to heat up the leftover chili?"

"Yes, thank you," Allie said.

"Will do," Blake said.

"Now what's got your panties in a twist?" Deke asked as soon as Blake disappeared.

"That's not something a guy friend says." Allie snapped another nail in place. "You'd best get to unrolling the next length."

"Not until you tell me what Lizzy's done now. Only she can put a look on your face that would melt the North Pole." Deke expertly rolled a length of paper out and cut the end with a box cutter.

"Mama and Lizzy are trying to fix me up with Mitch's cousin Grady."

Deke went back to the other end of the roof and started rolling out more paper. "You don't want to get tangled up with that guy. I know him, and believe me when I tell you his hat ain't coverin' up a halo but horns."

She snapped a couple of nails in the paper to hold it down so the wind wouldn't whip it off the roof before she answered. "Lizzy and Mama think he's a saint because he's a youth minister."

"Yep, but that don't make him any less of a devil when it comes to women. I've played poker with him and Mitch a few times, and he ain't a bit better than your ex. Steer clear of him," Deke said.

"Talk, Deke. I want to know about Mitch." She flipped the safety on the gun and rolled back on her butt. "Is my sister making a big mistake?"

Deke positioned half a dozen more shingles, then sat down beside her. "Well, Mitch and Grady were really players, but in the last couple of years they've had a come-to-Jesus experience, and now they're ready to get married. They've been bragging about how it's their biblical right to have someone cook and clean and do everything they say."

"Seriously?" Allie hissed. "I knew that Mitch was a snake. You should tell Mama."

Deke reached for the nail gun. "No way! She wouldn't believe me, and Lizzy would bury my body back in the mesquite so far that even the coyotes couldn't find me. I'm not sure where Katy stands where Grady is concerned, so I'm not sayin' a word. I sure don't want to be on either of their bad sides since I run a bill at both their stores. But, honey, you steer clear of Grady."

CHAPTER SEVEN

Blake brought a load of wood to the house just before eleven that morning but didn't take time to stack it. The steady sound of hammering up on the roof let him know Allie and Deke were hard at work as he hurried into the house. Blake threw a couple of logs on the fire so there would be a welcoming blaze, put on a pot of coffee, and slid the Mexican casserole into the oven.

Several vehicles pulled up in front of his house at exactly eleven o'clock, but he waited until someone knocked on the door to open it.

"Welcome to Dry Creek!" one of the dozen ladies standing on his porch said cheerfully. "We brought food so you'd have something to eat until you can get settled in."

Sharlene winked from back behind the woman.

Mary Jo smiled at him from the sidelines.

"Thank you all so much," Blake said. "Please come right in and excuse the mess. I'm not nearly unpacked yet. Can I get you ladies a cup of coffee?"

Sharlene ran her forefinger down his arm and locked it

around his pinkie. "I've been waiting for your call," she whispered.

Mary Jo pushed between Sharlene and Blake to hug him. "Welcome to Dry Creek. We're a friendly bunch, and we hope you do better on this ranch than the other folks have."

"I'm Dora June. This is Lucy." The woman with three chins made so many introductions so fast that he'd never remember all their names. "And now for the food! You'll have to freeze some of it, but I reckon you'll want to have my fried chicken for dinner since it's still hot."

"Why, Miz Dora June, how did you know fried chicken was my favorite food in the whole wide world? My mouth is already watering," he said.

"All cowboys like fried chicken." She beamed.

In a few minutes his kitchen table was filled with food, his counter space was covered with desserts, and a couple gallon jugs of sweet tea had been set in his near-empty refrigerator.

"I see my slow cooker in the fridge with leftover chili in it," Mary Jo whispered while the other women talked nonstop about how good it was to have someone living on the ranch. "All you have to do is call me when it's empty and I'll come get it, night or day."

Sharlene waited until Mary Jo moved to the side and looped her arm in Blake's. "And you've eaten my casserole already. I'll bring another one right over any ole time of the day...or night." She gave his right butt cheek a squeeze. "We might build up an appetite and then we could share it. I brought my pot roast today, and if you like it better, give me a day's notice."

Blake had fallen into a wild cowboy's paradise. He didn't even have to go bar hopping on the weekend. All he had to do was make a phone call, but...

Dammit! Why did there always have to be a *but*?

But, the voice in his head said loud and clear, *what if these women are looking for more than a one-night stand or a weekend romp in the sheets? What if they want a long-term relationship? Then you'll be up crap creek without any sign of a paddle because the whole town will turn against you for hurting their feelings.*

Lucy clapped her hands. "Okay, ladies. This man has work to do if he's going to get this place whipped into shape. Let's go on now. We will see you in church on Sunday, won't we, Mr. Dawson?"

"You are all such sweethearts to take care of me like this, and yes, ma'am, I will be in church Sunday. I might be twenty pounds heavier after eating all this good cookin', but I'll be there," he promised.

Lucy nodded. "You've got an open invitation to go home with me and my husband, Herman, for Sunday dinner anytime, honey. You might get lonely, and Herman can talk the legs off a kitchen table when it comes to ranchin' and cows."

"Thank you again for everything." Blake followed the parade back through the living room.

"You don't need to come out to the porch, cold as it is," Ruby said. "Just get on in there and open up that fried chicken and my potato casserole. They go right well together. And I do believe that Nadine sent her famous apple pie."

"I can't thank y'all enough for making me welcome," Blake said.

"Honey, I'd like to show you just how welcome you are," Sharlene said softly just before she followed the rest of the crowd outside.

Blake was still shaking his head, wondering how he was ever going to deal with so much temptation on every corner, when Deke pushed into the back door.

"We're at a stopping place. Mind if we come in and get warm? Wow! What is all this? Looks like a buffet for an army."

"Take off your coats and get comfortable. Make yourselves at home. Most of this will go in the freezer, but I understand the fried chicken is still warm and there is a potato casserole somewhere," Blake answered.

Deke headed for the living room. "Sounds like heaven to me."

Allie pulled off her gloves, tucked them in her coat pocket, and then hung it on the back of a chair. "Okay if I wash up at the kitchen sink? After we eat, I could help you put the other stuff in the freezer."

"Help yourself and thank you," Blake said.

"Ahhh," she said as the water went from cold to warm and then hot. "I need to do inside jobs in the winter."

"Speaking of that. Do you have anything lined up right now? I could sure use some help on the ceilings where the roof leaked through. Any advice you can give would be appreciated," he said.

She turned off the water and looked around for a towel. "Well, it should just take some drywall and paint. Probably not too expensive."

Blake picked up the hand towel from the cabinet and held it out toward her. "Would you be able to do the job? I'd be glad to help."

She turned around quickly and slammed right into his chest. "Oh, s-sorry," she stammered.

He ran the back of his hand down her cheek and looked

deeply into those brown eyes. He tipped her chin up with his knuckles and slowly bent to brush a soft kiss across her lips.

Never had a first brief kiss affected him like that, not in all the years he'd perfected his wild ways with women. The feeling was so new that he wasn't sure what to do with it. Did he apologize for kissing her or kiss her again with more intensity?

She took a step to the side, and her hand went to her lips. "I can work for you, Blake Dawson, but you cannot do that again."

"Are you seeing someone?" He handed her the towel.

She dried her hands and threw the towel over his shoulder. "No, and I'm not looking to be either. I was married at one time, and I loved that man with my whole heart. When the marriage ended, my nerves were shot. It's a long story and it's sure nothing to do with you, but..."

"Guess I got mixed signals. Can we at least be friends?"

"I don't know, but I..."

Two buts in less than a minute. Two women chasing him, ready and waiting for his call, and the one who had *but*s at the end of every sentence was the one who turned him inside out with a simple kiss. Oh, the irony!

"Hey, it smells good in here." Deke appeared in the doorway rubbing his hands together. "Blake, why don't you hire Allie to give this place a facelift while her business is slow?"

In a couple of long strides, Allie was behind her chair, her hands gripping the back where her coat hung.

"That's what we've just been talking about," she said.

Deke pulled out a chair and sat down. "Well, I'm going to be cutting wood if Blake was serious about the mesquite.

I can make more at that than helping you, but I will miss the dinners."

"If you are willing to clear mesquite, I will gladly provide dinner. You can eat with me and Allie every day," Blake said.

Deke glanced over his shoulder toward Allie. "You okay with that since I'm not going to be helping you?"

"Yes, of course," Allie said. "It's Blake's house and his food, not mine."

* * *

Allie was surprised that her voice sounded completely normal. Every nerve was humming loudly in her body. She pulled out the chair and sat down, glad to be off her weak knees. What had she done?

You took another job and Deke won't be there and you kissed that cowboy just like I knew you would. It was Lizzy's voice, no doubt about it, fussing at her. Allie hoped that when Lizzy did something stupid, she heard Allie's voice in her head telling her all about it.

Suddenly Deke touched her on the shoulder. "Earth to Allie," he said.

She was amazed to see that a disposable pan of fried chicken and one of potato casserole had been set on the table. Both Deke and Blake were looking at her like they expected her to say grace or do something.

"What?"

"Blake is going to say the blessing. Bow your head," Deke said.

A cowboy who said grace?

Her chin went down and she peeked out of one eye. Blake's

long lashes rested on his cheekbones, and that slow drawl sounded sincere when he said a quick blessing over the food.

"Now, let's eat," he said.

Allie picked up the potato casserole, heaped her plate, and sent it to Deke. "It smells really good. I'm sorry about a while ago. I was thinking about the ceilings. Do you want drywall, or would you like a framework and panels? That way, a panel could be removed and replaced if it got messed up and you wouldn't have to do the whole ceiling. They make the framework now to look like wood so it's not so modern looking." She was talking too fast and talking business when what she really wanted to do was curl up in the rocking chair in her room and think about that kiss.

"You weren't thinking about ceilings at all. Your eyes were all dreamy and soft, so you were off in Cinderella land. Did the prince ask you to dance yet?" Deke laughed. "But if that's your story, I'm sure you'll stick with it. You want a chicken leg or a breast or a thigh?"

She nodded. "Leg is fine."

"Who won?" Deke asked.

"Won what?" Blake asked before Allie could answer.

"Allie was fighting with herself again." Deke forked out a wing and a breast to lay on his plate. "She does that a lot. Lizzy or you? Who won?"

Allie managed a weak smile. "It was a tie this time."

"What were they arguing about?" Blake asked.

"Friday night." She answered honestly but kept her eyes on her food.

Blake passed a container of marinated vegetables to her. "What about Friday night?"

It didn't help that his fingertips brushed hers in the transfer.

Thank goodness there was food in her mouth, giving her a minute to think before answering.

"Her sister, Lizzy, the one you met at the feed store, is getting married this spring," Deke said. "Her boyfriend is Mitch, and his cousin Grady is the best man. Lizzy is trying to fix Allie up with him while he's in town this weekend. Why were you thinking about that, Allie? Did you change your mind?"

She shook her head. "Not in a million years."

"Good," Deke said. "I can get you out of that Sunday dinner real easy. I'll call and say that we have an emergency plumbing problem on Sunday right after church. Pipes could freeze right here at the Lucky Penny, and we wouldn't have a choice but to fix them. Might take all the way to supper to get the job done. I'll bring the beer. Besides, it could snow, and if it does, Mitch might not be able to get down here to go to church with Lizzy."

"Don't even suggest such a thing or it might happen," Blake said. "And I thought y'all were talking about Friday, not Sunday."

"She has to put up with Grady on Sunday at her mama's house since she won't go out with him on Friday. I'm her best friend, so I'm trying to help her out here," Deke explained.

Blake nodded. "So that's the reason you can't go get a burger with me?"

Deke chuckled.

Allie pointed her fork at him. "It's not funny."

"Yep, it is."

"Changing the subject here since my mama says it's not nice to make a lady blush," Blake said.

Allie could have planted a kiss right on those full sexy lips at that moment. She was sick of Lizzy's wedding plans, and she'd rather talk about busted sewer lines than those ugly orchid taffeta dresses Lizzy wanted her and Fiona to wear.

"Are you really going to start hauling wood off this place tomorrow?" Blake asked.

Deke refilled his plate. "Yeah, I am. And I got a feeling there'll be a lot more folks out there with chain saws. I bet Herman Hudson is the first one out here with his crew of grandsons. What do you think, Allie? You think that anyone can beat Herman when there's free wood to be had?" Deke asked.

Allie took a sip of the tea. Not too sweet but with enough sugar and strength to know she was drinking Southern tea and not murdered water. "We've got a lot of winter left, so he sure won't pass up a chance to get at this much mesquite for free."

She didn't want to talk about wood or anything else. She wanted to be back on the roof with her nail gun, working on the job where she'd have lots of time to think. Maybe even with her earbuds in place and listening to George Strait, who had helped her through the most difficult time of her life with the lyrics to his fifty greatest hits. Back when she first found out that Riley had been cheating on her for years, she'd leaned on country music to get her through those sad, tough times.

She stole a sideways glance toward Blake and found him staring at her. Their gazes caught above the fried chicken and time stood still.

* * *

Those dark eyes mesmerized him, and Blake wished she'd let him in long enough to see into her heart. He knew women, could look into their eyes, see past the glitter and glam, and know what they wanted from him. If it was a good time, he provided it. If it was a relationship, he was gone in a hurry. But this was something different. Could he really be courting a woman for friendship? If so, he was sure in virgin territory.

Deke pushed back his chair, picked up his plate, and carried it to the sink. "I bet that's Nadine's apple pie, isn't it?"

"That's what the ladies said. Help yourself to all you want. I hate apple pie. Ice cream is in the freezer if you want to top it off," Blake said.

Allie pushed back her chair. "I'm too full for dessert, even Nadine's pie, which I do like. I'm going back up on the roof. See you when you get done. Thanks for dinner, Blake. We'll discuss the next job after we finish the roof."

Blake waited until she was out of the house to ask, "What's her story?"

"Lived here in Dry Creek all her life, most of it over at Audrey's Place. Crazy the way that name has stuck for more than a hundred years."

"House is almost a hundred years old?" Blake rinsed dirty dishes and set them aside.

"Pretty close to that. Before the Depression it was a small hotel, but Audrey found out pretty quick that folks didn't have money for traveling. No one ever called it a brothel, but she hired six girls, gave them a room and three meals a day and a big cut of what they made. At least, that's the story. Who knows what is true and what is rumor around here."

Blake poured two cups of coffee and set one in front of Deke. "It looks like it held up good."

"Foundation is good and solid. Allie is afraid to knock out walls for fear the ceiling will sag. I told her that she couldn't knock them out because the studs are petrified by now," Deke answered.

Not caring that he was being nosy, he wandered into personal territory that went deeper than mere friendship. "Tell me more about Allie."

Deke dug into his pie. "She has two sisters. Lizzy, who you met, and Fiona, who lives down in Houston. Works for some big crackerjack law firm and is married to one of the partners. Allie's daddy was a carpenter, and she learned the trade from him. Married right out of high school. Divorced after two or three years. Can't remember exactly how long they were together, but he cheated on her. The rest you'll have to ask her. She's my best friend, and I'm not getting into any more trouble."

"Sometimes her eyes look sad," Blake said.

Dozens of wrinkles creased Deke's forehead when he frowned. "Allie? Sad? She's the happiest woman I know. She likes what she does, and she's the easiest woman in the world to work with and for."

"How long has she been a carpenter?"

Deke polished off his tea and refilled it one more time. "She started helping her dad when she was in middle school. I think she was about fifteen when she went on the payroll. She bought the cutest little pickup truck when she was sixteen. She's still got that truck somewhere over there at their place, but mostly she drives the business van these days."

Deke piled ice cream on top of the apple pie and carried it to the table. "When I was sixteen and she was twenty, she hired me to help her put the first roof on a house. It was her first solo job, and she was so nervous and—dang it, Blake Dawson, you got more out of me than I should have told. You interested in her or what?"

"She's going to be working on my house. I wondered if something about this place makes her sad, like her ex-husband lived here at one time. Or if maybe she used to sneak off and meet him here?"

"Oh, no! Riley wasn't..." Deke shook his head. "All I'm sayin' is that this house does not make her sad, and my lips are sealed past that. You want to know more about Allie, you go talk to her. She'd fire me on the spot for shootin' off my mouth. Now I'm going to change the subject. Are you going to tear up some more mesquite after dinner or start fixin' fence?"

Blake cocked his head to one side. "Why would you ask that?"

"There's the feed store truck coming down the lane." Deke pointed out the window. "I reckon it's bringin' all that barbed wire and those fence posts you bought. There are no secrets in Dry Creek, especially when it comes to the Lucky Penny. You might as well live in a glass house."

"Why are folks so interested?" Blake's skin crawled at the idea of people watching him through the windows of a glass house.

"Because you are the new guy in town, and they want to see if you'll last through the winter. They've probably already got bets on how long you'll stay. The ones who bet for you will be nice and the others, not so much. You'd better get out there and tell them where to unload that stuff or they'll drop it right in your front yard."

CHAPTER EIGHT

Allie hummed as she made her way to the kitchen that Friday morning. She was sure she and Deke could finish the roofing that day. Rays of sun poured into the foyer through the window in the door, and the aroma of fresh coffee floated from the kitchen. The humming stopped when she saw Lizzy sitting at the table. Their kitchen wasn't as big as the one over at the Lucky Penny, but their dining room could match it for size. Most of their meals they took in the kitchen unless they had company, and then Katy set the table in the dining room.

Allie liked the kitchen better, with its bright yellow walls and white woodwork. It brought cheer into the house on the darkest mornings. But the dining room, with its paneled walls and heavy curtains, told a different story. It said to sit up straight and be nice; there was company in the house.

"It's your morning to make breakfast," Lizzy said coldly. "I made coffee, but I'm not helping cook, not if you won't go with me and Mitch and Grady to dinner tonight."

Allie filled her father's favorite mug and sipped from it,

hoping that holding his old cup would give her the strength for yet another fight with her sister.

"Aren't you going to say a word? You know I'm right. That bad boy next door isn't for you, isn't interested in you other than maybe for a quick romp in the sheets, so wake up and smell the bacon," Lizzy said.

"What makes him a bad boy?" Allie asked.

"Sharlene and Mary Jo have been over there already, and he's been flirting with them. I heard he even called Dora June sweetheart, and she's sour as rotten lemons. If she smiled more than twice in a year, she'd probably drop dead. Sharlene says that she intends to bed and wed him by the end of the year, and you know how wild that girl is. Only a bad boy would take her eye," Lizzy answered.

"What I do or do not do with the cowboy next door is my business. I'm old enough to take care of myself." Allie sipped the steaming-hot coffee. "Besides, who died and made you God?"

"Don't blaspheme!" Lizzy raised her voice.

Irene shuffled into the room with Katy right behind her. "Don't yell in the house."

"Mama, talk some sense into your oldest daughter." Lizzy rolled her eyes.

"God is a lot farther away than the ceiling, so you might as well not be lookin' up there expecting him to leave important work to settle your fight." Irene went to the cabinet, poured a cup of coffee, and took it to the table. "Is Allie cooking this morning? If she is, I want pancakes."

Allie began to gather the ingredients from the refrigerator and pantry. "I'm tired of this fight, Mama. And yes, Granny, we are having pancakes if that's what you want."

"We need to get this settled," Lizzy said.

"Sounds to me like it is settled," Irene said. "Lizzy, you need to stop your whining and carryin' on like a two-year-old. Allie don't like that rascal Grady and neither do I. He's got wandering eyes and probably hands that match."

"Granny, he's a youth minister!" Lizzy protested.

"That don't mean anything, girl. There have been men since the beginnin' of time that wasn't worth a dime, and Grady is one of them. His ancestors probably spent a lot of time in this very house back when Audrey was doin' what she could to keep soul and body together," Irene declared with a frown. "And you can wipe that grin off your face, Allie. Ain't no good ever came from the Lucky Penny, so you need to be careful, too."

Lizzy exhaled so loudly it bordered on a snort. "I thought you'd want her to be involved with a decent man rather than someone who'll just run off and break her heart again."

Irene scratched her temple. "If you two want to fight, then take two butcher knives to the backyard, but remember, the one who comes back in the house had better have the strength to dig a six-foot hole because I'm not helping you. And remember, too, that the ground is cold and harder than a mother-in-law's heart."

Lizzy pushed her chair back. "I'm going to the store. I don't want pancakes."

Irene grabbed Lizzy's arm. "You are not going anywhere. You are going to sit down and behave yourself, and when Allie has breakfast ready, you are going to ask the blessing on it this morning. God needs to soften up your spirit or you'll never make a preacher's wife." Irene blew on her coffee and then sipped it loudly. "And it wouldn't hurt you to learn how to make decent pancakes. Allie's are light and fluffy. Yours are like shoe leather. If your marriage depends on your pancakes, Mitch will throw you out in the cold within a week."

Lizzy threw up both palms defensively. "Hey, why is this pick-on-Lizzy Friday? I don't think Mitch is going to leave me because my pancakes aren't perfect."

Allie pulled a cast-iron skillet down from the hooks in the utility room and set it on the stove to heat while she mixed up the batter. "I remember when you used to make pancakes for us girls at breakfast. And in the hot summer you let us pretend the big tub upstairs was our swimming pool, and you let us take our Barbie dolls swimming."

Irene's thin mouth broke into a lovely smile. "Remember when you played beauty shop and cut all their hair off, Allie?"

Lizzy raised a hand. "I do. I hated her for weeks for making my dolls look like boys."

"Boys?" The light went out of Irene's eyes as suddenly as if someone had flipped a switch. "I hear there's a new boy over at the Lucky Penny."

Allie crossed the room and wrapped her arms around her grandmother. Maybe a hug would bring her back for a little while. "Yes, there is, Granny. His name is Blake Dawson. You've met him."

Irene shook her head. "His name is Walter, not Blake. That's not a first name. It's a last name."

"Let's talk about my wedding. I think you'd look lovely in a dark purple dress, Granny, since the bridesmaids are all wearing orchid," Lizzy said.

Katy poured a cup of coffee and sat down at the head of the table.

"I thought you picked out pink for your wedding," Irene said. "When did you change your mind to purple? I've already bought my dress. Now what are we going to do? Besides, you know I hate purple. Always have," Irene said.

Katy patted her mother's shoulder. "Lizzy is mixed up. Of course she's using pink for her wedding."

"Good. I'm going to the bathroom to wash my hands. Will my pancakes be ready when I get back?"

"Yes, Granny," Allie answered.

"It was good to have her for a few minutes." Katy sighed.

Allie stacked three pancakes on the side of a plate and added as many sausage patties on the other side. "Mama, I've figured out the triggers that send her backward in time so fast these past few days. It's when we talk about Lizzy's wedding and the Lucky Penny. She keeps thinking about this Walter guy who lived there when you were planning your wedding and getting times all jumbled up in her mind."

"Makes sense," Lizzy said. "You shouldn't mention the Lucky Penny in front of her, and you shouldn't take that job. Which is more important? Having the money from the job, which you don't even need, or having Granny lucid for a little bit each day?"

"Then you shouldn't get married to Mitch. Which is more important to you? Marrying a man who's going to expect you to be this little submissive wife who bows to his every command, or having Granny lucid?" Allie shot right back at her.

"I'm marryin' Mitch whether you like him or not." Lizzy tilted her head like she used to do when they were kids and she knew she was wrong but all the angels in heaven couldn't get her to admit it.

One of Allie's worst fears was realized at that moment.

Lizzy was arguing too hard for Mitch. She had always been levelheaded when it came to business and relationships, seeing opportunities in business, knowing when a relationship was headed in the wrong direction. Her sister was marrying that snake-in-the-grass because she wanted to be married and any man would do—even a self-righteous prick who would make her life miserable in the end.

"And I'm going to work at the ranch next door," Allie said. "So I guess Granny is going to have lots of bad days."

* * *

Allie was on Blake's mind that Friday evening as dusk settled on the Lucky Penny. He was in one of the spare bedrooms, gazing at more unopened boxes, when someone rapped hard on the front door. Hoping that Toby had decided to surprise him by showing up that weekend, he turned around so fast that he had to catch himself on the wall to keep from falling over Shooter.

Shooter raced him to the door, but he wagged his tail when Blake threw it open to find Deke.

"Come right in. What's going on?"

Deke was dressed in creased jeans and a pearl snap plaid shirt, and his boots were shined. "Let's slip up over the county line and go have some barbecue." He winked.

"There's food in the house. We don't have to go out and buy more."

Deke chuckled. "Frankie's is way back in the woods and it's more than barbecue, but to get a drink, which is illegal right there, you have to buy some food."

"A bar! How far is it from here?"

"Maybe nine miles. Got to warn you, it's not a country bar. How fast can you be ready?"

"Give me ten minutes. Does it serve beer?" Blake was already on the move toward his bedroom at the end of the hallway.

"Yes, they serve beer, but you'll want to try Frankie's special brew and have some barbecue before you start lookin' at the ladies." The crunch of tires on the gravel outside brought Shooter's hackles back up for the second time. "Go on. I'll get the door," Deke offered. "It's most likely Herman asking how early he can be here tomorrow morning. He's real interested in getting all the mesquite he can to sell at his wood yard."

"He could have called. I put my number on the flyer." Blake's excitement level jacked up from the bottom of the barrel to cloud level in the time it took him to find a decent pair of jeans, dust off his boots, and change shirts.

Blake was on his way to the living room when Deke opened the door and said, "Come on in here out of the cold. Blake and I are about to take a ride. Want to go with us?"

"No thanks," Allie answered. "I came to do some measuring for supplies if that's okay," she said. "I can do it tomorrow, though, if y'all are going out."

"You're running away from family." Deke chuckled.

"Maybe…But I do need to measure the rooms to get an idea of how much drywall to buy."

"You might as well go with us if you are running from family." Blake grinned.

"And maybe Grady and Lizzy will get the message if they figure out you'd rather be with us than with them." Deke chuckled.

"I didn't come over here to crash y'all's party," she said.

Blake had always seen her in cargo pants and paint-splattered knit shirts, but tonight she wore skinny jeans, cowboy boots, and a knit top that stretched over her breasts and cinched in a tiny waist above well-rounded hips. Her hair, usually worn in two dark braids or a ponytail with a stocking hat stuffed down over them, hung to her shoulders in soft waves.

"I'm not taking no for an answer. You can measure tomorrow morning. We're going for a ride. Besides, you're dressed up. Be a shame to waste all that beauty." Deke placed his hands on her shoulders and ushered her out onto the porch. "I'll drive, Blake, since I know the way."

* * *

In minutes Allie found herself wedged between two big cowboys in the front seat of Deke's truck, heading north out of town. The sun was dropping quickly behind the gently rolling hills, and the moon had already made its appearance. Stars would be popping out soon, but right then that lazy part of the evening called dusk had settled in, and she didn't care where they were going as long as it took her away from Grady.

Deke turned the radio on to the country music station, but she couldn't concentrate on the songs that played one after the other. Not with Blake sitting so close that she could practically feel his pulse and especially not when they hit a bump in the road and it sent her sliding even closer to him.

She righted herself and listened to Lizzy's voice in her head lecturing her about how foolish she was to even go for a ride with those two bad boys. She pushed the voice away about the time they passed from Throckmorton County over into Baylor County, and her eyes widened, grew dry when she couldn't blink, and then she gasped.

"Good grief, Deke, are you headed for Frankie's?"

"I am." He grinned. "How do you know about Frankie's?"

"Everyone knows about it, but..." she stammered.

Deke patted her knee. "But no decent folks go there, right? Matter of fact, if Frankie don't know you pretty good, then you don't get anything but barbecue. He'll tell you that the beer and the liquor is for his personal use and isn't for sale. Don't worry, darlin'. Frankie knows me, and if I vouch for you two, he won't toss you out."

"What is this place anyway?" Blake asked.

"Private barbecue club, but I have a membership since Frankie buys his beef from me. Don't know who he gets the pork from, but they've probably got a membership card, too."

"Have you ever been there?" Blake asked Allie.

"I have not!"

Deke made a left turn and then a right before the road ended in a rutted trail that led another quarter of a mile through thick mesquite and scrub oak. Finally, he parked in front of a weathered old two-story house with dim lights showing through the downstairs window. "Well, y'all are going tonight. We're going to have some of the best ribs in the world, and then we're going to have a few drinks and maybe dance to the jukebox."

"Sounds like a bar to me," Blake said. "But it doesn't look like a bar."

"It's not a bar because half of it is in Throckmorton County and that's a dry county. The other half of the house is in Baylor County, which is semi-dry. They can sell beer in some parts of it but no liquor. Come on. Let's go have some fun," Deke said.

Allie could sit in the truck all evening or she could crawl out and go into an establishment even more notorious than

Audrey's Place. Teenagers were afraid to even whisper the name Frankie's for fear the wind would carry it back to their parents and they'd be put into solitary confinement until they were twenty-one years old.

Deke walked onto the porch with confidence, slung open the door, and held it for them to enter before him. "Hey, Frankie, these are my friends Allie and Blake."

Allie had always pictured Frankie as someone as big as a refrigerator with a scowl on his face and a shotgun in his hand. She was surprised when a little guy who barely came up to Deke's shoulder nodded at her. His baby face was round, and he wore little round wire-rimmed glasses. There were no wrinkles on his face, and his size made it hard to guess his age. She squirmed beneath his dark eyes when they scanned her and Blake.

"Any friend of Deke's is a friend of Frankie's, but the first three times you come through that door, he has to be with you. Understood?"

Allie nodded.

Blake stuck out a hand. "Pleased to meet you, Mr. Frankie. I hear you've got some of the best barbecue in the state."

Frankie smiled as he pumped Blake's hand a few times and then dropped it. "I'm Frankie, not Mr. Frankie. Mr. Frankie was my grandpa, and my daddy was Little Frankie. I'm just Frankie. And, son, my barbecue ain't *some* of the best. It is the very best. Now, what can I get y'all?"

"Ribs," Deke said. "We'll all have ribs and french fries tonight and maybe a double shot each of your famous brew."

Allie's eyes adjusted to the dim light and she scanned the room. The bar ran the length of the side where Frankie could watch the front door. A dozen chairs surrounded a couple of mismatched tables pushed up on the other side. It was small for a bar and barbecue combination but large for a living room. She could smell a delicious aroma of smoked beef and pork somewhere at the back of the house.

Everything was spotlessly clean. She could see the reflection of the bottles of liquor in the top of the bar. The hardwood floor looked as if it had been freshly waxed, and there wasn't a speck of dust anywhere. She'd always expected something a lot seedier when she thought of Frankie's, but then she'd painted a very different picture of the owner, too.

She propped a hip on a bar stool in between Blake and Deke. "Not what I expected."

"Me, either, first time I came here. I thought Frankie would be ten feet tall and bulletproof. I expect he's still bulletproof, even if he isn't that tall. The place will come to life in about thirty minutes. That'll give us time to eat, and then we can party. I'm taking home a woman tonight. How about you, Blake?"

"How?" Allie asked. "Y'all going to throw her in the back of the truck?"

"I'm just here for some beer and maybe a little dancing, not to take someone home," Blake answered.

"Why?" Allie asked.

"You sound like a newspaper reporter." Deke laughed.

Frankie carried three red plastic baskets to the bar, filled to the brim with ribs and steaming-hot fries, and lined them up. "Y'all's the first customers tonight. Now, what weight do you want that special brew, Deke?"

"Peach pie." Deke smiled.

"You got it." Frankie chuckled.

"Frankie has several famous brews, but I want you to taste

his peach pie first. He manages to make moonshine taste like fresh peach pie right out of the oven. But don't let it fool you. It's got more kick than pie," Deke explained.

Frankie reached under the counter and brought out a quart mason jar filled with an amber-colored liquid. Then he set three glasses on the bar and put a double shot in each. "Sip it. Don't throw it back. It's made to enjoy."

The door opened, and a couple of women wearing short skintight skirts, high heels, and crop tops plopped up on bar stools. One of them winked at Deke, and he smiled at her.

"How you doin', Prissy?" he asked.

"Right fine, darlin'. You?"

"Real good. You workin' or playin'?"

"Workin' tonight. You want to book some time?"

He held up his glass. "Naw, I'm just here for supper and some peach pie."

"Good stuff." She smiled, showing off a gold eyetooth. "How about your buddy?"

Deke shook his head.

"Y'all change your mind, I got room three booked, and Lacy here has paid for room four."

Lacy strutted across the bar and plugged several quarters into the jukebox. Etta James's soulful voice singing "At Last" filled the whole room.

Allie's eyes must've been the size of saucers because Deke poked her on the arm.

"I told you that it ain't a country bar," he said softly.

"I kind of gathered that," Allie said.

Blake held out a hand. "May I have this dance?"

"What about our food?" she asked.

"It'll keep."

Deke nudged her with his shoulder. "Go on. Have some fun."

She slid off the stool, and Blake picked up her hands and wrapped them around his neck. His arms rested loosely around her waist as he began to move slowly and smoothly around the dance floor. The lyrics of the song said that he smiled, and the spell was cast. Allie thought that truer words had never been spoken.

Instead of taking her back to the bar, he kept dancing when the first chords of guitar music started an old blues song, "Ain't No Sunshine."

"Do you listen to this music?" she asked.

"No, but my grandpa loves rhythm and blues, so I'm no stranger to it," he answered.

The third song was something fast and furious with lots of horn music in the background. Blake mixed swing dancing with something she'd never seen or done before. It took all her concentration to keep up with him, and when the song ended, she was breathless.

"Time for a sip of peach pie?" Blake asked.

* * *

This whole business of settling down might not be so tough after all, Blake thought. He could withstand the temptations of the local women if he could have some time at Frankie's occasionally. Allie had said she wasn't interested in any kind of relationship, so they could have good times with no strings attached. By spring he might be completely weaned away from the ways of his wild past.

When they'd finished their ribs and shots, the bar was

full of people. They moved from their stools to dance in the corner, where Deke ordered a round of beers. Prissy hugged up to a cowboy, and pretty soon they disappeared back behind a beaded curtain as "When a Man Loves a Woman" played on the jukebox.

"You like this place?" Allie asked.

Blake leaned close to her ear so she could hear him. "It's different for sure and beats unpacking boxes. What about you?"

"I'm glad I'm not here alone." She smiled. "Is that Etta James again?"

Blake nodded. "She's singing 'Damn Your Eyes.' Anyone ever tell you that you've got gorgeous eyes?"

"Not lately and certainly not anyone I would believe."

"Something's Got a Hold on Me," another Etta James tune, started as soon as the first one ended. Blake hugged Allie tightly to his chest and moved slowly around the floor.

"Do I have a hold on you?" she asked.

"Oh, honey, you don't have a clue," he teased.

The music stopped, and she hurried to the jukebox. She bent over it to see the song titles better, and there was that cute little denim-covered butt just tempting him. His mouth went dry and his pulse jacked up a few notches.

He vowed that he would not seduce Allie. He was trying hard to make her his friend, and that did not include benefits. She was an important part of his strategy to get past his wild reputation. He really, really needed for the folks in Dry Creek to see him as a responsible rancher, not a bar-hopping cowboy with nothing but a good time on his mind. No one in Muenster would take him seriously, and that had always bothered him.

The jukebox spat out "Lean on Me." Was she telling him something? She returned to her chair and smiled. "I remember some of these songs from when I was..." She clamped a hand over her mouth. "Granny had some of these on vinyl. I wonder if she was ever here."

Blake smiled. "Darlin', your granny has lots of secrets."

At midnight Deke handed Allie the keys to his truck and said, "Place closes at two. You can take my truck home. Just leave the keys on the front seat, Blake. I've got a lady who says she can make a mean breakfast come daylight." He grinned and disappeared.

"One more dance?" Blake asked.

Allie stood up and moved out to the middle of the empty floor as Sam Cooke sang "Bring It on Home to Me." She wrapped her arms around Blake's neck and smiled up at him. "It's not hard to imagine my granny in her best dress out here on this very floor dancin' with my grandpa to this song."

"Who says she came here with your grandpa? Maybe it was with Walter," he teased.

She leaned back and looked up at him. "I don't want to think about that."

Her dark brown eyes mesmerized him. He tipped up her chin and whispered, "Then let's think about this."

His lips closed over hers and his arms pulled her tighter against his chest. She tasted like peach pie moonshine.

"Have you always been such a charmer?" she asked when she finally pulled away.

"I'm sorry. I just got lost in the moment for a bit there. You don't have any idea how beautiful you are, do you, darlin'?"

"On that note, I think it's time for you to take me home." She blushed, shrugged, and threw up her palms all at once.

The gesture was so cute he wanted to kiss her again.

"I mean it," she said. "Take me home, so don't look at me like that."

The dance ended, and he led her out to the truck. He wished the whole way back through the rutted road and to the county road leading home that she was sitting as close to him as she had been on the way to Frankie's and reminded himself that she was just his friend.

CHAPTER NINE

Blake opened the door before she even knocked that Saturday afternoon. "Come right in out of the cold. Man, I'm glad y'all got the roof done. The weatherman just might be right, and we'll get that six inches of snow on Sunday."

"I won't take long. Just a few measurements, and then I've got to get to Wichita Falls for supplies before the weather hits." She pulled a steel tape measure from one of the pockets on her cargo pants and headed down the hall.

Deke pushed in the back door without knocking and yelled, "Hey, Blake, do you mind if I use your chain saw sharpener?"

"You sure can. I didn't think you'd be around today after last night."

"I'm energized and ready to work," Deke said. "I'm filling my travel mug with coffee. Once that snow gets here, the wood-cuttin' business will have to wait."

"Sharpener is in the barn," Blake said. "There's spaghetti sauce made from venison simmering in the slow cooker. One of the ladies brought it by when they delivered all that food. We can have it for supper tonight if y'all want to join me?"

"Sure, and maybe we'll go back to Frankie's after," Deke yelled, and the back door slammed behind him.

"How about you?"

"How about me what?" Allie asked.

"You gonna stay for dinner?"

She nodded. "Sure, I'd love to. Daddy hunted every year, so I was raised on wild game." She took a look around the place. "Okay, which room first?"

"My bedroom, though please excuse the mess. I'm still not unpacked."

"I'm not here to judge your housekeeping, Blake." She set about measuring the room and then pulled a notepad from her pocket to write down the measurements. "Color? And will it be for the whole house or different for every room?"

"What would you do if this was the bedroom you'd be sleeping in the rest of your life?" he asked.

That question put a visual in her mind that she had trouble kicking out. "Something neutral, like a soft ivory with white trim and doors. It would lighten up the place. Though honestly, anything would be better than this shade of pink."

Blake chuckled. "So you aren't into pink walls and lacy curtains?"

She thought carefully before she answered so she wouldn't go off on another tangent. "Pink and lace are more Lizzy's style. I was always running around behind Daddy and playing in the sawdust."

She forced her eyes away from the king-size bed with its tangled sheets. Thank goodness she had a notepad because she couldn't remember a single number she'd written down on it. She did recall something about sand-colored paint with white woodwork, but to be on the safe side, she probably needed to note that, too.

What was wrong with her? She couldn't even hang on to Riley, and he wasn't a tenth as sexy as Blake.

The back door slammed, and then Deke appeared in the doorway and pointed toward the ceiling. "I forgot to give you my notes." He read off a few as he handed them over to Allie. "The hall is four feet wide and twenty feet long. Living room is a twenty-foot square, so figure that many sheets. Oh, and one more thing. I can't go to Frankie's tonight. I promised my cousin and his wife I'd go to dinner with them."

She tucked his notes into her hip pocket. "Thanks, Deke."

"Y'all decided what to do with the floors?" Deke asked.

Blake shrugged and looked at Allie. "What do you suggest we do with this ratty old carpet?"

Deke went and pulled up a corner. "Looks like oak hardwood under it. I'd pull it up and throw it out. Wood floors are easier to clean. I took all the carpet out of my house a couple of years ago and ain't regretted it one time."

"Want me to rip it all up after I get through painting? If you do, then I won't have to cover the flooring to keep from ruining it," Allie said.

"That sounds good," Blake said. "How long do you think the whole job will take?"

"About a week if you will help me get the drywall up on the ceiling," she answered. "Trim work takes longer because it's tedious, and the doors will have to be sanded. But I'd say a week for each room."

"So roughly a month unless you have to take a day now and then to help take care of Miz Irene?" he asked.

"That's right." She bit her tongue to keep from spitting out a monologue about woodwork, floors, carpet, and anything else to keep her mind off that bed that was so close.

"Either of y'all want a cup of hot chocolate or coffee to warm your bones before you go back out in the cold?" Blake asked.

"Not me," Deke said. "I'm outta here. Got wood to get cut and ready to sell while the sun shines. Can't do much in that area if it's bad weather next week."

His boots didn't make a noise until he hit the kitchen floor, and then she heard the back door slam again. She tucked the notepad and tape back in her pocket. "I'll pass. I don't want to get caught in a rainstorm with drywall on the trailer."

Blake raised his arms over his head and stretched, working the kinks out of his back by bending to each side. Allie's eyes were glued to that broad chest and the way his biceps stretched the arms of the T-shirt. How long would it take her to strip it up over his head? How would it feel to curl up against his chest?

"What about fish?" he asked.

"What are you talking about?" Had she been so lost in her argument with herself or in the pictures she'd conjured up in her mind that she missed something about going fishing?

"You said you grew up on wild game. Did that include fish?" he asked.

She nodded. "Any kind long as it's cooked." She stood up and took a couple of steps toward the door. "Raw fish is called bait in our world."

Blake followed her. "Alora Raine? Where'd you get that name?"

"Is this twenty questions or something?" she asked.

He leaned a shoulder against the wall beside the coatrack. "It could be. I was trying to get you to stay longer."

"We'll have to play that game another time. I'll see you later. App weather forecast on my phone says no bad weather until tomorrow, so my stuff will be all right on the trailer until after church. I'll cover it with a tarp." There she went talking too much again.

Her arm brushed against his when she reached around him and picked her coat off the rack. The scent of his cologne mixed with a manly soap filled her nostrils every time she inhaled.

"Do you miss your family?" she asked as she slipped her arms into her coat and buttoned it up the front. One more layer of protection, not against him but herself.

"More than I thought I would. We went to my grandparents' house every Sunday for dinner after church." He straightened her collar. "Cousins fought. Men sat on the porch with a beer and talked crops and cattle. Women gathered in the kitchen to talk about girl things. I wasn't interested in the kitchen, but I learned to love ranchin' out there listenin' to those old men talk about cows and hay and spring plantin'."

The warmth of his fingertips on her neck sent electricity bouncing all around her. Did he feel it, too, or was it just her?

"But you did learn to cook," she said.

Blake stepped back. "Only because I had to. Most of my expertise starts with a big stew pot. I can't fry chicken that's worth eating and it's my favorite food. Deke says you hate to cook. Was he teasing?"

She slowly shook her head. "He was telling the truth. I hate to cook, but that doesn't mean I can't cook. I can fry chicken that will melt in your mouth."

"Biscuits?" His eyes twinkled.

She nodded.

"Gravy? The good stuff with no lumps?" A grin tickled his sexier-than-the-devil mouth.

Another nod.

"Will you marry me?" he asked bluntly.

Had he seriously just proposed? "I might fry chicken for you to celebrate when we finish this house, but I'm never getting married again."

"I don't take rejection well." He laid a fist over his heart and dropped his head in a fake pout.

Allie took another step toward the door. "Sorry about that, cowboy. You'll have to get over it."

He sighed. "Will you attend my funeral on Sunday? I promised my brother, Toby, if I ever found a woman who could fry chicken like my mama, I would ask her to marry me. It's going to kill me to tell him that the woman of my dreams has turned me down."

"You're full of horse crap." She laughed.

* * *

Allie deliberately stayed out late that evening, hoping to avoid Mitch and Grady. The Friday-night date with her sister and the two guys had been postponed at the last minute until tonight, so she didn't want to go home until she absolutely had to.

Instead, she decided a little retail therapy at the mall might be in order until she was sure they'd be out of the house. She meandered through three stores and bought a new pair of skinny jeans, a beautiful dark green sweater dress, and two shirts. Then she grabbed dinner on her own, wishing the whole time that Deke and Blake were sitting with her at the table.

It was a little after eight when she made it to Dry Creek and saw Mitch's truck right there in the driveway. She slapped her steering wheel, but the truck did not disappear.

She tiptoed across the porch and eased the front door open, then closed it behind her so carefully that it didn't make a bit of noise. She didn't realize she was holding her breath until it came out in a loud whoosh once she reached the landing. Quickly peeking over the banister to make sure her family hadn't heard her, she sucked in another lung full of air and hurried into her room. Without turning on the light, she slid down the backside of the door and wrapped her arms around her knees.

"Alora, let me in." A soft whisper on the other side of the door startled her. She hopped up and opened the door a crack to find Irene in her red flannel pajamas.

Her grandmother held up a package of chocolate chip cookies in one hand and a soda pop in the other. "I snuck in the kitchen and up the stairs and they didn't hear me."

"Who's down there?" Allie pulled her grandmother inside and flipped the light switch.

Irene crawled up in the middle of the bed and ripped open the cookie package. "Katy and Lizzy and those two men. Lizzy is dumber than a box of rocks."

Allie didn't care if her granny left her bed in a mess of crumbs or even if she spilled the can of soda pop. To have Irene there in her right mind might take her mind off Blake Dawson and that despicable Grady at the same time.

"I loved your grandpa. I really did," Irene said. "But there was a time…"

Allie waited for her granny to fall back into another time. She finished a cookie and reached for another one. "I forget things, Allie, but I want you to know something while my mind isn't all jumbled. Your grandpa started it when he had an affair with that woman from Throckmorton. But we got past it and fell in love all over again. We had four wonderful years before he died."

Allie crawled up on the bed with her grandmother. "It's okay, Granny. It's in the past, and Grandpa loved you."

"I know that and I loved him. I never did love Walter like I did your grandpa. I was getting even with him." She handed Allie a cookie. "But we need to talk about Lizzy. She is about to get into a mess. I never have thought that boy loves her like he should. She's marryin' just to be married. Leastways that's what I think, which ain't worth much these days the way my mind is working. I'm afraid she will regret it, and I can't tell her anything, so you're going to have to stop that wedding. You owe me this much because you wouldn't listen to me when it came to Riley. He was a sorry excuse for a man."

"I know, Granny." Allie nibbled on a cookie as she talked. "You were right. Riley thought he could change me and turn me into a little wife who stayed home and had dozens of babies for him. When I didn't get pregnant in those almost three years we were married, he blamed it on the work I do."

"Stupid fool. And then he left you. It wasn't your fault you didn't have them babies. It was probably his fault, the way he cheated on you. Here, have a drink of this soda pop and get the taste of his name out of your mouth." Irene passed the soda over to her.

Allie took a sip and handed it back. "Thank you, Granny."

"I don't want another of my precious babies to hurt like you did." Irene clamped her bony hand over Allie's knee. "If you love me and your sister, then put a stop to her marryin' that man."

"I'll do my best, Granny," Allie said.

Irene slid off the bed and tiptoed to the door, peeked out, and gave Allie the thumbs-up sign before she left. Allie threw herself back on the pillows and stared at the ceiling. Granny was worried about Lizzy, but the true message from her ten minutes of being lucid seemed to be that Allie needed to put the past behind her . . . after she got rid of Mitch, of course.

CHAPTER TEN

Several people turned around in the church pews that Sunday morning and stared blatantly; some whipped back to whisper behind their hands to the person next to them. Without even turning around, Allie knew exactly who had just walked in. The extra beat in her heart and the way her pulse raced told her it was Blake.

Grady scooted close to her and put his arm around her, his hand resting on her shoulder. Allie gritted her teeth and tried to shrug his arm away, but he was persistent. When the music director said that the congregation would sing, "Abide with Me," he held the hymnbook and pulled her even closer.

She didn't even try to sing. She didn't want God to abide with her that morning. She wanted him to strike Grady grave-yard dead in the pew where he sat or maybe send a bolt of lightning through the roof to turn him into nothing but ashes. She didn't even mind getting a little bit of scorch on her new, pretty sweater dress if the desires of her heart could be granted.

Her granny sang a different song, loud and clear in her

soprano voice. The folks in the church had long accepted that Irene Miller lived in many worlds each day and didn't pay a bit of attention to her that morning as she sang "I'll Fly Away," while the rest of the congregation sang "Abide with Me."

"You look really gorgeous this morning," Grady whispered when the song ended.

His breath was warm, and it was supposed to be seductive, but Allie wanted to brush it away like a fly that had lit on her earlobe after visiting a fresh cow pile. If she inhaled deeply, she could even smell the fresh cow manure.

"I'm looking forward to dinner," Grady said.

"Shhhh," Granny said. "No talkin' in church."

The preacher opened his Bible, cleared his throat, and said, "Good morning. We have a newcomer back there in the back row. Welcome to Dry Creek, Blake Dawson. We all know that you've bought the Lucky Penny, and we welcome you to our church. Now, this morning my sermon is from the verses that say that God will not lay more upon a person than they can endure and He will always provide a way of escape."

Irene tapped Allie on the knee and said in a very loud whisper, "I've got to go to the bathroom, and I don't know where it is." She frantically looked around everywhere, from the ceiling to the windows.

Allie laced her fingers in her grandmother's, and they stood up together. The preacher read verses straight from the Bible to support his opening statement as the two ladies, one in fear of wetting herself and the other giving thanks that God had provided an escape, made their way to the back of the church.

The ladies' room was located off the nursery, and two elderly ladies looked up from worn old rockers where they each held a baby in their arms.

"Good morning, Dorothy and Janet. Looks like you've got your hands full today," Allie said quickly so that her grandmother would know who the ladies were.

"We love babies. Hello, Irene. It's good to see you again," Dorothy said.

"I don't know you, so how can you say that you ever saw me in the first place?" She leaned toward Allie and whispered in her ear, "You'll wait for me, right?"

"I'll be right here, Granny. I'm not going anywhere."

Irene closed the door behind her, and Allie slumped down in a third rocking chair.

"She's not going to get any better, is she?" Dorothy said.

Allie shook her head. "The doctors say that this puzzle stage will get worse until she finally settles into one phase of her life. Probably when she was the happiest. She might not know us most of the time, especially if she stops when she was a young girl and we weren't even in her life then. We keep hoping one of the medications they are trying will work."

"I'm so sorry," Janet said. "We used to love having her help us here in the nursery, and we were all good friends. The three of us and Hilda, but Hilda's been gone now for years. Died of cancer back when she wasn't much more than forty."

Evidently Irene overheard the name *Hilda*, because when she came out of the bathroom with her skirt tail tucked up in the back of her white granny panties, the first words out of her mouth were, "Hilda, something ain't right with my clothes. Help me, please."

Allie didn't mind being Hilda if she didn't have to sit beside Grady anymore that day. "You want to stay in here or go back out into the church?" She stood up and put her grandmother to rights. "The preacher has another twenty minutes at the least before he winds down."

"Are we having fried chicken? Is that mean man coming to dinner?" Irene asked.

"What mean man?" Allie asked.

She popped one hand on her hip. "You know who I'm talking about. I'm not sitting on the same pew with him. I hate him."

"Then you do want to stay in here? And Mama put a pot roast in the oven for dinner, so we aren't having fried chicken." Allie sat back down in the rocking chair. The church was small, with two sets of pews, a center aisle, and just enough room on the sides for folks to get out of church single file. She didn't want to follow Granny, but then she didn't want to lead the way, either, because there was no telling what she'd do if Allie didn't keep a hand on her arm.

Irene shook her head. "I'm not a baby. We're both ten years old, and we don't belong in the nursery anymore. I'm going to listen to the preacher, but I'm not sitting on that pew." She marched out of the nursery like a little girl in a royal snit.

Allie jumped up and followed her right down the center aisle, which meant she'd have to skinny past Grady to get to the end of their pew. Irene made it to the back pew and stopped. She frowned as if trying to remember where she was and what she was supposed to do next and then cocked her head to one side.

"I'm sitting right here, and if you don't talk in church, you can sit beside me, Hilda. And I think I will go home with you today for dinner. Your mama makes good fried chicken," Irene said loudly.

The preacher never missed a single beat, but Allie did hear a few snickers in the crowd. That brought out her protective nature, and she would have marched forward and sat on the altar with her grandmother if Irene had wanted to do that. But instead Irene pushed past Blake and sat on his left. "You can sit on the other side of Everett. If he pulls your hair, kick him in the shins."

Allie slid in beside Blake. He was freshly shaved, and the smell of something woodsy, mixed with his soap, sent her senses reeling. She waited until Irene was settled and whispered softly, "Sorry, it's not a good day. It started off good, but it's gone to the devil in a handbasket."

Blake smiled. "I'm not a bit sorry. I may buy her an ice-cream cone after church."

"And where would you get that?" Allie whispered.

"Shhh. Everett Dunlap, you know better than to talk in church." Irene popped him on the shoulder. "And don't you dare pull my hair."

It was unsettling: one man's hand on her shoulder made her want to run; the other man sitting a foot away almost made her hyperventilate right there in front of her grandmother, the preacher, and even God. Life and fate were both four-letter words, and both should be put on the naughty list with the other cuss words.

Allie breathed a sigh of relief when they made it through the benediction without her granny announcing to the whole place that it was about time the long-winded preacher shut his mouth so they could go eat dinner. Everyone was standing up, and the noise level was rising by the second as folks talked about everything from the sermon to the weather and lined up in the pews to shake the preacher's hand at the door.

Blake extended a hand to Irene. "Thank you, ladies, for sitting with me."

She took it and nodded. "It was our pleasure, I'm sure. I don't believe we've met. Are you Hilda's uncle?"

"Isn't this Everett, Granny?"

Her grandmother's eyes went dark as she searched for a puzzle piece that would tell her who Everett was, then suddenly she clapped her hands. "Everett pulled my hair, and I kicked him. He tattled on me, but I didn't care. I think he likes me." Irene giggled. "But he didn't come to church today. I'm glad your uncle is here, though."

"I'm glad, too," Blake answered with a smile.

"Are you going to Hilda's for dinner, too?" Irene asked. "Her mama always makes fried chicken on Sunday, and my mama made roast beef today, so I don't want to go to my house."

"Your mama might want you to go home today since Lizzy has invited her boyfriend over for dinner," Allie said.

Irene looked up and waved at Katy. Above the noise of dozens of conversations, she shouted, "Mama, I am going home with Hilda and her uncle today. I don't like Lizzy's boyfriend or that mean man that runs around with him."

"Shhh, Granny," Allie said.

"We are all going home. You can ride with Allie," Katy said sternly.

Irene stopped in the middle of the aisle and glared at Katy. "When those two mean men go away, I will come home. Besides, I want fried chicken."

"I'd planned on driving over to Olney to a little restaurant that specializes in fried chicken on Sunday," Blake said quickly. "I'm sure my niece would enjoy her company, and I could have her back at your place by midafternoon."

"Yes, yes!" Irene clapped her hands. "Please let me go. I don't get to go to a café hardly ever."

"You put her up to this. You put the idea in her head," Lizzy hissed at Allie. "I will never forgive you for ruining my entire weekend."

"I did not. Next Sunday you can sit beside her and take her to the bathroom," Allie said.

Katy slipped her hand around Allie's arm. "This does not mean any more than taking care of your grandmother, does it?"

"No, ma'am," Allie said. "She'll make a scene if you don't let her go with me and Blake. She thinks I'm her childhood friend Hilda. They mentioned her name in the nursery, and that's probably what set her off."

Herman Hudson stepped out from his pew and fell in behind Katy, separating her from Lizzy and the two guys. "Blake Dawson, I hear you've got wood to give away."

"Yes, sir, I do," Blake said.

Herman stuck out his hand. "I'll be glad to take all you can pile up for my wood yard. You got a problem with me selling it?"

"No, sir, not one bit. I'd just be glad to get it cleared away and not have to burn it all up," Blake said.

"Then me and my kinfolks will be there soon as this snow stops. We don't mind workin' once it's on the ground, but when it's fallin', it makes it tough. Thank you, son," Herman said.

* * *

Irene wiggled in the back seat like a little girl eager to get to her destination. "We'll be there in a little bit, won't we? Can I have ice cream if I eat all my chicken?"

"Yes, you can, or whatever dessert you want," Blake answered.

"I like your uncle," Irene said.

The café had two empty tables when they arrived. The waitress waved them to one and said, "If you'll sit there, we'll save the bigger one for more folks. Be right with you."

The waitress finally got around to them, handing out menus, which consisted of one laminated page with the listings for breakfast on one side and lunch on the other. "What are y'all having to drink?"

"Sweet tea," Irene answered.

"Same here," Allie and Blake said in unison.

His leg touched hers under the table. That was all it took to flood her mind with pictures that she should not be entertaining after church or in a restaurant. Most of them did not involve clothing, menus, or even church music.

"We've got two specials today. Fried chicken tenders with hot biscuits, your choice of two sides, and pecan pie with or without ice cream for dessert. Second one is roast beef with all the same," she said.

"Fried chicken, mashed potatoes, macaroni and cheese, and I want ice cream on my pie for dessert," Irene said.

Blake handed her the menu. "Same only with okra instead of mac and cheese."

"Me, too, except I want corn casserole for my vegetable." Allie's arm brushed against Blake's when she gave the waitress her menu, and the pictures in her head became even more vivid.

"I'll have it right out." The waitress hurried off to seat a family of six at the larger table and clean off a small four-person table for another group just arriving.

"So what are you ladies going to do all next week?" Blake asked.

"School." Irene rolled her eyes. "I hope we don't have homework every night."

"Why is that?"

Allie had no doubts that Blake was a very good uncle to his nieces and nephew. He was a natural in the role.

Irene sighed dramatically. "If we have homework, then Hilda can't come and play with me after school. Her mama won't let her, and my mama makes me sit at the kitchen table until it's all done, and it takes hours."

"Do you like Dry Creek?" Blake asked.

Irene shrugged. "It's where I live, so I have to like it. Someday I'm going to move away to a big place, though. I'm going to live in a house in town so I can go to the movies and to a café and have coffee in the mornings."

Blake nodded seriously. "And do you like coffee, Miz Irene?"

"No, but I'll learn if I can move away from Dry Creek. Why are you asking me so many questions?" Irene asked.

"I want to get to know my niece's friend." He smiled.

Lord, have mercy! One more of those killer smiles and knee touches and Allie would need one of her mother's hot flash pills. Come to think of it, Blake should carry those little white pills in his shirt pocket and dole them out to the women he comes in contact with. One if he smiled. Two if he strutted past them in tight jeans. Go ahead and fill up a coffee cup with them if he kissed a woman.

The waitress brought their food and drinks at the same time, and Irene concentrated on her food. Allie was afraid to say anything at all because it could make her grandmother shift gears and suddenly not know either her or Blake.

"Allie." Irene touched her on the arm. "What are we doing here?"

Allie laid a hand over her grandmother's. "You had a forgetting moment, Granny. Deke's friend asked us to go to dinner with him, and you said you'd love some fried chicken."

"This is Blake from the Lucky Penny. He's not Deke's friend," Irene argued.

"Yes, he is. He and Deke are really good friends. Our fried chicken is here. Let's eat it before it gets cold," Allie said.

"I do like fried chicken. Did Grady and Mitch go home with Lizzy?" Irene asked.

Allie nodded.

"Well, I'm glad I came with you and Blake because I really don't like either one of those guys." Irene dug into her dinner with gusto.

Blake bit into a piece of fried chicken. "Is your chicken this good?" he asked Allie.

Irene laughed. "Oh, honey. Her fried chicken is even better than my mama's was. And her biscuits can make the angels in heaven weep for joy."

"Now you have to marry me." Blake grinned.

Where were those hot flash pills? She needed a mug full to eat like candy corn.

"No, she's not going to marry you. We might go to dinner with you when fried chicken is involved, but the women of Audrey's Place do not marry the men from the Lucky Penny, and that's a fact." Irene's mind and body both shifted from little girl to grown woman in the blink of an eye. "If we had some fried green tomatoes, this would be the ideal Sunday dinner."

Without another word, she cleaned up her plate and pushed it back. "Now I want pecan pie with ice cream."

Allie caught the waitress's eye, and the lady hurried right over to their table. "Ready for dessert? Three pecan pies with ice cream."

Irene giggled. "No, three *slices* of pecan pie with ice cream. I can't eat a whole pie."

"Yes, ma'am." The waitress patted her gently on the shoulder.

"Old people can say whatever they want and folks don't even mind," Irene said. "But I'm glad these people over here in Olney—we are in Olney, aren't we?"

Blake nodded. "Yes, ma'am, we are. I heard you liked fried chicken and that this place served up a good Sunday special."

"Well, I'm glad that we're here and not in Dry Creek. That café has been closed for years in Dry Creek, hasn't it?"

Allie's head bobbed. "Yes, Granny. You are remembering very well today."

"Some days are better than others," she said.

* * *

Floating from one time period to the next always exhausted her grandmother. The poor old dear curled up next to the window on the way home and went to sleep. What little Allie and Blake did say to each other was said in low tones so they wouldn't wake her. Twenty-five minutes from the time they'd left the restaurant, he drove past the church, the feed store, and the convenience store and on out to the lane that led back to Audrey's Place. He parked in front of the big two-story house.

Irene roused up and looked at the house as if seeing it for

the first time in her life. "Where are we? Why did you bring me here?"

Allie touched her on the arm. "We're home. Are you ready to go on inside and get warm in your own bed?"

Irene blinked several times and skewed up one side of her face as she finally found a place that made sense. "I'm not going in there. Not until he leaves. He shouldn't have slept with that woman, and I don't want to be married to him anymore."

"Who?"

Irene had settled on the time when her husband had cheated on her. "Your grandpa. He's in there trying to be nice to Mama so she'll make me stay with him. He's lower than a snake's belly, and I will get even. I can still turn a man's head even if I am almost forty."

Blake started to back the truck out of the driveway. "Where do you want to go? You name the place, Miz Irene, and I will take you wherever you tell me to."

"Granny, that is Mitch's truck. Remember? He's engaged to Lizzy," Allie said.

Irene nodded slowly. "That's right. I get things mixed up sometimes, especially when I first wake up. It's like I'm in another world. Let's sneak inside. We can't go anywhere else with this snow coming down."

When they'd left church, there was about a flake to the acre, as her father used to say when it was barely spitting snow. After they left Olney, the skies turned a solid gray and it started to get serious about the business.

"Come on in with us, Blake, but you will have to be very quiet." Irene's eyes twinkled as she put a finger over her lips.

Blake shut off the engine. "I should be going."

She folded her hands over her chest and glared at him.

"Nonsense. I'm not getting out of this truck if you don't go in with us."

Allie nodded ever so slightly when he caught her eye in the mirror again. "I guess you'll have to do what she wants."

"Thank you," Irene said. "Now, you can help me out, and I'll hold on to your arm so I don't fall going up the porch steps. You do remind me of someone, but I think he wore glasses."

Blake slung open his door and then opened hers. He looped her arm through his and held his hand over hers as he matched his step to hers.

Allie was on the other side, and Irene grabbed her hand. "I think we had a good time today, but I can't remember much about it. Is it Monday?"

"No, Granny, it's Sunday. We went to church this morning."

"That's right, and we sang 'Abide with Me,' didn't we? And now it's snowing like the weatherman said. Can we make snow ice cream tomorrow?"

"You had the prettiest voice in the whole church." Blake took the three porch steps one at a time, making sure her footing was steady before he went to the next one. "And I've got a real good recipe for snow ice cream. I'll make a big bowlful and bring it to you if Allie is too busy to make it for you."

"Thank you. I like that hymn. It was Mama's favorite. And I really like snow ice cream," Irene said. "You are a good man to help me inside, but now it's time to be quiet and not talk or we'll have to be nice to that sumbitch that Lizzy is engaged to marry. Some folks have to learn their lessons the hard way."

Allie opened the door, and they slipped inside the foyer and all the way back to Irene's room without getting caught.

When Audrey's Place was first built, the owners occupied the only bedroom on the first floor. Granny and Grandpa shared that room until he died, but now it was hers alone. She let go of Blake's arm and Allie's hand and eased the door shut. "They're in the kitchen. I'm safe now and I'm going to sleep awhile, so y'all can go on. Allie, don't you stay out late and, Blake, you see to it she's home by ten. Decent women are in bed at ten. And it feels like I had a good time today, so thank you for that."

"Yes, ma'am, I will see to it that she is," Blake said.

When they were in the foyer, Blake hugged her close to his side. "It has to be the scariest thing in the world for her. She's probably afraid to shut her eyes when her world is right because she's afraid she'll lose what control she has while she's asleep," he said. "Poor old darlin' is such a sweetheart when she's lucid. I would have loved to have known her before this disease started eating away at her mind."

Allie leaned into his shoulder, and it felt so right. "We never know what will set her off. She doesn't like Mitch or Grady, so that might have made her regress to her childhood so she didn't have to think about them. The doctor says one day she simply won't remember any of us, so we take the good when we can get it."

"Well, look who made it home." Grady's shifty eyes darted from Blake to Allie and back again. "I told Lizzy I heard you out here."

Allie put a finger over her lips. "Shhh. She's settled down for a nap. If she hears voices, it will upset her."

Grady's nose curled in disgust. "She needs to be put away in a place where they take care of people like her. It has to be draining on the whole family to put up with those tantrums when she goes back to being a child, if that's even what she does."

"What is that supposed to mean?" Allie asked coldly.

"She doesn't like me or Mitch. She's told him that she hopes he dies before the wedding, so I figure that she's playing the whole bunch of you. I'd be willing to bet that she wasn't a little kid at all this morning." Grady tilted his chin up like the know-it-all he thought he was.

"You really think so?" Blake asked.

"I don't think so. I know it, but right now I will speak for the family and say thank you for playing along with her and bringing Allie home early. I hear that you bought the Lucky Penny? How long do you think you'll last before you give up and go back to wherever you came from?" Grady asked coldly.

"I don't give up easy. When I want something, I work for it and treat it right," Blake answered.

"And," Allie said, "you don't need to speak for the family since you are definitely not a part of it."

Grady laid a hand on Allie's shoulder. "Now, don't get all huffy, darlin'. It's not becoming for a lady."

She shrugged his hand off and sucked in enough air to give him an earful of what she thought of him, but then Katy pushed past Grady and hugged Allie. "You are home. I heard y'all talking and wanted to thank you, Blake, personally for what you did today for my mother and daughter. We've been told to play along with whatever time frame she's in, and I'm very glad that you helped us out today."

"You are very welcome," Blake said. "I suppose I really should be going before the snow gets worse."

Snow!

God Bless Blake Dawson's soul!

It could be her salvation from that slimy Grady.

She hugged her mother and ignored Grady. "Granny switched gears about the time we finished eating and she wanted a nap. She's resting, so it might be best if y'all took your conversation back to the kitchen. I'm going to follow Blake over to the Lucky Penny to unload all the supplies I bought yesterday. They're under a good strong tarp, but if they get wet, it could be disastrous."

Blake nodded toward Grady and smiled at Katy. "It's been real nice meeting all y'all. I guess we'd best get going if we're to get things unloaded before the snow gets any deeper." He ushered her out of the house with his hand on the small of her back.

Allie could feel Grady's eyes boring holes into her, but she didn't care. If it wouldn't have wakened Granny, she would have liked to put a well-placed knee in his crotch when he made that remark about her grandmother. Watching him roll around on the floor holding on to his balls would have brought her so much satisfaction.

"Thank you. I don't think I could stay in that house another minute."

"Why?"

"When Grady looks at me, my skin crawls like it did—" she stopped.

"Go on," Blake said.

"Not today. I'm sorry we've ruined your whole Sunday, and now you'll have to help me unload wallboard and lumber," she said.

"Do I make your skin crawl?" he asked.

"No!" she said quickly.

He chuckled. "Then I don't need to know any more. I'll

follow your van and trailer to my ranch. That way, if anything flies off, I can stop and get it. Don't look like this is going to slow down any."

"My van is parked around back. I'll...well, crap...I'm still wearing my Sunday clothes."

The north wind had picked up and blew Allie's hair across her face, snowflakes as big as dimes sticking in it. Blake reached out and tucked the errant strands behind her ear. "And you look mighty lovely in that pretty dress. You drive over to my house, and I'll give Deke a call. We'll unload the trailer for you if you'll keep that dress on so I can enjoy the view a little longer."

"Does that pickup line work for you?"

He leaned on the hood of his truck and grinned down at her. "Don't know. You tell me." His eyes smoldered. "Is it worth writing down in my pickup line book?"

Allie giggled. "You've got a book?"

"That's classified information. See you at the ranch," he said with a wink.

As she drove from her place to his, she wondered how many names were in that book and how many pages were devoted to pickup lines. Could he tell by looking at a woman which lines he should use and which ones wouldn't work? Or did he fly by the seat of his pants, using whatever came to his mind in the moment?

Why did she care anyway? She slapped at the steering wheel, which seemed to be a regular thing these days. But dammit anyway! Blake infuriated her with his flirting. She wanted him to back off, but then she loved the excitement in his eyes, in his touch, and in his kisses. Her breath caught in her chest and her hands went clammy when she thought about that heat in his eyes just minutes before. It was one of those conundrums that made her dizzy. She couldn't have it both ways. Either she had to make him step back or trust him, and how could she do either one?

Deke was already waiting in the yard when Allie arrived in the van. It took some fast work, but everything was in the house before the snow changed to big cold raindrops falling from the sky in buckets. He and Blake shucked out of their coats and hung them on the rack. Blake headed for the sofa, and Deke headed toward the kitchen. "Anyone besides me want a beer?"

"Well, make yourself right at home," Allie scolded.

Deke landed a brotherly kiss across her cheek on his way to the kitchen. "Don't gripe at me like I was your little brother. If I can be called on to help a friend, then I can make myself at home, right, Blake?"

"That's right, and so can you, Allie." He turned around and went back to help her out of her coat.

There it was again when his hands brushed against that soft spot on her neck. An intensified surge of emotions rattling through her body, wanting more than a touch, more than a kiss. Then her brain kicked in quite loudly and reminded her that he was wild and wicked and not to be trusted. Which one did she listen to anyway?

"I hate Sunday nights," Deke said. "They are the most boring hours in the whole week."

"Why is that?" Allie asked, as breathless as if she'd had an actual argument with someone.

"The rest of the week we need forty hours in a day to get everything done. Friday we celebrate the week ending with a trip to Frankie's or a good cowboy bar and maybe Saturday night, too. But Sunday night is downright lonesome," Deke said.

"That's the gospel truth." Blake nodded in agreement. "At home at least there was family that stuck around until bedtime."

"We could make some popcorn and watch a movie and be bored together. It would keep Allie from havin' to go home." Deke sighed.

Allie would watch Shooter sleep if it would keep her from having to spend time playing Monopoly or watching the kind of movie Lizzy and Mitch picked out. She wished that Frankie's was open on Sunday evening. Listening to Etta James and Ray Charles, dancing with Blake, maybe indulging in just one more of those steamy kisses, watching Deke flirt with the women—now, that sounded exciting.

"I haven't got cable yet, but there are a few western movies that I brought along with me, and it would be good to have some company," Blake said. "Y'all want to follow me and we'll pick one out together?"

"How many did you bring?" Deke asked.

"A boot box full," Blake answered.

"Y'all choose. I'm going to the restroom," Allie said. "Meet you back in the living room."

* * *

"Allie is quite a woman," Blake said. "Beautiful, talented, and smart."

"Yep." Deke nodded. "I like this one." He held up *Quigley Down Under* starring Tom Selleck.

"That'll do fine. Between me and you, I'd rather be at Frankie's than doing this."

"Me, too, but Frankie is religious. He's closed on Sunday."

"You've got to be kiddin' me! Moonshine, hookers, and he's religious?" Blake drawled.

"There's layers to everyone, my friend. Frankie attends church over there in his community and leads the singin'."

Blake shook his head all the way up the hall to the kitchen. "So tell me about Allie's layers." He found a box of instant hot chocolate in the second place he looked and set three oversized mugs on the counter.

Deke put a bag of popcorn into the microwave. "She has a heart as big as Texas. She's a good sister even though she and Lizzy argue all the time. She's a right fine granddaughter and the best friend a man could have."

"I've never had a woman for a friend," Blake said.

"Then start with Allie. She's the best."

"Who is the best?" Allie's big brown eyes looked from one cowboy to the other.

"You are," Deke said.

"At what?" she asked.

"Being a man's friend. You're even better than my dog, and I really love that dog." Deke grinned.

She poked him on the arm. "Aww, now ain't that the sweet. What are we watching?"

"I picked out *Quigley Down Under*."

"Never have seen it. Can I help do anything?"

"Not a thing."

Allie sat down at the kitchen table and unzipped her knee boots. "I've had all of these I can stand for one day."

Blake took one look at her mismatched socks and chuckled. "Good-lookin' socks there, darlin'. They make the outfit."

She held up her feet and wiggled her toes. "I've got another pair like them somewhere in the house, but I can't find them. If Lizzy had pushed me toward Grady one more time, I planned to take off my boots in church to embarrass her."

"You are one wicked lady." Blake smiled.

"Not me!" Her smile was straight from heaven. "I'm just a carpenter who fixes roofs and does remodel jobs on houses."

"A beautiful, sexy carpenter who looks right gorgeous with a hammer in her hands," Blake said.

"Y'all going to jaw all day in there or are we going to watch our movie?" Deke called out.

"We're on the way, and I don't want to hear a word about my socks," Allie said as she made her way from the kitchen to the living room.

Blake kicked off his boots and settled on the other end of the long leather sofa from Allie. Halfway through the movie, she pulled her legs up and stretched them out toward him and he did the same, situating his on the outside. He moved his right one slightly so that it touched hers, and she didn't jerk it away or give him a dirty look.

That was progress.

A month ago he would have been telling some woman goodbye that he'd spent the weekend with. Or maybe she'd walk him to the door and tell him that it had been fun but one weekend of fun with him was all a woman could handle. Tonight he was almost shouting because Allie hadn't moved her leg away from his. Toby wouldn't believe it or understand if he tried to tell him, and forget about saying anything to Jud. He was the loudest of the three about staying a bachelor until his dying breath.

"I'm pausing the show for a bathroom break. I'll bring in some beers on my way back," Deke said.

Allie shifted positions, and her foot touched his hip. He picked it up, put it in his lap, and began to massage it, and suddenly things weren't boring at all.

"God, that feels good," she said.

"I'm not God," Blake said.

"You know what I mean."

He pulled the other foot over and worked on it. "You are too tense, woman. Loosen up and enjoy life."

She eased her feet back and tucked them under her, pulling the sweater dress down to cover them.

"He's right." Deke set three beers on the coffee table and settled back into the recliner. "You should have more fun."

"Y'all are ganging up on me," she said. "Turn the movie back on. I like Crazy Cora more and more as the story plays out. I don't think she's nearly as crazy as everyone thinks."

Layers, Deke had said. Was one of Allie's layers nothing but a protective coating against men since her husband left her?

CHAPTER ELEVEN

On Monday morning five inches of snow had turned the countryside around Dry Creek into a winter wonderland. The wind had died down, and there had been a glorious sunrise that morning. The weight of wet snow was heavy on the mesquite and scrub oak tree branches. Cardinals dotted the white landscape like little rose petals dropped from heaven to add color to the new monochromatic picture.

The beauty wouldn't last long. Cars, trucks, and other vehicles would soon leave their tracks. Animals would leave behind footprints. Cattle would stir up the snow, and by nightfall, if the sun stayed out, what was left would turn to mud that would freeze by morning. But later didn't matter as Allie drove slowly from Audrey's Place to the Lucky Penny. Right then, that moment, when everything looked like a fairy tale, that's what mattered.

The Lucky Penny house was empty when she arrived, and somehow it looked even worse without Deke and Blake there. Without those two big cowboys to talk to her or at least to each other while she listened, she noticed the ugly paint on the walls, the nasty stains on the ceilings, and the scuff marks on the woodwork even more.

She sighed when she reached the bedroom and then smiled. It reminded her of Cinderella in her rags, kind of like the muddy mess the snow would make when it melted. But in a week, the room would be the princess in all her glory with its new paint job, pretty new ceiling, shiny hardwood floors, and that big beautiful king-size bed taking center stage. Then it would be as fresh and pretty as the morning, with nothing marring the beauty of fresh-fallen snow.

The bare light bulb would be replaced by the six-blade oak fan with a lovely school-glass light kit. It had been the last one in stock and on sale at seventy-five percent off, so she'd bought it on a whim, and now she was having second thoughts. He might have asked what she'd do to the room if she had to sleep in it the rest of her life, but he hadn't meant she could go off half-cocked and buy something without even asking him about it.

First, she had to tear out the nasty old before she could put in the shiny new. She smiled as she thought of her father saying those very words every time they started a new job.

As brittle as the old drywall was, it wouldn't be nice and come down in four-by-eight sheets. It would fall in chunks of every size that would throw white powder and mildew dust everywhere. She shut the door and opened the window.

Sure it would get cold, but she'd dressed in thermal underwear, cargo pants, an old cotton western shirt, and insulated coveralls. She put her earbuds in and pushed the button on the little MP3 player tucked into her pocket.

George Strait entertained her as she brought down the ceiling a piece at a time and then went back to remove all the nails from the ceiling joists. It was close to noon when she finished. The room was still filled with a fog of white powder, and the old carpet would never be usable again, not with that much white powder ground down into the fibers.

With the music in her ears, she didn't know anyone was in the house until Blake touched her on the ankle. She jerked the earbud out and frowned. "You scared me. Don't sneak up on a woman holding a hammer."

He grinned. "Sorry about that. I called your name when I came in and a couple more times as I came this way. Want some help? The dozer is bogging down in the snow. Deke and Herman have plenty to keep them busy with what I've already got piled up. Even with the snow, it's not as cold as it was over the weekend."

"There isn't any wind. That makes a difference. Got a hammer?"

"Of course."

She nodded. "Then, yes, you can help get these nails out, and then we'll be ready to hang the Sheetrock after we have dinner."

He was only gone a few minutes before he returned wearing a pair of coveralls like hers and carrying a hammer. "Seems colder in here than it does outside, don't it?"

"Yep," she said.

His biceps strained the seams of the camouflage coveralls as he popped one nail after another from the ceiling rafters. Keeping her eyes uplifted and concentrating on her own job was not easy for Allie. More than once, she found herself pausing to stare at the ease with which he reached up with that heavy hammer, hung the claw on a nail head, and pulled it free without so much as a grunt.

Riley had hated quiet. If they had nothing to talk about, then he turned on the television. Even if he didn't watch it, he wanted noise at all times. Blake seemed perfectly comfortable working in silence with her, and she liked that. The screeching sound of nail after nail coming out of an old rafter was better than music.

That's when she remembered the MP3 player in her coverall's pocket, pulled it out, and turned it off. She was returning it to her pocket when they heard a loud rapping on the front door.

Blake laid the hammer on the floor. "Be right back. Can't imagine who is here."

The claw of the hammer was hung in a nail when Allie heard a familiar raspy giggle. She eased it back down and laid it on the top of the ladder. Two backward steps and her boots hit the floor. Five steps forward and she opened the door a crack and peeked. Yep, she'd been right. It was Sharlene, and she was handing off a six-pack of beer to Blake.

She patted his cheek affectionately. "I was up in Wichita Falls over the weekend and thought you might need this. I know you have lots of food, but a man cannot live by bread alone. He must have beer."

"Thank you." Blake's smile lit up the whole dingy room. "Bless your heart for thinking of me. And truer words were never spoken. I'll put this in the refrigerator. Want a cup of coffee to take the chill off?"

"No, darlin', not today, but I'm still waiting on your call." Sharlene rolled up slightly on her toes, cupped his face in her hands, and kissed him long, hard, and leaving no doubt tongue was involved. "Although I might be willing to be late if there was something more than coffee involved."

Allie had to fight the sudden urge to throw her hammer at Sharlene. She did owe Blake. He had, after all, helped her pull nails for the last hour and a half, so she should help him out of the pickle. But then who's to say he wanted out of the situation? A streak of hot jealousy shot through her veins as she slammed the door into the bedroom and headed up the hallway.

"Hey, Blake, is it time to put in one of those casseroles?" She talked loudly and put on her best innocent face. "Oh, hello, Sharlene. I was in the back room with the door shut and didn't realize you were here. Blake, which casserole did you want tonight?"

"I-I was just leaving," Sharlene stammered. "You think about what I said, darlin'." She winked at Blake and hurried out the front door.

"What took you so long?" he asked.

"Was it good?"

Blake frowned. "What?"

"How does kissing a smoker taste? I always thought it would be like licking the bottom of an ashtray," she said.

Blake's laughter echoed off the walls.

"What's so funny?" she asked.

"You are funny, and you are right. I need a glass of sweet tea to get the taste out of my mouth. Want one?"

"No, I'm going to finish up that last corner so we can hang drywall after we eat. Holler when dinner is ready." She returned to the cold room, shut the door firmly, put her earbuds back in place, and went back to work. When Mr. George started singing "You Can't Make a Heart Love Somebody," tears came out of nowhere and streamed down her face. She crawled off the ladder, pulled the mask off, threw it on the floor with the broken wallboard, removed a glove, and brushed the tears away with her bare hand.

The lyrics reminded her of what Riley said when he finally admitted that he was having an affair. He said it was all her fault because she wouldn't stay at home and be a wife, especially since she couldn't be a mother. When she hadn't gotten pregnant in those two years, he said he'd go to the doctor for a checkup. He came home with the news it wasn't him so she didn't need to go. And like the lyrics of the song said, she couldn't make him love her.

She hadn't cried that day, so why were the tears flowing now? She slid down the wall, bowed her head, and listened to the next song—"Today My World Slipped Away."

The song fit that day when Riley told Allie all about his new love, Greta. Riley said they had looked at each other across the top of that new Ford Mustang he had just sold her and he was smitten. She was the most beautiful, feminine woman in the whole world, and he had found his soul mate. Of course, it did help that she was a trust fund baby and he would be cashing in on that dividend check that came every month.

Why did she have to face off with all those memories that day? She wiped the tears again, leaving streaks of dust and grime on her cheeks. Her father's words came back again, telling her to finish tearing out the old so she would be ready for the shiny new. Until that moment, she hadn't realized how tightly she'd held on to the past, to the anger and the pain, but it had to go.

She raised her head and stared at the big gaping hole where the ceiling had been. Trusses, the bottom of roof decking, ceiling joists—all visible, but the old ugly stuff had been ripped away. It was symbolic of what she had to do to move on with her life.

The old had been torn out of her heart and soul, but suddenly fear gripped her when she thought of taking a step forward. She'd been in limbo for so many years, she didn't know if she could trust her feet to take even a baby step, she was so scared of falling on her face...again.

She looked out the open window at the bright sunshine and then up at the rafters. Instead of an answer to the multitude of questions plaguing her, she heard the back door slam and heavy footsteps coming down the hallway. She swiped a hand across her face to get rid of the last of the tears and stood up.

"Can we open the door?" Deke yelled.

She made her way across the cluttered floor. "It's a mess. Enter at your own risk."

The door eased open and warmth flowed in. Deke's silhouette filled the doorway. Leaning against the doorjamb with one leg slightly bent in those tight jeans, he was almost as dirty as she was. Twigs and leaves stuck to his flannel shirt as well as his hair.

"You got a lot done to be workin' alone." His gaze started at the hole where the ceiling used to be, traveled to the open window and carpet, and then slowly inched its way from her work boots to the top of her head. He grinned when he saw all the white dust in her hair. "Wow, Allie! You're going to grow up to look like your granny."

"Thank you so much for that, Deke! I may look like shit, but I got the worst of the job done, and Blake helped me pull nails for more than an hour. That helped a lot." She smarted off back at him.

"Hey, I'm statin' facts, not startin' a fight," he said.

"Good, because I'm sure not in the mood for a fight!" She pushed her way past him. "See y'all in the kitchen after I clean up."

When she looked in the mirror above the wall-hung sink in the bathroom, sure enough there was Irene Miller staring back at her. The streaks from tears mixing with dirt and dust had created pseudo-wrinkles down her cheeks. Her dark hair had a coating of white dust all the way to her scalp, and her eyes were slightly swollen from crying.

That she looked like shit didn't bother her half as much as the fact that Sharlene had seen her looking like that. She stripped out of her coveralls and left them lying on the bathroom floor. Her work pants and T-shirt were in good shape since they'd been covered up. However, the insulated underwear was getting pretty warm now that she was out of the chilly room. So she took off everything down to her underpants and bra and picked up a washcloth to work on her face.

One more glance in the mirror and she realized that she'd never brush all that grime from her hair. She found towels on the shelves above the toilet, along with shampoo. She pulled the curtain around the tub and hoped that the drain didn't clog. She hated doing plumbing work.

"I promise to wear a hat next time I take down drywall." She stepped into the tub and let the hot water rinse away tears, dirt, and dust from her body and hair.

When she finished, the woman in the mirror smiled at her. "Hello, I haven't seen you since before you married Riley. I thought I'd lost you forever."

The grin widened.

She redressed, leaving her work boots sitting on the floor

beside her coveralls and long underwear. The phone in her hip pocket rang at the same time she stepped out into the hallway.

"Hello, Mama," she said.

"I need you to stop what you are doing by one o'clock. I have to take your grandmother to Wichita Falls this afternoon for a doctor's appointment. I forgot all about it until I looked at the calendar. You'll need to mind the store." Katy sounded frantic.

"It's okay, Mama. I'm at a really good stopping point. I've got the ceiling down in the master bedroom." Allie stopped and leaned against the wall. "Is one early enough? I can come on right now if you want me to."

"The main roads are clear from here to there, but we're in for more snow tonight. I just want to get up there, get it done, and get home before the roads get slick. I'm not lookin' forward to driving in it. Are you eating dinner with Blake and Deke?" Katy asked.

"Yes, but I could eat whatever you've made in the store. It's no big deal," she answered.

"Go on and eat your dinner. One o'clock will be fine. Thank goodness the sun melted some of this already," Katy said.

Allie ran a hand through her hair and realized she hadn't taken time to brush it. "Want me to take her?"

"No, I have to be there to sign papers and talk to them about a new medication they want to try. See you in an hour."

She went back to the bathroom, ran the brush she found on the shelf beside the shampoo through her damp hair, and put it back on the shelf. Then she padded to the kitchen in her socks.

"Cinderella emerges." Blake set a pot of beans on the table.

"I thought I heard the shower pipes rattling. Did you find everything you needed?"

She nodded. "Maybe I should have asked."

Blake patted her on the shoulder. "Friends make themselves at home. Your timing is great. Food's on the table. Beans with ham hock, fried okra, and sweet potato casserole."

Allie pulled out a chair and eased into it. "I'm hungry. You won't get any fight out of me."

"I'll do the honors." Deke picked up a ladle and filled Allie's bowl first. "Herman showed up this morning with a crew, and I swear he's cutting and stackin' wood as fast as Blake and the bulldozer can pile it up."

"How are you doin' with the wood business, Deke?" Allie scooped sweet potatoes onto her plate and added several spoons of okra to the side before passing both off to Blake.

Their fingertips brushed, and sparks danced around the room. Life wasn't fair. Not thirty minutes ago Sharlene had her tongue in his mouth, and yet a simple touch had created enough electricity to jack her pulse up. Her mind wandered, and she had to play fast catch-up when it came back to the kitchen and Deke was answering her question.

"I'm selling everything I cut to Herman right in the field. We made a deal. He's giving me five bucks less a rick than if I hauled it to Wichita Falls, but when you consider the time and the gas, I reckon I'm probably making money rather than losing it."

She nodded, but her thoughts skipped backward to what her father said when they started a new remodeling job. Was Blake the new that she was supposed to be thinking about now that she'd erased the old?

Deke went on. "But it's going to snow again this afternoon,

so when it starts we'll help you get the mess cleaned up in the bedroom and maybe even put up some ceiling. Chain saws and snow in our eyes don't go together."

"I have to go babysit the store this afternoon so Mama can take Granny to Wichita Falls for a doctor's appointment," she said.

Blake nodded. "When it starts snowing, we'll come to the house and do some work here."

Deke motioned toward her bowl. "We throw it out the window, and if Allie will trust us, we can put up the drywall."

She shook her head. The beans were good, but she couldn't eat a second bowl. "That would be great, but after that last time, don't you dare touch the bedding and taping."

Blake raised his eyebrows in question.

"I decided to surprise her once," Deke explained. "And I had to sand it all off smooth so she could do it right. Some folks have an easy touch with that shit. Some of us flat out can't do it."

"You said it's a two-person job. I'll help Deke, and we won't touch the bedding and taping. How's that?" Blake asked.

"That'd be great! I'd have a big jump on tomorrow if you'll help with that," she said.

"When are you going to start fencing, Blake?" Deke asked.

"After I get the first eighty acres ready to plow up and plant, then I'll repair what fence there is around that portion so that Toby can bring cattle in the summer."

"So, partner number two gets here in the summer?" she asked.

Blake nodded. "We will start getting the next couple of pastures ready for when Jud arrives in the winter with the next herd. At that time, we'll work on the rest of the ranch. It'll take a couple or three years to get it in top shape, but we've got a schedule lined out."

"Then your brother and cousin will live here in this house with you until they get something else built?" Allie asked.

"Yup, though they've already picked out spots to build when the time is right. Of course, Allie, if y'all ever want to sell your twenty acres, we'd sure like to buy it."

Allie started shaking her head the moment he said the word *sell*. "Audrey's Place will never be for sale. It's our heritage, and we'll pass it on down to our own kids."

"So you're planning on having children?" Blake asked.

"One of us will." She wasn't going to discuss that issue at the dinner table.

"If they're going to have their own places, I don't suppose Jud and Toby will care how you're remodeling here at the Lucky Penny?" Deke asked.

"I don't think either of them would care if it was painted bullfrog green as long as it was cool in the summer, warm in the winter, and had lots of food in the freezer," Blake answered.

Allie giggled. "How about pink with purple trim?"

Blake laid a hand on hers. "Now, that, darlin', we might all balk at. Would you leave your van and trailer so we can throw the trash out on it? You can take my truck into town this afternoon." He removed his hand and refilled his glass with sweet tea.

She swallowed hard and nodded. Holy smoke! Of all the cowboys to be in her sights when she finally let go of the past, it had to be Blake Dawson.

CHAPTER TWELVE

The aroma of chili met Allie when she entered the convenience store, and she groaned. If she hadn't eaten those beans, she could make herself a chili pie with corn chips, cheese, and mustard, but now she was too full.

Katy picked up her coat and Irene's from the back of a chair behind the counter. "The lunch run is over and there's still some left, so if latecomers want a chili pie, you could probably still make about half a dozen, and the doughnuts have been there since early this morning, so sell what's left at half price and—"

"Mama, I've got this," Allie butted in. "Go on and don't worry about anything. And if she's in a good mood after you leave and it's not snowing by then, take her somewhere to eat. You could use some downtime, too. You are frazzled."

"I don't usually forget these things." Once she and Irene were buttoned up, Katy led her mother toward the door.

"I can walk on my own," Irene protested. "Don't know why we have to keep going to this doctor anyway. He don't give me pills or shots or do a thing for me. My hip still hurts, and he don't even check it."

"It's not that kind of doctor, Mama," Katy said.

"A doctor is a doctor, and he should treat a person's illnesses no matter what. Allie, I've got a bag of them white doughnuts in the back. You can have one, but if you take any more, you are in trouble," Irene said.

Allie hugged Katy and opened the door for them. "You've had so much on your mind, it's a wonder it hasn't shut down. Go and don't drive fast."

"Thanks, darlin'." Katy blew a kiss her way.

Katy's car had barely cleared the parking lot when a bright-red SUV pulled up, and Allie slapped her forehead and swore under her breath. She didn't want to deal with Sharlene and Mary Jo this afternoon. Not after that morning.

The two women pushed their way into the store and hung their coats on the long line of hooks right inside the door. Sharlene's slim body looked great in skinny jeans and a tight knit shirt. Mary Jo, the brunette with blue streaks in her hair, had put on a few pounds since high school, but she still had curves that made men turn for a second look.

Allie wanted to hide in the back room because there she was in the very worst pair of cargo pants she owned, a faded red T-shirt, hair that hadn't been styled, and no makeup. For the first time in years, it mattered to her what she looked like, and she didn't enjoy feeling like the ugly duckling at a pretty white swan convention.

"Nadine is on her way." Sharlene smiled at Allie. "She's always late. You look different than you did a couple of hours ago."

"Amazing what a little soap and water can do. What are y'all doing in Dry Creek on a Monday afternoon?" Allie asked.

"We all called in sick. Don't tell on us." Mary Jo laughed.

A second van came to a halt in the parking lot, and Nadine

hopped out with an orange Texas Longhorns umbrella over her head.

"Alora, darlin', would you please get us three big cups of coffee and a dozen of those doughnuts on the counter? And come on back here and sit with us? It's been too long since we've all four sat down and had a good old gossip fest." Nadine set the umbrella by the door and peeled back her yellow slicker to reveal red hair straight from the bottle.

"Make four of those chocolate," Sharlene yelled. "And Nadine is right. We haven't talked in forever."

Forever, her ass! They'd never been friends, not in high school, not since, and the only reason they wanted her to join them was to talk about Blake Dawson and the Lucky Penny. Besides, she and Sharlene had seen each other a couple of hours ago.

"And four of them can be maple iced," Mary Jo said. "The weatherman is saying the sun will come out later today and the main roads will be cleared, but I'll never understand why they go to the trouble when there's more on the way. I heard that it's already starting down around Abilene. Supposed to be here by suppertime and give us another four inches."

Mary Jo giggled. "I want more than four inches if I'm going to be snowed in with a cowboy. Tell me, Allie, what would I get if I got stranded with Blake?"

Nadine pulled out the fourth chair and patted the seat for Allie.

Allie fought the blush, but she lost. It was on the tip of her tongue to tell Mary Jo to ask Sharlene, but she bit her lip to keep from spitting out the words.

"I think we've embarrassed her." Sharlene giggled. "But we do want to hear more about Blake Dawson and his brother.

Blake is hot enough to make a virgin sin, and I lost my V-card years ago. If Allie hadn't interrupted us this morning, I might have more to tell you." Sharlene went on to tell about how she was about to get Blake in a horizontal position when Allie came out of the bedroom looking like a bag lady.

Mary Jo laid a hand on the extra chair. "We really do want you to join us, Alora, even if you did upset Sharlene's plans. You do know she's got her eye on that cowboy, and it's not a short-term deal she's lookin' for."

Nadine fanned herself with the back of her hand. "I get hot flashes every time I get a glimpse of him. I needed a fan Sunday in church, and it was a place of worship, so I shouldn't be letting a cowboy affect me like that! And you got to sit with him when your granny went all wonky. What was that like? Did you feel the heat from all that testosterone?" she asked and went on before Allie could answer. "Bobby Ray says that he won't last at the Lucky Penny and it might be best if he don't, because there's liable to be a dozen marriages on the rocks if he sticks around very long."

"You are in love with Bobby Ray and planning to marry him. How can you talk like that?" Allie asked.

"I'm not dead. A dieter can look at the candy counter, you know." Nadine huffed.

"I work for Blake. End of story," Allie said bluntly.

"I'd gladly work under him." Sharlene giggled.

"Or on top of him," Mary Jo said.

"I've got news," Sharlene said. "Y'all remember Oma Lynn who graduated a year before us?"

"That tall blonde with braces who had two left feet?" Mary Jo asked.

"That's her. Well, she works at the Muenster bank and

she says Blake Dawson...Isn't that the sexiest name ever? It sounds like a name you'd hear on the CMA awards. I wonder if he sings." Sharlene sighed.

Nadine polished off a doughnut and reached for a bear claw. "I bet he could make my body sing."

"Ain't no doubt." Mary Jo's laugh was high pitched.

Allie was torn between wanting to hear what they had to say and hiding in the back room out of sheer embarrassment. They were acting like they were still cheerleaders at Dry Creek High School. She sat down in the spare chair and crossed one leg over the other.

"Well, anyway, I called Oma Lynn to catch up. She was so happy to hear from me that she didn't even know I had an agenda." Sharlene reached for the last bear claw. "So I skirted around the issue and said that some dumb cowboy had bought the Lucky Penny. And she dived right in without me sayin' another word. She said that they call him the wild cowboy and his younger brother, Toby, is the hot cowboy and the cousin, Jud, is the lucky one."

Nadine almost choked on a bite of her bear claw. "Oh. My. Goodness! Do you mean there's one even hotter than Blake? And they've got a cousin?"

"That's what Oma Lynn said," Sharlene said as she nodded. "And that his brother is going to show up here in the summer and the three of them are determined to turn that ranch's luck around. And one more thing—if I don't land Blake Dawson, then y'all better stand back because I will get Toby or Jud."

"Well, I can't wait to see the other two," Mary Jo said. "And now we want to hear about Blake. No detail is too small. How does he like his coffee? Black? With cream or sugar? Is he really wild? I heard he and Deke took some woman to Frankie's this weekend."

Allie leaned on the table with her elbows. "Who was the woman?"

Mary Jo shook her head. "We can't find out, and believe me, we've tried hard to get someone to tell us."

Sharlene shook her head slowly. "I wouldn't even go there."

"Me, either. I've heard all kinds of things happen at Frankie's." Mary Jo shivered.

"You got any idea who they were having a threesome with?" Nadine asked.

All eyes turned to Allie. She squirmed in her chair and said, "You'll have to ask them. They don't tell me their dark secrets. Mainly we talk about drywall, paint, and shingles. Oh, and whatever food he brings out of the freezer for dinner."

Allie's phone rang, and she fished it from her pocket. "Excuse me. Y'all need more coffee, help yourselves."

It didn't take a psychoanalyst to know they were talking about her and Blake when their loud voices dropped to whispers once she left the table.

"Fiona, thank you, thank you!" Allie said.

"For what?" her sister replied.

"The gossip triplets are here," Allie answered.

"What are they doing at the Lucky Penny?"

Allie sat down in the metal folding chair behind the counter. "Mama had to take Granny for an evaluation, so I'm minding the store this afternoon."

"Don't they have jobs?"

"They all called in sick," Allie answered.

"Lizzy has called me a dozen times in the past three days

tattling on you for being really rude to some guy named Grady," Fiona said bluntly.

Allie nodded to herself. "If that sorry sucker was the only man left on earth, I still wouldn't like him."

"And Blake. If he was the last man on earth?" Fiona asked.

"I'd jump his bones." Allie laughed.

"Mama and Lizzy are afraid you are really going to fall for him. You aren't going to do that, are you? That place has never brought anything but bad luck to anyone who was affiliated with it, so think before you jump," Fiona begged.

Allie rolled her eyes toward the ceiling, then looked outside. The sun was still shining brightly in Dry Creek. It was hard to imagine that in a few hours the sky could go all gray.

"Allie, are you still there?" Fiona yelled.

Allie held the phone out from her ear. "I'm here. What if Blake is the one?"

"I hear he's got a reputation for wild cowboy ways, so he's definitely not the one for you, sister. After that crap with Riley, you're too responsible for that kind of relationship," Fiona said.

Well, that put the tally up to four who thought she was nothing but a plain old Jane who could never even get a wild cowboy to kiss her.

"Changing the subject. Remember when I told you when Riley left you that if Greta could break up a marriage, then she'd better watch out because someone could come along and Riley would leave her behind, too? Do you remember Denise Wilson who graduated with me?"

Allie didn't want to hear about Riley. He was the old that she'd taken care of that morning. Strange as it was, she'd rather be at the table with the gossip trio than listen to stories about her ex, but Fiona was only trying to help.

"She had an older brother who was Riley's friend, right?" Allie asked.

"That's the one," Fiona said. "She works at the dealership, and rumor has it that Riley has been sneakin' around with Denise's younger sister, Suzanne. The kid won't listen to a thing. She's quit college and says that she's ready to settle down and be a mama."

"Whoa! Is she pregnant?" Allie gasped.

"Not yet, according to Denise, but she and Riley have been going at it hot and heavy for more than a month. I've got to get to work now, but tell me that even though he's hot, you're not interested in the cowboy, and I'll tell Mama and Lizzy. That way, they'll stop calling me," Fiona said.

Allie propped her feet on the counter. Crap! She was even wearing work boots, and all three of those women at the table had on cute cowboy boots, with their fancy jeans. "He's hot. I'm not interested."

"That don't sound like you mean it."

Allie laughed. "Okay, he's scorchin' hot. But I've got better sense than to get tangled up with someone that close to home. He's my friend, and I like him." No way was she mentioning Frankie's because her sister wouldn't only tattle, but she'd also make arrangements to send Allie off to a convent.

"You are interested. I can hear it in your voice. Dammit, Allie!"

"Tell Mama and Lizzy that I'm not interested in him, and they'll leave you alone," Allie said. "And now I'm hanging up."

Allie hit the END button as Lucy Hudson walked into the store.

"Hey, Miz Allie, where's your mama?" She made her way to the milk and soda pop case.

"She had to take Granny up to Wichita Falls for a doctor's appointment."

"Ain't nothing else wrong with Irene, is there?" She carried two gallons of milk to the counter. "Don't have to buy this often, but my milk cow ain't makin' as much as she did a month ago, and them grandboys who are stayin' with me and Herman use a lot of milk. Might have to buy us another cow pretty soon."

"Granny is going for a routine checkup. That all you need today?"

"That's it. No, wait a minute. I'd better get a pound of bologna to make sandwiches for the boys tomorrow if the weather is fit."

"Won't take a minute. You sure a pound is enough?"

"Best make it two pounds. Them boys can put away the groceries," Lucy said.

Allie sliced and wrapped the order in white butcher paper, wrote the items on a yellow sales pad, and Lucy scribbled Herman's name on the bottom. Allie filed it under H with the rest of the Hudson bills for the month.

Lucy leaned over the counter and whispered, "I hear Sharlene is making a fool of herself with Blake and that Mary Jo ain't far behind her. Them two ain't cut out for ranchin'. It takes a strong woman to be a rancher's wife, and them two are all about themselves, not helpin' a man make a livin'. You need to warn him or talk to Deke and get him to talk sense to that boy."

Allie was about to say it wasn't her place to warn Blake, but Lucy inhaled and went on. "I like Blake and I hope he makes a go of it on the Lucky Penny. I'd hate to see him fail because he wound up getting roped by a woman with dollar signs in her eyes."

Allie nodded.

"Tell your mama and granny hello for me. I hope they get home all right. It's going to get slick out there," Lucy said.

"I will." Allie nodded.

Lucy winked, gathered up her bag of groceries, and hurried out to her truck.

* * *

"Well, that's done," Deke said, and looked up at the ceiling. "All ready for Allie to start beddin' and tapin' come morning. Let's go to the store and get a cold soda pop. I bet Allie is bored to death on a day like this, and she'll be glad for the company."

"Sounds good to me. Do they let dirty old cowboys like us in the store?"

"I expect we can go without shinin' our boots," Deke said.

The first flakes of snow were drifting down from the sky by the time they arrived at the store. Deke removed his weathered old cowboy hat and yelled, "Allie, if there's any doughnuts left, put my name on them and bring them to the"—he cleared his throat and coughed—"back room, where me and Blake are going to have a cold soda pop."

Allie cocked her head to one side. "What are y'all doin' in town?"

"We put in some hard work, so we came to get a cold drink, darlin'." Blake grinned. "I could've cut more wood, but me and Deke decided to surprise you. The new drywall for the ceiling is up. Looks bad right now, but Deke tells me your magic touch tomorrow will do wonders."

Blake noticed Sharlene at the table, and was that Mary Jo?

"What is going on?" Blake asked when he and Deke had

passed through a curtain into a back room. A twin bed was set up on one side with a recliner beside it facing a small television. Four chairs surrounded a table for four in the middle of the room. The blinds had been raised to let as much natural light as possible into the room.

Deke set two bottles of Coke on the table and explained the situation. "Irene stays in here part of the time, so they made it comfortable for her. But your question is about Sharlene, Nadine, and Mary Jo. Don't never encourage them with even a smile. Steer clear of them. If you need any help, call me. They are trouble."

"Is this the voice of experience I hear?" Blake grinned.

"It's the voice of my older brother's experience. I learned from his mistakes, and I'm passin' that bit of information down to you. Not only are they on the prowl most of the time, but they kiss and tell, and they are Dry Creek's biggest gossips. And I heard Sharlene has already said that she's going to marry you, by hook or crook," Deke answered.

"Allie, darlin', we need to pay our bill. We're going to Wichita Falls for a spa afternoon. You want to go with us?" Nadine called out.

"Got to keep the store for Mama. Y'all have fun and be careful. You might get stuck up there if the weather gets really bad," Allie said from behind the counter.

Nadine giggled. "That is exactly what we are hoping and why we packed our bags in case of emergency."

Mary Jo handed her a twenty-dollar bill. "Are you sure there's nothing goin' on with you and Blake? I'm paying for everything today, so take it all out of this."

Allie rang up the amount in the cash register and made the right change. "Smart ladies to go prepared."

"You didn't answer my question," Nadine said.

"Like I told you, I work for him. Deke helps me out when he can like he does on all jobs." If there was something going on, those three would be the last people on earth that Allie told.

"Good. I'd hate to see you get involved with the wrong person again like you did with Riley. Y'all never did go together. And believe me, honey, that cowboy is way too much for you to handle, especially since you couldn't handle Riley." Nadine laughed.

Tally was growing. Now it had five people on the list.

CHAPTER THIRTEEN

Allie had been working all day Tuesday, cutting and putting up insulation, and she itched from her scalp to her toes, some of it real but a lot of it imaginary since there was no way the insulation had gotten down into her socks and work boots. But still, it would be nice to take a quick shower before supper, so she dropped all those itchy clothes on the floor and pulled the curtain around the tub.

Blake had taken a pan of pulled pork barbecue from the freezer and had invited her to stay for supper. Her mother, sister, and grandmother were at a ladies' meeting down at the church and they'd be there until well after nine, so no one would even know she'd spent the evening with Blake.

"Hey, throw your clothes out here in the hall and I'll put them in the washer. They'll be clean and dry by the time we finish supper." Blake's deep voice carried through the thick bathroom door. "My robe is on the hook on the back of the door. You can wear it until your stuff is ready."

She stood behind the door and shoved all her things out to him. Dammit! Now he'd know she wore plain white bras without a bit of lace and matching cotton bikini underpants. Nothing sexy about her; not one thing to catch a wild cowboy's eye.

The robe smelled like a mixture of Blake's shaving lotion and soap, so she pulled it closer and inhaled deeply. Making sure it was securely belted around her waist and nothing was showing that shouldn't be, she glanced at her reflection in the mirror.

She felt totally naked even though she was covered from head to toe. The woman in the mirror with no makeup and wet hair wore white cotton underpants and a white bra and Blake would know it by now. There wasn't a thing she could do about it, so she took the first step toward the kitchen.

"Come on in, Allie. I'm putting the food on the table," Blake called out.

She opened the door and sniffed the air. "Smells good."

Everything was normal when she got to the kitchen. Supper was on the table in disposable aluminum foil pans. A washer was running in the background, and the coffeepot gurgled out the last bit of water. It was merely another meal at Blake's place, but without Deke there and Allie wearing nothing but a robe—well, that changed things a lot.

"Beer or sweet tea? I made a fresh pot of coffee for after with dessert, which is peach cobbler that came with the church ladies."

"Sweet tea," she answered. She didn't want a thing that Sharlene had brought into the house. "I love peach cobbler. I bet it's Ruby's recipe. That's what she always brings to church suppers."

"You look downright adorable in my robe, and I bet you feel a lot better with all that insulation washed off you," Blake said. "After your things get washed and dried, let's go outside and build a moon snowman."

"A what?" she asked.

"A snowman by the light of the moon."

She smiled. "That sounds like fun. The snow is wet enough to pack good and solid, and there's enough to make a good snowman."

"You look beautiful," he said abruptly.

"I got to admit, I feel more than a little vulnerable, so you might want to keep your wild ways under wraps," she said honestly.

How did the conversation go from snowmen to her so quickly? She felt a blush coming on, but she wasn't the only one with high color in her cheeks. Grown men did not get flustered, but Blake did. Then he laughed. "And what makes you think I've got an ounce of wild in me? I'm only a rough old cowboy trying to turn a ranch around and get the town of Dry Creek to accept me."

Allie sat down. "Oma Lynn. You ever heard of her?"

Blake's heavy dark brows drew together until they became one long line. "You mean the sweet lady who works at my bank in Muenster? Why are you asking about her?"

Allie dipped into the pot and filled up her bowl with pulled pork. "She grew up right here in Dry Creek. Sharlene, Mary Jo, and Nadine have gotten the scoop on you from her. She spilled the beans about you being the wild Dawson, your brother being the hot one, and your cousin being the lucky one."

Blake raked his hand down over his face. "I guess a man can't outrun his past, can he?"

"Just how wild were you?"

"Just how married were you?" he fired right back.

"Touché," she said with the briefest of nods.

"Guess we're both lookin' to make changes in our lives and forget the past," he said.

Did Allie hear him right? Did he say he wanted to make a change in his life? Could that possibly mean that Sharlene or Mary Jo weren't in his sights for a one-night stand or even more?

"Yes, sir. Would you please pass the cheese?"

He handed her the plate. "Anything for a beautiful lady. Thanks for having supper with me, Allie. The evenings get long if you and Deke aren't around."

Every time, without fail, that he called her beautiful, her pulse raced, and her heart threw in an extra beat. She took a deep breath before she spoke so he wouldn't know how he affected her. "I know exactly what you mean about getting lonesome. Lizzy is so involved with wedding plans, and the evenings are tough for Granny. If she does have a lucid moment, it won't be after dark. And Mama gets dragged into the wedding business, so even though there's four of us over at our place, I still get lonely."

He gave her one of those brilliant grins that electrified the whole room. "Well, darlin', you are welcome here anytime of the night or day." He stood, walked over to move Allie's clothes from the washer to the dryer, and then came back to the table.

She drew his robe even tighter around her chest, glad that the plush material covered up the effect he had on her aching breasts. She was flirting with the devil, but he was so enticing that even a glance drew her to him like a wayward moth to a flame. Allie had sure never been any kind of saint, but she really should slow down and quit taking such giant steps toward the fire.

"You've got that faraway look on your face again. Is Lizzy arguing with you?" Blake asked.

"No, she's been quiet this evening. It was me fighting with me," she said honestly.

"About what?"

Blake picked up a pickle and bit into it. "Want to talk about it?"

"No, I'm tired of analyzing everything to death."

Blake handed her the rest of the pickle. "It's dill, and I thought it was a sweet pickle. You finish it. You like dill."

Without even thinking about it, she popped the rest of the pickle into her mouth. Was that something that friends did? She didn't share her food with Deke, and they'd been friends for more than a decade.

She was still chewing when the front door burst open and Irene stomped in wearing a pair of bright-red rubber boots, a cowboy hat, and a long denim duster, all covered with snow.

"Walter, where are you?" she yelled.

Allie jumped up so quickly that the robe's belt loosened and the top fell back, showing the top half of her breasts. Blake and Allie met Irene in the living room, and she took one look at Allie, doubled up her fist, and shook it at Blake.

"You cheated on me, Walter! And now you're goin' to pay the price for doin' that."

Allie took a step forward and grabbed her grandmother's hands. When she did, even more of the robe fell away from her body.

"Granny, this is Blake, and I'm Alora Raine. I'm your grand-daughter, and this man is not Walter," Allie said sternly.

"You are naked under that robe," Irene hissed.

Allie continued to hold her hands. "Yes, I am. I've been working in insulation all day, and my clothes are in the dryer right now. I'll get dressed as soon as they are done. Let's call Mama to come get you."

"My mama has been dead for years, so you can't call her. Silly girl, there ain't no phones in heaven." Irene eyed Blake seriously. "You aren't Walter, are you? Who are you again?"

"I'm your new neighbor, Blake Dawson. Allie is doing some carpentry work for me," he said.

Allie groaned when she heard a vehicle coming to a stop outside. Thinking about having to explain to her mother why she was wearing nothing but a robe was enough to make her want to run home in four inches of snow in her bare feet. If that old adage about how man plans and God laughs was true, then the Almighty must be howling up in heaven right now.

High heels on the wooden porch didn't sound like her mother's footsteps, but then, maybe Katy had gotten dressed up for the church thing and hadn't had time to kick off her Sunday shoes. It didn't matter if she showed up in rubber boots or her best dress shoes as long as she took Granny home and didn't throw a hissy about the way Allie was dressed.

Allie let go of her grandmother's hands and put the robe to rights. The cutesy little rap on the door sounded like da-da-da-da-da and then a da-da, which should have alerted Allie that it was not her mother.

Blake yelled for the visitor to come on in. The door swung open, and a cold north wind pushed Nadine into the room. She wore her best Sunday coat and high-heeled shoes, and she carried an apple pie in her hands.

"Blake, darlin', I brought you a pie. Oh!" She looked from Irene to Blake and then to Allie. "I didn't know you had company."

Irene poked her on the arm. "What are you doing here? Does Bobby Ray know you are out at this time of night flirtin' with a married man? He'll call off the wedding if he finds out, and I'll tell him next time I see him."

"Blake is married?" Nadine frowned.

"I'm *not* married," Blake answered.

Nadine shoved the pie into his hands. "I just dropped by to bring you another apple pie and welcome you to Dry Creek."

"Thank you," he mumbled.

More noises out in the driveway meant Katy was really coming to take Granny home this time. After all the stuff with Nadine, it would be wonderful to get the whole ordeal finished and go home with her mama and Granny. Hopefully, her things would be dry by then.

The knock came on the door, and Blake opened it.

"May I help you?" he asked.

"Nadine?" Her fiancé, Bobby Ray, pushed his way past Blake and into the house. He stopped so quick that his boots squeaked on the floor. His eyes went straight to Nadine. "What are you doing here? You're supposed to be at that ladies' thing at the church."

"I came to see Allie," she said quickly. "She wanted to taste my apple pie, so I brought one to her."

Bobby Ray, a tall man with a full black beard and a beer belly, crossed his arms over his chest. "Why here and not over at Audrey's Place?"

"Lizzy was at the church meeting and said Allie was doing

some work here, and when I called her, she said to bring it here," Nadine lied.

"I asked about the pie recipe when she and Sharlene and Mary Jo came in the store yesterday for coffee. It's awful sweet of you to bring one to me," Allie piped up.

Bobby Ray tilted his head toward Blake. "Why is Blake holding it, and why are you dressed like that?"

"He's holding it because"—Allie nodded toward her grandmother and lowered her voice—"my granny thought it was for her, and she hates apple pie. She's on a tear tonight, and we were afraid she would throw it at Nadine and ruin her coat." The sentence came out in a rush. "And why I'm dressed like this isn't a bit of your business, Bobby Ray."

"That's right." Irene slapped him on the shoulder. "What exactly are you doing here?"

"I don't believe this cock and bull story one bit about bringing that pie to Allie. I came over here to ask Blake if I could cut up some of that wood he's givin' away for free. I didn't come to fight with you, Nadine." Bobby Ray eyed Nadine closely.

Blake set the pie on the coffee table. "You're welcome to all the wood you want. Herman and his crew have been taking a lot of it but, believe me, there is plenty more on the way soon as I can get it dozed down."

Allie heard another vehicle. It had to be her mother this time. Or maybe it was all the ladies of the church bringing another round of food to replenish what Blake had used. It didn't matter. Tomorrow morning the fact that she was in his house, wearing his robe and nothing else, would be the headlines of the gossip vine.

This time there was no knock. A tall blonde plowed into the living room. Wearing a floor-length black leather coat, tight skinny jeans, and a gorgeous red sweater, the woman ignored everyone. She set her eyes on Blake and made a bee-line for him, slung her arms around his neck, and kissed him. It wasn't a sister kiss but a long, lingering one that involved lots of tongue.

When the kiss broke, her eyes lit on Bobby Ray, standing there with his hands in his pockets and looking at the ceiling. "Bobby Ray Wilson. I haven't seen you in a whole month, darlin'. What are you doing here? I swear the world gets smaller every day."

Bobby Ray stammered, "What brings you here, Scarlett?"

"Long story, but it don't have anything to do with us, darlin'. I told you that we were through the last time I saw you, remember? I don't date married men or engaged ones. You were a naughty boy. You should have told me you were engaged before we spent the weekend together," Scarlett said.

Nadine drew back her fist, and if Blake hadn't taken a couple of long strides forward and blocked it, she would have broken Bobby Ray's nose.

"Turn me loose. He's in here blaming me for cheatin', and I didn't, but he did," Nadine screeched.

"Who is that screeching harpy, Blake?" Scarlett asked.

"This would be Bobby Ray's fiancée, Nadine," Blake said.

Scarlett slapped a hand over her mouth dramatically. "Oops."

Nadine shook free of Blake's grasp and tiptoed so that her nose was only inches from Bobby Ray's. "You aren't worth this. I'm going home to cool off, and we'll decide tomorrow if we are still engaged or not."

"That would be the pot calling the kettle black after this little escapade, wouldn't it? You're running around taking pies to men after dark. I bet you didn't make me a pie, did you?" Bobby Ray said.

Scarlett ignored them and pointed at Allie. "And this one wearing my favorite robe, sweetheart? Who is she?"

Allie would have taken the robe off and stomped on it with dirty boots if she'd had another piece of clothing underneath. "I'm Alora Raine Logan. I happen to be working on this house, and it's none of your business why I'm wearing this robe."

Scarlett looked down on Allie, her blue eyes so cold that Allie could feel the chill behind them. Her voice was sweetly sarcastic when she said, "It's nice and warm, isn't it? At least I've always found it to be just the ticket after a long bath."

Allie met the challenge without backing down an inch. "Who are you?"

"I'm Blake's wife, and this is my yearly booty call," she said.

CHAPTER FOURTEEN

The entire room went so quiet that Allie's ears ached. Did that woman just say she was Blake's wife? Allie whipped around and stared at him.

"Ex," Blake said quickly.

A loud rap on the doorframe took everyone's attention in that direction. Katy Logan stepped inside without waiting to be invited. "Have you seen...? Oh, there you are, Mama. It's time to go home now. What the...?" Katy's eyes came close to popping out of their sockets when she saw Allie.

"It's a long story," Allie said. "Come on, Granny. I think it's time for us to go home."

Irene sat down in the rocking chair. "Why? I like this party. It's exciting. When are they bringing out the birthday cake and ice cream? I want cake."

"We've got chocolate cake waiting for us at home. I'll get my boots, and I'll see to it your robe gets brought home tomorrow," Allie said coldly without even looking at Blake.

"Allie, let me explain," he said.

Her shoulder bumped his as she stomped toward the

bathroom to get her boots, but she didn't look back. "Enjoy your booty call. I'll get my boots and get out of your way."

"Is this your new girlfriend?" Scarlett asked above the argument still going on between Bobby Ray and Nadine.

"That is none of your business. All of you need to leave," Blake yelled above the din.

"Well, Walter, don't go screamin' at me like that. You invited me for cake and ice cream. I didn't bring all these other fools. It's not my fault," Irene huffed.

Allie marched back up the hall in boots that were unlaced, took her grandmother's hand, and helped her up out of the rocking chair. "Come on, Granny. We'll have cake and ice cream, and you can even blow out the candles."

"Is it my birthday?"

"Not yet, but we'll practice for when it is," Allie said.

* * *

The moment they were alone in the house, Scarlett draped her arms around Blake's neck and rolled slightly up on her toes to kiss him on the lips. One hand braced against his chest while the other one worked on his belt.

"A year is too long," she whispered. "We have to start taking care of this every six months."

He pushed her away and ran a palm over his mouth, wiping the kiss away. "Get out, Scarlett, and don't come back."

"You can't resist me. You never could, so don't give me that song and dance. I've looked forward to this for a month. We always get together right after New Year's to celebrate the fact that our parents were smart enough to get our drunken marriage annulled," she whispered.

He opened the door and pointed. "Out!"

She didn't budge. "You can do a lot better than that mousy-lookin' little creature."

"Out!" He raised his voice so loud the second time he said the word that Shooter whimpered.

"Okay, then," she growled. "Since you are in a mood, I'll leave, but I don't believe that woman can tame you. That can't be done, and I'm proof of it." She stormed out the door and slammed it behind her.

Blake made sure the deadbolt was set and threw himself back in the recliner. "Maybe this place is unlucky after all," he sighed.

Shooter gobbled down the apple pie and licked the glass pie plate clean. Then he curled up in front of the fireplace, his big brown eyes looking up at Blake.

"You're not in trouble, boy. I was going to heave the thing out in the yard," Blake mumbled.

Shooter's tail wagged a few times.

"Now I have to explain the whole thing to Allie," he whispered as he petted the dog.

The doorknob rattled, and Deke yelled from the other side, "Hey, man, are you alone in there?"

Blake rushed to the door, unlocked it, and slung it wide open. "Where were you thirty minutes ago when I needed you?"

"What do you need done?" Deke asked. "Or are we going somewhere to dance and flirt with the ladies?"

"I needed you to referee." Blake ushered him inside and told him the rest of the story.

Deke removed his coat and tossed it behind the recliner. "Man, I can't believe all that happened tonight, but I'm glad that Allie and even Irene were here when Nadine showed up. If you'd been alone and Bobby Ray hadn't decided to come around and ask about firewood, you'd have been in trouble."

"If I can tell Scarlett to go away, and Sharlene and Mary Jo, I reckon I could get rid of that redhead." Blake plopped down on the sofa. "There's still food on the table if you're hungry."

"Already ate, but don't put it away. I might get into it later," Deke said. "Do you like Allie? I mean as in *like* her, not as in like her as a friend and neighbor? It seems to me you might have developed some feelings for her."

"Why are you asking?"

The dog on the television barked, and Shooter's head popped up. "See, even Shooter thinks something is going on and he's voicing his opinion. The reason I'm askin' is because she's like a sister to me and I don't want to see her hurt, and you just now told me about this once-a-year booty call and I bet this is the first time you turned it down."

"I could never hurt Allie. I..." Blake hesitated. "Yes, I do like her a lot."

"You'd best be real sure before you make that statement because as good of friends as we've become, if you make her cry, I'll have to hurt you," Deke said seriously.

Blake went to the kitchen and brought back two open beers. He handed one to Deke and downed a third of his before he settled into the rocking chair in front of the blazing fire. "You don't scare me as much as this feeling inside me. I didn't move here with intentions of getting involved in any way with a woman. I should back away from her completely. She's already got baggage in her past, and she don't need an old cowboy like me, and besides, my brother and I have a rule about dating women too close to home," Blake said.

"That's not your decision to make. It's Allie's."

"After tonight I'll be surprised if she even comes back to finish the bedroom."

"Man, I would have loved to have been here to see it, but I'm more than a little mad at you for kicking that tall blonde out in the cold. I would have gladly let her come to my house for the night." Deke laughed.

* * *

"Start talkin'," Katy said the minute they were in the house.

Irene clapped her hands like a child. "Cake and candles, and ice cream."

"We'd better take care of this first or she'll be a nightmare the rest of the evening." Allie led the way to the kitchen. She found a package of two chocolate cupcakes in the pantry, unwrapped them, and put them on a decorative disposable plate before carrying them out to the table where Irene waited.

"Candles?" She frowned.

"Right here." Katy brought them to the table with the container of ice cream.

Allie poked a candle in each cupcake. "Now blow 'em out, Granny."

"Practicin' for my birthday, right? That means you have to sing to me." Irene giggled.

"You get them both with one breath and we'll sing," Katy said.

"What's going on? It's not Granny's birthday." Lizzy was carrying a thick three-ring binder with everything from pictures of centerpieces to candles to honeymoon places, all arranged neatly with tabbed dividers.

Allie hated the sight of the *wedding book,* hated everything about it, from the pictures of the lavender dresses to the tuxedos that Mitch and Grady would wear. The wedding would be held in the Dry Creek church, with the reception in the fellowship hall, not in a big-city cathedral.

"I thought we'd talk about the ribbons for our bouquets tonight, but I see you are all busy." Lizzy pouted.

"We are practicin', and if you don't like it, go away," Irene said.

"Practicin' what?" Lizzy asked.

"Granny's birthday," Allie answered.

She blew out both candles, and Katy started the birthday song. Lizzy and Allie sang with her all the way to the end.

Lizzy poked Allie on the arm. "What are you doing in a man's robe, and why does she think it's her birthday?"

"It's a long story. Come on upstairs to my bedroom while she eats and I'll tell you." Allie didn't want to confide in her sister, but by morning the rumors would have the story blown so far out of proportion that she might as well come clean.

Lizzy followed Allie to her bedroom and sat on the edge of the bed. "Well?"

"I'm going to get dressed first, so be patient." She stepped inside the big closet and shut the door. Like always, she'd held up good under pressure, but now that it was over, her hands shook and her stomach hurt. Her skin turned clammy and tears filled her eyes, but she refused to let them spill. She pulled on a pair of underpants and an oversized nightshirt that stopped midway down her thigh.

"You going to take all night in there?" Lizzy called out.

Allie pushed the door open and lay on the bed, curled up

in a C with the pillow under her head. "Might as well stretch out here beside me. This might take a while."

Lizzy fell back on the bed. "What have you done? Don't tell me that was Blake's robe you were wearing down there. I thought it was one of Daddy's old ones, but it was that cowboy's, wasn't it?"

"It is and there's a reason I was wearing it, but believe me, sister, I will not be wearing it ever again." She told the story from the time she finished the room, only leaving out the way his robe touching her bare body made her feel.

"Oh, my!" Lizzy gasped. "Do you know what the gossip hounds are going to do with that before morning? To get the heat off herself, Nadine will call Sharlene and Mary Jo, and they'll spread the news to everyone else, and by morning you will be having an affair with that cowboy. You might as well have gone on and slept with him."

"Well, ain't that just the ticket! Now that I have your permission, maybe I should go over there and boot that tall woman out of his bed and have a turn with him," Allie said sarcastically.

"Oh, hush! That hussy really said that she'd worn that robe?" Lizzy hissed.

Allie nodded. "She did."

Lizzy slid off the bed. "Put on some jeans and some boots. We are going to burn the thing out in the backyard right now. I may not agree with you very often, but you are my sister, and no one is treating you like that."

"That won't solve anything. She is part of his past, like Riley is mine," Allie said.

Lizzy went straight to the closet and picked the robe up from the floor. "I don't care what she is or what Riley was.

There's going to be a robe burnin'. I'll do it if you don't want to." She paused. "Oh. My! You have fallen for that cowboy, haven't you?"

Allie shrugged. "I like spending time with him, but I wouldn't say I've fallen for him. That involves more than wearing his robe while my clothes are in the washing machine. Which reminds me, why wasn't Granny with you at the Lady's Circle meeting?"

Lizzy glared at the robe now lying on the floor. "No one showed up, so we came on back home. We didn't have a meeting after all."

"Nadine said she was there, and you told her I was working over at the Lucky Penny."

Lizzy's eyes rolled toward the ceiling. "Before or after Bobby Ray showed up? She was trying to save her own skin, and you helped her out, so she owes you big time. And don't change the subject. Answer me."

Allie sighed. "You sound like Granny when your voice goes all high and squeaky. I like Blake. He's a good person, Lizzy. Tonight wasn't his fault. It was one of those cluster things that happen all at once."

"Depends on the booty-call woman, don't it? I wonder if he sent her packing, or if she's over there right now." Lizzy's fists were clenched. "Lord, I'd like to hit her or him or even Nadine. Do you realize what kind of gossip is going to be going through town by morning?"

"I need to sort it all out. Can you give me a few days to do that before you start fussing at me about it? Or before you go hittin' someone? Remember you're going to be a preacher's wife."

Lizzy set her mouth in a firm line. "Fire starts in ten

minutes. That's how long it will take me to stuff this in the fire pit and douse it with gasoline."

"Wait till I get my jeans on. If that woman had it on her body, then I want to see it burn," Allie said quickly.

"That's my sister. The one I knew before Riley broke her heart." Lizzy grinned. "Promise me that you won't ever go back over there?"

Allie left the bed and jerked on a pair of jeans. "Oh, no! I've got things to say to him, so I definitely will go back to his ranch."

"You like him more than a little bit if he makes you that mad," Lizzy said.

Allie pulled her dark hair up in a ponytail. "Maybe so. I'll have to figure it out, but right now we've got a robe to burn. Wonder if he'd like to see it or maybe smell the smoke?"

"Wind is blowing toward the south. Call him once we get it lit and tell him to step out on the porch," Lizzy answered. "He'll probably tell you to keep your scrawny hind end on your side of the fence from now on."

They set the robe on fire, and despite feeling childish and more than a little bit like a teenager instead of a twenty-eight-year-old woman, Allie called Blake. He answered on the first ring, and she told him what she and Lizzy were doing.

"Fine by me," Blake said. "But next time you need to wash some insulation out of your clothes, you won't have a robe to wear, so maybe you should bring an extra set of clothing over here—just in case you need it—or else you'll have to run around naked. I have no problem with that. None whatsoever."

"I will always have an extra set of clothing from now on," Allie shot back.

"Then that means you're going to finish the job you started?" Blake asked.

Allie drew in a long breath and let it out slowly. "I don't let anyone keep me from doing a job. Just tell her to stay out of my way tomorrow morning."

"She's gone, and I don't expect she'll ever come back. Deke says to say hello."

"Hello, Deke, and good night, Blake."

She pushed the END button and bit back the grin so that she wouldn't have to tell Lizzy what he'd said.

CHAPTER FIFTEEN

Allie called Blake the next morning to tell him that she had to mind the feed store because Lizzy had come down with the flu overnight. That meant Katy took Granny to the convenience store with her and Allie would be on the other end of the block at Lizzy's store all day. The sun was out again, but the temperature was below freezing, so there wouldn't be a lot of melting going on that day.

She got his voice mail and left a short message.

She tried again at midmorning but got the same message, and her mind immediately went to the tall blond bombshell who might have returned and sweet-talked her way into Blake's bed. It was his bed and his life so it wasn't a bit of her business, but that didn't keep the envy at bay. Besides, she'd known Blake less than two weeks, so what gave her the right to be jealous?

Wearing his robe did not give her any rights over him. Lighting it up might have burned any bridges between them anyway. She grabbed a dustrag and went to work on the shelves in the Dry Creek Feed and Seed Store. As much as she hated cleaning, she needed something to do so that the hands of the clock would move. Starting on the side where all the supplies were kept, she straightened, wiped out a month's worth of dust, and grumbled.

Of all three Logan sisters, Lizzy hated cleaning the most. And yet Mitch expected a spotlessly clean house and three meals on the table and Lizzy to wear high heels the whole time she was making that happen. After the first week, she'd kill him. Poor old sumbitch had no idea what he was getting into.

"Anybody here?" A voice startled her so badly that she threw the dustrag straight up with a squeal. Gravity brought it back to Lucy's hands, and she held it out to her.

"Just because I caught the thing don't mean I'm going to use it," Lucy said with a giggle.

Allie laid the rag on the shelf. "What can I do for you today, Miz Lucy?"

"I need to buy a chain saw blade for Herman. He called me when I was elbow deep in makin' bread for the week to tell me to bring a new saw blade out to the Lucky Penny for him. Thinks he can't waste a minute coming to town to get it, but it's okay to interrupt what I'm doin'," Lucy fussed.

"Got to cut wood while the sun shines. This is just the middle of January. We could have lots more winter before the robins come around to stay," Allie said.

"And it would be a sin if one chunk of mesquite wasn't in his wood yard." Lucy winked. "Men! Never will understand them. While I'm here, I need a new extension cord."

"The big orange industrial one or one of these brown and white ones?" Allie pointed to the shelf where they were displayed.

Lucy glanced back toward her office. "Give me one of them white ones then. And put it on our ticket. Where's Lizzy?"

"She's down with that stomach virus that's going around, but it only lasts a couple of days, so she'll be back by Friday." Allie rang up the bill and laid Herman's copy on the counter.

Lucy scribbled his name on the bottom of the ticket. "Tell her to get well soon and to keep that sickness at Audrey's Place. Us old folks don't bounce back like the young do. And I sure hope Irene don't get a dose of it."

Allie filed the ticket in a box under the counter. Lizzy could take care of entering all that into the computer later. It was double work, but the old folks in town didn't trust the new way of doing business, so Lizzy and Katy both still made out handwritten tickets for them.

Lucy pointed to the radio on the counter. "I'm glad that Lizzy plays old country music in here. I hate going into a store and that new stuff is playing. It makes my ears hurt."

"Daddy always had the classic country station playing," Allie said.

"I know he did. I liked it then and I still do. It don't get no better than Conway and Loretta." Lucy smiled. "You know folks in town say you are on a fool's mission fixin' up that house for Blake, don't you?" Lucy changed the subject abruptly.

"I'm not surprised. Hey, do you remember someone named Walter who lived on the Lucky Penny maybe thirty years ago?" Allie asked.

Lucy nodded. "Remember him well. Tall, lanky old boy with dark hair and glasses. Him and his mama bought the ranch and lived there a year, maybe two, and then like all the rest of the folks who've lived there, they moved on. Can't recall his last name, but his mama was one of them women that always had something wrong with her. I wanted to wring her neck for pretending to be sick all the time. Woman who could eat as much as she could at a church social, there couldn't have been a thing wrong with her. She just had to act like that to keep Walter under her thumb. Tell all the ladies at Audrey's Place I hope they stay well."

Allie plopped down in the lawn chair behind the counter. "So, Walter isn't a total figment of her imagination."

"No, Walter was very real," Lucy answered and waved as she left the store. The business phone rang, and Allie reached for the cordless sitting beside the cash register. "Dry Creek Feed and Seed," she answered.

"I forgot to tell you that the vet supply guy isn't coming this month and what's on the shelf is all we've got until he gets here the first of February," Lizzy said. "If someone needs more than what's there, I can make a run up to Wichita Falls, but it'll take me a couple of days to get it."

"Drink your hot tea and stop worryin'. I can run this store for a day or two," Allie said. "Lucy is the only customer that you've had, and she bought an extension cord and a blade for Herman's chain saw."

"Mitch was coming into town to see me tonight and now he can't," Lizzy moaned. "I don't want him to get sick with whatever this is I've got."

"None of the rest of us have caught whatever you have. Maybe it's not a bug but wedding jitters. Or maybe you're pregnant," Allie said with a wicked grin.

"Alora Raine Logan!" Lizzy yelled into the phone.

Allie held it out from her ear. "Are you telling me it's not possible? Mercy, Lizzy! You've been dating this man for a year."

"We entered into a covenant when we got engaged. We will abstain until our wedding night," Lizzy said.

"Well, that explains a lot." Allie laughed. "Your hateful mood. And your sharp tongue and that hangdog look on your face all the time. You need to get laid."

"I'm abstaining for the Lord," Lizzy growled. "You are doing without because you..."

Allie's jaw set in anger. "Because I'm ugly as a mud fence? Because I have no sex appeal? Because I am a carpenter? Be careful, Lizzy. I'm minding the store for you, and I could re-arrange everything or maybe I could shuffle all the stuff in the bill box under the counter."

"You wouldn't dare!" Lizzy huffed.

"Oh, I would, and you know it," Allie said.

"Mitch is going to be your brother," Lizzy reminded her.

Allie shook her head emphatically even though no one could see it. "He's going to be your husband, not my brother, and I will be every bit as nice to him as you were to Riley."

"I never did like that man," Lizzy grumbled.

Allie stood up and carried the phone with her to the first round rack of clothing. "Point proven. I'm going to work on straightening and putting up stock on the clothing side. You need to look around before you order. You've got four orange hoodies in a two-X size and only one in a small."

"Those will be gone by the end of next week and the small will still be hanging there. I ordered it for Sharlene's brother, and he broke his leg and can't hunt this year. Thanks for the cleanup. Bye," Lizzy said in a rush and the phone went silent.

Allie didn't need an explanation of the quick end to the call and hoped that she didn't catch whatever sent Lizzy to the bathroom every fifteen minutes. She looked back through the clothing area of the store. Hunting jackets, hoodies, jeans, and one rack of cute little western shirts for women.

"I need coffee before I tackle getting all this dusted and straightened," she said.

After a quick trip to the office/kitchenette, she propped a hip on the tall stool behind the cash register. She had taken the first sip when the door opened, and she looked across the store into the eyes of her ex-husband, Riley. His light brown hair was longer, almost touching his shirt collar, and he'd gained at least twenty pounds, most of it around his midsection right above his belt. All in all, he looked like he'd aged ten years, and that put a big smile on her face.

"Hello, Allie." He smiled back at her.

She wiped the grin off her face instantly. "What brings you to Dry Creek?"

His soft-soled shoes didn't make a sound as he crossed the floor. She didn't recognize that shaving lotion, but it smelled like he'd taken a bath in it, and it cost a buck ninety-nine at Walmart.

"I came to talk to you, darlin'," he said smoothly.

She recognized his attempt at seduction and crossed her arms over her chest. "That ship sailed a lifetime ago, Riley. I don't have anything to say to you; nor do I want to hear anything you say to me."

"But all ships eventually come back home after their adventure." He placed his palms on the counter and locked gazes with her.

Riley had been her high school sweetheart. He'd made her feel special. She'd landed the quarterback of the football team, and he'd treated her like a queen. They'd married right before her nineteenth birthday and divorced about the time she was twenty-two.

"I understand you've been flirting with the new owner over at the Lucky Penny and got caught last night." His smile was so sarcastic that it chilled the whole store.

The Riley she married, the one who'd looked into her eyes with such love on their wedding day, was not the man on the other side of the counter. This was the same stranger who came home one day and told her he was in love with another woman. There was no way he could ever, ever worm his way into her heart again.

She sipped her coffee. "I understand you've been keeping even later hours with a minor and that your nights are a lot hotter than mine."

"She's of age," he protested. "And I didn't come here to talk about Suzanne."

"What did you come to talk about?" Allie asked. "Do you need a sack of chicken feed or maybe an extension cord? I can help you with that, but anything else you'll have to get from your wife or your newest soul mate."

His thin mouth clamped shut until it was nothing more than a slit. Fantastic! Paybacks could be so sweet.

"I want to talk about us," he said through clenched teeth.

Allie shook her head. "There is no us. Hasn't been in seven years. What I do or don't do isn't a bit of your business."

"Come on, Allie. We've been in love since we were in grade school," he said.

"Like I said, that ship sailed. Matter of fact, I believe it sank in a storm, and there's nothing left of it," she told him. "I'm looking ahead, not behind."

"We were good together. We could be again." His voice

dropped to a whisper. "We could start fresh like Bobby Ray and Nadine."

"Bobby Ray." She frowned. "So, he came running to your house when Nadine threw him out last night, did he?"

Riley reached across the counter and touched her cheek. "Bobby Ray stayed with me last night. Nadine cheats on him, too, so she doesn't have room to complain. I'm sure that somewhere in our marriage you had a little fling."

She slapped his hand away. "Do not ever put your hands on me again. If you touch me again, I will knock you on your butt and enjoy every minute of it," she said.

"I came in here to remind you of the good times when we were married. I gave you advice about things back then, and from what I hear, you need someone to step up to the plate again."

Allie laughed out loud.

"What's so funny?" he asked.

"You are a regular comedian today," she said between giggles. "Go home, Riley. It's been over with us for a long time. And you weren't giving me advice. You were putting me down that last few months so you wouldn't feel guilty about cheating on me."

"I want you back, Allie. I'll treat you right this time. I'll let you work," he begged.

She shook her head slowly from side to side. "Sometimes it's too late to do what you should've been doing all along. Door is closed, Riley. Let me work, indeed! Have you lost your mind?"

His face turned scarlet with rage. "Don't you talk to me like that, and don't laugh at me."

The cowbell attached to the front door rang loudly, and

Nadine walked in and popped her hands on her hips. "What are you doing in town, Riley? And don't be givin' me that look. I heard that Bobby Ray holed up in your place last night. He's back home now, but we've had a come-to-Jesus talk."

"He came to give me a second chance," Allie said. "You want to spread the news so Suzanne knows what kind of man she's quittin' college for?"

"She can sure do better than you." Nadine got right into Riley's personal space and poked him in the chest.

"I don't know what gave Suzanne that idea. I'm a happily married man. I dropped by because I was in town." Riley pulled himself up to his full height of five feet eight inches. "I'll be going now. I don't have to take abuse from either of you."

"No, but I reckon Greta and Suzanne might have some that you'll have to take when they both hear you've been down here trying to get back with your ex," Nadine told him.

He almost made it to the door when Irene rushed inside and stopped right in front of him. She stomped one foot on the wooden floor.

"What are you doin' in my store?" she demanded. "I hope the good Lord strikes you graveyard dead. And God hears the prayers of little children and old women, so you'd best get on out of here."

"I'm leaving." He turned back to give Nadine an evil smile. "You ever tell her about us?" The slamming door echoed through the store like a shotgun blast.

Irene turned on Nadine. "Did you go to bed with him, too?"

Nadine blushed and covered her face with her hands. "I'm so sorry, Allie."

"Before or after we were married?" Allie asked.

The sobbing started.

"I asked a question," Allie said loudly.

"After," Nadine sobbed. "But only two times. He said that you couldn't keep him happy and wouldn't even sleep with him after the first week of marriage. But I wasn't the only one, Allie."

"Sharlene?"

Nadine dropped her hands and nodded. "But before y'all were married."

"And Mary Jo?"

"Right before Greta," Nadine whimpered.

Irene threw up her hands in disgust and went straight back to the office, where she sat down and turned on the television. Allie could barely think straight, but she made a quick call to her mom to let her know Granny was safe and sound before turning toward Nadine.

Nadine was frozen in the spot where she'd been standing when Riley was still there. "I am so sorry. I came to town to fess up to you. Honest, I did. I heard you were runnin' the store for Lizzy because she's sick, and I came in here to tell you that I won't be flirting with Blake Dawson anymore. I didn't know you were interested in him, and I feel so guilty for what I did with Riley. I'd never do that to you again, Allie. You deserve better."

Allie should feel something other than indifference. Four women including Greta had slept with her husband either before or after she'd married him. One was standing right there within slapping distance. She should hate her, but the only thing she felt for Nadine was pity. "Well, thank you for that, but you should be thinkin' about your wedding instead of my feelings."

Nadine took a step toward the counter. "You have always been too nice. We were all so jealous of you in high school and then afterward when you married Riley. Every girl in school was in love with him, and he chose you. We all hated you for that."

Allie wasn't in a hugging mood, so she hoped Nadine didn't come around the end of the counter and expect to have a girly-type hugging fest. "Don't look like much of a catch now, does he?"

Nadine's chin quivered, and more tears rolled down her cheeks, leaving long streaks of black mascara in their wake. "I'm bored. I want my own café, but that's not going to happen. Bobby Ray wants me to quit my job when we get married. If I'm bored now, just think what it will be then. I'm so jealous of you. Always have been because you have something that is yours and you work for it and you are happy."

Allie's mind went into high gear. "Rent one of the empty buildings and put in a café. We could use one in Dry Creek. You might not make a million dollars a year, but it will give you something to do. I've eaten your cookin' at the church socials, and you're good at it."

"I'm not as smart as you. I can cook, but a business requires book work, and I never was real good in school," Nadine said.

"Sharlene is good at bookkeeping. She works at a bank and could help you with that," Allie said.

"Do you really think I could do this?" Nadine whispered.

"Yes, I do," Allie said.

Nadine cocked her head to one side. "You reckon your mom would rent the old café building to me? It's already set up with a kitchen. Would take a lot of cleanup, but it would cut down on start-up cost."

"Go ask her. She might even rent to own so that if you get it going good, you could buy the place from her," Allie answered.

"Why didn't I think of that rather than hating you for having what I wanted?" Nadine asked.

Allie laid a hand on Nadine's arm. At first the woman

flinched, and then she grabbed the hand and brought it to her cheek. "Like I said, you've always been too nice."

"I can be a real witch. Ask my sister if you don't believe me. Or ask Deke or Blake. But the past is gone, and today is all we get. You might want to talk to Bobby Ray before you talk to Mama. He's a lot like Riley in that he expects his little woman to stay home and raise kids."

Nadine took a deep breath. "Right now is the perfect time to do this because he won't tell me no. Not after last night. Thank you, Allie. You might have saved my sanity."

Allie looked out the front window at the buildings across the street and imagined all of them with clean windows and prosperous businesses. "Think Sharlene would want to rent one of the buildings? Or maybe Mary Jo? We might turn this town around if all the women who are bored had something to keep them busy."

"Lord, honey, Mary Jo can cook, but not like Nadine. But, oh, my gosh, Allie, she might put in a beauty and barbershop combination in the old barbershop. I'm going to talk to her and Sharlene, too." Nadine clapped her hands like Irene did when she got a chocolate cupcake.

Allie followed her to the door. "Just remember, you aren't going to get rich here in Dry Creek, but it might make you feel a lot better."

The door had barely shut behind her when Allie's phone rang. She recognized Deke's number and answered after the second ring.

"Are you holding a grudge? This isn't like you, Allie," Deke said bluntly.

Riley? Nadine? How did Deke know all that so quickly? "Grudge for what?" Allie asked.

"Why didn't you show up for work this morning? Blake told you he kicked that ex of his to the curb after you left, and I believe him," Deke said.

Blake yelled in the background, "Hey, Deke, I've got five messages from Allie. Her sister is sick, and she's down at the feed store. I left my phone on the kitchen table this morning."

"What's the matter with Lizzy? Did she finally wake up and realize that she's engaged to a jerk, and it made her sick to think about what a fool she's been?" Deke asked.

Allie popped up on the counter and sat crossed-legged. "I want to go back to what we were talking about before. Why did you take Blake's side first? I've been your friend a lot longer than he has."

"Yes, you have, and that's why I didn't like it when you were sinking back into that ugly mood you got in after the divorce," Deke said. "I was afraid you'd lose your mind that first year after Riley left."

Allie didn't want to talk about the past. "So I'm ugly?"

Deke lowered his voice to a whisper. "I did not say that. I said you were in an ugly mood, and you're not going to twist your way out of this. If you didn't like Blake—and I mean as more than a friend—you wouldn't be carryin' on like this."

"You are acting like a girl." She laughed.

"I'm your best friend, and I just want you to listen to me. Just don't ask me to be your bridesmaid when you get married again. I draw the line at that," he said.

"Darlin', I'm not getting married again, and if I did, it would involve a twenty-minute trip to the courthouse in Throckmorton, not a big wedding. Go eat your dinner and get back to work. With any luck I'll be back on the job tomorrow morning."

Deke lowered his voice to a whisper. "The ex-wife did not come back last night. And Bobby Ray spent the night at Riley's place, but he and Nadine made up this morning."

"Gossip travels fast," she said.

"Nothing speedier in the whole world, especially with the help of a cell phone and texting. Got to go," Deke said.

"Bye, Deke," she said, feeling much better than she had. "Thanks for the call."

"You betcha, and Blake is yelling for me to tell you that he will call you back soon as we get done eating dinner," Deke said, and the call ended.

Allie's coffee had gone lukewarm, but she sipped it anyway. The first tinkling, haunting sounds of the piano announced a song by Conway Twitty started on the radio. She tapped a finger on the counter to the beat in her head. He sang about standing on a bridge that just wouldn't burn. Allie shut her eyes and pictured an old wooden bridge. Riley stood on the other end with his arms open wide, a smile on his face, beckoning her to take the first step. In the vision, she took out an imaginary chunk of blazing firewood and set the thing on fire.

"Goodbye, past. Hello, future," she mumbled.

* * *

Blake was in the bulldozer with Shooter right beside him when he called Allie. She was out of breath when she said, "Hello."

"Busy at the feed store today?" he asked.

"Quiet except for a little drama this morning, and then I had a run this afternoon to deliver a load of feed. I was in the back of the store making tickets for half a dozen ranchers who were loading their trucks when I heard the phone. I'd left it on the counter beside the cash register," she explained.

"I can call back," Blake said.

"It's okay. I can talk," she said. "Everything is taken care of right now. Granny is watching television and eating doughnuts in the office, while Mama is taking care of the usual school lunch rush. Hey, guess what? Nadine may open up a café here on Main Street."

Blake put the phone on speaker so he could talk and drive at the same time. "I wanted to tell you that Scarlett left right after you did last night. I guess a person can't run from their past, can they?"

"Riley came in here this morning wanting to give me a second chance," she said. "Guess this was the day for drama, but then I heard that old song by Conway playing on the radio. Remember 'A Bridge That Just Won't Burn'?"

"No, but I can understand the title after last night," Blake said. "Are we okay, Allie, until we can talk face-to-face?"

"Did you hear what I said? He wants to give me a second chance, not me give him one." Allie's tone changed.

Blake chuckled. "Now I understand."

"I'll be back at work tomorrow or Friday at the latest. My goal is to have your bedroom done by Saturday evening," she said. "We can talk then."

"And then you'll go out with me for dinner and a movie. Maybe up to Wichita Falls?" he asked.

"Tell you what. I'll go out with you when I have that room done. It can be our celebration," she answered.

"I could help you so it will be done by Saturday night," Blake offered.

"Great!" Allie said. "I have a customer, so I'd best get off the phone. Thanks for calling, and yes, we're okay for right now."

Another rancher needed a pickup load of feed, and that didn't take long. Allie checked on Granny and then went back to her stool. She should have been dancing a jig around the store that Blake had asked her out, but instead she had a rock in her chest.

"It's because I'm falling right back into the same pattern I had with Riley. He calls the shots, and I do the dancing," she mumbled.

"No, you are not going dancing," Granny said at her elbow and startled her. "You are not going to a bar where folks hug up tight to each other. Your sister is marryin' a preacher, and you'll ruin her reputation. I'm going back over to your mama's store. She made pinto beans and ham this morning, and I'm hungry for more than doughnuts."

Allie helped her into her coat and followed her to the door, stepped outside in the bitter cold, and watched her until she was safely inside the convenience store, and then Allie went back to her fretting stool. She told herself it was only dinner and a movie with a friend, not a date. Even after all those hot kisses, it still wasn't a date. She'd ask Deke to go with them to prove that it was friendship and not the beginnings of a relationship.

CHAPTER SIXTEEN

Blake made sure his phone was fully charged and in his shirt pocket instead of leaving it on the kitchen table. He could hardly believe that it was Friday. In ten days his house had gotten a brand-new roof and his bedroom was getting a fine remodel. Things were falling into place even better than he could have hoped for when he first moved to the Lucky Penny. He had missed seeing Allie the past two days while she worked at the feed store, but he hoped she'd be back at the Lucky Penny that day.

He'd barely crawled up into the cab of the dozer when the phone rang, and he hurriedly pulled it from his pocket when he saw that Allie was calling.

He answered before it rang the second time. "We've got to stop all this talking on the phone. I miss you, Allie. I miss seeing your smile and having you sit beside me at the dinner table. I miss talking to you. It's not the same around here without you, and Deke is getting depressed. Poor old Shooter misses you, too."

"I'm at the feed store today," Allie said. "Lizzy finally felt well enough to go to work, but Granny is lethargic, so Mama took her back to the doctor to make sure she's not coming down with the stomach bug. She was afraid to let it go over the weekend. You and Deke want to come into town for dinner? We've got a big pot of taco meat simmering, and we're serving tacos with pinto beans and dirty rice. I'll treat today. If you wait until the school rush is over, I'll take my lunch break and eat with you guys."

Blake smiled and nodded to himself. She talked too much when she was nervous. He wanted nothing more than to hug her, to calm her from whatever was creating turmoil in her life, but most of all he wanted to be near her again. Even if he couldn't kiss her or hold her, he wanted to share space with her, be able to look at her. It seemed like a hundred years since that craziness when Scarlett showed up at his house and even longer since Allie stormed out past him in that robe. He was glad she'd burned the thing. He never wanted to see it again.

"What time? Can I bring the beer?" he asked.

"Twelve thirty or after, and yes on the beer. I can't sell it, but I could sure drink one with dinner. Looks like our bedroom celebration will have to wait until the first of the week. There's no way I can get it finished by Saturday," she said.

"Bedroom celebration, darlin'?" he asked.

"We're going out to celebrate finishing your bedroom. Did you forget? I thought we'd ask Deke to join us, so he won't feel left out," she said quickly.

"No, I hadn't forgotten. I was teasing you and, darlin', I don't do threesomes," he said with a chuckle. "I'll see you at dinner. I'll be the one with three beers and a lean and hungry look on my face."

In the middle of the morning, he got a text message from Toby saying that he was leaving Muenster as soon as he could get away that evening and driving up to the Lucky Penny for the weekend.

He couldn't wait for Toby to see the progress that had been made. But most of all he wanted to introduce him to his Allie.

"My Allie," he muttered. "I only wish she were mine."

* * *

Allie was so busy making lunches from eleven thirty until five minutes before the final bell rang down at the school that she didn't have time to look up. When the store finally cleared, she sat down at a table and propped her legs up on an empty chair.

She wished she was painting walls at Blake's place rather than running the store, but family helped family, even when they didn't like it. Too bad Lizzy and her mother didn't know a hammer from a dishrag so they could return the favor when she needed help.

"Hey," Deke called out as he and Blake pushed their way into the store. "Looks like we timed it about right. There's some big black clouds gathering up down in the southwest, and I got a text from a friend in Throckmorton who says we've got freezing rain on the way by midnight, so we're in for a blast. Cold wind is coming down from the north and rain from the south. Won't be no more workin' outside today."

Allie's heart kicked in an extra beat when she saw Blake, and her pulse went from low to high gear in less than five seconds. It was the first time she'd seen him since that horrible night. He stopped a few feet from her, and she searched his expression, hoping that they were truly all right and the whole scene wouldn't be awkward between them.

"The weather teaches us we're not in control. Take off your coats and hang them on the rack in the back. Dinner is on the stove. Help yourselves." Allie's voice sounded normal despite the way her heart was flopping around like a fish out of water inside her chest. She started to get up, but Blake shook his head.

"Keep your seat. I'll bring you a plate. One or two tacos?" He smiled and erased all doubts from her mind.

She held up four fingers. "No beans and extra dirty rice, but I'll make my own plate and we'll take them to the back room, where it's a little more private."

"She's bored." Deke laughed. "When she's bored, she gets cranky and picks fights if you don't feed her. When she's nervous she talks too much. She's not made to run a store. Hey, neither Blake nor I can work outside anymore with this weather comin' on, so how 'bout I run the store for you and you go on home with Blake and do some paintin'. It might keep you from gettin' too cranky."

Allie jogged over to Deke, put her arms around his neck, and hugged him like a brother. "I love you, love you, love you! You are my very best friend, and I owe you one."

"I could tear out some hallway ceiling while you paint." Blake removed three beers from the pockets of his work coat and set them on the table. A twinge of jealousy had reared its ugly head when she told Deke that she loved him and said that he was her best friend. Blake wanted that spot even if he wasn't going to admit it out loud.

"That sounds wonderful. Now let's eat so we can get out of here and go to work," she said.

Blake nodded toward the doughnuts. "Can we have them for dessert?"

"No!" Deke called out from the back of the store. "You'll want ice cream to chase the picante sauce that we're going to put on these tacos. Katy makes it from her own special recipe, and believe me, you will want ice cream. We'll each pick a pint of our favorite flavor from the freezer."

Blake removed his coat and hung it on the back of a chair. Then he followed Allie into a back room, where a table for four was pushed against one wall and a desk over on the other side. When he sat down next to her, his leg was jammed tightly against hers, and electricity that had nothing to do with the thunder and lightning outside jump-started her pulse to racing again just when she thought she had it under control.

"Damn fine tacos," Deke said between bites. "Herman and his boys are practically carrying off ever' bit of the mesquite that Blake is clearing out. I've made a good livin' sellin' my wood around town to folks this week, but this damn weather will slow us down for the rest of the week for sure. Freezing rain on top of snow makes a big mess."

Blake finished his first taco and took a sip of his beer. "Once things thaw out, it's going to be easy to turn the land the way they're cleaning it up. I might even have eighty acres in alfalfa when Toby brings in the first round of cattle. We can put them on forty to graze and make hay from the rest. Then come fall when Jud gets here, we'll have more land ready. It's going better than I could have hoped. These are good tacos. What's your secret, Allie?"

Allie picked up her second one and turned to look at Blake.

"Not my secret but Mama's. She makes her own seasonings for the meat, but there's a possibility that she won't be cooking much longer here in the store."

Deke frowned, drawing his forehead down to turn his hazel eyes into slits. "I don't want to hear that. What are we going to do for a place to have coffee or to grab food at noon if Blake ain't cookin'?"

"Nadine is opening up the old café. Hopefully by the end of the month. It all happened really quick. She's leased the building from Mama, and if things go well after the first year, she's going to buy the building," Allie said. "And she's trying to talk Mary Jo into putting in a barber and beauty shop across the street."

Deke held up a finger. "And Sharlene? I imagine she'll want something to do, too."

"Nadine is talking to her about a day care center in the old clothing store. It's got a lot of room and it wouldn't take much to convert it, and Sharlene is real good with kids."

Blake glanced out the window. "Wouldn't it be something if all these empty buildings were filled with businesses in a year or two?"

Deke chuckled. "You best hope for one miracle at a time. Turning the luck of the Lucky Penny is enough for you to worry about right now."

CHAPTER SEVENTEEN

Herman waved from the window of his trailer loaded high with mesquite wood when Allie and Blake passed him on the way to the ranch. Travis Tritt was singing "Love of a Woman" on the classic country radio station, and Blake kept time with his thumbs on the steering wheel.

Allie tapped her foot to the beat and was so wrapped up in her relief to get away from the store that she didn't realize they were at the Lucky Penny until Blake parked the truck and jogged around the front end to open the door for her.

She stepped out in four inches of snow that wasn't so pretty anymore with tire tracks zigzagging everywhere across it. Shooter bounded off the porch, his tail wagging as if it were a lovely spring day. A rabbit peeked out from behind a fence post, and the dog went into instant point, quivering only slightly until the bunny bounded and the race was on.

"I vote that we build a snowman before we go inside to work," Blake said. "I don't know about you, but the last time I built a snowman I was still a kid."

She pulled her gloves from her coat pocket. "We've had

snow and ice and bad weather in this part of the state, but the last time my sisters and I built a snowman was the year before I graduated from high school. Fiona was still in junior high, and I really thought I was too old to play in the snow."

"And today?" Blake asked.

"You got a carrot for his nose?" She grinned.

"I sure do. Let's build him in the backyard. That way, I can see him from the kitchen windows," Blake said.

The wet snow packed together beautifully. Soon she had a start the size of a basketball, and she started rolling it on the ground. When it was big enough for a base, she looked over her shoulder to see that Blake had already positioned the bottom of the snowman in the middle of the yard. From the size of what he'd made, her donation would be the midsection.

Wiggling her shoulders to get the kinks out, she looked for him but couldn't see him anywhere. She hadn't heard the back door open or close, so he wasn't in the house, but then she'd been thinking about burning bridges again. Suddenly two strong arms wrapped around her waist from behind. Shooter bounded up to them from the back of the house. When he threw his paws up on her chest, the momentum took all three of them to the ground.

Shooter popped up and sent snow flying in an instant mini blizzard when he shook from head to toe and then raced off to chase after something else.

When the snow settled, Allie was on her side, pressed against Blake's long, muscular body, and his arms were tight around her. She rolled over and brushed flakes from his thick eyelashes.

Blake pulled her even closer. "It makes for a cold bed, but I like the way you fit into my arms."

"Me, too," she whispered. "But right now I feel a freezing mist starting to fall. If we're going to finish this old boy so he can get a coating of ice over him tonight, we'd best get on with it. You've got the bottom layer ready. I've made the middle. All we need to do is put them together and make him a head. Then it won't take long to put a hat and scarf on him and give him a face. And I'm talking too much again."

"Nervous?" He pulled her up with him when he sat up.

"Yes."

He tipped up her chin with his fist and kissed her. The heat when their lips met came close to melting all the snow in the whole state.

When he broke the kiss, she leaned against his shoulder, every nerve ending standing on edge, every hormone begging for more. She didn't care what common sense said, she wanted him to kiss her again.

"You don't ever have to be nervous around me, Allie," he whispered.

Instantly he was on his feet with his hand extended toward her. She put her glove in his and wasn't the least bit amazed at the effect even that much of a touch had on her.

"Let's get this snowman done so we can get inside," he said.

When they were finished, the snowman was six feet tall and quite the cowboy with his red plaid scarf and old straw hat. He had a carrot for a nose, blackened wood chips for the eyes and mouth, and mesquite limbs for arms. A coating of freezing rain was already putting a shine on him when Allie and Blake hurried into the warm house.

The second the door shut behind Blake, he wrapped his arms around her and hugged her tightly to his chest. "I miss you so much when you aren't here every day," he whispered into her hair.

"Me, too," she said softly.

"I want more than friendship, Allie." His voice was hoarse with emotion.

"How much more?" She tilted her head back to see his face. His dark lashes fluttered and his mouth opened slightly. She tiptoed and moistened her dry lips with the tip of her tongue. His lips found hers in a hard, demanding kiss that made her knees go weak. Her arms snaked up around his neck, and she arched her body against his so tightly that air couldn't find a way to get between them.

His eyes were closed as the kisses grew even hotter. His hands found her cheeks and gently held her face still as he made love to her mouth.

"Oh, my!" she panted when he finally scooped her up in his arms. "I feel like my insides are a boiling pot of heat and desire."

His chuckle was as hoarse as if he were a lifetime smoker. "Is that a pickup line, Allie?"

"It's a fact. Where are you taking me?" she asked. "Please say it's to your bed because Shooter is on the sofa."

"Say no now if you are going to," he whispered.

"I couldn't say no even if I wanted to," she said softly.

Instead of turning into the room where his king-size mattress took up most of the floor, he carried her into the bathroom and set her on the floor. "You are simply beautiful, Allie. We've got all afternoon, so I want to make this last. First, a nice warm bath together."

"Are you serious?" she asked.

"Anything worth doing is worth doing right."

* * *

Allie awoke to the click of the clock as another minute passed. With a start, she sat straight up in bed, only to find herself alone. It was straight-up five o'clock. Had she dreamed the whole afternoon—their bath, the beautiful lovemaking afterward, cuddling together in the afterglow? If so, she didn't want to wake up. No one had ever made her feel so cherished before.

"Hey," he said from the doorway. "We got so involved that I forgot to tell you that my brother, Toby, is on the way for a visit. He'll be here in half an hour."

"I had no idea we slept so long! I've got to go home." She was frantic. She didn't want to be there when his brother arrived, especially not with a smile that she couldn't wipe off with a dose of alum-laced lemonade.

"You don't have to." He wore his jeans but no shirt and held a brown robe in his hands. "I got it for Christmas, and I promise it's never been on another woman."

"It'll have to wait. I really have to get dressed and go home." She hopped up from the bed and stood before him, comfortable in her nakedness. "And before you offer to drive me, I think it would be best if I walk. I need to have a reason for the blush on my face."

He opened his arms, and she walked into them. "You are amazing as well as beautiful, Allie. Can you come back later and meet Toby? He's staying all weekend."

"Of course," she said. "Bring him to church on Sunday. It will show the folks in Dry Creek that y'all ain't as wild as they heard. I hope they don't ask me any questions. I'd hate to lie right there in the church house about how hot and wild you are," she said.

He laughed out loud. "Please let me take you home."

"No, sir. I meant it when I said that about this blush on my face. I can't hide my smile, and Lizzy will gripe until she runs out of breath. It's not that far, and my knees aren't so weak that I can't climb a fence."

"I'll build a stile over it next week," he said.

"You will not! Everyone in town would talk about why. Besides, as wonderful as this was, we both need to think about where we are going, Blake. It might be smart for us to stop now."

"What?" He frowned.

"A few more weeks of something that hot will set one or both of us on fire, and all they'll find will be ashes and teeth." She grinned.

CHAPTER EIGHTEEN

The Bent Spur, a cowboy bar that Toby and Blake found just over the border into Wilbarger County, Texas, was hopping that Friday night. The parking lot was full enough that they had to park Toby's truck at the outer edge and the music so loud that Blake felt the ground pulsating under his boots.

"We'll have to remember this place. I already like it," Toby yelled above the din when they pushed open the double door and joined the noisy crowd.

A tall blonde dressed in skintight jeans and a top that dipped low enough to reveal two inches of cleavage, with a provocative look in her eye, quickly crossed the floor in a man-teasing wiggle and ran a hand down Toby's forearm. She looked up at him, batted her blue eyes, and smiled brightly.

"Hey, cowboy. Wanna dance?" she asked in a husky voice.

"Absolutely, sweet darlin', but let's get a beer first," Toby said.

The woman looped her arm in Toby's and wove her way through the line-dancing couples to the bar, with Blake bringing up the rear right behind them. Toby ordered two beers, and the woman asked for a double shot of Jack on the rocks.

"Hey, what are you doin' here?" Deke turned around on the bar stool.

"Toby, this is Deke. Deke, my brother, Toby. And this is?" Blake nodded toward the blonde sitting beside him.

"This is Lisa," Deke said. "That would be her twin sister with the double shot of Jack sitting beside Toby there."

"Fine way to start the night," Toby said.

"Depends." Blake sipped his beer.

"You sick or something?" Toby asked.

Blake smiled and held up his beer in a toast. "Been workin' hard all week."

Toby frowned. "You've never been too tired to party after a week's work before."

The blonde wrapped her arms around Toby's neck. "Forgot to tell you my name and here you already bought me a drink. I'm Laney, darlin', and I understand that you are Toby. If you ain't the hottest thing I've ever seen. Come on and dance with me, cowboy."

Toby set his beer down on the bar, winked at Blake, and two-stepped across the floor with the woman who'd pressed her body close to his.

Conway Twitty's voice sang "I See the Want to in Your Eyes." When Twitty mentioned that he saw the sparkling little diamond on her hand, Blake instinctively looked for a ring on Laney's finger.

"Neither of them is married," Deke said. "Hey, girl, this here old cowboy's feet are aching to dance." He held out his hand to Lisa, she threw back the rest of her drink, and they disappeared into the crowd of dancing folks.

A short redhead popped her butt on the bar stool Lisa had vacated and smiled at Blake. "You must like Conway and old classic country music."

"What makes you think that?" Blake asked.

"You're keeping time with your thumb on your beer glass," she said.

"I do like him." Blake nodded. The lady was a cute little thing and her eyes said that she was interested, but Blake wasn't interested.

She leaned closer to him and touched his cheek with her fingertips. "Well, darlin', so do I, and for the next half hour that's what we're going to hear because I plugged a bunch of money into the jukebox. Buy me a drink to celebrate our mutual love of Mr. Twitty?"

Blake held up a hand, and the bartender quickly made his way to that end of the bar. "This Conway-lovin' lady would like a drink."

"Long-neck Coors, in the bottle," she said.

Blake laid a bill on the bar and pointed to his glass. "Refill, please, of the same."

"I'm Kayla. Thanks for the drink. You could ask me to dance," she said.

"Got two left feet," Blake said. What was the matter with him? He should already be on the dance floor with Kayla wrapped around him like a pet python.

She took his hand and tugged at it. "I don't believe you."

"Don't say you wasn't warned." He took another sip of his beer and let her lead him out onto the dance floor.

She melted into his arms as the jukebox played "Rest Your Love on Me."

She rose on her toes and breathed into his ear, "Like the

words of the song say, I'd like to put my worries in your pocket and rest my love on you all night. I see some sadness in those green eyes, cowboy. Let me make you happy tonight."

"I bet you tell all the old ugly cowboys that," he said.

"Darlin', whoever told you that you are ugly has rocks for brains." She laughed. "You didn't tell me your name."

"Blake Dawson."

"Blake and Kayla. Goes together real good, at least for one night."

A tall brunette moved into Kayla's place and looped her arms around his neck when the song ended, and Conway started singing "House on Old Lonesome Road."

"It's my birthday, and my friends dared me to come over and dance with you," she whispered. "I have a boyfriend at home."

He twirled her out and brought her back to him, and even dipped her at the end of the dance. "Happy birthday, darlin'. Your boyfriend is one lucky feller."

After the dance, he made his way to the men's room, where he checked his reflection in the mirror. It was the same face that he shaved every morning, same dark hair, and same green eyes, so why wasn't he having a good time? He felt his forehead. No fever, so he wasn't sick.

Singing "I May Never Get to Heaven," Conway's voice came through the speaker above his head. The lyrics said that he might never get to heaven, but he once came mighty close. Blake shut his eyes and visualized Allie lying next to him. Could that have really been only a few hours ago? It seemed like nothing more than a dream or a little taste of what Conway was singing about. Any of the women he'd met that evening would give him a good time, but all he wanted was to go home to Allie.

"Where you been?" Deke motioned him to the end of the bar and pointed at the empty seat on the other side of Toby. "Me and Toby been havin' us a good time."

Six weeks ago, he would have been in heaven, but that night, even with the toe-stomping line dancing, he felt as out of place as a hooker in the front row of a tent revival. Then, of all things that Mama Fate could throw at him, Blake Shelton started singing "Home."

Blake fished his phone out of his back pocket even though it hadn't vibrated or rang. "Excuse me. I have to take this, so I'll step outside."

He sucked in the cold, clean night air and leaned against the porch post. The lyrics of the song said that he felt like he was living someone else's life, that another day had come and gone and he wanted to go home. He talked about being surrounded by a million people and yet he felt all alone.

And why did every song remind him of Allie in some way?

Another song started, but the last one about going home was stuck in his mind so strongly that he couldn't hear anything else. He wanted to be home with Shooter, maybe working alongside Allie. Pulling nails out of the ceiling made him happier than he was right now.

"Looks like I've turned into the designated driver," he muttered.

Toby poked his head out the door and asked, "Something wrong? The redhead said you got an important call."

"Nothing's wrong." He paused. "Actually, everything's wrong. Think you could catch a ride home with Deke? I'm just gonna head home," Blake said.

"Sure thing. I know he won't mind. We might even leave here and go find a quieter place with Lisa and Laney," Toby said.

"Have fun," Blake said. "See you at home. Keep in mind that you're sleeping on the couch."

* * *

It wasn't fair.

Lizzy had flat-out sabotaged Allie, and she was miserable sitting in the living room watching a boring movie with Grady and Mitch, but there wasn't anything she could do to get out of it. And it was Friday night! She could be with Deke and Blake like last week.

As luck would have it, Granny had even turned in early and wasn't wandering through the room. She'd tried to get her mother to stick around and watch the movie with them, but oh, no, she went to bed with a book. So now Allie was stuck on the sofa with Grady's arm around her.

She made an excuse to go to the bathroom and slid down the back of the door, sitting on the floor with her knees up and her face buried in her hands. A few hours ago, she'd been sleeping in Blake's arms with the most beautiful afterglow in the whole world surrounding them.

"You okay in there?" Lizzy asked from the other side of the door.

"No, I think I'm getting that bug you had," Allie said.

"Well, crap! You and Grady were having such a good time. I guess you'd best go on up to your room, so you don't give it to him and Mitch," Lizzy said. "I should've known you were catchin' it when you came in from the Lucky Penny with scarlet cheeks. Grady will be disappointed."

"Sorry," Allie lied.

She waited until she heard the drone of Lizzy's voice in the living room, then stood up and snuck up the stairs to her room. Once inside her room, she couldn't sit still. Pacing from one side to the other, she wondered what Blake was doing right then. Were he and Toby watching some old western movie and drinking beer? Was Shooter as glad to see Toby as he was to see her nearly every day lately? Or were they all three out with a flashlight showing Toby all the work that Blake had gotten done the past few weeks?

She turned on the radio to the classic country music station and curled up in the old overstuffed rocking chair in the corner, slinging her legs over the arm. Granny had rocked her to sleep in this same chair when she was a little girl, and it always brought her comfort to sit in it, but not that night. She went to the window, pulled back the curtain, and looked outside and then picked up a book from her nightstand. It didn't interest her, so she put it back.

The DJ announced that the next hour would be a tribute to Alan Jackson and if anyone had requests to call in. Then he started playing "Small Town Southern Man."

She couldn't listen to the song because it was too sad in light of how badly she wanted Blake Dawson to be that small-town Southern man who'd be content with a wife and small-town living. She turned the radio off and hit the POWER button on the television remote.

"Evidently, I'm supposed to listen to this," she mumbled as Alan Jackson's video for the same song showed up on CMT.

Tears rolled down her cheeks as she watched the video from beginning to end. She wanted what those two people had in the video, which portrayed their lives from the time they danced together the first time until the day that death came calling for the small-town Southern man.

She wondered if Blake Dawson could ever be tamed into a man who'd only love one woman. And if he could, would she ever trust him? It seemed as if everywhere she looked these days, someone was cheating on the person they'd vowed to love forever.

The next video was Blake Shelton's "Goodbye Time." Every single word scared the crap out of her. She had to see Blake tomorrow, to explain that the sex they'd had could never happen again because she couldn't bear to spend years with him only to wake up one day and have him tell her that the feeling was gone.

Someday, when she was an old woman with gray hair, sitting on the porch and watching the seasons come and go, she would remember this beautiful day when a man made her experience that wonderful thing called afterglow. She'd smile and hold it close to her heart and be grateful that it was untarnished and beautiful.

She fell asleep in the chair as Miranda Lambert sang "The House That Built Me." Her last thought as her eyes drooped was that Audrey's Place had built her and it was where she belonged . . . forever.

CHAPTER NINETEEN

A loud clap of thunder awoke Allie with a start. She grabbed a pillow and crammed it over her head, but the next lightning flash only heralded a rolling thunder that sounded as if it was dumping a load of potatoes on top of Audrey's Place. Her phone rang right at the end of the noise. She pushed back the covers and threw the pillow in the direction of the rocking chair.

"Why are you calling me?" Allie growled into the phone.

"Good morning, sunshine." Lizzy laughed. "Breakfast is ready and I don't want to eat alone, and I didn't want to come back upstairs. Mama and Granny have already left for the store. Crawl out and come on down here. I made crunchy French toast."

Allie's stomach growled. "I'm on the way."

The sun peeked from behind a bank of dark, fast-moving clouds, sending a few rays through the glass in the front door. Allie stopped long enough to stretch and feel the warmth on the foyer floor against her bare feet.

Lizzy stuck her head out of the kitchen. "Your toast is

getting cold. Weatherman says we've got more bad weather on the way later this afternoon. Be glad you are at least working inside over there at that abominable place."

So much for hoping that Lizzy was ready to bury the hatchet. She had an agenda up her sleeve, and that was the reason she'd made Allie's favorite food. Suddenly her favorite breakfast didn't sound so good after all.

Lizzy did give her time to sit down and at least get the first bite in her mouth before she pulled out a chair across the table from her, sucked up enough air to deliver a Sunday-morning sermon, and started talking. "I knew you weren't sick. You flat-out lied to get out of spending time with Grady. And all for nothing because I've already heard the gossip this morning, and your little Lucky Penny bubble is about to bust wide open."

"What are you talking about?" Allie asked.

"Blake's brother arrived last night, and the two of them and Deke went bar hopping up near Wichita Falls. Deke brought a tall blond hussy home with him. I did have such hopes for him turning his life around when he started coming to church pretty regular, but now that the infamous wild Dawson has become his new best friend, I swear, he's on a joyride straight to the devil's front door," Lizzy said.

"Are we being judgmental this morning?" Allie was sure glad the gossips hadn't been hiding outside the window when she and Blake had been tangled up in his sheets.

"I'm stating pure facts and I'm tellin' you that..."

"What if I told you I spent yesterday afternoon having amazing sex with Blake Dawson?" Allie butted in before Lizzy could say another word.

Lizzy slapped the table hard enough that her coffee sloshed

out. "Now look what you made me do. Sometimes you make me so mad I could shake you, Alora Raine."

Allie shrugged. "It's a sister thing or maybe it's a middle-child thing. Do you think maybe you should see a therapist for your control issues?"

Lizzy jumped to her feet and grabbed a fistful of paper towels. "It's not a middle-child thing. Fiona doesn't make me as mad as you do. There's no way you really slept with Blake Dawson. One, you're too smart to do something like that after the Riley thing, and two, he's a one-night-stand kind of guy. You're not his type."

"Deke says the same thing, so I guess if Lucifer's protégé—that would be Deke—and God's right arm—that would be you—say it's so, then it must be true." She continued eating her breakfast, but down deep she wondered if Toby and Blake had brought home women from the bar, too.

"Go on and ruin your life again," Lizzy huffed. "I'm trying to warn you, but I can only be the watchman. I can sit in the tower and tell you what I see coming, but I can't make you steer clear of it."

Allie picked up her empty plate and headed to the sink with it. "Well, sister, you enjoy the view from your tower. I'm heading over to that abominable place to paint. See you at supper."

* * *

Allie parked beside a truck but didn't pay a lot of attention to it, figuring it was Toby's. A streak of lightning so close that the air crackled sent her running to the porch. She slipped inside the front door to the sounds of people talking in the kitchen.

She quickly removed her yellow slicker, hung it on the coat-rack, and replaced her rubber boots with her work boots.

Shooter hopped off the sofa. Tangled sheets and a blanket gave testimony that Toby hadn't gone back to Muenster early that morning and was one of the voices in the kitchen. She thought that she recognized the other voice as Deke's. She didn't really care how much testosterone was sitting around the table; she only wanted a cup of hot coffee to wrap her hands around before she started to work in Blake's bedroom. She intended to have the walls and trim painted today. The doors would have to wait until Monday, but by the middle of next week her goal was to have that room completely done and the living room and hall ceilings ready to texture. Then she and Blake would really have something to celebrate.

Her line of thinking stopped abruptly when she walked into the kitchen and saw the man at the stove had a woman draped around him like a snake, one hand on his butt, the other pressed against his chest as she kissed him.

Allie whipped around, feeling a blush burning her cheeks, only to see Blake sitting at the table with another blonde who looked almost identical to the one plastered against the man she could only assume was Blake's brother, Toby. She risked another quick glance and saw that Toby had the same face shape, hair color, and smile as Blake, but his eyes were blue and he had a faint white scar across one cheek.

"Where's Deke?" she asked, her brows furrowing into a single line.

"At home, I guess." Blake quickly pushed back his chair and stood up. "Allie, I didn't know you were coming to work today."

"Evidently you didn't," she said. "I'll get a cup of coffee and go on to the bedroom to work. Y'all don't let me interrupt."

Her work boots sounded like shotgun blasts with every step as she crossed the kitchen, poured a cup of coffee, and carried it down the hallway. She shut Blake's bedroom door behind her and sat down on the dirty carpet with a thud, hot coffee sloshing out. Her hands shook so badly that she finally set the cup down and put her head in her hands.

"Allie? Can I come in, please? We need to talk," Blake said from the other side of the door.

"It's your house," she said.

He slipped into the room, shut the door behind him, and sat down in front of her, keeping a foot of space between them. Before he could say a word, another knock on the door startled both of them. "Hey, is Walter hiding in there? I've got a sweet little lady out here hunting for him. I told her we don't have a Walter here, but she doesn't believe me."

Blake rolled up on his feet and offered her his hand. "What you saw wasn't what was happening."

She ignored the hand and got up on her own, leaving the coffee behind.

Irene slung the door wide open and marched inside with her hands on her hips. A pair of Lizzy's designer jeans hung on her thin hips and the red-sequined top that Allie wore to the church Christmas party a few weeks before had slipped off one shoulder, letting a white bra strap shine right along with her veined skin. Her thin gray hair hung in wet strands and the makeup she'd applied streaked down her face, settling in the wrinkles. The jeans were soaked as well as the sequined top, and her poor frail body had a faint blue cast from the cold wind and rain.

"What are you doing with another woman in this house, Walter? Three of them to be exact, counting this one here in your bedroom!" Irene stopped for a breath and slapped Blake on the arm. "You've got some explainin' to do. I don't know why I even bother with you. It's a wonder your mother hasn't taken a fryin' pan to all these women."

Toby cocked his head to one side just like Allie had seen Blake do when he found something amusing. Well, her grandmother was not funny, and the disease that was eating holes in her memory wasn't a bit comical.

"Breakfast is served. Laney and Lisa are already digging in. There's plenty for all y'all," Toby said.

"Is this one of your lazy brothers? Where is your mother?" Irene demanded.

"Granny, this is not Walter. It's Blake Dawson and his brother, Toby Dawson. I'm Allie, your granddaughter, and those women in the kitchen are not here to see Walter," Allie said.

"I'm ready to go home now. I'm cold and I'm hungry." She looped her arm through Allie's and marched past Toby, with Blake right behind them. They'd barely made it to the living room when Katy knocked softly on the door, pushed it open, and sighed.

"I figured I'd find you over here. Good grief, Mama! If you don't catch pneumonia from running around in that getup, it'll be a miracle. I'm surprised you didn't fall and break a hip on the ice." She grabbed Allie's yellow slicker from the coatrack and slung it around Irene's shoulders.

"Allie was in the bedroom with that man," Irene tattled. "And I'm not old. I can climb over a fence any old day of the week, and the ice broke when I stepped on it, so stop your bitchin'."

"It's the room I'm working on," Allie explained.

"Introductions?" Toby asked.

"Sorry." Blake grinned sheepishly. "This is Allie, the woman who's redoing the house and who put the roof on for us. This is Katy, her mother, and this is Irene, her grandmother. Ladies, this is Toby, my brother and business partner in the Lucky Penny."

So, she wasn't his friend Allie, or his neighbor Allie. Heaven forbid that she might be his girlfriend Allie. Oh, no! She was the woman who was redoing his house. Lizzy had been right all along. Allie didn't have enough sense to know not to wade right into hell.

Toby kissed Irene's hand, shook hands with Katy and with Allie, and said, "I'm right pleased to make your acquaintance, ladies."

Irene's eyes started at Toby's toes and traveled slowly up his long legs to the top of his head.

"Who are these women?" Irene nodded toward the two women who were headed out of the kitchen.

"Just some friends of me and Deke," Toby said.

"Lord, help us all," Katy moaned. "Allie, you'll have to stay home with her today. You know how she gets after she runs off and comes over here. I can't manage her at the store, and Lizzy sure can't keep an eye on her on a Saturday at the feed store. That's her busiest day."

"I thought she was with you at the store. Lizzy said you'd taken her," Allie said.

Katy shook her head. "I did, but she stole my car keys, slipped out the back door, went home and obviously changed her clothes, and here she is. I had to get Nadine to loan me her van to come get her. The car is parked at home. You can come get me at five."

"I'll be there." Allie nodded. "Go on back to the store. I'll take her home and get her warmed up."

"We need to talk," Blake whispered.

"Nothing to talk about." Allie took off her work boots and slipped her feet back down into the rubber boots.

"Later?" Blake raised an eyebrow.

"Probably not," she said.

He pulled a heavy jacket from the rack and held it out to her. "I tell you, it's not what it looked like. Take my coat. You can't go out there without something to keep you warm. That rain is cold."

She shook her head. "I come from sturdy stock. I'm not sugar or salt, so I don't melt in cold rain. See you in church tomorrow."

"And you and your brother are welcome to come home with us for lunch," Katy said as she escorted Irene out onto the porch. "I won't take no for an answer."

"We'd love to have Sunday dinner with y'all," Toby said.

"Tell Deke, too," Katy said over her shoulder.

"You sure you want to do that?" Allie asked Blake.

"Wouldn't miss it for the world, would we, Toby?" Blake said.

"We'll be there," Toby answered.

"Now can you please get rid of your and Deke's women so we can take a drive around the ranch? It might be sleeting, but you can still see what I've gotten done around here." Blake talked to Toby, but most of it was for Allie's ears.

"Lookin' forward to it, ma'am." Toby nodded toward Allie.

Blake laid a hand on her shoulder. "I did not..." he started. She shrugged it off.

"I don't care." She closed the door behind her.

CHAPTER TWENTY

Is that the woman who's got your heart in a twist?" Toby asked.

"What makes you think that?" Blake asked.

"You've got that look in your eyes," his brother answered.

Blake shrugged.

A lot of good it would do him if he did fall in love with Allie. She'd declared that she didn't care. Just when he was ready to get into a serious relationship with a decent woman, she said that she didn't care. Blake Dawson, the player, had been played.

"What's on your mind, big brother?" Toby asked. "What happened in that bedroom?"

Blake shook his head. "I'm not totally sure, but I believe the tables got turned on me, and it's one strange feeling. I don't want to talk about it right now. We don't have time for women."

"Except for Laneys and Lisas, right?"

"Not even for that if we're going to get this place in shape in four years like we said we'd do," Blake said.

Toby headed for the kitchen. "Man, I'm not goin' celibate

for four years, not for this ranch, not for you, and not for anyone. And you ain't, either, because when you go a month without a woman you get cranky."

"Who's goin' a month without a woman?" Lisa asked. "We've been poutin' because it's time for us to go. We've both got appointments at eleven in Wichita Falls, and the roads are probably getting icy. But don't pout, darlin's. We'll be in touch." She blew them kisses as the two women left the house.

"Dammit!" Blake doubled up his fist and hit his palm with it as soon as the women were gone. "I don't want those two comin' around here. I'm trying to build a relationship with the community." *And Allie.*

Toby laid a hand on Blake's shoulder. "I won't let it happen again. Let's go eat breakfast if there's anything left for us. And then we'll take a look at what you've done. I'd planned on helping you clear off some mesquite or repair fence, but it's rainin'. I guess we could tear down the ceilings in the hall and living room," Toby said.

"And put up the new," Blake said. "Even if my carpenter doesn't come back, that would be a start. You any good at bedding and taping?"

"I got the bedding part down real good, but like I said, I'm not into the kinky stuff." Toby chuckled. "Why wouldn't Allie come back?"

"I'm not sayin' another word except that you have not lost your touch with these biscuits, brother," Blake said.

* * *

Lizzy met her mother, grandmother, and sister at the door. She clucked her tongue like an old hen when she saw her grandmother wearing jeans and a sparkly top, with a yellow rain slicker flopping open with every step. "I'm not even going to ask. I'm going to work, and we'll talk about it this evening."

Katy glanced nervously toward Allie. "Store should have opened thirty minutes ago. If I don't get down there, the gossip will be flyin' over town like Santa Claus at Christmas."

"I've got it. Both of you get going. I'll get her dry and fed, and then I'll watch her like a hawk. It's not my day to clean, but I'll take care of the house for you, Mama." Allie shooed them both out the door.

She needed something to keep her mind occupied that day. She'd never known such jealousy as she did when she saw those women looking so cozy in Blake's kitchen. She hadn't even been that angry when Riley came home and told her that he was in love with another woman.

"I'm frozen." Granny shivered. "Help me get out of these clothes and into a warm shower. Why'd you tell me to wear this anyway? You know I'm old."

Allie pulled the ruined sequined top up over her grandmother's head and marched her to the shower. When she was tugging the jeans down from her granny's hips, she realized the old girl had on two different shoes. One was a brown sneaker that belonged to Katy. It was laced properly and tied in a perfect little bow. The other was a lovely black-velvet flat that Lizzy kept for special occasions. Lizzy would gripe for days, but there was nothing to do but toss them in the trash now because they were ruined.

"Granny, where did you find this shoe?" Allie asked.

"Me? You're the one who put me in that ridiculous outfit and then let me go out in the weather, so don't ask dumb questions. I've got more sense than to pick out stuff like that," Irene fussed. "I can take off my own underpants and bra. You put a towel on the vanity, and when my bones are warm, I'll come out and get dressed."

Allie sighed. "Okay, Granny."

Allie laid out a towel and a warm sweat suit, then sat down in the rocking chair beside the window in her grandmother's room. She could hear her grandmother singing something about the love of her life. Allie wondered if it was something she made up or if the song had been popular back in her younger life.

Leaning her head back and staring at the ceiling, she replayed that introduction. She was the carpenter, nothing more or less. Blake didn't throw an arm around her shoulder or even wink when he said that. The moment had brought the truth to the surface: she was nothing more than another notch on his bedpost.

The headache started with a jabbing pain in her right temple and traveled across her forehead around to the back of her skull. She shut her eyes and put her hand over them to keep out the light. She didn't even try to open them when she heard the shower stop or when her grandmother grumbled about the ugly pink sweat suit that was laid out for her.

She did open them when her granny kicked the rung of the rocker. "What's wrong with you? Surely you haven't let that boy next door get in your pants and give you a guilty headache. If you have, I hope you used protection because your sister will have a hissy fit if you get pregnant."

"Granny, come sit down at the vanity and let me blow-dry your hair and curl it for you. It looks pitiful," Allie said.

Irene clapped her hands. "And my fingernails and toenails, too. Let's have a beauty shop day. I could trim your hair and put it up in sponge rollers."

Allie wouldn't let her grandmother near her hair with a pair of scissors, and she doubted if there were any sponge rollers left in the house. It had been years since she'd seen even a stray one.

"Let's do you all up pretty first, and then we'll talk about my hair and nails. It might be time for dinner by then, and I was thinkin' about chocolate chip pancakes," Allie said.

Irene clapped louder. "I like it when you stay home with me, Allie. I can't remember too good these days. Sometimes whole days get away from me, but I do remember having fun when we get to spend a day together."

Allie gave her a hug. "You smell like baby powder."

"It's a nice clean scent that goes well with any perfume," Irene said seriously. "I bet I've told you that a hundred times."

Allie led her to the vanity and set her on the cute little brass stool with a pink velvet pillow. "Yes, you have, but it takes a lot of tellin' for me to remember. Now, while I do your hair, you can tell me stories about when you were a little girl."

Irene prattled on, telling tales of her childhood that Allie had heard dozens if not hundreds of times. Letting her own mind wander while she curled her grandmother's thin gray hair and did her nails with the bright-pink nail polish that she liked, she kept going over and over the details of that morning. Did she miss a sly wink? She slowed the memories of what had happened that morning down and could honestly say that he had not even looked her way when he introduced her as the woman who'd been working on his house.

"And then you grew up and married that rotten man." Granny's final words brought her back into the present.

"Yes, I did." Allie's phone rang the moment the words were out of her mouth.

Granny stuck out her lower lip in a pout. "This is supposed

to be our day. Don't you dare invite that boy from next door over here. He'll get in our way and ruin everything."

Allie checked the ID, hoping it was Blake, but no such luck. "It's Fiona, Granny, not Blake."

"Give me that phone." The older woman jerked it out of her hand. "Fiona, Allie did my hair and my nails, and I'm all pretty for you to come home this weekend. Are you on the way? I miss you so much. When was the last time you came home? It's been five years, hasn't it?"

A pause and Irene set her mouth in a firm line. "You were not home at Thanksgiving. I might be old, but I ain't stupid. I know…Who is this? I don't want any magazines, so stop calling here."

And like that, in the blink of an eye, Irene was off in another time warp. "Take this phone and tell those people that I'm sick to death of them buggin' me about magazines. And they are not getting my credit card number, either."

"Fiona?" Allie said. "Are you still there?"

"Mama called and told me about Granny running off again this morning. I bet she was a sight in that getup. And she said that Blake looks at you like he could eat you up—her words, not mine. And that she invited him to dinner tomorrow after church so she could see y'all together. She's worried about all this, Allie," Fiona said.

Allie had forgotten about dinner the next day. She couldn't face Blake that soon. She would plead a headache, which might not be a lie the way it was pounding right then, and stay home from church. As soon as the family left, she would run away to Deke's and stay there all day.

Fiona raised her voice. "Are you still there? You didn't hang up on me, did you?"

Allie heard the cling of a cash register in the background and lots of people talking at once. Fiona worked in a prestigious law firm in Houston, so why were there noises like a fast-food place in the background?

"Where are you?" Allie asked.

"At work," Fiona said quickly. "Well, not actually at work. I'm at a coffee shop right next door, getting a midmorning cup of coffee."

Allie tried to blink away the headache, but it didn't work. "I thought I heard cash register noises."

"Got to go. Just wanted to let you know that Mama is watching you close. See you at the wedding this spring," Fiona said.

Allie hit the END button and shoved her phone back into her pocket. She heard a soft snore, more like a kitten's purr, and turned to find Irene curled up on her bed in a ball, sound asleep. Figuring it was a fine time to straighten her grandmother's room and keep an eye on her at the same time, Allie hurried off to the utility room for her basket of cleaners.

"Poor old darlin'," she mumbled, "it has to be hard on her doing all that time travel. I cannot imagine living in so many worlds every day."

She'd finished cleaning the bathroom and had started dusting all the empty perfume bottles on Irene's dresser, when her phone rang a second time that morning. Expecting it to be Lizzy after she got the gossip of two women keeping three men company the night before, she was surprised to see Blake's number flashing on the screen.

"Hello," she answered cautiously. "If you're calling about the bedroom, I told you in the beginning that I'd have to take days off for family pretty often."

"We're going to take down the ceiling in the hall and living room and put up the new drywall. I'm not getting into the bedding and taping, though. We figure we can do this much, and come Monday it will be ready for you. Deke is coming over soon as he gets his chores done to help us, too. But that's not why I'm calling. We need to talk, Allie."

"You're coming to Sunday dinner. We'll talk then." She picked up a tarnished silver hairbrush and dusted under it.

"Are we still on for a celebration when you finish the bedroom?"

She had to scramble to hold on to the phone and the brush at the same time. "I have no idea. Wouldn't you much rather go to a bar than have dinner with me?"

"What are you so mad about? It's me who has the right to be mad since you said you didn't care. What am I, Allie? A notch on your bedpost?" His tone turned edgy.

She shut her eyes against the headache that threatened. "I'm not fighting with you on the phone, Blake Dawson."

"Then I'll come over there, and we can fight in person."

She didn't want to see him or talk to him until the steam stopped pouring out of her ears. Notch on her bedpost, indeed! If they compared, hers would have two notches where his would look like a carved-up totem pole.

"I think we'd both best cool off before we see each other," she said tersely.

"Maybe so. I'll see you in church," he said, and the phone went dark.

CHAPTER TWENTY-ONE

Allie woke up with the determination that she would not go to church and she would not have Sunday dinner with her family. She planned a shopping trip to Wichita Falls, where she would check out all the after-holiday sales and maybe take in an afternoon matinee.

She dressed in a pair of jeans, a sweater, and cowboy boots, glanced at herself in the mirror, and decided she looked just fine for a shopping trip.

"Making a statement, are you? Letting everyone at church know that you are just a carpenter?" Lizzy said from the doorway.

"I'm not going to church," Allie answered.

Lizzy crossed the room and hugged Allie. "I heard about what happened yesterday morning, and I was right. Blake was just leading you on."

Allie changed the subject. "You look pretty this morning. Red has always been your color."

Lizzy smoothed the front of the red sweater dress. "I came

to borrow a scarf from Fiona to dress down all this red. It's kind of loud for a preacher's wife, don't you think?"

Allie brushed past her on the way out of the room. "You already toned it down with those black leggings and boots. And you'd better remember to put whatever you borrow right back where it was. I'm pretty sure that Fiona takes inventory every time she comes home."

"How we could all three have the same parents is a complete mystery," Lizzy said. "Oh, yeah, I invited Grady and Mitch to Sunday dinner. Mama said she's invited the neighbors. I figure it will be a good time for you to see the difference between a man of God and a wild cowboy."

Allie bit her lip to keep from smarting off and had a change of heart about going to church. If she didn't go, Blake would think she was running from him. If she did go, she'd have to endure the business of talking to him as well as Grady.

She rolled her eyes toward the ceiling. *Why does life have to be so complicated?*

She still hadn't made up her mind what she was going to do when she reached the foyer. Granny sat ramrod straight in the chair beside the credenza. She was dressed in a cute little navy blue pantsuit, and her shoes matched. Her hair was combed back in waves, and her lipstick had settled into the wrinkles around her mouth.

"I don't want to go to church," she whispered.

"Me, either. Let's run away," Allie said softly.

"We can't. We are strong women, and we don't run from our problems," Granny said.

"What is your problem?" Allie asked.

"I forget where the bathroom is at church, but I can depend on you to remember, can't I?" Granny kept whispering.

Allie sighed. "Yes, Granny, I will sit beside you and remember for you."

* * *

Snowflakes drifted to land among a few dead leaves, blown in from the scrub oak trees across the street from the church that morning. Would winter never end? Allie was so ready for spring, for the sound of birds chirping instead of sleet pounding on the metal house roof, to sit on the porch swing in the evening instead of having to be inside all the time.

Allie, her mother, and her grandmother had all ridden together in Katy's vehicle. Lizzy had tried her best to fix it so that Allie would ride in the back seat with Grady in Mitch's truck, but Allie had sidestepped the issue by saying that she'd help with Granny.

When they reached the church, Allie manipulated it so that she sat on the end of the pew next to her grandmother. Katy was next in line and then Lizzy with Mitch beside her and Grady on the far end. Lizzy didn't spare a bit on the dirty looks, but Allie could endure those if she didn't have to sit beside Grady.

She glanced over her shoulder after the announcements were made and the preacher was making his way from the short deacon's bench to the pulpit. Deke, Toby, and Blake were all sitting in the back pew. It was the first time that antsy feeling hadn't forewarned her that he was in close proximity. Did that mean that whatever they had—friendship, relationship, or one-night fling—was over?

Deke waved.

Toby smiled and nodded.

Blake looked straight ahead.

She whipped around, and from that moment, the preacher might as well have been reading the dictionary because Allie didn't hear a single word.

She liked Blake as a person, as a hardworking rancher, but she was not going to be the friend who hopped over the fence for booty calls whenever Blake wanted a quick romp in the hay. If that's what he wanted, he could call his ex-wife, Scarlett, to warm up his bed.

She'd followed her heart when she married Riley and intended to be his wife until death parted them. But she'd learned after two years that physical death wasn't the only way to end a marriage. It could simply die in its sleep or it could be murdered by a two-timin' husband.

That antsy feeling that said someone was staring at her made her look over her shoulder. Blake's lips curled into a smile when their gazes locked and held for several seconds. When she started to turn back around, she caught Grady's gaze from the other end of the pew. It had the intensity of a hungry hound chasing a rabbit and made her skin crawl.

Trust my heart when it failed me? Trust my sister's advice when it makes me want to run for the hills? Maybe I should simply forget all about men and become a nun. I bet a convent could use my skills as a carpenter.

* * *

Allie didn't even care that she was so angry at her sister or that the little dinner place cards done up with hearts were a cute idea. She was sitting smack-dab between Grady and Blake, and Lizzy had done the planning.

Every ugly deed does have its comeuppance. Lizzy got hers because the only place left for her to sit was between generic old Mitch and Toby Dawson. It would serve her sister right to be as miserable as she was.

Her mother sat at one end of the table. Granny sat at the other end, and on each side there was a sister between two men. If that didn't set Granny off into another world where she talked about Walter, nothing could.

"Nice to have a full table today." Granny picked up the basket of hot rolls, put two on her plate, and passed them to her right. "Lizzy, why are you sitting between a preacher man and a hot cowboy? Are you trying to figure out which one you like best?" She leaned forward and whispered, "I'd take the hot cowboy. He'll be more fun."

It was as if someone had pushed a MUTE button. One second conversation flowed, then presto, everything went quiet. The silence was every bit as deafening as it had been over at the Lucky Penny when Scarlett announced that she was Blake's wife.

Toby finally broke the awkward silence. "Did you make these biscuits, Miz Irene? They taste just like my granny's, and everyone loves hers down around Muenster."

Allie passed the green beans to Toby. "They're real good. Katy cooks them with lots of bacon and onions."

"Thank you," Toby said.

Allie caught Lizzy's sharp intake of breath when Toby passed the bowl off to her. She took out a heaping helping of beans and gave them to Mitch. And nothing happened when Mitch's fingers deliberately covered Lizzy's: zilch, nada, nothing at all. So, Toby's touch affected Lizzy, did it? Yes, sir, paybacks were terrible.

Before the beans made it to Allie, Grady slipped his hand on her thigh and squeezed as he whispered, "You look lovely today, but I like you all dressed up much better than in jeans. You should do it more often."

Zilch. Nada. Nothing at all, other than a major irritation until she picked up his hand and put it back in his lap. "Thank you, but I'm much more comfortable in jeans."

"Why are you talking about britches at the Sunday dinner table?" Granny asked. "In my day, ladies wore dresses, and they only put on britches to ride horses or do chores outside on the farm."

Blake's knee pressed against Allie's, and his simple touch jacked up her blood pressure. She felt like Abigail in her favorite LaVyrle Spencer novel, *Hummingbird*. The sensible choice was the man Abigail was nursing back to health in the downstairs part of her house. But the one who made her heart sing was the bad boy upstairs with a bullet hole in his body. The one who called her Abby and set her free from the strict rules of society, the one she couldn't wait to talk to every day.

Grady called her Alora. Formal. Rigid.

Blake called her Allie. Sensible. Happy heart.

She understood the character Abby so much better that day than she did back when she read about the character in the book years ago.

"Penny for your thoughts, Allie," Blake said.

"I'll pay a dollar for them, Alora." Grady grinned.

Allie glanced at Lizzy. "I might sell them to the highest bidder and use the money to buy whatever is making my sister blush."

"I'm not blushing. It's hot in here from all the cooking," Lizzy stammered.

"Does Walter still live at the Lucky Penny?" Irene blurted

out. "Has his mother died yet? I get confused about time, and I can't remember if he moved."

Allie leaned forward, ignoring both men, and said, "No, Granny, Walter moved years ago. I don't know if his mother is still living or not."

"Probably is unless someone drove a stake through her heart. I might take a Sunday-afternoon walk over there and see if Walter is still there," she said.

"Not today, Mama. You have to stay here and chaperone the kids while I drive up to Wichita Falls for supplies. When are you moving to the ranch, Toby?" Katy asked.

"I'm hoping to be here by the first of June. With two of us and a hot summer, we should get lots done. Then our cousin Jud will join us about Thanksgiving time," Toby answered.

Katy nodded. "Sounds like you've got things planned out pretty good."

Irene shrugged. "Who are we talking about?"

Mitch narrowed his eyes at the elderly woman.

Irene raised her voice. "Don't look at me like that. We don't like each other, but this is the Sunday dinner table."

Blake reached over and laid a hand on Irene's arm. "I hear that you took care of Allie and her two sisters right here in this house while Miz Katy worked. Tell me some stories."

She gave Mitch a dirty look and smiled at Blake. "They were a handful for sure. When there's three, there's lots of whining and giggling."

Irene's mind stayed crystal clear as she told stories from the past. Blake's laughter was genuine. Mitch's lack of even a smile showed that he was bored. When they'd finished eating, Katy brought out two pies—apple and cherry—for dessert, along with a container of ice cream and caramel topping.

"Lizzy likes her apple pie with a crown." Irene smiled. "That's what she called it when she was a little girl and said apple pie was princess food and the ice cream was the princess's crown."

"Me, too," Toby said. "But Blake likes cherry better. He never did like apple pie. That's when the family knew for a fact there was something wrong with him. All cowboys love their mamas, pretty girls, and apple pie."

"Two out of three ain't bad, though," Blake said.

"Not me. Too many fat grams and calories," Mitch said and glanced over at Lizzy. "We have to be careful with our desserts, or we'll be as big as circus clowns, won't we, darlin'?"

Allie placed a well-directed kick right on his shin and immediately apologized. "Oh, excuse me. I'm so sorry." She flashed a sarcastic smile across the table.

He glared at Allie. "I think Lizzy and I will forgo dessert and have coffee in the living room while we set up the Monopoly game."

"Yes, darlin'." Lizzy pushed back her chair.

He did the same, stood up, and slung an arm around Lizzy's shoulders.

Allie couldn't understand why Lizzy put up with such a controlling man.

"How about you, Allie? Shall we take our coffee to the living room with them?" Grady asked.

"Oh, no! I'm having both kinds of pie with ice cream. I'll save you a chunk of apple for later, Lizzy," she called out.

Lizzy shook off Mitch's arm and gave Allie a weak grin as she poured two cups of coffee. She handed one to Grady before she followed her fiancé out of the kitchen.

"So, what are you guys doing this afternoon?" Katy asked

Blake. "I hear you tore out some ceiling and put up some new yesterday."

"We are going to take advantage of the sunshine and look at the ranch." He turned slightly and touched Allie on the arm. "Want to go with us?"

"I promised I'd watch Granny this afternoon," she answered, "so I can't leave."

Irene pointed at Allie. "It's not nice to whisper. Who is that sitting beside you anyway? Is that one of Walter's kids? When did he get married?"

"This is Blake Dawson," Allie said. "He lives over at the Lucky Penny now."

"I'm confused again," Irene said.

Blake smiled at her. "It's okay. We all get things mixed up some of the time."

"You are a good boy," she said. "I want cherry pie with ice cream and chocolate syrup on top."

*　*　*

Toby was in the truck with the motor running, but Blake lingered behind to talk to Allie. "I really want to explain about yesterday. Deke took a woman home and she had the car for her and her friend, so she came to get her sister..."

Allie held up a palm and said, "Enough. I told you I don't care."

"And what does that mean?"

"It means..."

"Hey, Alora, darlin'." Grady pushed his way out the door and in between them. "We're waiting on you. We can't start the game without you."

"I'll be there in five minutes," she said.

"Go on now since you don't care," Blake said bluntly.

"Care about what?" Grady asked.

"Nothing," Allie answered quickly.

"Guess that sums it up then." Blake settled his black cowboy hat on his head and marched off the porch, his boots making a cracking sound on the wood with each step.

"Is that over now?" Grady asked. "It needs to be. He's not the man for you, darlin', and I'm glad that you don't care about him. Now come on inside with me and I'll show you a proper good time." He slung his arm around her.

She shrugged it off but not before Blake turned around. The expression on his face said that he was finished with her, that it was over and done with, and all that was left was Grady.

Sensible.

Sad heart with no song.

"Y'all are going to have to play without me," she said around the lump in her throat. "I promised to read to Granny while she falls asleep for her Sunday nap. If she isn't restless, I'll check in with you later."

Grady kissed her on the cheek. "Okay, sweetheart."

She shivered from disgust instead of desire and wiped it away with the back of her hand as she went to the kitchen. Katy was busy clearing the table. Half of Granny's pie was done, and she had that blank look on her face that said she wasn't sure where she was.

"Go on, Mama. I'll do this while I wait on her to finish. You can be halfway to Wichita Falls by the time that happens, and I need something to do," Allie said.

"Have you been crying?" Katy asked.

"Not yet, but I might start when the anger dies down. Blake and I had an argument."

Katy hung a kitchen towel on the hook. "About what? Are you going to finish the job over there?"

"I told him I didn't care and..."

"Care about what?"

Allie put a hand on her forehead, but it didn't ease the pain throbbing in her temples. "I'm not sure. It's complicated."

Katy handed her the dish towel. "You'd best uncomplicate it before Grady pushes his way into your life. I pray every night that you don't let him talk you into a relationship."

Allie shivered. "You'd rather have Blake than him? And yes, I am going to finish the job. Whether we are friends or not doesn't mean I can't work for him."

"Honey, I'd rather have Lucifer than Grady. He's got shifty eyes." Katy cut her eyes toward Irene. "You'll have to keep a close watch on her."

"I'm going to read to her and then sit in the rocking chair in her room and reread that LaVyrle Spencer book about Abigail this afternoon," Allie said.

Katy nodded. "And figure out what you meant by you don't care, right?"

"I hope so, Mama."

Granny was asleep before Allie finished reading the first page of *The Velveteen Rabbit,* which was her new favorite book these days. The roles had been reversed because Allie remembered Granny reading that book to her when she was a child.

When she heard the first soft snore, she put the book aside and picked up *Hummingbird* by LaVyrle Spencer. After reading five pages and not comprehending a single word that she'd read, she laid it aside and decided to straighten Granny's closet.

But first she was going to call Blake and try to explain to him what she meant when she said she didn't care. It wasn't that she didn't care for him, but that she didn't care who Toby and Deke slept with and that Blake didn't owe her an explanation for their actions. There, that was easy enough to put into words, now, wasn't it? And then she was going to confront him about the way he'd introduced her to his brother. He didn't have to say they'd slept together, but he sure could have done better than saying she was the woman who was remodeling the house.

She hit the right number and the call went straight to voice mail. No way was she going to talk to a recording about something that important. She waited two minutes and called again. Same thing.

She ended the call before the message even finished and called a third time. This time, Blake answered.

"This is not a good time, Allie," he said gruffly.

"I don't care."

"You say that often, don't you?"

"What?" she asked.

"I don't care."

"I meant I don't care if it's not a good time. We need to talk, Blake."

"This time I don't care to hear the explanation. We need some breathing space before we talk again. That dinner was the most awkward thing I've ever had to endure." The line went dead, and she flung the phone onto the bed.

"Dammit!" She wanted to scream, but the whisper had to do. Waking Granny always made her cranky.

She slung open the closet doors, sat down on the floor, and started arranging the piles of shoes into some kind of order.

She found three bars of soap tucked down in the toes of shoes that Granny hadn't worn in five years or more. A shoebox held a ziplock bag full of miniature chocolate bars that had long since gone white with age, two washcloths, and a can of root beer.

When she'd first started hoarding things, they'd asked the doctor about it and discovered it was a symptom of the disease. Folks got paranoid and thought people were stealing their possessions, so they hid them.

Then she found a full bottle of Jack Daniel's in one boot and a bottle of Patrón tequila in another boot. Granny must have found them in Fiona's room because Katy didn't drink, Lizzy was too self-righteous to even have a beer these days, and Allie sure hadn't brought the bottles home.

She opened the bourbon first and took a long swig and then tried a taste of the tequila. She liked the bourbon better, but it might hurt Mr. Patrón's feelings if she didn't share her attention between him and Mr. Jack.

A sip of Jack for the wild cowboy.

A sip of tequila to wash the youth director out of her world.

Equal time, she thought as she twisted the cap off the Jack for another gulp.

"Bless Granny's heart for hiding things," she said as she leaned against the wall and got serious about the sharing process.

CHAPTER TWENTY-TWO

A picture of Nadine with that apple pie in her hand snuck across Allie's mind. She tucked her chin to her chest and glared at the tequila bottle in her left hand. How had she drunk half a bottle of that, too? Did Nadine drop by and help her?

"Well, here's to Nadine and apple pies that Blake doesn't like. But he likes pretty girls and his mama." She clinked the two bottles together in a toast. "Some friend I am. Nadine has been down there working on that rotten old building for days, trying to turn it into a café, and I haven't even stopped by to check on her."

"Who are you talkin' to?" Granny asked as she slung her legs over the side of the bed. "I'm going to the kitchen for more pie. Want me to bring you some?"

"No, thank you. I'll be right behind you."

Allie frowned as she held on to the furniture and walls and made her way to the door. Lizzy could watch Granny for the rest of the afternoon. After all, she was only playing that boring-as-hell game of Monopoly. Poor darling Lizzy wasn't ever going to experience the kind of sex that Allie had had with Blake. She loved her sister even if they weren't best friends. They should fix that, and Allie would make the first step. She carried the two bottles out into the foyer and yelled her sister's name.

"You are drunk. On a Sunday, no less," Lizzy said when she saw her sister leaning against the wall.

"Shhhh, don't yell. Mitch will hear. He'll pray for me, and I don't want anyone to know that I've been drinkin' on Sunday." The words were slurred, but at least she was standing on her own two feet.

"Mitch and Grady left a long time ago. Granny and I are about to have a slice of pie. She said you were cleaning her closet. You smell like a liquor store." Lizzy's pert little nose curled up. "You were supposed to be watching Granny, not getting drunk."

Allie giggled. "I'm not drunk, and I love you, Lizzy. Don't marry Mitch. You won't ever have mind-blowing sex with him or know what an afterglow is. He's boring as a board game." She hugged her sister. "Let's bury the hatchet and have a drink to toast being best friends." She held up the two bottles and clinked them together. "Which one will it be? Señor Patrón or bad, bad boy Jack Daniel's?"

"Neither one." Lizzy made a grab for the liquor. "Give me those bottles and go sleep it off in your room."

Allie hugged the bottles to her breast like long-lost relatives. "Oh, no! I'm going to town to have a drink with Nadine. I'm dis...dish...appointed in you, Lizzy. Nadine will be my best friend if you won't, and you ain't going to be happy ever, not ever."

"You can't drive drunk," Lizzy protested.

"I tell you, I'm not drunk, but I will be by the time I

finish up my visit with these two. You take care of Granny. If she runs away, you'll answer to Mama." Allie picked up her purse from the foyer table and staggered out the front door. She heard Lizzy talking to her mother on the phone, but her sister could talk to Jesus, God, and Moses for all she cared. She needed a best friend, and Nadine would be glad to drink a toast with her.

Besides, she hadn't been a good friend to the woman. No doubt, Nadine would be at the store building because she wanted to open the café in another week. The most important thing in the world was for Allie to tell her that all cowboys didn't like apple pie. They liked their mamas and pretty girls, but some of them liked cherry pie or maybe even lemon meringue, but not to depend on apple pies. A friend would be honest with Nadine and tell her that.

She put the bottles between her legs and started the engine. She shook her head and admitted that she was pretty well drunk. But she had things to say to Nadine, and it wasn't so far into town that she couldn't walk.

When she made it to the end of the lane, she stopped and looked both ways. Left was town. Right was the Lucky Penny Ranch. "Am I getting a foggy brain, like Granny?" she asked.

She couldn't remember where she was going. It had something to do with apple pie, but Blake didn't like apple pie. She twisted the cap off the Jack and took a long gulp. Everything was clear as a bell—she was going to the Lucky Penny—and the whiskey didn't even burn. She could hold her liquor. All she needed was bad boy Jack to clear her mind.

She started off to the right and was freezing when she made another right into the Lucky Penny lane. She parked and got out of the truck, taking the whiskey with her. She dropped the bottle, and it broke into a dozen pieces when it hit a rock.

* * *

Blake and Shooter were alone in the house. Toby had gone home a couple of hours before, and the house was too quiet. As if the universe realized that he was lonely, someone pounded on the door.

He jogged across the room, threw open the door, and said, "Come in. Did you drive?"

"I'm cold, and I think I'm drunk." Allie leaned on the doorjamb. "It's okay if you don't like apple pie." She fell into his arms.

A bottle landed on the porch. The Patrón landed right side up, resting there as pretty as if it were sitting on the top shelf behind a fancy bar.

Blake scooped her up in his arms and carried her into the house. She was snoring loudly and smelled like a whiskey barrel when he laid her down on the mattress. Shooter sniffed her, tucked his tail between his legs, and made a beeline for the living room.

Blake chuckled, and she roused slightly.

"Blake hates apple pie, Nadine. He loves his mama, though."

"Shhh! Close your eyes," he said.

She sat straight up without opening her eyes and began weaving from side to side. "I'm not drunk, and I don't care." She slurred her words, but Blake understood most of them. "Poor Lizzy."

He swiftly removed her sweater and unzipped her skirt

before sliding it down her legs. She opened her bloodshot eyes and cocked her head to one side. "I love you, Blake."

He whipped his T-shirt off and pulled it over her head, pushed her back onto the pillows, and covered her up with a blanket. "Sleep, darlin'. Tomorrow you'll have a headache, but you won't remember much of what you said. What on earth made you hit the bottle anyway?"

"Apple pie," she mumbled. "You don't like apple pie."

He lined a small trash can with a plastic bag and set it beside the bed. Then he removed another T-shirt from a dresser drawer, jerked it over his head, and covered her with another blanket. Her hands were so cold that they made him shiver when he tucked them under the covers. He picked up the book he'd planned on reading that evening and settled himself on the other side of the king-size mattress. She wouldn't remember saying that she didn't care, but that was okay. She was beside him, and for right now, she said she loved him.

The sun had sunk below the window ledge when the notion struck that he should at least tell the folks over at Audrey's Place where their prodigal daughter had landed. They probably didn't need to know that she was passed out cold and snoring like a two-ton grizzly bear.

He laid his book to the side and reached for his phone on the nightstand. It slipped out of his hands and skittered its way across the hardwood floor. Allie roused up and opened one eye. "Ouch. My head hurts. Afterglow isn't supposed to give me a headache."

He slid off the mattress, picked up the phone, made his way around the bed to her side, and kissed her on the forehead, but she was already snoring again. He called her number, but it went straight to voice mail. Then he remembered the number on the side of the van and called it.

"Hello." Irene's thin voice filled his ear. "Who is this?"

"This is Blake Dawson from the Lucky Penny. Could I talk to Katy or to Lizzy?" he asked.

"I don't know you, and who is Katy? Are you the law?" The click of her hanging up the phone receiver banged in his ear.

"Guess some folks still have a dial-up phone." He called the number again.

Irene screamed into the phone, "If this is the law, you can quit calling here. We ain't runnin' moonshine no more."

He could hear Lizzy yelling in the background. "Granny, who is that? Is it Nadine? Is Allie with her?"

"Who is Nadine, and what are you talkin' about? It's the law," Irene said.

Lizzy's frazzled voice finally asked, "Nadine, is Allie with you?"

"This is Blake, Lizzy. Allie is over here," he said.

"She's drunk, Blake. Bring her home," Lizzy demanded.

"She's out cold and moving her will probably make her start upchucking, so why don't we let her sleep it off over here," Blake said. "I've got a good recipe for a hangover that I'll give her when she wakes up."

"Please don't tell anyone what happened. I'm marryin' a preacher, you know," Lizzy said.

"Wouldn't dream of saying a word," Blake said. "I'll drive her home when she's sobered up tomorrow morning."

"She's trying to ruin me," Lizzy got out before Irene wrestled the phone from her.

"Walter, is that you? I told you not to call this number. What are you thinkin'?" Irene's shrill voice blasted through his ears.

"Give me that phone, Granny," Lizzy demanded.

The loud bang in his ears said that Irene hung up a second time.

He tiptoed to the kitchen and made himself a sandwich, carried it to the living room, and turned on the television. The weatherman said that they'd have thunderstorms through the night and most of the day on Monday. He watched two episodes of *Family Feud* and a couple of reruns of *NCIS*, but his mind kept running in circles and Allie Logan was right in the middle of all of it.

Shooter went to the door and whined, so Blake let him out for his evening run.

The dog finished his business and dashed into the house, almost tripping Blake on his way to the kitchen.

"You don't have to break my leg. I wouldn't forget your midnight snack," Blake said.

Shooter sat up on his hind legs and begged.

"Okay, you rascal." Blake laughed. "You get two pieces of bologna for that trick. But when you're too fat to run this spring, it won't be my fault."

* * *

Allie's eyes popped open and then snapped shut again as she grabbed her head and rolled up into a ball. Her mouth was dry and tasted like a dirty bathroom smelled. She tried to swallow but gagged instead. Clamping a hand over her mouth, she tried to get up and rush to the bathroom, but knew she wouldn't make it. She grabbed the trash can beside her bed and dry-heaved until her sides ached, but nothing came up.

She'd never had the flu like this before, and she did not

have time for it now. She had to paint Blake's bedroom and then texture the ceiling in the hall and living room. She set the trash can back on the floor and fell back on the bed.

Shooter bounded across the floor and onto the mattress, started at her chin and slurped all the way to her forehead, his dog food breath causing her to gag again. How in the devil did Blake's dog get in her house and to her bedroom?

She pushed him away and opened her eyes slowly, shielding them with her hand against the light pouring in the window. Then a streak of lightning lit up the sky, followed quickly by a boom of thunder that made Shooter drop and shove his head under the covers.

"That's loud." She moved her hands to her ears. "Oh. My! I'm in Blake's bed. How did I get here, and what have I done?"

"You want the truth or a pretty princess story?" Blake asked.

Her chest tightened at how sexy he was, standing there like a mythical god with pajama pants riding low on his hips, a T-shirt stretched out across his muscular chest, and his feet bare. His hair was tousled like he'd gotten out of bed. Did they have sex?

"Truth?" She pulled herself up and propped her back against the pillows.

"Don't even want a little bit of the pretty story?" he asked. "I worked one up for you about a princess who was poisoned by her wicked sister who was going to marry a preacher."

The laughter made it past her chest and partially out of her mouth before it stopped, and she grabbed her head again. "Just the truth."

"You got drunk, and I think you walked over here. You passed out cold in my arms. I put you to bed, and now it's time to get rid of the hangover." He poured honey from a cute little bear-shaped bottle into a spoon and said, "Open your mouth."

She clamped her mouth shut and mumbled, "Will it make my headache stop?"

"It's the first step. Open up." He started toward her mouth, and she obeyed. She didn't care if it was arsenic, as long as it made the throbbing between her eyes stop without killing her.

"Don't move. Next step is coming up. I'll be right back."

Shooter peeked out from under the covers.

Blake returned with two cups of steaming-hot coffee and handed her two aspirin, his fingertips tickling the palm of her hand. She tossed them into her mouth and swallowed them with the first sip of coffee.

"Geez, this is strong enough to melt the enamel off my teeth!"

"That's what makes it work," Blake said. "I have a four-step hangover cure perfected."

"I don't know if anything will cure this," Allie grumbled.

"Where did you even get the liquor?" Blake asked.

Allie shut her eyes tightly. "Granny hides things. I found it in her closet when I was straightening her shoes. Where is it?"

"The tequila is in the kitchen. Was there more?"

She groaned. "Jack Daniel's, but I dropped it because my hands were cold. I've never been this drunk, and believe me, I won't be again. What happened?"

"We had a great talk and cleared up that stuff about you saying you didn't care, and then you did some real good snoring."

She couldn't remember anything about a talk of any kind. She remembered finding all sorts of things in the closet and drinking from the two bottles. Then there was an argument with Lizzy in the foyer. And then she was going to talk to Nadine, but nothing about a talk with Blake came to mind.

"We did?" She opened one eye.

Blake grinned. "Of course we did. You drink the rest of that and don't move. I'll bring the third dose in a few minutes."

As he left the room, a clear memory flashed, and both eyes opened wide. Shooter moved over and laid his head in her lap. She propped up enough to continue to sip her coffee with one hand and scratch his ears with the other.

"Scrambled eggs and toast." Blake returned carrying a plate of food.

Was he trying to kill her? "I can't eat eggs. My stomach can't handle them. I'll try a few bites of the toast."

Blake picked up the fork. "No, ma'am. You will eat every bite of the eggs. There's only two."

"I can feed myself," she protested.

"You handle the coffee. I'll do the feeding." He grinned.

What a sweet man, she thought.

There was something intimate about a man feeding her breakfast in bed, even if it was a hangover cure. Not once in the two years she'd been married to Riley had he ever brought her breakfast in bed or fed her. But she didn't want to think about Riley; she wanted to focus on the man feeding her the hangover cure.

"No!" she said.

He put another bite into her mouth. "No, what?"

She swallowed quickly. "We are fighting. You shouldn't be nice to me."

"We got all that settled last night," he said.

"I don't remember it, and until I remember, it's not settled. Four steps? What's the last one?" she asked.

"A banana and then a warm shower," he said. "Don't snarl your pretty nose. Trust me! It works."

She blinked several times. "How did you figure all this out?"

"Internet," he said. "After a few hangovers, I did some research and found a combination of cures that works. You plannin' on usin' it real often?"

She shook her head very slowly. "I like a beer. I even like a shot of Jack. I'm not so much into tequila, but it was there, and I didn't want it to feel left out. But until right now, I've never been drunk, and believe me, it isn't ever happening again."

He put the last bite into her mouth and kissed her on the forehead. "Good girl. Now for the final step, and then you can take a shower. There's an extra toothbrush in the cabinet. Still in the bubble pack. I'll get another pot of coffee going while you do that."

Her eyes fixed on him as he left the room again. Surely she hadn't merely dreamed that they'd had sex on this very mattress. She drew her eyebrows down and flinched when that brought another pang between her eyes. What was today? Had she been there a day? A week?

Shooter hopped off the mattress and made his way up the hallway, probably to stretch out in front of the fireplace since the lightning and thunder had stopped. Was that an omen? The storm was over and it was time for her to go home and face the music from her family, and why was it thundering at this time of year? There was snow on the ground for heaven's sake.

She would eat the banana, and she'd have a shower and gladly brush her teeth, but then she and Blake were going to have a talk. And this time she would remember every word, every nuance, and every expression on his face.

"Every single word," she mumbled.

"Word about what?" he asked. "It's snowing again, and you're in no shape for texturing a ceiling, so I vote we cuddle up on the sofa and spend the day together. We can turn off our cell phones and pretend we're stranded on a desert island."

"How long have I been here?" she asked.

"Since late last evening. Today is Monday," he answered.

Had they cleared things up? If not, then why was he being so nice?

"I've always wanted to get lost on an island," she said. "Hand me that banana and get the canoe ready for us to row to the island."

Did she say that out loud? What was the matter with her? They still had to clear up a lot of things before she cuddled with him on the sofa all day.

He tossed the banana toward her. "This is all working. My headache isn't nearly as bad," she said.

"I'm the hangover guru. Stick with me and I'll take care of you," Blake said with a smile.

CHAPTER TWENTY-THREE

Hot water washed away more of Allie's headache, but it didn't do much to take away her guilt. What had she been thinking? She'd been put in charge of her grandmother for the afternoon and she'd failed...again.

Alora Raine Logan was a failure. Stripped stark naked, standing under the shower spray at the Lucky Penny, which was every bit as appropriate as an AA meeting for alcoholics, she admitted that she had failed. Failed in her marriage— couldn't hold Riley's interest. Failed as a daughter—proved she couldn't be trusted. Failed as a sister—weekends were the only time Lizzy got to spend with Mitch.

"Sorry feller that Mitch is, he's *her* fiancé." Allie wiped at the tears streaming down her cheeks.

She slid down in the bathtub and curled up in a tight little ball, sobbing as the hot water streamed over her body. She didn't hear the little plastic rings holding the shower curtain slide across the rod. She had no idea anyone was in the bathroom until Blake was in the tub with her. Still dressed in pajama pants and a knit shirt, he sat down behind her and gathered her into his arms. One minute she was sitting on the hard porcelain of an old bathtub, and the next she was curled up in his lap, her cheek against his chest.

She started to say something, but he put a finger over her lips.

"The depression is the alcohol talking, not sensible Allie Logan. Whatever happened is water under the bridge. Burn the bridge and forget the past," he whispered.

His words were so soft and poetic that they brought on a fresh batch of tears. She didn't care if it was just another line he'd used. Didn't care…they were the words that had started all this to begin with.

"I do care," she said between sobs.

"About what?" He brushed strands of wet hair from her face.

She took several seconds to get her thoughts together. "I care about Lizzy and Mama and Granny. I don't care if you are telling me pretty words that you've told lots of women before me. I don't care about your past. I'll burn those bridges for you if you'll hand me a stick of firewood and a match."

How he managed to stand up in a slippery, wet tub with her in his arms, then step out without falling, was a miracle. But suddenly she found herself wrapped in that brand-new robe he'd talked about and her hand was in his, letting him lead her to the living room. He tossed a quilt over the sofa and motioned for her to sit. She obeyed without arguing, and he carefully brought the ends of the quilt up around her legs.

"Don't go away." He smiled.

Leaving wet footprints on the floor and dripping water as he disappeared into his bedroom, he whistled a tune that she recognized as "Honey Bee" by Blake Shelton. In a few minutes he returned, dressed in gray sweat bottoms and a long-sleeved thermal shirt. He carried a towel in one hand and a hairbrush in the other.

"Slide forward about a foot," he said.

When she did, he settled in behind her, one long muscular leg on each side of her body. He towel-dried her hair and then massaged her scalp with his fingertips. Her body felt like a rag doll, and yet every nerve was on high alert, wanting more, begging for his wonderful hands.

"Mmmm," she murmured.

"Is it making it better?" he drawled.

He started brushing her hair, and a whole new set of emotions surfaced. She was afraid to move an inch for fear she'd find out this was all a dream and she would wake up with that grinding hangover, or worse yet, in her lonely bed at home.

His hands grazed her cheeks as he pulled her damp hair back to run the brush through it. Then he leaned forward and kissed her softly on the side of her neck.

"We were going to talk," she whispered.

"We are talkin', darlin'. We'll use words when necessary," he said softly.

No one had ever cared enough about Allie to sit in a tub with her when she was crying or brush her hair, much less talk to her without using words. Sitting there with her eyes shut, feeling Blake's long legs against her body, she couldn't help but wonder if the third time was the charm. First, there was Granny's Walter. Then, there was Katy's Ray. And now, there was Blake, who was the third. If it was a real fairy tale, the prince would come along and win the princess.

"Now, that's as far-fetched as anything can be," she murmured to herself.

"What?" he asked.

She clamped a hand over her mouth. "Did I say that out loud?"

"You did. Want to explain?" he asked.

She shook her head and leaned back so she could look up into his eyes. "Where are your glasses?" She'd do anything to change the subject.

"My hands are seeing for me this morning. They tell me that you are beautiful beyond words." He smiled, then reached behind him to the end table and put his glasses on. "Usually, I have my contacts in, but glasses come in handy when my allergies act up."

"I like them on you. They make your eyes even greener."

"Then I'll throw away my contacts and wear them every day just for you," Blake said sincerely.

In all the fairy tales she'd read or that Granny had read to her in her youth, the prince had never worn glasses or been nearsighted. This had to be reality.

"You don't have to do that, Blake. Do you always believe what your hands say?" she teased.

"Not always, but my heart never lies to me, and it's in agreement with my hands," he whispered.

"Oh!"

He stopped and kissed her hair. "I'm sorry. Did I hit a tangle?"

"No, I should call Mama and Lizzy. It's a wonder they haven't called out the militia already," she said.

He pulled the brush to the end of her dark hair and then laid it on the end table. "I talked to Lizzy last night and your mother this morning. They know where you are, that you are alive, and that I'll bring you home sometime later."

She readjusted her position until she was sitting in his lap, tilted her chin up, moistened her lips, and wrapped her arms around his neck. "Thanks for letting them know."

Suddenly lips met lips in a fiery kiss that erased the argument. Tongues did a mating dance that included forgetting and forgiving, leaving Allie and Blake in a wonderful vacuum with room for only two beating hearts. The heat between them burned away the bad feelings, and nothing mattered but the future.

"Wow! Just wow," he said.

"I like you, Blake Dawson." She stood up and then settled down on the sofa with the robe covering her legs. Her heart said that she loved him, but she wasn't totally sure that there weren't a few drops of whiskey and tequila left in her blood that might be influencing the major organ in her body.

"I like you, too, Allie Logan," he said, and smiled.

"Why?"

"You said it first, so you have to tell me why you like me first. And I'm leaving my glasses on so I can see you, because your face does not lie."

"Oh, really?"

"Yes, ma'am." He stared into her eyes. "Just how far does this 'like' business go?"

She inhaled and let it out slowly. "It's real hard for me to trust anyone, and I have commitment issues after two years with a husband who left me for another woman. He was a lot like Mitch. He manipulated me into giving him what he wanted and made me feel guilty when I didn't cave in. The only thing I refused to do was quit working, and that was a big thorn in our marriage."

"Sounds like he was controlling," Blake said.

"He was, and I was young, naive, and very stupid," she

said. "I didn't know that it was mental abuse. He'd sigh and say that he wished I would dress better. But it wasn't all bad all the time. I guess that's why I didn't see the infidelity when it was right before my face."

"That's just wrong," Blake whispered coldly.

She could feel the last of the ice chipping away from her heart. Was this what it was like to have a best friend, someone a person could tell anything to?

"I don't think my heart was broken but more relieved that I didn't have to keep fighting over my working situation," she said. "But my pride was in shambles. It was a long time before I went out on a date, and I figured out real quick that I didn't believe anything he said. It wasn't him but me. I didn't trust men."

"And now?" Blake asked.

"I like you and I trust you, but I want to know why you introduced me to your brother as the woman who was fixing this house instead of your friend or, since we'd been to bed, as your girlfriend," she said.

He took her hands in his. "It was an awkward situation, Allie. Those women from the bar were in the kitchen. Your granny showed up looking like a half-drowned old madam. Don't look at me like that. You know I'm tellin' the truth. And then your mother came to get her. I wanted to tell you that I hadn't slept with you and then turned around and spent the night with one of those women, but I couldn't with all of them standing so close. And I didn't think you'd want them to know that we'd had sex, and I didn't know how to introduce you. And I'm battling this idea of us when you live so close."

"What does my living close have to do with anything?" she asked.

"If things didn't work out between us and there were hard feelings, well"—he paused and took a deep breath—"we are neighbors. It's complicated."

Sitting there with her small hands tucked into his big ones felt right, as if that's the way life should be. "I don't want you to leave the Lucky Penny, so please make it work. I've opened my heart to you. That's why I like you, Blake. I can talk to you. I can argue with you. I can be drunk and you don't judge me. You don't talk down to me or make me feel like less of a woman because of what I do."

He dropped her hands, then leaned forward to bookcase her face in his hands. "You've had Deke as a best friend, but I've never had a best friend who was a woman, so this is all new territory for me. Why do I like you? Let me count the ways."

She looked up at him. "You don't have to be complimentary. Just knowing that you consider me a best friend is enough for me."

He captured her hand midair and kissed the knuckles. "What I feel for you goes far above 'like,' Allie Logan. I don't know if it's love because I've never really been in love before. But believe me when I tell you that I admire you for what you do. I think it's downright sexy the way you can crawl up on a roof or fix a ceiling and, honey, those cargo pants turn me on."

"Kind of like that song 'She Thinks My Tractor's Sexy'?" she said. "Only in reverse? He thinks my cargos are sexy?"

"You got it." He nodded. "You can do all those things, and then, when we are in bed, you make me feel like I'm the greatest lover on earth."

Allie's smile grew wider. "That's because you are. And

speaking of that, since we're best friends, does that mean we can't see if you're still that great in bed? Like right now?"

"Allie, I want more from you than booty calls. If we weren't both close to thirty, I'd say this is where I'd ask you to go out with me." He chuckled.

She pulled both her hands free and cupped *his* cheeks in them. "We haven't even been dating. You know that commercial that says like comes before love?"

His hands covered hers. "I've seen it on television a couple of times."

Allie leaned forward and kissed him on the tip of the chin. "I'm not so sure I believe that. I think maybe they get mixed up sometimes and sometimes they arrive at the same time, but right now I don't want to think about any of it. I want to go to bed with you."

CHAPTER TWENTY-FOUR

Blake and Deke had already gone when Allie let herself into the house and went right to work that Tuesday morning. At noon the ceiling was painted, the walls were finished, and she was working her way around the floor doing the woodwork. The doors to the bedroom and closet had been removed and were resting on sawhorses in the third bedroom. She'd painted one side of the doors, then worked on the ceiling, and she planned to paint the other side before she left that evening. Then, the next day, she would hang them before she started texturing the hallway and living room ceiling.

She'd really dodged a bullet the day before with the gossip hounds in Dry Creek. The big news in town right then was the grand opening tonight of Nadine's new café. It had only taken a lot of elbow grease and a big trip to the grocery wholesale store to get the place up and running. Katy had helped her cut through a ton of red tape to get a license, and rumor had it that Sharlene and Mary Jo were taking vacation time from their jobs to help out the first week as waitresses and dishwashers.

Of course, Nadine's business venture was only part of what was keeping all the phone lines heated up that week. Sharlene was still thinking about cleaning up the old clothing store for a day care center because she was tired of the banking business, and Mary Jo was continuing with plans for putting in a beauty and barbershop combination in the building between the café and the feed store.

Some folks thought they were destined for failure. Others cheered for the ladies and whispered over the backyard fences that Blake Dawson might be the luckiest thing that had happened to northern Throckmorton County in several decades. He was the only thing that had changed in town the past several years and look at what all was happening.

Allie wished all three of them the best of luck in their ventures and could have personally hugged them for taking some of the heat from the rumors away from her that week. She was picturing three stores on Main Street with clean windows and folks fanning in and out of the new businesses when she came to the end of the baseboards and stood up to paint around the door facing.

She caught a whiff of woodsmoke but figured a draft had sent it from the fireplace to her nose. Paintbrush loaded, her hand was headed toward the middle of the door trim when two hands snaked around her waist. It startled her so badly that she squealed, flipped around, and threw up the brush, sending a broad swath of white paint across Blake's face. White went ear to ear, across his mouth, chin, and below his nose, before she dropped the brush on the toe of his right boot.

He pulled her tightly against his chest, tipped up her chin, and kissed her, smearing wet white paint all over her face. She tasted woodsmoke, cold winter air, and a hint of black coffee mixed with paint. Who would have ever thought that that mixture could be an aphrodisiac? She rolled up on her toes and then remembered Deke.

Sweet Jesus in heaven! She had to get to the bathroom and wash all that paint off her face before he saw it or else he'd have a million questions and at least that many lectures all ready to deliver.

"Deke?" she whispered.

"Is on the way. He wanted to finish up the cord of wood he was working on so that Herman could take it out of the field. Weatherman says it's going to snow more, starting tonight and going through tomorrow. Never seen winter like this in central Texas before, but when it's cold outside we have to get warm inside, don't we?" Blake pulled her back to his chest.

"You got that right, but first we've got to get the paint off before Deke gets here," she said.

"Hey! This room is almost finished, and it looks great." He took a step back and looked around at the fresh sandy-colored walls and white trim work. "I can move my furniture back in tomorrow evening, soon as we pull up this nasty carpet. That means we've got a date, right?"

"Thursday evening?" she asked.

"I'll pick you up at seven at your place." He led her to the bathroom and turned on the water in the wall-hung sink and wetted a washcloth.

"Here, let me."

She turned her face toward him, and he gently wiped away most of the paint from her face. Allie's breath caught at his intense stare, and it took every ounce of her willpower not to melt into his arms.

"Hey, where are y'all?" Deke called from the living room, breaking the spell.

"Cleaning up Blake," Allie yelled back.

"You're what?" Deke wasted no time getting down the hall. He stopped at the bathroom door and leaned a shoulder against the jamb. "What happened?"

"Never scare a woman who's holding a paintbrush," Blake said.

Deke laughed out loud. "Just be glad you didn't run into her freshly painted wall." He left the bathroom and peeked into the bedroom. "Lookin' good. You'll have it done by quittin' time today. It's amazing what a coat of paint and a new ceiling does for a room, ain't it? I'm going to wash up in the kitchen sink, and then I've got something to tell you."

Allie picked up the washcloth again and wiped away more paint. Cupping his chin under her hand sent waves of desire through her body.

"I've got the bowls on the table. Y'all going to take all day in there?" Deke shouted.

"Almost done," Allie yelled back. "Be there in two minutes."

"Make that three or four. Get out the cheese, salsa, and chips." Blake raised his voice and bent his head to give her a blistering-hot kiss that took her breath away.

"Wow," she muttered.

"It never gets old or dull, does it?" Blake whispered.

"Hasn't yet," she said.

"If you ain't here in thirty seconds, with or without paint all over your face, I am eating alone. You've had time to take off the first layer of skin, Allie," Deke called out.

When they reached the kitchen, she sat down in her chair. "You must be hungry, Deke."

Deke got busy dipping tortilla soup into bowls. "I'm always starving by dinnertime. And, Allie, I know y'all are more than friends, so you don't have to find excuses to stay in the bathroom and make out."

"What?" Allie sputtered.

"It's all over your face, and Blake's been whistling more than usual and, well, I'm your best friend, Allie, so I know. Now let's eat before the food gets cold. I'm hungry, and talking about hungry"—he blew on a spoonful of soup—"Nadine is having her grand opening tonight. She's serving hamburgers and two blue plate specials. It's not a big menu, but tomorrow she's adding to it. We're going. My treat for all the food I've been getting here and, Allie, this was your idea, so you need to be there."

"So that's what you wanted to tell us?" Blake asked.

"Yep. Now admit it. I'm right. You two are dating," Deke said.

Allie downed the rest of her sweet tea. "Blake and I are more than friends."

Deke reached for the salsa and added a tablespoon to his second bowl of soup. "I knew it. Have you told Lizzy and your mama?"

"Not yet. I thought maybe since we're best friends you'd do that for me," she teased.

"Oh, no, I want to be out of the county when you tell Lizzy."

* * *

Allie wasn't a bit surprised to see that Lizzy had gotten all dressed up in a cute little pencil skirt and a turtleneck sweater in the same shade of brown as her eyes. She'd even added a clunky gold necklace to the getup. She'd abandoned her cowboy boots for a pair of spike-heeled dress boots. Her dishwater-blond hair floated in curls on her shoulders, and her makeup was perfect. Mitch expected her to look beautiful when they went out, and she did everything to please him.

Lizzy gasped when she saw Allie wearing a snug pair of skinny jeans, a formfitting sweater that accentuated her curves and her tiny waist, and a pair of cowboy boots that Lizzy had never seen.

"What?" Allie asked.

"Did you change your mind? Please tell me that you did and you're going with me and Mitch and Grady." Lizzy smiled.

"I'm going to the grand opening, but I'm not going with you. And for the last time, Grady is out of the question. I'm going with Blake Dawson."

Lizzy fell back in the old rocking chair and threw her hand across her eyes in a dramatic gesture that did Scarlett O'Hara justice. "I knew it. I told Mama nothing good would come from you going over there to work. You are weak and you can't say no."

Allie frowned and held up her hand like a little girl in the classroom. "Hello. My name is Alora Raine Logan, and I fall over backward for any sexy cowboy who pays attention to me. The youngest sister is the smart one. The middle sister is the strong one. I'm the failure."

Lizzy dropped her hand and glared at Allie. "That is not funny."

"There's the doorbell, so that will be Blake. See you at Nadine's. I hope she made her famous apple pie for tonight." Allie picked up her coat and purse and left Lizzy sitting there speechless for the first time in her life.

Katy had already opened the door, and Blake was standing at the foot of the stairs when Allie started down. Her breath caught in her chest at the sight of him there in his bulletproof jeans bunched up over the tops of black boots so shiny she could see the reflection of the foyer light fixture in them. He held his black hat in his hands, his eyes locked with hers, and his smile said more than words could ever get across.

He handed her a tiny stem with a little white daisy-looking flower at the end. "I should have brought flowers, but I didn't have time to go into town, so this will have to do. Mama calls them snow flowers because they bloom in the winter. I found it this evening right up next to the house. You are stunning tonight, Allie."

"Oh, Blake, it is beautiful. I'm going to press it and keep it forever," she said. "Hold my coat and give me a second to put it in water until I get home tonight." She hurriedly put the flower in a small glass of water, went back to the foyer, and turned to Katy.

"Are you and Granny going to have supper at Nadine's?" she asked.

"No, she's already in her room watching episodes of *Designing Women*. I'm going to make myself a sandwich and catch up on quarterly taxes while things are quiet," Katy said. "Give Nadine my best and tell her I'll be there for lunch tomorrow. Lizzy and I are going to put a sign on our doors and take a thirty-minute lunch break. That way, all the schoolkids will go to Nadine's, and it will stir up a little more business for her."

"You've cooked your last time at the store, then?" Blake asked.

Katy smiled. "Yes, I have, and I won't miss it a bit."

Blake and Allie walked out to his truck, fingers laced together, ignoring the cold weather and smiling at each other. He opened the door for her and settled her into the passenger seat. They rode in comfortable silence almost all the way to town, and then Deke called to tell her that he was already at the café and was holding a table for the three of them and one of Herman's granddaughters. She was between jobs and came to visit for a couple of weeks.

"Kelly?" Allie asked. "You better be careful. Herman will skin you alive if you mess with her. She's his favorite since she's the only granddaughter."

"It's not a date, only a chair at a table. She was waiting. It's a packed house, I'm tellin' you," Deke said. "And Nadine has apple pie. I told her to save three pieces and one of pecan for Blake since he hates apple pie. It's going fast."

Blake had to park all the way down at the end of the block and across the street. Dry Creek usually rolled up the sidewalks at five o'clock, when Katy and Lizzy closed up shop, and there wasn't another car seen on the street until the next morning. But that night there wasn't a parking place on either side of the wide street.

Blake crawled out of the truck, shook the legs of his jeans down over his boots, and circled the front to open the door for her. They walked across the street hand in hand, and when he tried to pull away as they entered the café, she tightened her grip.

The place was almost as noisy as a rock concert until they saw that Allie was with Blake and holding his hand, and then the only racket that could be heard was the pots and pans in the kitchen area.

Allie marched right over to Nadine's mama, who had held

the crown for the biggest gossip in Dry Creek for nearly three decades, and laid a hand on her shoulder.

"Hello, Willa Ruth. Have you met my boyfriend, Blake Dawson? He's been to church a couple of times, but I don't think everyone has been properly introduced to him. Blake, darlin', this is Nadine's mama, Willa Ruth. She taught Nadine everything she knows about Southern cooking, so this should be written up in the magazines before the year is out."

"I'm right pleased to meet you, ma'am." Blake nodded. "Deke is waiting for us, so I expect we'd best get on over there. I'm looking forward to a lot of good meals right here."

Willa Ruth mumbled something that sounded like she was pleased to meet Blake and then threw her hand up over her mouth to whisper something to the women sitting with her at the table.

Between that area and the corner Deke had saved, Allie stopped by two more tables to introduce Blake as her boyfriend. By the time they were seated with Deke and Kelly, the whole place was buzzing. Allie didn't need a PhD in rocket science to know exactly what they were saying or that a few of those phones up to their ears were calling everyone else in town to give them the news.

"Well, that was pretty bold," Deke said.

"Did I hear you right? Did you say that Blake is your boyfriend?" Kelly asked.

"I think she did," Blake answered seriously.

"I wouldn't have a bit of trouble crawling up here on this table and telling the whole place if you were my boyfriend." Kelly pushed back her red hair and batted her thick lashes at him. "But I don't mess with another woman's feller."

Lizzy, Grady, and Mitch pushed through the door, and Deke

nodded that way. "She's liable to tear the place apart when… and there is Sharlene whispering in her ear right now."

Everyone in the place saw Lizzy's expression, but Allie smiled and blew her sister a kiss from across the room. With those mixed signals, the poor old gossip hounds wouldn't know what to say or do next.

"So, I'm your boyfriend?" Blake leaned around the corner of the table and kissed Allie on the cheek. "I'm lucky to have a girlfriend as beautiful as you are."

Kelly sighed. "Rotten luck! I would've gone to cut wood with Grandpa, but I was lazy and look what it got me."

"I'll be your boyfriend as long as we are at this table," Deke said.

"Why not longer?" Kelly asked.

"Because your grandpa would make sure they never found my body, and that would make Allie sad since she is my best friend," Deke answered.

"Quite the charmer, you are." Kelly smiled.

Deke gave her a crooked little smile back. "Do my best, darlin'."

Blake glanced at the menu, which was stuck between the sugar bowl and napkin holder. "I like being your boyfriend, but you could have given me a little notice."

"You brought me flowers. Doesn't that mean we are in a relationship?" she asked.

Before he could answer, Mary Jo appeared at the table with a little order pad and pen. "Well, you stirred up things. Nadine says to thank you because gossip is good for business."

"I want a hamburger with mustard, fries, and a Dr Pepper. Not diet," Allie answered. "Tell Nadine she's welcome. We are glad to be a help."

"Make that two," Blake said. "Double meat and add cheese, please. Sweet tea instead of a soda."

Deke nodded. "I'll take what he's having."

"Me, too," Kelly said.

"How long has this been going on?" Mary Jo used her pen to point at Allie and Blake.

"A while," Allie answered.

"Some women have all the luck, and just so you know, Sharlene is not a happy camper." Mary Jo rushed across the room to take Lizzy's order.

* * *

Blake walked Allie to the porch and then caged her by putting a hand on the wall on either side of her. "As your boyfriend, I do get a good night kiss, right?"

She stood on tiptoe and wrapped her arms around his neck. "I'm sorry. I should have told you I was going to do that. Everyone was staring at us, so I figured I'd give them something to talk about. If you don't want a commitment, then please at least play along with me until after Lizzy's wedding so I don't have to deal with Grady anymore."

His lips came down on hers, sweet and gentle at first, then more demanding. Her breath came out in short raspy gasps when he finally pulled away.

"Why didn't you think of this sooner?"

"We can break up after the wedding," she said.

"We'll cross that bridge when we get to it. I'll see you tomorrow at noon, and remember, since the room is done, we have a date on Thursday night. I'm thinkin' some dancin' at a honky-tonk."

"Sounds good to me," she said. "Good night, Blake."

He tipped his hat brim toward her and whistled all the way to the truck.

Allie took a deep breath and pushed the door open to find both her mother and Lizzy sitting on the bottom step of the staircase. She exhaled slowly and smiled brightly.

"I guess you heard the news," she said.

"You could have told us yourself," Katy said. "Not that it's a big surprise, but to announce it like that—have you lost your mind?"

"No, I'm weak. Ask Lizzy if you don't believe me," Allie answered.

Lizzy rose to her feet. "Are you doing this so you have an excuse not to go out with Grady?"

Allie put her foot on the first step of the staircase. "I'm dating Blake, plain and simple, and if you would please relay that to Grady so he'll leave me alone, I will love you forever. Lizzy, the next time you call me weak, you might do well to remember this night."

"I know I've been mean, but it's only because I worry about you, and I'm sorry," Lizzy said.

"Alora, are you sure about this?" Katy asked.

"I am, Mama, and, Lizzy, thanks for the concern. Family is always there when friends and marriages collapse and, Lizzy, we'll be here for you no matter what, just like y'all are for me," Allie said and then went straight to her room and shut the door. She removed her clothing down to her underpants and pulled on a soft nightshirt before slipping between the covers.

She'd made the first call in saying that she and Blake were in a real relationship when she didn't know if they were or not.

She'd changed the whole course of her world in a single night, and now she had to face the consequences.

She turned the switch on a bedside lamp, putting the room in soft shadows. She'd had more fun these past couple of weeks than she'd had in her whole life. What she and Blake had might not last forever, but she'd never know if she didn't give it a shot. And besides, Allie liked her life that night. She liked what she was doing and who she was sharing it with, and that was all that mattered. She shut her eyes and dreamed of Blake Dawson.

CHAPTER TWENTY-FIVE

Allie left the Lucky Penny on Wednesday afternoon in a nasty mood. She'd gotten the ceilings in the hallway and the living room bedded and taped, ready for the texturing the next day. That should have made her happy, but it didn't. She'd spent most of the day in the house all alone without even Shooter to talk to. She was in a horrible mood and hoped that Lizzy and Mitch had already left for midweek church services.

There had been a note beside the coffeepot that morning saying that Deke had a couple of cows delivering calves, so Blake had gone to help with the birthing process. Allie had lived in a rural community her entire life, so she understood that friends helped friends.

At lunch she had heated up a bowl of leftover tortilla soup from the day before and ate it at the cabinet straight from the pan. While she was washing up, she got a text saying that one calf was on the ground but the other heifer was still in labor. Nothing about missing her or a mention of the date planned for the next night.

Snow fell in big fluffy flakes, melting as soon as it hit the warm van windshield on her way home that evening. The clock on the dash said that it wasn't even five o'clock yet, which was hard to believe with the darkness surrounding her. She followed Lizzy's truck and her mother's car down the lane, and they all parked side by side right next to the gate leading into the yard.

"I hate snow," Irene declared as she held tightly to Katy's arm. "Old people shouldn't be out in this crap. I'm not leaving the house tomorrow, so y'all best make some plans. I could break a hip."

Allie raced ahead, unlocked the door, and held it open for her mother and grandmother. Irene was still grumbling about the cold when out of nowhere a snowball hit Allie smack in the side of the face. She slammed the door and whipped around in time to dodge the second one, which hit the house with enough force to send it flying apart and peppering down into her hair.

Lizzy was scraping up snow around the fence post and patting it together to make another one when Allie bailed off the porch and tackled her, landing them both in the half inch of snow already lying on the ground. She scraped up all she could hold in one fist and smeared it over Lizzy's face. Then her sister did a roll and came up with a leg on either side of Allie's body and pinned her hands down above her head.

"You are right," she panted.

"About what? That this is cold?" Allie laughed for the first time that day.

"No, about needing family. Mitch is leaving for three weeks, I have to give up my honeymoon for God, and I'm so mad I'm not even going to church tonight," Lizzy said breathlessly.

Allie freed herself from her sister and leaned against the fence post. "Explain, please."

Lizzy scooted over and shared the post with Allie. "A mission trip to Mexico has come up suddenly, and he and Grady are going. But that means he won't have time off left for our honeymoon, so I have to sacrifice it for him to do his mission thing. And like I said, I'm upset beyond words."

Allie caught a snowflake on her tongue. "You are kiddin' me, right?"

"I wouldn't joke about something this serious. We were planning a trip to Cancun, where the weather would be warm, and I already bought two sweet little bathing suits, and now we'll be going straight to his apartment after the wedding. No honeymoon because his vacation time has to be spent on a mission trip to help build a new school. And I can't gripe about it to anyone because he's doing it for God, and you were right. If I didn't have you tonight, I'd be…well, I'm just glad you are here, and I don't even care about you liking Blake anymore."

Allie put her arm around Lizzy's shoulders. "I'd be mad, too."

Lizzy grabbed her sister's hand and squeezed. "Thank you. I'm sorry about being so ugly these past weeks. This is probably my punishment for trying to run your life."

"No apology necessary. Let's go make supper, and if it keeps up, we'll make snow ice cream for Granny." Allie hopped to her feet and pulled Lizzy up with her. "You cussed. You fell off the wagon."

"The words I used at the store when he called me and said he was leaving in two hours blistered the paint on the walls," Lizzy said.

"Two hours! And he bombed you with all this on the

phone? That means he's already headed to Dallas to catch the plane, right? What did you say?"

Lizzy slung the door open and led the way into the warm house. "I kept my cool and said that of course God's work should come before our honeymoon. And then I hung up and cussed until I ran out of words and cried until I ran out of tears. I'm glad I didn't have many customers, or the gossip would be so hot that it would melt the North Pole."

Both women removed their coats and hung them on the rack inside the door, kicked off their boots, and tossed their stocking hats on the foyer table. Pots and pans rattled in the kitchen, and the sound of Katy and Irene discussing supper floated out into the foyer.

"Does Mama know?"

Lizzy shook her head. "No, but she will in a few minutes. I might as well fess up because it will be all over town by bedtime."

"Why don't you stay home with Granny tomorrow, and I'll work the store for you?" Allie said. "That way, you can put at least one day between you and the gossip."

"You'd do that for me?"

Allie laid a hand over Lizzy's. "That's what sisters are for."

* * *

Blake had awoken in a black mood on Wednesday morning. When Deke called to ask for help, he'd agreed gladly, hoping that being around cattle and new baby calves would get him out of the funk.

It did not!

Thursday at noon, when he went to the house for dinner,

leaving two big piles of mesquite with three inches of snow on top of them, he finally got a handle on his problem.

It was Allie! And he fully intended to straighten it out that night when they were on their first and maybe last date. He pushed back his half-eaten roast beef sandwich, laced his hands behind his neck, and looked up at the kitchen ceiling with all its rusty brown circles. If she quit, he and Toby would have to finish putting up new drywall and they'd have to learn to texture the living room and hall.

"And insulation." The minute the words were out of his mouth, his arms began to itch.

That afternoon Herman and Deke showed up to cut firewood. There was at least a day's worth out there piled up, and Blake planned on clearing more land that day. Snow on the ground wouldn't keep him from working. Sleet falling out of the sky was a different thing.

The dashboard clock said it was five o'clock when Blake parked the dozer. In another two weeks, if this weather cooperated, he'd begin to till the ground, then put in a crop of wheat and one of alfalfa. Not long after that, Toby would arrive with cows and there wouldn't be many days that they'd have the luxury of stopping before dark.

Deke waved and crossed the field. "Hey, the calves are doing fine. Looks like that little bull might be breeder stock. I'll have to decide later, but he's got some fine shoulders and good markings."

"Good. Never knew how much I missed working with cattle until yesterday. I can't wait until the Lucky Penny is in full swing." Blake fell in beside him, and together they walked back to the house with Shooter dashing on ahead of them.

"So you and Allie got a date tonight to celebrate your

bedroom getting finished. Where are you taking her? Dinner and a movie?" Deke asked.

Blake shook his head. "We do that all the time right there at the house. I'm thinking about a honky-tonk, where we can have a drink and dance."

"Then let me suggest Cowboy Heaven. It's this side of Wichita Falls, it's got a nice dance floor, and it's not too loud. I take the women I really want to impress up there," Deke said.

"Directions?" Blake asked.

"You'll see the signs for it soon as you cross the county line. It's right on the highway to the right. Big parking lot and a sign that stands tall. Can't miss it," Deke said. "Have a good time. I'll expect a full report tomorrow. No, don't tell me a thing. If Allie's able to come to work, I'll know by lookin' at her face if she enjoyed the evening. See you tomorrow, but it won't be until midmorning. With this weather, I'm throwing out a lot of hay."

Deke veered off toward his truck, and Blake went on to the house, through the back door, and straight to the bathroom. He shucked out of his clothes while the shower water heated and then stood under it for a long time, trying to figure out exactly how to approach Allie. He liked her. He might even be in love with her, but he was a man and he did not stand behind a woman's apron strings for protection.

He dressed in a fresh pair of starched jeans, straight from the cleaners back in Muenster, a plaid western shirt, and his most comfortable black boots. He had already picked up a western-cut leather jacket when Shooter whined.

"Fine friend I am. You need to be fed, and I need to stoke the fire before I leave so you don't freeze," Blake said.

Shooter wagged his tail and headed off toward the kitchen,

where his food bowl and water dish stood empty. Blake took care of both containers, then filled a third one with dry food. "That should hold you until I get home, and then I'll get out the treats."

The big yellow dog was too busy gulping down the food to even wag his tail.

* * *

Allie opened the door at the same time Blake raised his hand to knock and motioned him inside. "I have to get my coat and purse and I'm ready."

He took the dark brown suede jacket from her hands and held it for her. "You look absolutely beautiful tonight. Deke says that we should try out Cowboy Heaven. That sound good to you?"

"I love that place. They make the best cheeseburgers in the state, and the dance floor is great," she said. "And you look pretty sexy yourself, cowboy."

She leaned in for a kiss, expecting something that would knock her socks off, but all she got was a quick brush across her lips and then there was nothing but quietness. For a man who could talk the horns off an Angus bull when they hadn't been together in a couple of days, Blake was too quiet. He kept his eyes on the road, and his thumbs weren't even keeping time to the music.

Something wasn't right.

For the first time since she met him, she wasn't comfortable. Forget the old proverbial elephant in the room. There was an angry Angus bull standing between them that evening. What had she done wrong? No, she wasn't going there. She'd always figured she'd done something wrong with Riley and then did her best to fix it. She went over the past couple of days, and she hadn't done or said anything. She crossed her arms over her chest and looked out the side window. He could open up and talk, or it would be one long evening.

They went from Dry Creek through Elbert and up to Olney with neither of them saying anything except a few comments about the songs on the radio. Allie looked up and saw the Archer County sign, and then all chaos broke loose as blizzard-like conditions complete with high winds and near zero visibility hit them head-on.

The radio emitted one of those long bleeping noises, and then an announcer said that the bad weather had taken a turn and Highway 79 was now closed at the line between Archer and Young Counties. People were advised to only get out on the roads in case of emergencies.

"How far over that line do you think we are?" Blake asked.

"Five miles, maybe. Sign right there says it's twelve more to Archer City," Allie answered. "I can't even see the white lines on the road."

"Neither can I, but I think we might be the only vehicle out here. Is there a motel in Archer City?" he asked.

"A small one. Not fancy. Not a chain." She gripped the armrest so tight that her fingers ached.

"We don't need fancy. We have to find a place to hole up until this passes through and they clean off the roads."

The radio emitted another bleeping noise, and the newest flash was that the storm was heading straight for Throckmorton County. All schools had been closed, and again people were urged to stay inside.

"I hope there's a room at that motel," Blake said.

"I hope we make it there without bogging down in this stuff. I've never seen a storm like this before," she whispered. "I feel like I'm in an igloo."

Blake kept both hands on the steering wheel and his eyes straight ahead, even though the headlights created a kaleidoscope that was constantly moving and came close to blinding him.

"I've been in a hateful mood for two days," he said.

"Me, too. What's your problem?"

"I want to know if you're just using me to get Grady out of your life and off your back until Lizzy's wedding and then planning to end this relationship."

"No, I'm not using you, Blake. Why would you think that?"

"It's doubt creeping in because I'm falling in love with you." He eased up on the gas.

She turned around in the seat as far as she could without undoing the seat belt. "This isn't the time to tell me this."

"Why, because we might slide off in a ditch and die?" he asked.

"Exactly," she said.

He turned to face her, and his foot leaned too heavy on the gas. The truck slipped from one side of the road to the other before he got it under control and moving forward again at a trusty fifteen miles an hour.

She folded her arms over her chest and said breathlessly, "Let's wait to talk about this until we are stopped at the motel."

Blake glanced over at her. "I wanted you to know in case we do wind up in a ditch and freeze to death in each other's arms." He cleared his throat. "I've flat out fallen in love with you. I think it was love at first sight and I've been fighting it, but it's the way it is, and I want you to know."

For a few seconds, she wasn't sure that she would ever breathe again. Then she inhaled deeply and said, "Were you going to tell me before we got in this situation?"

One of his shoulders jacked up an inch or two. "I don't know, Allie. I only figured it out tonight, and I'm tired of fighting with myself. I know it's only been a few weeks, but my mama said that I'd know when the right woman came into my life. And I know, so I have to spit it out and say it."

"That's not so romantic for a man who's got the reputation you do," she said. "Look, that sign we just passed said it was only two more miles. We could walk that far."

"Not without frostbite. And my reputation is what scares me, Allie. What if you have second thoughts about someone like me?"

"I won't. I promise," she whispered.

She loved him, too, but she couldn't say the words. They were there, but they wouldn't come out of her mouth.

* * *

Ten minutes later, she pointed to a flashing VACANCY sign above a motel, and he eased off the road into a parking lot so deep with snow that his front fender pushed it out of the way like a plow. He brought the truck to a long, greasy, sliding stop in front of the motel and waded through the snow to the office, where the lady told him that they had three rooms left. One was a king-size, nonsmoking room. The other two were double queens. He opted for the king-size bed and asked if there was a pizza place that made deliveries in the bad weather.

"A lot of the town is without power, so we filled up

real quick. Those that do have electricity are takin' in their relatives, and all the businesses are shut down," she said as she ran a key card through the machine. "Here are your keys and, honey, right not far from your room is the ice machine and vending machines. Soda pop, juice, bottled water in one. Candy, chips, and those cute little energy bars in the other. That's the best I can do for you tonight."

"Does it take credit cards?" he asked.

She shook her head. "Only coins. Need change?"

He flipped a twenty-dollar bill onto the counter. "Turn it all into whatever I need."

She counted out fifteen single bills, then picked up a plastic cup with the motel logo on the side and filled the thing with five dollars in quarters. "That should do it."

He picked up the cup. "Thank you. Do you have complimentary toothbrushes and toothpaste? We were traveling to Wichita Falls when this thing hit us. We don't have anything but what we're wearing."

"Right here, and here's a customer packet with shaving equipment, deodorant, toothbrushes, and such. Holler right loud if you need anything else." She handed him two bubble packs, each containing a toothbrush and a tiny tube of toothpaste. "Oh, and we do doughnuts, bagels, and coffee for breakfast from six to nine in the morning if my husband can get out to the pastry shop to get them and if it's open."

Blake started toward the truck to open the door for Allie, but she pushed her way out of it, stepped out into knee-deep snow, and yelled above the howling wind, "Which way?"

He pointed and bent against the swirling cold chilling him to the bone. He found the room, only a couple of doors down from the office, and slipped the key card into the slot, hoping the whole time that the thing worked. He could have shouted when the little green light popped on and Allie hurried into the room.

It wasn't the worst room he'd ever rented, but it lacked the luxury of where he would have taken Allie if he'd had a choice. It was warm, had a television and a big comfortable-looking bed. The warmth and bed were more inviting than anything after hunching over that steering wheel for what seemed like hours.

"I'll take that trash can and go get supper," he said. "I'm going to fill it up so if you've got a preference, holler right now."

"Vending machine?" She removed her gloves and warmed her hands over the wall heater.

"That's right, darlin'. Big juicy hamburger will have to wait until another night. This date has changed course," he said.

"I don't care. Bring me some of all of it and I'll be happy. I'm so glad that we're safe in a room. Oh, I've got to call Mama. I didn't even tell her which way we were going," she said all in a rush.

"You call. I'll be back soon as I spend all my money." He grinned.

* * *

Katy answered on the third ring and started talking before Allie could say a single word. "Where are you? If you went north, then find a place and hole up until this horrible storm passes. I've never seen anything like this in our part of the world. It's so bad out there, I can't even see the edge of the porch from the window."

"I'm in Archer City, and we've gotten a motel room. It took forever to get this far, but I'm safe and warm. Blake has gone to buy out everything in the vending machine, so I'm not going to starve," she said.

"Stay put and..." The line went completely dead.

When Allie looked at her phone all she got was a no service signal. Evidently, the wind had played havoc with the towers between Archer City and Dry Creek. She laid the phone on the nightstand, removed her coat, and hung it in the closet. An extra blanket, tucked away inside a zippered bag, rested on a fold-up luggage rack. She removed it and tossed it on the bed. Then she kicked off her boots and wet socks and set them under the desk.

A shiver running from her backbone to her toes let her know that the legs of her jeans were every bit as wet as her socks. She undid her belt buckle and shimmied out of the jeans, hung them in the closet, and caught her reflection in the mirror across the room. White cotton bikini underpants when she knew she was going on a real date; she slapped her forehead with her palm.

"Allie, open the door. My hands are full, and I can't knock," Blake called out.

She did double time from heater to door and slung it open to find the abominable snowman on the other side. The wet snow had stuck to Blake's eyelashes, and his black cowboy hat had an inch lying on the brim. She grabbed his arm, pulled him inside, and slammed the door shut, but not before a gust of wind blasted her with a face full of cold white snow.

She took the trash can full of vending machine goodies from his arms and set it on the desk. "Get undressed. Hang everything in the closet. I'll put a towel on the floor to catch the drip. Then get under the covers, Blake. You have to be chilled to the bone. Even your jeans are soaked."

His teeth chattered as he reached inside the closet and brought out the rest of the hangers. "I've got a better idea. I'll get undressed in the bathroom and hang all my wet things in the shower, but I will take your advice and get under the covers. I don't think I've ever been this cold and I've ranched through cold winters my whole life. But I do like that outfit. Did you bring it special in your purse in case we had to stay in a motel tonight? This is some first date, Allie."

"I bet we don't ever forget it." She smiled.

The black hat came off first, and he hung it on the showerhead. Allie fought the urge to hum the stripper song as he removed one article of clothing at a time. When everything was off, he threw back the covers on the bed and crawled in between them, shivering.

"How'd you get so wet through?" Allie asked.

"It's slippery out there," he answered, "and the soles of my boots don't have the traction that my old work ones do. When I was going to the vending machine, I fell twice."

"Are you okay?" Dammit! What if he'd cracked his head on something and died out there in the snow and she'd been too stubborn to tell him that she was in love with him? He would have died without knowing, and she would have never forgiven herself.

"Nothing hurt that you cuddled up next to me in this big bed wouldn't heal." One hand came out from under the covers to pat the place beside him. "I need body heat."

In seconds the rest of her clothing was tossed toward the desk and she was shivering in his arms. "You could have told me the sheets had been stored in the freezer."

"My love will warm things up real fast," he said.

She looked up into his green eyes. "About that? Are you sure that what you said wasn't...?"

He put a finger over her lips. "You know my reputation, Allie. You know what kind of cowboy I've been. But what you don't know is that I've never, ever meant anything more than I do now."

"But you were ticked at me," she said.

"I was," he said. "But it was male pride getting in the way and doubts that I could ever deserve a woman like you."

"And now?" She pressed even closer to him.

He buried his face in her hair. "Now I feel free. I'm happy. I can't imagine life without you in it. I was terrified I'd wreck the truck and hurt you."

He held her close, and she reveled in his warmth. Within moments, she could hear his breathing, soft and even.

"Blake?" she whispered.

"Sorry, darlin'," he mumbled. "Seems all that adrenaline plumb wore me out. Maybe we could take a quick nap?"

"Sounds like a good plan to me," she said. But she hardly had the words out before his eyes fluttered shut.

The hotel phone ringing startled Allie out of her sleep. For a moment, she forgot where she was, and then she felt Blake's naked body wrapped around her and remembered the whole evening. She opened one eye and checked the clock. 11:11. That meant she could make a wish and it would come true, a superstition, but she and her sisters had believed it since they were kids.

She brought one hand out and reached for the remote phone receiver. "Yes?"

"This is the front desk. I got a call from a feller named Deke saying to tell Blake Dawson that he has Shooter at his house.

Cell phone towers are down all around us, so he couldn't get through to you that way."

"Thank you," Allie said.

"Weatherman says that it's supposed to let up by midnight, but I wouldn't bank on the roads being cleared tomorrow. Y'all want me to pencil you in for another night?"

"Yes, please," Allie said.

"Will do. If you need anything, I'm right here all night."

"What was that all about?" Blake asked.

"Deke has Shooter at his place. Evidently, he found out from Mama that we're in the motel in Archer City and got the number to call here so you wouldn't be worried," she answered.

"Hungry?" he asked.

"Me or Shooter?" she asked.

"You." He grinned.

"Yes, but not for food. Blake, I love you, too," she said. The words came out so slick that she didn't realize she'd said them until his lips were on hers.

CHAPTER TWENTY-SIX

Blake could hardly believe it was already February. Allie had said that she loved him and things had been good since those three wonderful days in the motel when they'd lived on vending machine food, takeout pizza, and lots of sex. Two weeks had passed since then, and their relationship had grown deeper with the passing of each day. The next step was to pop the question and open a pretty red velvet box to reveal a ring, wasn't it?

All those sparkling diamonds displayed in a jewelry store window had always made Blake shield his eyes and hurry across the street. But now a ring was all he could think about. He wanted to spend the rest of his life with her, but was he rushing things? Buying the ring didn't mean he had to give it to her before summer. Six months seemed like the appropriate time to wait between the "I love you" and the "Will you marry me?" He would have months to plan the perfect setting and the ring would be ready for that magical moment.

The plan had to be right because thinking the words

didn't give him hives. Only the online jewelry stores had so much to offer that he couldn't choose, and then he worried that he might select something similar to her first wedding rings. He worried with it all afternoon and finally decided the only thing to do was ask Lizzy and hope she didn't pull out the gun from under the counter and start shooting.

"Hey, gorgeous!" he yelled down the hall toward Allie as he and Shooter came through the kitchen door. "I'm going to Lizzy's store. You need me to pick up anything?"

Allie's head bobbed down from an exposed rafter in the living room ceiling. "Not a thing. Lizzy is lonely with Mitch away. Want to ask her to join us for supper at Nadine's tonight?"

"I'll ask her. See you later. Be careful up there." He blew her a kiss.

Luck was with him. No one was in the store when he arrived that chilly February afternoon.

Lizzy looked up from the counter and smiled. "Fence posts?"

"Wedding rings," he said.

"I don't sell those things."

"Lizzy, I love Allie and I want to spend my life with her."

"Don't tell me. Tell her."

"I need rings, and I need help before I do that."

Lizzy smiled. "I can't believe I'm saying this, but I believe you and I'm happy for you both. Now, what can I do?"

* * *

Allie sat between Blake and Deke in the back pew at the church on Sunday morning. One arm around her shoulders pulled her close enough to hear the steady rhythm of his heartbeat. His fingers interlaced with hers shot delicious little tingles throughout her body. This was the man she'd fallen in love with, part dependable and the other part pure sexy pleasure.

The preacher took the podium, opened his Bible, and looked out over the congregation.

Blake squeezed her hand. "Bet he speaks from that love chapter in Corinthians. Valentine's Day is a week from today."

"As all you folks know, Valentine's Day is next Sunday," the preacher said.

"Glad I didn't make that bet," Allie whispered.

"And the ladies tell me that we're having a potluck in the fellowship hall immediately after church that day. Everyone is invited, and I'm sure there will be plenty of food. Nadine has said she's not opening the café that day, so y'all best plan on having dinner here with us." He chuckled. "And now if you will open your Bibles to the love chapter in Corinthians and follow along with me while I talk to you about what all love can do in your lives, both in relationships and friendships…"

"Two for two." Blake kissed her on the earlobe and the tingles turned into hot little sparks.

Allie wished they were anywhere but church. She blushed and Blake chuckled.

"Thinking something that will bring down lightning?" Blake asked.

She brought his ear close to her mouth. "More like it would rain brimstone down through the roof."

The preacher finished his sermon by saying something

about love and then said, "Don't forget the social potluck next Sunday, and now I'm going to ask Blake Dawson to end our service with the benediction."

Everyone stood, and Blake, bless his cowboy heart, said a two-minute prayer without missing a beat.

"That was downright mean," he said as soon as everyone else echoed his amen at the end of the prayer. "I bet he saw us whispering."

"I'm just glad he didn't ask me to do it," Allie said.

* * *

Blake was so nervous that he could hardly be still during Sunday dinner at Nadine's after church. It had more to do with the ring box in his pocket than the four women sitting around the table with him. Having it in his pocket made him want to put it on her finger. He wondered how in the world he'd ever wait six months.

"So, one more week and Mitch is coming home, right?" Blake asked Lizzy.

She nodded. "The day after Valentine's Day, less than a month from our wedding day. The church is planning a wedding shower the week after he gets home."

"And where are you going to live?" Blake asked.

"He rents an apartment in Wichita Falls, not far from the church where he hopes to fill the preacher's shoes in the summer when he retires. Right now he helps out when the preacher needs to be gone or wants a week off," she answered.

Blake nodded, his mind on the ring. "And you'll commute to work?"

"It's a distance, but..." She shrugged.

"If the weather is bad, she can always stay with us," Katy said.

"That's a silly notion if you ask me, which nobody did," Irene piped up. "They could live halfway between the two places or he could commute, but oh, no, not Mitch. He's got to be in control."

"Granny!" Lizzy exclaimed.

Allie raised an eyebrow in Blake's direction. "Looks like you stirred up a hornet's nest."

"I'll fix it," he whispered, and then said, "Miz Irene, can you believe that it's such a beautiful day when two weeks ago the whole area was covered in a foot of snow?"

"It's Texas. If you don't like the weather, stick around. It will change. And the only thing that's dependable in this place is that in the summer it's going to be hotter'n anything you can imagine. I'm hungry. Is Nadine having to wring that turkey's neck and pick the feathers before she can make my turkey and dressin' dinner plate?" she answered.

Katy laughed. "At least it won't be that frozen crap that you hate, Mama. I think the waitress is bringing our dinner right now."

"Well, I hope so. I'd like to live to see my sixtieth birthday."

"Granny, you will be seventy-one on your birthday," Lizzy said.

Mary Jo set their plates in front of them. "Be careful. The plates are hot."

"I'm old, not stupid," Irene said.

"And don't you look beautiful today." Mary Jo stopped to give her a hug.

"Granny, you were rude," Lizzy said.

"For that smartass remark and since you are bound and

determined to marry that worthless wannabe preacher, you can say grace before we eat this good food."

Lizzy dropped her chin and said softly, "Father, thank you for this food. Forgive Granny for her dirty language and the rest of us for our sins. Amen."

"That wasn't a prayer. God didn't even hear that short two sentences," Irene fussed.

"It's enough, Mama. Eat your dinner," Katy said.

Irene picked up her fork. "Okay, but if I die tonight and Saint Peter won't let me in the pearly gates because I ate unblessed food, then I'm going to tell him it's y'all's fault."

Blake chuckled. "I think I'm fallin' in love with her."

Irene's head popped up. "Who's fallin' in love with who?"

"No one, Granny. I hear Nadine made cherry pies and she's got ice cream and chocolate syrup," Allie said.

"I said that I was falling in love with you," Blake said.

"I'm old. You're not in love with me. You are in love with Allie."

Blake nodded. "You are right. I have fallen in love with Allie. I'm in love with this woman, and I don't care who all knows it."

Irene clapped her hands. Allie blushed.

"Hey, if you can declare that I'm your boyfriend right here in the middle of this café, I can tell the whole world I'm in love with you in the same place." Blake leaned to his left, tipped her chin up with his fist, and kissed her right there in public.

"Well, would you look at that, Katy? I think he means it." Irene giggled.

"I was going to wait for a private moment, but this seems

like a perfect place and time." He pushed back his chair and dropped down on one knee. "Allie Logan, I love you. Plain and simple, and I can't imagine life without you. Will you marry me?"

He flipped open a red velvet ring box to reveal a brown diamond solitaire ring surrounded by more than a dozen sparkling clear diamonds. "I chose this because it's the color of your eyes."

"Yes!" she said without hesitation.

He slipped the ring onto her finger, picked her up out of the chair, and swung her around the floor several times before his lips settled on hers. Most of the folks in the café clapped. The ones who didn't were already talking on their phones.

* * *

Later that afternoon, Allie held the ring up to catch the sunlight pouring into the bedroom. "I can't believe you proposed right there in public."

Blake wrapped his hand around hers and brought the ring to her face. "That brown diamond is the same color as your eyes. Darlin', it was either propose or explode. I knew I wouldn't be able to swallow that good food until I asked you to marry me."

"We need to talk," she said.

"Oh, no!" He fell back on the pillows. "I hate it when you say that."

"Well, we do."

"Please don't tell me you aren't going to marry me." He groaned.

"Oh, honey, I'm going to marry you, but I'm fixin' to give you a way out if you don't want to be burdened with what I'm about to say." She swallowed twice and started three times, but the words wouldn't come out. "Blake, this is tough."

Blake propped up on an elbow. "Just spit it out."

"Riley and I had wanted children, but it never happened, and Riley said it was my fault," she said slowly.

"And what has that got to do with us?" he asked.

She shrugged. "I'm three days late, and we haven't even talked about kids because I told you I couldn't have any. But I've never been late, and now I'm thinkin' maybe Riley lied to me about going to the doctor to get tested." She stopped to catch her breath.

Blake pulled her into his arms and kissed the top of her head. "I want kids, but I want you more. If you are pregnant, then I hope it's twins, so we'll get a jump on a house full. If you aren't and you really can't have them, then someday in the future we might discuss adoption if you want them."

She pushed back and let the tears loose to stream down her cheeks. "I love you with my whole heart, and what you just said makes me say yes to your proposal all over again. Let's get married this week."

"Sounds great to me, but don't take the test until afterward. I don't ever want you to feel like I married you because I had to. I'm marrying you because I love you, Allie." He kissed away her tears.

"You are trying to make a ranch here. A wife wasn't in your four-year plan, and I know a baby wasn't."

"We'll take them when we get them, and if we never get

them, then we have each other. Did you have your mind set on a big wedding?"

"Nope!" she said loudly. "Let's go get a license at the courthouse before Friday, get married on Sunday morning after church, and the potluck can be our reception. I want to be a wife, not a fiancée."

He laid a hand on her flat stomach. "I love you, Allie."

"I love you, too, Blake," she said.

CHAPTER TWENTY-SEVEN

Y ou cannot wear that." Lizzy was absolutely aghast that Sunday morning. "You are getting married, not going to stand on the street corner to solicit business."

"It's Valentine's Day. I like red, and Blake is wearing a red tie so this is it. Now, let's go to church and have a wedding afterward, and then we can eat all that lovely food. And, Lizzy, thank you one more time for helping me move all my things over to the Lucky Penny. I can't believe I'll be waking up tomorrow in my new home."

Lizzy laid a hand on her shoulder. "Or that it's this close to Mama and Granny. I envy you, sister."

Allie turned around and hugged Lizzy tightly. "I'm not going to think about you having to live all the way up there in the city. I'll miss you so much."

"Don't talk about it or we'll both cry and mess up our makeup. I've got to stand up beside you at the wedding, and I don't need to have black streaks down my face. Who is Blake's best man? Deke?"

Allie took a step back. "No, it's his brother, Toby."

"Well, you will have a few months before he moves in to enjoy the honeymoon." Lizzy sniffed. "At least Mitch and I won't have another person living with us."

"But Grady will be there every day, I betcha. And with Deke in and out every day, we're already used to an extra person around," Allie told her.

* * *

Allie's hands started to sweat when the preacher took the podium. He laid his Bible down but didn't open it and smiled out at the congregation. "Today we aren't going to have a service, but we are going to have a wedding. In my opinion, there isn't a better way to celebrate Valentine's Day than to unite two people who are very much in love in the bonds of holy matrimony."

"I thought he was going to preach first," Blake said.

"So did I." Allie nodded.

The preacher's wife hit a few keys on the piano, and Lizzy stood up in her cute little off-white lace dress. She pulled a small bouquet of tiny little white flowers mixed with half a dozen red roses from a small cooler at her feet. The white ones reminded her of that tiny little snow flower that Blake had brought her that day, and the roses—they reminded her of the roses that grew on the barbed-wire fence between the Lucky Penny and Audrey's Place in the summertime.

Folks looked around to see where Mitch was, and from the expressions on their faces, Allie could tell that they thought Lizzy was the bride. But then Lizzy laid the bouquet on the altar and took her place on the stage.

Blake and Toby rose to their feet at the same time. Some folks might say they walked up the aisle, but from where Allie sat, there was no doubt that it was a Texas cowboy strut or swagger. It definitely covered much more than a walk. She waited until they made it to the front to start down the aisle.

Blake caught her eye, and everything else disappeared. She didn't hear the whispers about her tight red dress or the gasps, or even thumbs working frantically as some of them typed text messages. All she saw was the man she loved, the wild cowboy she'd been waiting on her whole life. She picked up the bouquet and joined him on the stage.

"You are beyond beautiful today. Words could never describe what a stunning bride you are," he whispered.

"I love you," she said, loud enough for everyone in the church to hear.

"Dearly beloved, we are gathered here today to unite Alora Raine Logan and Blake Alan Dawson in holy matrimony..." the preacher said.

"I just realized what your initials are," Allie whispered. "I really did fall for a bad boy."

"And I fell for an angel." He grinned.

She handed Lizzy her flowers and held both of Blake's hands in hers. Six weeks ago, she hadn't even known this man, and now she was standing right there before her friends and family, saying that she would love, honor, and cherish him until death parted them. Not one doubt filled her heart when she said aloud, "I do!"

The ceremony ended with a prayer, and the preacher said, "You may now kiss your bride, Blake."

She wasn't expecting him to bend her backward in a true

Hollywood kiss and then sweep her feet off the floor and swing her around the stage twice before he set her down and kissed her again.

But he did, and the whole congregation applauded.

"I am the happiest man right now on this whole planet," he said.

"And now the bride and groom and these two young people who have stood with them to witness their marriage vows are going on to the fellowship hall. Give them five minutes to catch their breath, then we'll join them," the preacher said.

Lizzy handed Allie the bouquet.

Allie turned around to loop her arm in Blake's, but he shook his head. "Not that way, darlin'. We are doing this our way."

He scooped her up in his arms and carried her out of the sanctuary and down the short hall to the place where the potluck was set up.

"Would you look at this?" He grinned.

Allie was stunned. Red roses decorated tables covered with white cloths. A gorgeous three-tiered cake decorated with roses and snow flowers sat on a round table with a lovely silver punch bowl.

"Mama, Nadine, Mary Jo, and Sharlene got together yesterday and did all this," Lizzy said.

"It's gorgeous," Allie said.

"I guess I'd best tell you that the church was packed this morning because my family brought campers and RVs and they set up last night on the Lucky Penny," Blake said. "Surprise! You get to meet them all in about two minutes."

Allie was sure she'd faint dead away right then, but she stiffened her legs and made her knees stop knocking together. "Bring 'em on. I tamed the wildest cowboy in Texas. I'm not afraid of anything."

"That's my girl," Blake said.

* * *

An hour later, when everyone had gone through the buffet line (some more than once) and it was almost time to cut the cake, Allie looked around for Lizzy and couldn't find her. There hadn't been a formal table for the wedding party so she figured Lizzy had opted to sit elsewhere, but something wasn't right. Allie could feel it deep in her bones.

"I'm going to make a trip to the ladies' room, darlin'. I'll be back soon, and then we'll cut the cake so folks can have a piece of it," she whispered.

"Don't take that test without me standing right beside you," he said.

She kissed him on the cheek. "Wouldn't dream of it."

She found Lizzy curled up around a toilet in the handi-capped stall in the bathroom. Her eyes were swollen, and she'd cried so hard that she had the hiccups. She threw her arms around Allie's knees and sobbed.

"What happened? Did Mitch die?"

"No, worse," Lizzy said. "But I didn't want to ruin your wedding day."

Allie sat down on the floor and held her sister tightly. "How much worse?"

"He's not going to marry me, Allie. The preacher's daughter went with them on the mission, and he says he's found his soul mate. That after praying"—Lizzy gagged, but nothing came up—"about it, both of them praying about it, they realize God meant them to be together and for them to preach at the little church in Mexico, so they aren't coming back to Texas. They're going to be missionaries."

Allie hugged Lizzy even tighter. "Oh, Lizzy, I'm so sorry. That was cruel of him to do this with a phone call."

Lizzy nodded. "He said I was never cut out to be a preacher's wife anyway. What am I going to do?"

"Give me your engagement ring," Allie said.

Lizzy pointed at the toilet. "I flushed it."

"That's even better. You are going to get up, wash your face, and use the makeup kit in my purse to fix things as best you can. Then we're going back into the church, and we're going to cut my wedding cake. You aren't going to say a word, but when people start to notice that your ring is gone, you are going to say that you broke it off with him because you found out he had another woman on the line. Do you understand me?" Allie said sternly.

Lizzy nodded. "It's almost the truth, and it will save all that sickening sweet pity, won't it?"

Allie pulled Lizzy up and marched her to the sink. "Work some magic in five minutes. The gossip fiends will come looking for me if I'm not back by then."

Lizzy washed her face with a brown paper towel and then applied makeup. When she and Allie walked out of the bathroom, they both wore smiles. Maybe Lizzy's didn't reach her eyes, but no one would notice.

"And here is our bride and her lovely sister," the preacher said loudly when they reached the fellowship hall. "Let's cut into that cake and see if it's as good as it looks."

Allie reached for Blake's hand, and he raised an eyebrow.

"Later, darlin'. More than one prayer got answered today." She smiled up at him as they crossed the floor to the cake table.

"You took the test?"

"Not yet. It's waiting at home, and I'll explain the rest later."

"And after the cake cutting," Katy announced, "Allie and Blake will have their first dance as a married couple."

Allie picked up the long knife with a lovely cut-glass handle. "The mamas went all out, didn't they?"

"Mamas are like that." Blake kissed her again, and the whole crowd applauded. "Don't worry, I chose the song."

"You knew?" Allie asked.

"Not until late last night. Let's get this cake cut and dance so we can go home, Mrs. Dawson."

When the first strands of music started, Allie's eyes widened out as big as saucers. "Is that what I think it is?"

"Not the conventional wedding music, but it's our music, and the words remind me of..." Blake said.

Allie put her fingers over his lips and blushed. Blake twirled her out on the area cleared out for a dance floor and danced with her just like they'd done at Frankie's place while Etta James sang "Something's Got a Hold on Me."

"And now for my choice." Allie put her arms around Blake's neck and swayed with him to "I Cross My Heart" by George Strait. "And yes, I knew last night, too. Lizzy told me."

She glanced over at her sister sitting in a folding chair, a smile plastered on her face even though it didn't reach her eyes. That's when Toby stood up, shook the legs of his jeans down over his boot tops, and held his hand out to Lizzy.

Allie could have kissed her new brother-in-law as he drew Lizzy into his arms. Lizzy frantically looked across the room to her sister.

Allie nodded and winked. She and her sister might fight. They would definitely argue, but as sisters, they still had the ability to comfort and convey messages with a glance.

Lizzy relaxed in Toby's arms and followed his expert steps around the room as the rest of the floor filled up with folks dancing to the next song on George Strait's CD, "I Swear."

"I do swear to love you with every beat of my heart until death parts us just like George is singing," Blake whispered.

Allie rolled up on her toes and kissed him and hoped that someday her sister found a man just like Blake Dawson. One who, like George Strait sang about, would love her with every beat of his heart.

* * *

It was midafternoon when Blake picked up Allie for the second time that day and carried her across the threshold into the ranch house. He didn't stop at the bedroom but took her straight to the bathroom before he set her down. "I love you, Allie Dawson, but I can't wait any longer."

She followed the directions on the paper and laid the stick on a paper towel on the counter. With a hand on either side of her face, Blake looked deeply into her eyes. "Neither of us will look until the time is up."

The seconds dragged, but finally she covered his hands with hers. "Okay, here goes. Oh, Blake, it's positive. Three weeks. Must have happened that first time."

She'd wondered all week how she'd feel if she was really

pregnant or how he'd feel. And now the answer was there. She was going to be a mother. She was carrying Blake's child. And she was filled with an indescribable mixture of awe and happiness. And his face registered absolute pride and joy.

"Lord, help us if this baby gets your wild cowboy ways and my temper," she whispered.

"Now, wouldn't that set Dry Creek on its ear." He chuckled. "Darlin', you have given me the best wedding gift a man could ask for."

BUTTERCUP FARMS

As horse trainer Lucas Ryan helps a special little boy, he finds his heart opening to all kinds of new opportunities.

CHAPTER ONE

Lucas Ryan's mama, Pearl, had a plaque on the wall that read, *Home is where the heart is.* He wasn't sure if that was true where he was concerned. He'd been roaming around the world for the better part of twenty years now, and if he had a motto, it would probably be *Home is where you hang your hat.*

Lucas had always been more comfortable with horses than with people—even with his two brothers, Jesse and Cody— so he had mixed feelings about moving back to Honey Grove, Texas. Visiting the family was great, but after a few days, the wanderlust started calling his name again. Sometimes he stopped by the ranch in between his gigs as a trainer for cutting horses, and even though he hung his hat on the rack beside the back door, it still didn't seem like home.

He had planned to move back to help his brothers on the family property, the huge Sunflower Ranch, back in the summer, but then a six-month job that paid so well he couldn't turn it down had come up. Now he had an offer to go to Ireland—one of the places on his bucket list—to work for a year. As he hooked up the horse trailer to the back of his truck, he wondered if he really wanted to put a few more dollars in his already fat bank account or if it was an excuse not to move back to Honey Grove. For a long time, he had told himself that he wanted to learn more about training horses before he went home. There was always some new technique to pick up. Lately, though, he felt a yearning for more than bachelorhood whenever he spent time around his two older brothers and their wives.

The time had finally come when he had to either sign on the dotted line for the Ireland job or else make good on his promise to go home. As luck would have it, his brother Jesse had called him a couple of days ago and told him how much the family was looking forward to having him on the ranch during the holiday season.

"We can sure use some help around here," Jesse had said. "With the holidays coming on, a lot of the hired hands are wanting to be with their families, and it's stretching us out pretty thin. I don't want Dad to think he needs to go out in the cold in his condition."

"I'll be there soon as I can," Lucas had promised, and a Ryan didn't go back on his word even if his hand itched to sign a contract.

Lucas hunched his broad shoulders against the howling wind and held on to his hat. A strand of light brown hair fell across his forehead. He removed his hat, combed his hair back with his fingertips, and resettled the old worn black hat that had been with him for more than a decade more comfortably on his head.

"Am I doing the right thing?" he asked himself as he headed back to the barn to get his horses. On one hand, he couldn't wait to get to Sunflower Ranch to have some of his mama Pearl's cooking, visit with his father, Sonny, and see the rest of the family. Then there was the other side, which had been fussing at him about a trip to Ireland, a place he'd always wanted to see.

In his mind, he knew that commitment to family would put him on the ranch forever, and, to a drifting cowboy, that was more than a little scary. Lucas wasn't sure that he was—or ever would be—ready to put down roots. According to the rancher in Ireland, the job was his anytime he wanted it, so even though he was going home, he could keep that on the back burner.

His father had MS, but he was managing it, and Jesse and Cody were there to take care of the ranch, so when it came right down to the brass tacks of the issue, Lucas wouldn't really be needed at the ranch when the holidays were over. Addy, Jesse's wife, was a nurse, and she took good care of his father. Cody's wife was a veterinarian, and both she and Addy were good ranch hands. They were all getting along fine without him living on the place.

Maybe it was the crow's-feet around his eyes that reminded him he wasn't getting any younger and made him think—even for a minute—that he was ready to settle down. Or it could be the fact that he had begun to get pretty danged homesick for the first time in all the years he'd been gone.

I want to be there for Dad, but I feel like a fifth wheel when I'm around Jesse and his family, and Cody and his new wife, Stevie, he thought. *I'm not sure I'm ready to settle down to a family or even if I want one, but the yearning is there.*

If you are arguing with yourself, you better be careful. His father's voice popped into his head when he entered the barn and headed back to the stalls where Winnie and Buttercup were waiting.

"I don't know if I'm ready for this or not, but I can't disappoint the folks another time. Besides, Jesse and Cody shouldn't have to bear the entire burden of taking care of the ranch. It wouldn't be fair for me to inherit the same portion as they do if I don't help," he told Winnie, his Appaloosa horse, as he tossed a bright blue blanket over the animal and fastened the straps under her belly. "It's a little warmer than this in north Texas, and when we get to the Sunflower Ranch you will have a really nice barn to stay in when the weather is bad and a big pasture to run when the sun is shining."

When he led Winnie out of the barn, he saw the foreman of the Pine Valley Ranch leaning against his truck's back fender. Lucas hated goodbyes. He thought he had taken care of all that the night before when he and his bunkhouse buddies had shared a few drinks and promised to stay in touch.

"Any way I could talk you into sticking around?" Eddie asked. "I'll double your salary if you'll sign on for another six months."

"I appreciate the offer, but my folks are expecting me to be in Texas by suppertime." Lucas busied himself getting Winnie into her side of the double trailer and making sure she was comfortable before he closed the door.

"Well, son"—Eddie straightened up and stuck out his hand—"you've got a job here any time you want or need one. We'll miss you."

"Thank you. I'll keep that in mind." Lucas shook with him and appreciated the fact that the man just turned and disappeared into the darkness without trying to talk him into staying for breakfast.

He went back into the barn and flipped a red blanket over Buttercup's back. He had chosen the two Appaloosa horses to train as therapy horses a few years back because they were so good with children. After he bought them, he'd accepted only jobs that he could drive to and bring his horses with him. But the Irishman had offered to pay for his horses to be transported across the Atlantic and give them free room and board on his ranch—that made turning the job down even tougher.

"If all goes well, we'll be in Honey Grove by suppertime," he said as he fastened the blanket and led Buttercup out of the barn. "This could be the last time you have to get into this trailer. Hopefully, by springtime there will be some little kids that will come around to get acquainted with you."

He took time to close the barn door, and then he and Buttercup walked out across the crunchy, frozen grass together. When she was tucked into her side of the trailer, he took out his phone and checked off the list that he kept for the days when he left a job. Saddles were in the storage room at the front of the silver trailer. His personal belongings were in duffel bags in the back seat of the club cab truck—not much accumulation for a thirty-eight-year-old cowboy.

The wind whistled through the cab of the truck when he opened the door. He quickly slid under the steering wheel, slammed the door shut, fastened his seat belt, and started the engine.

"Just another place to leave behind," he whispered around the lump in his throat. Lord have mercy, he hated making friends and having to say goodbye. He removed his cowboy hat, laid it over on the passenger seat, and smiled.

"Right fittin'," he whispered, "a pickup truck has been my home for almost two decades, and other than dozens of bunk-houses, my cowboy hat has ridden beside me every mile. It's where I've hung my hat, so I probably should call it home."

He adjusted the rearview mirror and stared at his reflection for a moment. The eyes were the same light brown they had been almost twenty years ago when he had left Honey Grove to go to Wyoming to work on a horse ranch. His hair—blond or brown, depending on who was judging—was a little longer than it had been back then, but he hadn't been in the military like his oldest brother, Jesse. Ranchers didn't care if their hired hands had a crop of hair that hung down their backs, if they were bald, or even if they had a mixture of both. Lucas smiled at his reflection when he thought about Buster, one of the guys in the last bunkhouse, who had only a rim of gray hair that was so long that his braid reached halfway down his back. He glanced down at the dashboard—6:30 a.m., December 10— not quite two weeks until Christmas.

"Enough procrastinating," he told his reflection. "You are going home whether it's where your heart is or not. Your traveling days are over, and you'll be hanging your hat in the old bunkhouse, where you will be living alone."

By the time he reached Erin, Tennessee, a beautiful sunrise filled his side window. Of all the things he missed about Honey Grove, Texas, the sunsets were what he missed the most. He and his dad had spent many evenings out behind the barn— sometimes not saying a word—and enjoyed the beauty of the land as the sun made its nightly descent out there beyond the scrub oak and mesquite trees.

"I'm hoping that we can have more days like that while he's still able to enjoy them," he said as he hooked up his phone to Bluetooth and listened to his playlist—a combination of old country songs that he'd grown up hearing and the newer ones that he liked.

When he reached Interstate 40 and made a turn toward

Memphis, "Sand in My Boots" was playing, and Lucas nodded in agreement with the lyrics when they mentioned that all the vocalist was taking home was sand in his boots.

"I may not have been to the beach, but all I'm taking home is worn-down-at-the-heel boots and a nervous stomach at the idea of settling down," he muttered.

His hat didn't have anything to say about that, so he settled in for the long nine-hour trip. Before he had gone very far, a few snowflakes began to swirl around and shoot up past his windshield—nothing to be worried about. They brought back memories of the times when they'd gotten snow in Honey Grove. Hard winters meant freezing weather and ice but seldom snow.

He visualized his dad standing at the kitchen window and saying, "Boys, we've got snow. It's just a flake to the acre, but it's sure enough snow."

Lucas had seen real snow in his travels since those days. He'd seen snow that was belly deep on horses in Wyoming. On the flip side, he had ridden through sandstorms in Arizona, and he had spent time on every continent in the world. Still, nothing compared to a Texas sunrise or sunset—winter or summer—in any of those places.

Maybe the reason for that is because you shared so many with your dad. His mother's voice whispered so softly in his ear that he whipped around to see if she was sitting behind him.

"Maybe so, Mama," he said.

* * *

On some days, Vada Winters swore she would never forgive her ex-husband, Travis, for leaving her and their then three-year-old son, Theron. Other days, she was glad he was gone. If Travis couldn't deal with Theron's special needs and super intelligence, they were better off without him. But, boy, it was exhausting some days to handle everything on her own.

Since their divorce seven years ago, her ex had moved to West Virginia, remarried, and started a new family. He still paid child support, but he hadn't come around to see Theron or even called to talk to him in all those years.

Of course, when Theron was having a bad day, Vada wished that she, too, could run away from all the stress and anguish of not knowing how to help her son better fit into the world.

She took Theron's bowl of dry cereal to him—no milk, no sugar, no fruit—just Cheerios in a bowl with a bottle of orange juice on the side. She went into his bedroom, and the blinds were closed. Only the light from his computer screen made it possible to see anything at all. His back was ramrod straight, and his eyes never left the screen. He wore sweatpants and a hoodie with the hood pulled up. Vada glanced down at his screen, and it looked like his normal classwork, but today was Saturday.

"Good morning, son," she said cheerfully.

"Mornin'," he answered. "I'm researching ways to help kids like me who are really smart."

"That's good. Let me know if I can help." She set his food down on the edge of his desk and left, easing the door shut behind her. The coffeepot had just gurgled out its last drops when she made it to the kitchen. She poured a mugful and sipped on it while she made herself a scrambled egg sandwich. She had just sat down at the table when someone knocked on the door, and a familiar voice yelled.

"Hey, Vada, it's cold out here," Stevie called out. "Can a wayfaring stranger find a warm fire?"

Vada hurried to open the back door. "Come in, girl. I'm so glad to have company this morning. Coffee is ready. Can I make you an egg sandwich?"

"I brought pastries from the doughnut place." Stevie held up a paper bag and crossed the room to the table. She removed her heavy coat, hung it on the back of a chair, and poured herself a cup of coffee. Taller than Vada by several inches, Stevie had red hair and bright green eyes and was married to Cody, the middle son in the Ryan family.

Vada opened the bag and put the pastries on a plate. "Thank you for these. You must've read my mind. I wanted a doughnut for breakfast, but I was too lazy to get dressed and drive up to Main Street to get one. What are you doing out this early on a Saturday morning?"

Stevie carried her coffee to the table and took a seat across from Vada. She blew on the hot liquid and then pushed a strand of curly red hair behind her ear. "Vet duty. Joe Don Clement's old mare needed help to birth her colt. Little filly was healthy, and the mama took to her once it was on the ground."

Vada sat down, ignored her sandwich, and picked up a doughnut with maple icing. "Sounds like you had a good start to the day."

She and Stevie had gone to school together right there in Honey Grove and graduated almost twenty years ago. Vada had married Travis Winters, her high school sweetheart, right after they had finished college. Stevie had gone to a different university, and their paths hadn't crossed again until this last year.

Aren't you glad that she came back to Honey Grove, and y'all became good friends when you really needed someone? Vada's grandmother's voice popped into her head.

"Yes," she whispered.

Stevie had dunked a maple glazed doughnut into her hot coffee and taken a bite. "I'm sorry. Did you say something to me?"

"No, I was talking to my grandmother," Vada answered. "She was such a big part of my life until she passed away last year that I can still hear her voice sometimes."

"I understand," Stevie said with a nod. "My mother pops into my head all the time. I'm grateful for those times."

"Me, too." Vada bit into her doughnut and sighed. "This is still warm."

"Yep, I brought it straight from the bakery to here," Stevie said between bites. "There's also a couple of bear claws and doughnuts with sprinkles for Theron."

"I'll offer them to him and hope he will eat one. He's on a Cheerios kick right now. Breakfast and supper. Dinner is a grilled cheese sandwich and a cup of hot chocolate. No vegetables and no fruit."

"Is he still diving into his online courses like a hungry coyote?" Stevie asked.

"Yes, and as soon as he finishes one, he's ready for me to pay for another one. Right now he is conquering online chess in addition to his studies, but it's been weeks since he's gone outside. Sometimes he *will* come out of his room for dinner, but he hasn't now for several days," Vada said. "I'm at my wit's end, Stevie. Thank God I've got a job I can do from home."

"That's one of the reasons I came by today," Stevie said between bites. "You remember Lucas? He's Jesse and Cody's younger brother, and he graduated from high school a year behind us. He's been training cutting horses since he left Honey Grove, but a few years ago he got into horse therapy for kids. He was working on a ranch, and the foreman's son was super intelligent like Theron, but his social skills weren't the best. The foreman was paying for the boy to get therapy with horses, and Lucas got into it. He's taken a few online psychology classes since then and is ready to put in his own business when he gets back to Texas."

"Sure, I remember him. A quiet kid who always seemed to be in the shadows of his older brothers," Vada answered. "What's he got to do with anything?"

"He's on his way back here to stay," Stevie told her. "He left Tennessee this morning and is coming back to Honey Grove with two horses that he's trained as therapy animals. He'll be working on the ranch with his brothers, but he wants to build up a practice to help kids like Theron."

"With horses?" Vada could hear the disbelief in her own ears and caught just a brief glimpse of a motion in her peripheral vision. When she glanced that way, there was nothing there, so she chalked it up to the sunshine coming through the windows and making patterns on the wall.

"It's not a new thing," Stevie said. "I understand that folks have been using animals to bring children with all kinds of disabilities out of their shells for a while. I thought maybe you might bring Theron out to the ranch on Monday morning to see what Lucas can do."

"Honey, I would try anything at this point, up to and including standing on my head in hot ashes, but what makes you think a horse can help when every therapist I could take him to, or pay to come to the house, from here to Dallas, hasn't done much good?" Vada asked.

Stevie shrugged. "Never know until you give it a try. If it works, you might have a Christmas miracle. If it doesn't, at least you've gotten Theron to go for a ride in the country.

Lucas will be here around suppertime today. Can I tell him that you'll bring Theron out to the ranch on Monday morning? Say around ten o'clock?"

"Like I said, I'll try anything," Vada answered. "I can't see where a horse could do what a trained therapist can't, but anything is worth a shot."

Stevie pushed back her chair, crossed the room, and brought the coffeepot to the table. She topped off Vada's mug and refilled hers. "Lucas has a lot of patience, and kids are drawn to him. He was awesome with Addy and Jesse's twins the last time he came home."

"But they're just over a year old. Theron is ten," Vada said.

"And Mia is almost twenty, and she still adores her uncle Lucas," Stevie argued.

Vada chuckled and touched her mug with Stevie's. "Here's to Lucas being right. I bet Pearl is excited that all her boys will be home for good and just in time for Christmas. And how is Sonny?"

Stevie picked up a bear claw and tore it in half. She handed off the part in her right hand to Vada and answered, "Sonny's meds are working very well. His MS isn't any better, but it hasn't gotten worse in the past few months. Pearl is ecstatic about Lucas coming back to the ranch permanently and has been cooking for days. You've been to the ranch, haven't you?"

Vada shook her head. "Nope. I was too busy with Travis in high school, and by the time I came back home to Honey Grove, my old friends hardly even remembered my name. You can't know how glad I am that our paths crossed that day in the grocery store."

"Me, too. I love my Ryan family, but I sure appreciate our

friendship," Stevie said and then frowned. "I never asked, but what caused the problem between you and Travis? If that's too personal or painful, then just say so."

Vada wasn't sure she wanted to get into those details, but after a moment's hesitation, she took a deep breath and let it out slowly. "It makes more sense to me to talk to you than to talk to a horse, I guess," she said with a smile.

Stevie chuckled. "Thanks for that, but you might find talking to an animal is a help. Sometimes I go out to the barn and tell Dixie, my alpaca, all about my frustrations. She's a danged fine listener."

"I bet she is," Vada said. "Okay, here goes. Travis and I wrote down our plans for our whole life when we graduated from high school. I mean we really wrote them on paper, and we followed them to the letter. We would get married when we finished college and had good jobs. We would start our family when we had been married four years, and then we'd have another child two years later."

She paused and took time to eat a couple of bites of the bear claw. "Everything went just like we planned. We had Theron, a beautiful baby boy, but looking back, I could see that something wasn't quite right from the beginning. I started working from home because he was so difficult, and we couldn't keep a nanny. I thought maybe he was on the autism spectrum, but when I had him tested, we found out that his IQ was off the charts. He was three when Travis said he couldn't take the stress of having a kid who was more interested in books than playing with toys. He had already packed up his personal things, and everything he wanted from our apartment was in his truck. I was thirty years old and had a three-year-old child who required most of my attention"—she paused—"and didn't know what I was going to do. I called my grandmother, and she said that I should move back to Honey Grove and told me I could live in her rental house. My company didn't care where I lived just so long as I got my work done. Been here ever since."

Stevie finished off her coffee, went to the cabinet, and brought back the pot to refill Vada's cup and her own. "What happened next?"

"I moved here and took him to the four-year-old program at the school. He was already reading at a fifth-grade level by then, so he was bored out of his mind, and I guess the word is that he retreated into himself. The teachers didn't know what to do with him. He didn't want to play with the other kids, which I understood. Why would a kid with fifth-grade intelligence want to even talk to kids who couldn't read or do math problems? I took him home after the first two months and let him learn at his own speed. That fed his antisocial behavior, and now he's even looking into ways to help 'kids like him.'" She air-quoted the last three words. "He doesn't like to come out of his room because everything in there is put in its place. His OCD is almost as bad as his intelligence is good, if that makes sense."

"Well, at least he realizes he's got a problem, and that's the first step toward getting any kind of help," Stevie said. "Thank you for trusting me enough to share that story. I've always wondered if Theron might be autistic; now I just realize that he's probably the person who will grow up and design the rocket that puts a man on Mars."

"Just telling it to someone other than my grandmother is kind of cathartic, so I appreciate you for listening," Vada said. "Maybe horse therapy will work for Theron if talking to an animal makes him feel better."

"I bet you miss your grandmother as much as I miss my mother, and the therapy might work since he's evidently looking for ways to help himself and others," Stevie said.

"Yes, I do"—Vada nodded—"but I'm sure glad that you and I are friends."

Stevie stood up, then bent and gave Vada a hug. "Me, too, and like I've told you a million times, you are welcome to come out to the ranch anytime—with or without Theron."

"And like I've told you a million times," Vada said, smiling, "it's tough enough to get Theron to go outside. Being around that many people would send him swirling into a dark hole."

"I'll be sure to tell everyone on Monday to let Lucas be the only new person Theron meets," Stevie said.

"Thank you—again." Vada pushed back her chair and walked Stevie to the door. "I'll see you on Monday if Theron will agree to go see the horses, but don't expect a miracle."

Stevie stopped at the back door and said, "Mia and I have vet appointments all day, but I'll call you that evening to see how things went."

"Fingers crossed that I'll be able to tell you good things." Vada watched her drive away and then closed the door and went back to the table.

Even though the idea of horse therapy was new to her, she crossed her fingers in hopes that it would help Theron to overcome being in a crowd. She finished off her breakfast, loaded and started the dishwasher, and headed down the hallway to her home office. She opened the door into Theron's bedroom and was surprised to see the lights on, the window blinds open, and his hood thrown back to show his pretty blond hair.

"I'll be in my office if you need me," she said.

"I'm doing research," he said without looking up.

She sat at her desk, opened her computer, and brought up the day's work for the insurance company out of Dallas that she'd worked for since she graduated from college. A picture of Theron as a baby sat beside her computer, and next to it, the latest one of him taken last Easter with one of his rare smiles. He had been born just a few days after her twenty-sixth birthday. Who would have thought that by the time he was crawling, he wouldn't want anyone other than Vada to hold him—and that included his father? Or that by the time he was three, he wouldn't function well with anyone else around him other than Vada?

She glanced over at the last picture taken of her grandmother. She had done her best to make their holiday together last year special for Vada—and for Theron. She had always been patient with him, understood that he had difficulties with his peers, and had told Vada that God must trust her a lot to give her such a special child.

"It's going to be tough without you this year, Granny." Vada wiped a tear from her cheek. "I probably won't even put up a tree. Theron hates anything that changes in his world, so what's the use."

Don't give up hope. Miracles happen during this season; her grandmother was back in her head.

CHAPTER TWO

Lucas had slept in bunkhouses for most of the past twenty years, and the one he awoke in on Monday morning wasn't all that different. A living area with a couple of bunk beds shoved over to one side. A door that led to a large pantry and another one into a bathroom. The kitchen was part of the open living space and had a table and chairs for four people, and there was a separate bedroom and bathroom for the foreman which he'd figured he might as well take since there was no one else to claim it. For just a split second, he had trouble remembering where he was when he opened his eyes. He was used to sleeping in a bunk—if he was lucky—or in a sleeping bag out under the stars, not in a king-size bed that felt like it covered an acre of ground.

He remembered that Theron was coming that morning and bailed out of bed so fast that he scared the ranch hound dog, who'd been sleeping on the rug beside the bed. "Sorry about that, Tex. I got excited about a kid coming out here for his first session in horse therapy."

He remembered Vada from high school and almost blushed

when he thought about the crush he had had on her. Not that he ever approached her or even spoke to her all that often because she and Travis Winters, the star of everything in school, were a couple, and she only had eyes for him.

Tex growled and headed toward the door without even looking back.

"Guess you aren't interested in hearing me talk about how I've always measured every woman I dated by what I thought Vada would be like?" Lucas plodded along behind him and let the dog outside. "I built her up in my head to be a perfect woman, and now no one else has a snowball's chance in hell of measuring up to that."

Tex took off in a dead run around the bunkhouse without even so much as a growl.

Lucas closed the door, went back to the bathroom just off his bedroom, shaved, combed his hair straight back, and stared at his reflection in the mirror. "She's only here for therapy for her boy. Remember that, and don't get all shy and bashful around her."

His reflection didn't have a single bit of advice for him, so he got dressed and headed out to the kitchen to make himself some breakfast. He had worked on huge ranches and hung his hat in both small and huge bunkhouses. He had stayed in this very one a couple of times when he had come home the past year, but that morning when he made an omelet, it felt emptier than it ever had before.

He had gotten in so late the night before that he put the horses in the barn and then went straight to the bunkhouse. Stevie had called him about the time he hit the Texas line and told him about the child who needed help, and he was too excited to get much sleep and up too early to join the family for breakfast. He would get hugs from them all when he saw some lights come on in the ranch house, but right now he was hungry. At the news of having his first horse therapy client, he'd been too excited to eat supper. He'd just finished slipping the omelet out of the cast iron skillet and over onto a plate when he heard Tex scratching at the door.

"Great timing," he said as he slung the door open to let the dog back inside. "I suppose you want a bite of my breakfast, right?"

The noise that Tex's claws made when he marched across the wood floor into the kitchen area echoed through the place. Lucas thought of grumbling cowboys fussing at one another for snoring or telling tales about the night they'd just had with some lady they'd met at a local bar, and the bunkhouse seemed to get even emptier.

Even though he was the one who sat back and listened most of the time, he missed the hustle and bustle of what had become his normal routine. Tex sat down beside his chair and waited for Lucas to share a few bites with him.

"I'm not really a people person," Lucas said as he put a forkful of the omelet in his mouth and then gave Tex one, "but I'm figuring out real quick that I don't like to be alone either."

When he and Tex had finished breakfast and he had cleaned up the kitchen, Lucas put on his coat and hat and headed outside with Tex right behind him. Lucas made a left turn when he reached the fork in the path—one led to the ranch house where Jesse and Addy lived with their family, and the other one led to his folks' place. Tex turned around after he'd gone a few feet down the well-traveled path toward the ranch house and bounded back toward Lucas.

"So you decided to have a second breakfast with Mama and Dad, rather than Jesse and Addy, did you?" Lucas chuckled.

Tex barked his answer and took off in a trot toward Pearl and Sonny's house. Sunflower Ranch had four dwellings on it—the original ranch house where Jesse lived with his family, the foreman's small house where Pearl and Sonny now lived, Stevie and Cody's place across the section line road, and, of course, the bunkhouse. Lucas had spent a lot of time sitting on the former foreman's porch and in Henry's house when he had been a teenager. Henry had been the ranch foreman long before the three Ryan brothers had been adopted and had been more like a favorite uncle to all of them than a hired hand. It still didn't seem right that he had left Sunflower Ranch for a cabin in the Colorado mountains.

Lucas didn't knock on the back door but stuck his head inside and yelled, "I smell coffee and bacon."

"Come on in and pour yourself a cup," Sonny called from the table where he sat with his morning newspaper. "Breakfast is on the bar. Your mama hasn't learned to cook for two yet, so there's always plenty."

Lucas removed his coat and hat and hung them on an old, familiar rack beside the back door. "Mama's food is the best in the whole world," he said as he crossed the floor and kissed his mother on the cheek, then gave his father's shoulder a gentle squeeze. "I've eaten in too many bunkhouses to count, and Mama's food tops them all, but I've already had breakfast."

"Oh, hush up with all that talk. It's just breakfast." Pearl's smile said that she had enjoyed every compliment. "Cody came by earlier and grabbed a couple of biscuits. He said that you've got your first customer in the therapy business today."

"How does that work, son?" Sonny asked.

"I've talked to Theron's mama, Vada, on the phone," Lucas explained as he poured himself a cup of coffee and then grabbed a blueberry muffin, "and she gave me a little information about the boy. He's ten years old and has been diagnosed as super intelligent with social issues. Sometimes that goes along with folks who are smarter than their peers. He can take care of himself, but change is hard for him. He doesn't like to talk to anyone but his mother, and he lives in a solitary world." He sat down across from his mother and took his first sip of coffee.

"And how do you propose to help with that?" Sonny asked.

"Mostly, I've worked with Down syndrome kids and those with low self-esteem," Lucas answered. "So I'll have to feel things out as we go. I'll introduce him to Buttercup today, and if things go well, maybe I'll bring Winnie out to meet him later on down the road, just to show him that he can accept change. If he just wants to watch me brush and talk to the horses this first time, that's fine. We'll go at his speed, whether it's slow or even slower. I don't expect a lot on the first day."

"What about other people being there?" Sonny asked.

"Not for a little while and then only if he shows signs of improvement. It will most likely be a long process," Lucas answered. "Horses don't see a kid who is different in any way. They just see a child. Somehow, children with their own challenges understand this, and it helps them to heal and eventually have positive relationships with people, even if it's just a few folks."

Pearl nodded. "I can understand that. When you came to our family, it seemed like Champ, the old ranch dog we had at the time, helped you."

"I loved that dog, and he took a lot of my secrets to the grave with him. From my research." He took a bite of his muffin and a sip of coffee. "I don't know what you put into these, Mama, but they are the best in the world."

"Love, son," Sonny said. "She puts love in all her cooking. Now tell us more about these children you hope to help."

"I've discovered that a child with problems needs to learn to have a relationship with himself so that he can accept change and figure out how to live in the world," Lucas answered, and wondered if he was talking about himself as much as about the kids he worked with.

"So your goal for today is simply to meet Theron and let him look at the horses?" Sonny asked.

"That's right, Dad," Lucas answered.

"And later, maybe in a few weeks, I can meet him?" Sonny asked.

"I hope so," Lucas answered. "Once he's adjusted to having me around, I'd like for you to be the next person he meets."

"I'll be looking forward to it," Sonny said.

"Do you remember Vada from high school?" Pearl asked.

"Of course," Lucas said. "It's not like Honey Grove High was that big." Lucas almost blushed. There was no way he was going to admit that he had had a serious crush on Vada all those years ago and that he still dreamed about her.

"It was such a shame she lost her grandmother last year. We miss her at church. It can't be easy for Vada, working at home and being closed off from the world so much. I'll gladly pay for these therapy sessions," Pearl offered.

"There is no charge," Lucas said. "If I build up a client list that takes all my time, then maybe I'll figure up a price for my services, but right now I just want to help kids."

"That's pretty generous, son," Sonny said, "and it makes me proud of you."

Lucas pushed back his chair and took his coffee mug to the dishwasher. "Thanks, Dad, and thank you, Mama, for the offer to pay for the sessions. I hate to eat and run, but Jesse wants me to help herd some cattle from one pasture to another. It's been a long time since I did that job on a four-wheeler rather than a cutting horse."

"You brought two horses back home with you," Sonny reminded him.

"Those are therapy horses." Lucas chuckled. "They wouldn't know how to herd cattle. Their job is to make friends with kids and let them learn to ride."

"Kind of like kids," Sonny said with a broad smile.

"How's that?" Lucas asked with a frown.

"You've raised those horses to be therapy horses, and that's what they are. I raised three sons to be ranchers and be danged if they don't all three go off and be doctors, military, and horse trainers," Sonny told him. "I wouldn't be surprised if either Buttercup or Winnie became a good cutting horse if you gave them a chance."

"But then we all come back home to be ranchers. What is it that the Good Book says about raising a child up for a few years?" Lucas put on his coat and settled his old, worn hat onto his head.

"It says, 'Train up a child in the way he should go: and when he is old, he will not depart from it,'" Pearl said.

"And y'all did a good job of it. Ranchin' is in our blood, and we just can't get away from it," Lucas said with a smile.

* * *

Vada wasn't hopeful when she awoke that Monday morning. She had learned not to tell Theron about any kind of outing—even a simple trip to the backyard—until a few minutes before the event. If she did, he fretted about it until he was a wreck when the time came. That morning she was surprised when he came out of his room and sat down at the table. He had his fidget toy in his hands, but he wasn't playing with it.

"Cheerios?" she asked.

"Bacon, please, and eggs." He kept his eyes on the table.

"Scrambled or fried?" Vada asked and then wished she could take the words back. Choices would not be a good thing that morning.

"Do horses eat scrambled or fried?" he asked.

"I think they eat hay or grass. I know they like carrots and apples," she said.

"Scrambled then, and I will need an apple to take to the horse," he said.

"What horse?" Vada almost dropped the whole carton of eggs she was taking from the refrigerator to the counter.

"The one we are going to see today. I looked horses up on the computer. I think I will like them," Theron said. "They are supposed to help kids like me."

Vada was both excited and shocked, almost speechless. "How did you know about horses?"

"I heard you talking to Stevie and to someone else about going to see a horse this morning at ten," he answered, "so I did some research."

"You've had therapists, Theron, and..." Vada stumbled over the words.

"I don't like people. They scare me and the ones my age bore me. That's not nice to say, but they do..." He paused, and Vada half expected him to go back to his room, but he went on. "The therapists you took me to and the ones that came here want me to talk about the way I feel. They want me to say more than I just feel alone and lonely." He raised one thin shoulder and looked up at her.

Vada had almost forgotten how pretty his brown eyes were. "Well, I don't expect Buttercup—that's the horse's name that you will meet today—will expect you to talk if you don't want to."

"Are there more animals where we are going?" Theron asked.

"I understand there's a dog named Tex, a cat and some kittens in the barn, and alpacas." Vada thought she was dreaming until she took the bacon out of the microwave and a bit of the grease popped onto her finger. It burned badly enough that she knew she was wide awake.

"I will research those and see if they help kids like me," Theron said.

Why didn't I think of that before? Vada wondered. *If any animal would help him, then he could have a cat or a dog.*

Hope. Miracles. Magic. 'Tis the season for all of it, her grandmother whispered softly in her ear.

She whipped up two eggs and scrambled them in a bit of butter. "Do you want the horse to help you, son?"

Theron picked up the plate of bacon and carried it to the table. "Yes, I do. Will there be people there?"

"Just Lucas. He owns the horses and lives on the ranch," Vada answered.

Theron got two plates from the cabinet and cutlery from the drawer. He set a perfect table, poured a mug of coffee for his mother, and set a bottle of orange juice beside his plate.

"Lucas won't want me to talk a lot like the therapist did, will he?" Theron began to work with his fidget gadget.

"I don't think so," Vada assured him. "I knew him a long time ago, and he was kind of shy back then. I imagine he'll just want to tell you about the horse."

He laid the fidget toy to the side and began to eat his breakfast. That he even came out of his room was a miracle. That he talked to her that morning gave her hope. She wondered if a bit of holiday magic could really be waiting for her out at Sunflower Ranch as she sat down at the table and had breakfast with her son.

When he had finished his food and drank all his juice, Theron carried his plate to the dishwasher and then sat back down at the table. "I might like Lucas if he doesn't ask me how I feel about every little thing."

"That would be good," Vada said.

"If this helps me, will we go back for more therapy?" he asked.

"That will be up to you," Vada answered.

CHAPTER THREE

Lucas brought Buttercup out into the corral, brushed her coat until it was shiny, and then put the bridle and lead rope on her. "Theron Winters is coming to visit you today," he told the horse. "You will need to be patient with him. I understand that he doesn't talk much except to his mother, and that's only occasionally."

The horse nuzzled Lucas on the neck. He pulled an apple from his coat pocket and fed it to her. "I hear a vehicle coming now. I've never dealt with a child just like this, so maybe you could calm me down, too. And just between me and you, I haven't seen Vada in many years, and I'm as nervous as a long-tailed cat in a room full of rocking chairs."

Lucas glanced over Buttercup's back when the car came to a stop right outside the corral fence. A minute passed, and no one got out of the vehicle. His hands began to sweat inside his work gloves. Another minute went by, and he figured that maybe today Theron would just look at the ranch through the window, and he wouldn't get to see Vada at all. The sun seemed to hang up there in the clear blue sky and not move for a while longer. Then the passenger door opened, and a small, thin boy got out and walked slowly over to the fence. Vada came out from the driver's side and stood beside the car, as if she were waiting for Theron to bolt and run at any minute.

Her dark brown hair was pulled up in a ponytail that hung halfway down her back. She wore sunglasses, so Lucas couldn't see her pretty, aqua-colored eyes, but she seemed slimmer than he remembered her being in high school.

That was almost two decades ago, the pesky voice in his head reminded him, *and her living situation hasn't exactly been wonderful.*

He didn't say anything at all to Theron but simply walked Buttercup over to the fence and stood to one side. The plan for that day was to let the horse and child get to know each other. Whether Theron wanted to say anything to Lucas was up to him.

"Buttercup or Winnie?" Theron whispered.

"This is Buttercup," Lucas answered.

The horse hung her head over the top railing and waited.

"Can I touch her?" Theron asked.

Lucas nodded.

Theron put what looked like a small toy into his coat pocket and stroked Buttercup's head very gently. "My name is Theron Winters. I want to be your friend so you can help me."

Buttercup moved forward a few more inches until she could lay her head on Theron's shoulder. He untied the string that had tightened up the hood of his jacket until just his nose and eyes were showing and flipped back the hood.

"I think maybe we can be friends. Can I come inside the fence?" he asked, but he kept his eyes on the ground.

"That would be fine," Lucas said. "Would you like for me to stay, or would you rather I left you and Buttercup alone?"

Theron didn't raise his eyes. "Just me and Buttercup."

Lucas put one hand on the fence and hopped over it. Theron crawled between two rails and went into the corral with the horse and picked up the lead rope. Lucas didn't realize that Vada had jogged over from her car to the fence until he caught a whiff of coconut that reminded him of riding on the beach in Florida.

"Please, tell me he won't get hurt," she whispered. "It's so wonderful to see him trying something new. If he got hurt, he would revert to where he was."

"Buttercup is trained to do this," Lucas assured her. His heart skipped a beat and then began to race. "From what you told me about him, I wasn't expecting even this much progress in one day."

"Neither was I," Vada said. "He's been researching horse therapy since he overheard Stevie and me talking, and then he eavesdropped on the conversation I had with you. You can't begin to imagine how big of a step this is for him."

"And for you?" Lucas wished she would remove her sunglasses so he could see her eyes. So much could be determined by a person's expressions and whether their eyes twinkled or were sad.

"Even bigger for me," Vada answered in a voice barely above a whisper. "It's bordering on huge and unbelievable." She pointed toward the corral. "Look at that. Buttercup is letting him lead her around the corral, and I can tell he's saying a few words. Can you hear what he's saying?"

"Nope, and we don't need to." Lucas could hear pain and fear in Vada's voice and wanted so badly to comfort her with an arm around her shoulders. "That is between the two of them. Buttercup is a good listener."

Vada finally removed the sunglasses and stared at her son. "I can't believe what I'm seeing."

Her eyes were the same as he remembered. They had a few crow's-feet around them, and today they weren't twinkling, but then they weren't sad either—more like totally amazed.

"He must want to be helped to be willing to do this," Lucas said. "That goes a long way in the process. Today he can stay as long as he wants, and anytime he asks to come back, give me a call. I'll have things ready by the time you arrive, but I don't take appointments. This is totally up to him."

Vada looked up and locked gazes with Lucas. He could have dived right into her eyes like he would a pool of clear water and stayed there forever, but she blinked and turned back toward the corral.

"That's so generous of you, Lucas." Her voice hadn't changed one bit. It still reminded him of good whiskey mixed with honey—a little on the edgy side with a dose of pure Southern sweetness added to it.

"Maybe so." He propped a boot on the bottom rail. "But it brings me a lot of pleasure to help a child."

Tex ambled up from behind the barn, his head down and tail wagging. He slipped under the bottom rail and followed alongside the horse for a couple of minutes before Theron saw him. The boy stopped in his tracks. Buttercup did the same thing and waited patiently.

Lucas held his breath until Theron dropped to his knees in the dirt and held out a hand. Tex stretched out on his belly beside Theron and wagged his tail so hard that dust flew up around the child.

"I like you, too," Theron said as he stroked the dog's head. "Buttercup told me you wouldn't bite me. She's real smart."

"Talk about a miracle," Vada whispered. "If I wasn't seeing it with my own eyes, I wouldn't believe it." She rounded her vehicle, opened the trunk, and took out a couple of folding chairs. "How long can we stay?"

Lucas popped both open and waited for her to sit in one before he eased down in the other one. "As long as it takes. Theron will decide when he's ready to leave, not us. I should've remembered to bring chairs, but I didn't expect this much progress in one day."

"I keep chairs in the trunk and snacks in the back seat just in case he wants to stay longer when I can talk him into going to the park," she said.

"With other kids there?" Lucas asked.

"Oh, no, usually late in the evening, and then he doesn't play on the equipment," she answered. "He sits in the chair and looks at the stars. Sometimes he'll have a bag of chips and a travel mug of hot tea. He's partial to herbal peach, and, forgive me, I talk too much when I'm nervous."

"No problem." Lucas could have listened to her read the dictionary and asked for her to read it again when she finished. "I usually clam up when I'm nervous. That's why I get along with the animals better than people for the most part."

"I remember you being shy in high school," Vada said.

"Not shy so much as I just liked to watch people and try to figure out what made them the way they were. I don't imagine any of y'all would have liked to have known what I thought." He wasn't sure why he hadn't lost his ability to speak around Vada. Maybe it was the fact that Theron was doing so well, or that he needed someone to talk to as much as she did.

"Probably not. We might not have liked what you saw in us." She smiled. "Am I keeping you from other appointments or jobs?"

"This is my job for today or any day that Theron needs to come out here," Lucas said. "Someday, when he's comfortable with me, I can show him the ranching business, and he can meet the family, but only in small doses at first."

"Do you really think that day will ever come?" Vada asked.

"That's the end game. He might never be comfortable with a room full of people or with strangers, but I'd like to introduce him to one person at a time later on down the road," Lucas explained. "Again, that's all just future goals and will be done on his schedule. My dad, Sonny, already has dibs on being the first one to meet Theron. He's good with kids and he's patient. He had to be to raise three wild boys."

Theron draped an arm around Tex and sat there with him until the dog got tired of being still and ran out of the corral toward the side of the barn where the alpacas were and turned around to bark at Theron.

"I think Tex is asking Theron to follow him, so Tex can introduce him to the alpacas." Lucas chuckled.

"Looks like a horse and a dog might be enough for one day." Vada nodded toward the corral, where Theron stood up, dusted off the seat of his jeans, picked up the rope, and began leading Buttercup around the corral again.

Lucas could see the child's mouth moving as he whispered to the horse. He wondered if he should say something to Vada or not, but he was so comfortable sitting there beside her that he didn't want to break the spell.

After another half hour, Theron brought Buttercup to the fence, whipped his hood back up over his head, and crawled between the railings. He went straight to the car and got inside without saying a word to anyone.

"Is that usual for him?" Lucas asked.

"Usually he'd not even get out of the car. On a rare day, it might mean that he would stare at the horse and the dog for a few minutes and then tell me to take him home. There he would go into his room to either play his games, do his on-line schoolwork, or research something. He loves to learn and is constantly looking up something. The past couple of days, he's been all into horse therapy," Vada explained as she stood up and folded her chair.

Lucas did the same and took her chair from her hands. "I'll put these away. How does he do on his schoolwork?"

"If he went to public school, he would be in fifth grade, but he's doing advanced studies in eleventh-grade work right now. I expect he will graduate in another year and begin working on his first online college degree." Vada followed him to the back of the car.

"That's genius level." Lucas couldn't hide the shock in his voice.

"He loves to learn about all kinds of things. By his next visit, he'll be able to tell you things about horses that even you probably don't know."

"What are his favorite subjects?" Lucas asked.

"Science and math," Vada answered.

"If he keeps going at this pace, he'll have a degree before he can drive," Lucas told her as he closed the truck lid. "I bet he would be an asset on a ranch like this one."

"Most likely he'll have at least one doctorate before most kids graduate from high school. His intelligence level is off the charts. Lucas, I can't tell you how much I want this to help him with his other issues, or how much today has meant to us." Vada laid a hand on Lucas's arm.

Heat shot through his body at her touch. "It meant as much to me to see him get this far in one session with Buttercup and Tex." Lucas hoped his voice didn't sound as hoarse to Vada as it did to his own ears. "I'm just glad to be able to help, but I'm not doing much. Buttercup is doing most of the work," Lucas said. "I'll be looking for your call later today."

"Why today?" Vada asked and removed her hand.

"Theron is going to want to come back tomorrow," Lucas said. "I can feel it in my bones."

"I hope your bones are right." Vada smiled brightly as she got into her vehicle.

"So do I," Lucas whispered as he watched her drive away.

* * *

Vada thought she had already had her Christmas miracle when she slid in behind the steering wheel and started the engine— but she was wrong.

"Talking to Buttercup and the dog made me hungry." Theron removed the hood and glanced over at his mother. "Can we, please, get a hamburger and a chocolate shake and go to the park?"

"Of course." Vada could almost hear her heart humming.

"When can we go back?" Theron asked. "I forgot to tell Buttercup about my class schedule for next semester and that I will finish my high school courses in three more semesters."

"Lucas says you can come anytime, and the dog's name is Tex," Vada told him.

"Tomorrow at one o'clock. Tex sounds like a good name

for a cowboy's dog," Theron said. "I will have my schoolwork done by then. I like Tex for a dog's name." He turned and looked out the side window.

"I'll let Lucas know that we'll be there about one o'clock. I'm glad you've had a good day with the horse. So, you think Buttercup is a better therapist than the ones you've seen in the past?" Vada drove into town and pulled in behind one other car in the line for the drive-up window.

"Yes, she just listens and doesn't ask me how I feel about you or being so smart, or anything like that. I like her a lot, and Tex is a good dog. I talked to him some, too," Theron answered. "I didn't know that I liked dogs and horses, but I do. I'll have to do some research on them when we get home."

The place wasn't too busy, so they got their order and were on their way to the park when Theron straightened up in his seat and asked, "Can we move out to that ranch so I can talk to Buttercup and Tex anytime I want?"

Vada opened her mouth to say something, but words wouldn't come out. She remembered the day they had moved from Dallas to Honey Grove with a shiver. Theron hadn't done well with the change. He liked his things neatly arranged in his room, and having to get used to a new house and a different bedroom took a while. All this progress in one day was more than she could take in, and all because of a horse? Surely, she had to be dreaming.

"Do you mean forever or just for a weekend?" Vada asked as she snagged a parking place at the park in front of the swings, where several little kids were playing. Mothers, grandmothers, or maybe some of them were nannies, watched from the benches not far away. "You do know that there's a big family that lives on that ranch, don't you?"

Theron removed the paper from his burger and held the sandwich in one hand and his fidget toy in the other. "How many is a big family? Is it like infinity or all the stars in the sky? Or is it just, like, fifteen?"

"Not as many as the stars," Vada answered. "Pearl and Sonny are the older folks. They're about Granny's age. Then there's Jesse and his wife, Addy, their daughter, Mia, who is about twenty years old, and their twin boys, who are a year old. Cody and Stevie, and now Lucas. I would imagine in the summertime that they would have extra hired hands."

Theron nodded and kept eating. When he finished his burger, he wadded up the paper and put it back in the sack and picked up his chocolate shake. "Maybe just for one week, and maybe I wouldn't have to be around anyone but Lucas."

Vada ate her burger slowly and enjoyed being outside, even if it was in a warm car. "I would love to go to the ranch for a week, but since it's your idea, you should ask Lucas about it."

Theron set the shake in the cup holder on the console and began to work overtime on his fidget device. "Can't I just ask Buttercup?"

"Buttercup lives in the barn." Vada hoped she wasn't pushing his or her limits too far, especially after such a phenomenal morning. "This is wintertime, and it's cold outside. We would need to live in a house. I'll ask Lucas to rent the bunkhouse to us for a week if you will ask him if we can have a few days out there."

Theron kept his eyes on the device. "Will Lucas be in the bunkhouse?"

"I don't know about that," Vada said. "He lives there now, but he might go stay with his folks while we are there. That's something we would have to work out with him."

"Can we go home now?" Theron whispered. "I need to research bunkhouses before I ask Lucas."

"Yes, we can." Vada started the engine and backed out of the parking spot.

Theron put his toy away and pulled his hood up over his head, but he didn't tie the strings under his chin. They had barely made it back to the house when Stevie pulled up beside them. Vada motioned for her to come inside and hurried to unlock the door for Theron to escape to his room.

"Come on in," Vada said.

"I haven't got but a minute, but I wanted to see how things went," Stevie said. "I've called Lucas like a dozen times, but every time it goes right to voice mail. I expect he's talking to Sonny."

Vada removed her coat and led the way to the kitchen. "How about a cup of hot tea or chocolate to warm up your bones?" A vision of Lucas's smile popped into her head at the mention of bones. He'd said he could feel it in his bones that Theron would want to come back to the ranch the next day.

"Don't have time for that," Stevie said. "I really do have only five minutes, so please talk fast. How did things go?"

"Shockingly well. Spectacular by Theron's standards. He wants to go live on the ranch for a week." Vada couldn't believe the words were coming from her mouth. "That horse and dog did more in one day than all the therapists I've tried could do in all these years. I really think that he's ready to *want* help."

"That's great!" Stevie said. "I'm so happy for him. Want me to talk to Lucas about Theron coming out to the ranch for a week?"

"No, I'll call him," Vada whispered, and shifted her eyes down the hallway to be sure Theron wasn't eavesdropping, "but I told Theron that he has to ask Lucas himself before we even consider it. It's a big step and a hard choice, but if he's ever going to get any better..."

"I understand." Stevie laid a hand on Vada's shoulder. "Let me know if I can help in *any* way."

"Thank you." Vada pulled out a chair and sank down into it. She still felt like she should pinch herself to be sure she wasn't dreaming. The old Theron would never, ever—not in a thousand years—have done some of the things he had done that day.

She took her phone from her purse, shoved it into the hip pocket of her jeans, and tiptoed down the hallway. That there was a light showing under his door was yet another surprise. When she reached the bathroom, she closed the door behind her and sat down on the vanity stool. Then she turned the water on in the sink and called Lucas.

"Hello," Lucas said.

He might have traveled all over the world, but he still had a deep Texas drawl that she could listen to for days on end. She had always been intrigued by him back in high school, but seeing him at the ranch, there had been a little spark between them. It was wild to even think like that, and most likely the little jolt she'd gotten when she touched his arm came from the fact she hadn't dated since her divorce.

"This is Vada," she said.

"I figured it was either you or Theron, since your name came up on the caller ID," Lucas said.

"Theron may change his mind tomorrow, but on the way home he told me that he wants to come to the ranch and stay a week," she blurted out. "He hates any kind of change, so I'm shocked that he even said that."

"It can be arranged and would be good for him to be here so he could go out to the corral anytime he wanted," Lucas said. "When does he want to move in?"

Vada took a deep breath and let it out in a loud whoosh. "He has to ask you himself. We need to agree on a price. I feel bad running you out of the bunkhouse," she said.

The line was quiet for a long while, and then Lucas said, "That's asking a lot of the little guy."

"Maybe so, and I'm walking on new ground here, but..." She hesitated.

"I understand. You are his mother, and you know him well, so I'll abide by whatever you think is best," Lucas said. "But only if I can stay in the bunkhouse. It would crowd Jesse and Addy to have me in the ranch house, and Mama and Daddy only have one bedroom, so I'd be on the couch."

"Is it all right if we come to the ranch at one o'clock tomorrow then, even if he doesn't make the call?" Vada asked.

"I'll be waiting, and I hope he asks me, because I could use some company. I thought I wanted privacy, but I'd forgotten how lonely it can be to have a whole bunkhouse to myself," Lucas told her. "I've been used to living with several other cowboys, and this one feels pretty danged empty."

"You do realize I'll be with him?" Vada was suddenly more than a little nervous about sharing a house with Lucas for a whole week.

"I was counting on it." Lucas chuckled.

CHAPTER FOUR

Theron came out of his room on Tuesday morning wearing jeans, a black T-shirt with a bright-colored symbol of an atom on it, and no hoodie. "Could we have waffles and sausage for breakfast, please?"

"Of course." Vada still felt like she was living in a dream. "Hot tea or juice?"

"Milk," Theron said. "I read that a growing person my age needs more calcium for the bones, and sunshine to get the D vitamin. I should have researched this before now."

Vada popped a package of sausage links into the microwave and put two frozen waffles in the toaster. She tried to remember a time when her son had come out of his room two days in a row, but she couldn't.

"I am ready to move to the ranch for one week," Theron said. "I researched what I would need, and I have my things laid out on the bed. I need a duffel bag or a suitcase to put them in. After I eat, I will call Lucas and ask him if we can come today. I will need his phone number."

To Vada's knowledge, Theron had never used his cell phone

for anything other than playing games or as a research tool, so she wasn't sure he would even know how to use it to make a call.

"It will be easier if I talk to him on the phone," Theron said.

"And if he says no?" Vada asked.

"Then I will put my things away," he answered, "but I think he will say yes."

From the time he started talking at a year old, he used very proper English—when he wanted to say something. To hear him verbalize as much as he had the past two days was mind-boggling.

Vada wrote Lucas's number on a scrap piece of paper and slid it across the table to Theron. "Here you go. Let me know what he says so I can get my things together, too."

"I will," Theron said with a brief nod. "My research says kids like me have trouble with change, but I need to work through that."

"I'll be right there beside you, son." Vada blinked back tears as she got the sausage out of the microwave and put it on a plate. "If it gets to be too much for you, we can get in the car and come home."

Theron nodded but didn't say anything. Vada decided that she wouldn't start packing to be away for a whole week until after Theron had really made the call. Her heart hurt for her son, knowing how much courage he would have to muster up to even poke the numbers into the phone.

* * *

Lucas's phone rang and he answered it without checking the caller ID. "Good morning."

"This is Theron," the voice in his ear said. "May I come stay on the ranch for a week so I can see Buttercup and Tex every day?"

"I think that would be a very good idea." Lucas did a fist pump and mouthed, "Yes!"

"May we come this morning?" Theron asked.

"Of course, but you should know the place where I live has only one bedroom. You and your mama can have the bunk beds in the living room, or you and I can take them and let her have the bedroom. You decide which would work better for you," Lucas said.

"I have researched both bunkhouses and bunk beds, and I will take the top bunk. Mama can have the bottom one. Older folks might hurt themselves if they fall out of a top bunk," Theron said.

Ouch, Lucas thought, but he said, "That sounds like a fine idea. Then you will be here in just a little while?"

"Yes, sir," Theron answered. "Will you tell Buttercup and Tex that I am on the way?"

"I will certainly do that," Lucas said. "Be sure to bring a warm coat and boots. A cold front is headed our way."

"I have researched the weather, and I am ready," Theron said. "Goodbye."

Lucas started to tell Theron goodbye, but when he looked down, the phone screen was dark. "Man, that had to take a lot of courage," he said.

"What took courage, and who were you talking to?" Mia, his niece, asked as she tossed the last bag of cattle feed into the bed of the ranch's old work truck.

"Theron Winters wants to spend a week in the bunkhouse," Lucas said.

Mia closed the truck's tailgate. "Is he coming today?"

"Yes, he is," Lucas answered.

Mia rounded the truck and slid into the driver's side. "Then we better get this feed out to the pasture. You need to be here when he arrives, or he might change his mind. This is a good thing you're doing for him."

"I wonder if he's moving too fast," Lucas said as he settled into the passenger seat and wondered just how things would go with Vada living in the same house with him, "but he seems determined to be here a whole week. I'll be happy if he lasts a couple of days this first time."

Mia started the engine and backed the truck out of the barn. "I hope I get to meet him while he's here."

"Me, too." Lucas nodded. "He's super intelligent but isn't comfortable around people."

Mia drove down the pathway that was just a couple of ruts in the pasture. "There was a kid like that at college. He was maybe fourteen and taking advanced classes. I kind of felt sorry for him. He didn't fit in, and it was plain that he just wanted someone to talk to." She pulled up to the place where they needed to dump feed and pointed to the cattle that had fallen in behind the truck. "Looks like we've got a waiting line. Maybe if Theron gets more comfortable at being around people, we can bring him out here some morning."

A blast of cold air that could be promising sleet or snow hit Lucas in the face when he opened the truck door. "I'll take care of this. You keep the vehicle warm."

Mia shook her head. "I'm not just a pretty face, Uncle Lucas. I'm a ranch hand." She slid out from behind the wheel and hopped up into the truck bed. She set one bag up on the end, pulled a pocketknife from her back pocket, and slit the top open. "There now, it's ready for you to dump."

Lucas carefully hefted the bag to the ground and pushed several cows back so he could get to the feeder. "You really are more than a pretty face."

"That's what I keep telling my boyfriend, Beau," Mia said as she got another bag ready for him. "I can't wait for you to meet him, Uncle Lucas. He'll be here for Sunday dinner day after tomorrow. He missed last week because he had to take his grandpa to a rodeo. They invited me to go, but I wanted to be here with you on your first real day back at the ranch."

"Well, thank you, darlin'." Lucas took care of the last bag and tossed the empty bag in with the others in the back of the truck. "It sure was nice to sit down to Sunday dinner with the whole family. I can't believe how much the twins have grown. They're walking and trying to talk."

"Oh, they're talking," Mia said with half a giggle as she jumped out of the truck's bed and went back to the cab. "It's just that they have a language of their own and only communicate with each other. I hope Beau and I have twins someday."

"Oh, so you're plannin' babies before the wedding?" Lucas teased as he got back into the truck.

"No, sir!" Mia gasped. "We're not plannin' either for a while, but we know we love each other and all that's on the calendar down the road. He's a good man, Uncle Lucas, and he treats me right."

"That's what matters." Lucas wondered if he'd ever find someone to share his life with—that would be on the calendar for a long-term relationship—as Mia said.

* * *

Vada packed jeans, sweatshirts, and casual clothing for the week. She thought about adding something for church but figured it would just take up space. She hadn't been to Sunday services since her grandmother died. When her granny was alive, they had switched off attending Sunday services. One week, Vada went to morning worship, and Granny attended the evening service. The next week, they swapped. Common sense told Vada that she sure couldn't leave Theron alone, especially in a new and strange place, and there was no way he would go with her.

She was only mildly surprised when she rolled her suitcase into the living room and found Theron sitting on the sofa. His feet were planted in front of him, and his hands were folded in his lap. His computer case and a smaller case that matched hers were beside the door with his coat, gloves, and the watch cap her mother had knitted for him lying on the top of it.

"I am ready." Theron pulled up the hood of his gray jacket and then pushed it back again. "I will put on my cap when we get there. I wonder if Buttercup's ears get cold. I will have to research that tonight. I wouldn't like for her to be cold just for me."

Vada pulled her suitcase over to the door. "She might be in the barn in her stall since it's so cold. Are you going to be comfortable spending time with her in the barn?"

"Yes, I am," Theron answered as he stood up. "I will talk to Buttercup wherever she is. Do you think Tex comes into the bunkhouse to get warm? I read about ranch dogs when I did research. I hope he gets to come inside when it's cold."

"We can ask Lucas about that," Vada answered.

When they were in the vehicle and she'd driven to the end of the lane, he pulled out his fidget toy and played with it, but he didn't pull the hood up on his jacket. She drove past the empty corral, and Theron straightened up in his seat.

"I guess she's in the barn," he said. "I can see her today, can't I?"

"I'm sure Lucas will arrange it so that you can." Vada parked in front of the long, low building that Stevie had described when she gave her directions to the bunkhouse. "Are you sure about this, Theron?"

He took a deep breath and let it out slowly. "No, I'm not sure about it, but I want to get better. I don't like people looking at me like I'm weird."

"Do you really think they do that?" Vada hoped that she wasn't treading on thin ice.

"I can feel how people see me, Mama," Theron answered. "Lucas and Buttercup don't treat me like I'm different. They see me as a ten-year-old boy, not a genius."

"Then I guess the next thing for us to do is go inside," Vada said.

"First we knock on the door and wait to be invited in," Theron told her. "That is what my research says about going to another person's home. It's rude to just walk in. I don't want to do something that will make Lucas think I'm weird."

Vada felt a slight prick in her heart for not teaching Theron the proper etiquette about going to see other folks. In her defense, she hadn't thought that Theron would ever leave the house or face a situation like this.

"That's right," Vada said. "Do you want to knock, or shall I?"

"I should do it." Theron opened the car door. "It will help me to get better if I learn this. It can't be harder than analytical psychology."

"Is that where you got the idea to come out here for a week?

Is this one of your experiments?" Vada got out of the car and removed her suitcase from the back seat.

Theron got out of the car and took out his suitcase. "I've been studying the relationship between consciousness, which is what makes me sink back into myself and not let others inside to be a part of my life, and subconsciousness, which keeps me from being social." He stopped to inhale deeply again. "I figure I have to balance those two things, so yes, I suppose it is a bit of an experiment. Buttercup understands me, and I can talk to her about the correlation between the two. Sometimes I don't need an answer to my questions. I just need to ask them so I can figure them out in my head."

Vada wasn't sure she understood a word of what he had said other than something about not being social. If it helped him come out of his shell, she was all for whatever conscious or subconscious signs he got, and for a horse that listened to his intelligent one-sided conversations.

She knew by the way his hand trembled that it took a great deal of determination for him to raise his fist and knock. In just seconds, Lucas threw open the door and motioned them inside. "Come on in. Tex is waiting in the living room, and I've got a pot of tea ready with some of my mama's sugar cookies on the table."

"That is very good," Theron said. "A host is supposed to offer a guest a beverage and a snack. I like hot tea. What kind did you make?"

"Earl Grey," Lucas answered.

"That's a good one for this time of day," Theron said. "Is it okay for me to look around before we have a break?"

"Of course it is," Lucas answered.

Theron parked his suitcase at the end of the bottom bunk,

dropped down on his knees, and stroked Tex's head before he even took in the rest of the place.

"You look like you just saw a ghost," Lucas whispered for Vada's ears only.

"I just found out that he's been studying analytical psychology on his own. I always know what high school classes he's taking, but I don't know what he's 'researching.'" She air-quoted the last word.

"Buttercup's a real smart horse," Lucas said with a smile. "She can listen to intelligent conversation or to babbling that doesn't amount to anything at all."

Theron rose, crossed the big room that served as a kitchen as well as a living and dining area, and stopped at the end of the sofa. "I have not been in very many houses, but I like this one. I'm ready for tea now."

"I'm glad. Shall we sit around the table for tea?" Lucas asked.

"I would like that," Theron answered. "And then can I go talk to Buttercup? Is she in the barn where it's warm?"

"Yes, she is. Your mama and I can go with you out there, and you can spend as much time as you want with her." Lucas poured three cups of tea and motioned toward the cream and sugar. "I like it plain, but you can fix yours however you like."

Vada pinched her leg, and it hurt, so she knew she wasn't dreaming. This child that she had all but given up hope of ever leaving her house was talking to a man he'd only met one time. She glanced over at Lucas and caught his eye. She wasn't a bit surprised at the flutter in her stomach, or that her breath caught in her chest.

Good for you, her grandmother's voice popped into her head. *It's about time you were attracted to a man, and I knew these boys. They've grown up to be good men.*

But, Granny, I have to think of Theron, she argued.

Yep, but the way I see it is that he is beginning to think for himself, her grandmother said.

She didn't have an argument for that. She took a sip of her tea and took in the whole bunkhouse with one glance. She could see into the bedroom. Lucas's bed was made so tightly that she could bounce the old proverbial quarter on it. The bunk beds were straightened so well that she would have sworn that Theron had taken care of them. A blaze burned in a big stone fireplace that sat across the room from the sofa and a well-worn coffee table.

Just the basics, she thought. *Maybe Theron and I both need just the basics.*

CHAPTER FIVE

Vada awoke to a whispered, one-sided conversation between Lucas and Tex, along with the smell of bacon and coffee. Her first thought was that she was dreaming. She hadn't woken up to someone in the kitchen since she was eighteen years old and left home for college. Her father had owned an air-conditioning and heating business in Honey Grove, and her mother worked in the office for him. She had grown up eating a big breakfast because that's what her folks both liked. They had died together in a car accident the year before Travis divorced her, and she still missed them terribly. She opened her eyes slowly to find it wasn't a dream.

"Is this a bunkhouse breakfast?" Theron rubbed sleep from his eyes as he crawled down the bunk bed ladder.

Lucas turned around from the stove and nodded. "Cowboys need a good breakfast so they can get lots of work done. I'm making bacon and eggs, oatmeal, and hot biscuits this morning. Does that sound good to you?"

"Yes, sir," Theron said. "Can I help? I know how to set the table."

"That would be great." Lucas reached up into the cabinet and took down plates and bowls. Then he pointed toward a cabinet door. "Silverware is in there. Napkins are in the holder on the table."

Vada threw her legs over the side of the bed. Lucas crossed the room in a few long strides, dropped down on his knees in front of her, and held out a bedroom slipper. She blinked back tears as she slipped her feet down into the fur-lined booties.

"That's called spoiling a woman," she said with a smile—still unsure if she was awake or if this was a beautiful dream.

"The woman is so worth it," Lucas whispered.

He held out a hand, and she put hers in it. He pulled her up to a standing position and gently squeezed her fingers. "Now your feet won't freeze. These old wood floors are cold in the wintertime. Did you sleep well?"

"Yes, I did," she answered. No one had been that concerned about her since—well, she couldn't remember a time. "What can I do to help with breakfast?"

Lucas turned and went back to the kitchen. "You could get the juice and the jellies out of the fridge."

Travis had never cooked breakfast or even helped her with Theron. He had dang sure never raced across the room to put her house shoes on her feet. He came from a family where the housework and raising babies were women's work.

"Hey, Theron," Lucas said, "you are doing a great job. Did your mama teach you to set a nice table like that?"

"I researched it, but Mama said that we didn't need to set it like the queen of England." Theron beamed. "So, we just make it look like this at home."

Vada's eyes popped wide open, and she glanced across the open space to the kitchen area. Theron was talking to Lucas as if he were an old friend. Maybe her grandmother had been right when she said that Christmas was the season of miracles.

"Well, it looks mighty fine. What have you asked Santa to bring you for Christmas?" Lucas asked.

"Santa is a myth. But…" Theron paused.

Vada didn't realize she was holding her breath until her chest began to ache. Theron had never asked for anything for Christmas. She'd bought him games and given him gift cards to buy whatever he needed for his computer and wrapped new pajamas up for under the tree.

"But…" Theron repeated, "if…" he stammered, "if I could have what I wanted, I would ask for a pair of cowboy boots like yours, with square toes. The pointed-toed ones are not good for a growing boy's feet, and maybe a cowboy hat, a black one like you wear."

"I see." Lucas whipped up eggs to scramble. "Is there a reason you would want those things?"

"Because I want to ride Buttercup," Theron answered.

A strong sense of dread filled Vada's heart when she thought about having to leave the ranch in a few days. The different setting and spending time with that horse every day had brought her son out of his shell. Would he go back to his old hermit ways after they went back home?

Lucas filled a mug with coffee and handed it to Vada. "Just like you like it—black and strong."

"Thanks—again," she said, "Granny used to say that weak coffee was just murdered water."

She couldn't help feeling a special thrill when his fingertips brushed hers, the warmth shooting right through her.

At last, someone likes you and Theron as well. Her grandmother was back in her head.

Theron waited patiently at the table with his hands folded in his lap. Lucas seated Vada and then took his chair at the head of the table. "I will say the blessing this morning," Theron said.

Vada almost fell out of her chair when Theron began, "Thank you to God or the universe or whoever is out there for this breakfast and for my mama, for Lucas, and for Buttercup. Amen. And one more thing, thank you for Tex. He is a good dog."

He looked up and said, "What?" just like a regular ten-year-old would. "I learned how to say a blessing on the Internet. I was practicing. Did I do it right?"

"You did just fine," Lucas said with a nod as he passed the platter of bacon and eggs to Vada.

That was another first in her world. Her ex-husband would have taken out a portion for himself before handing it to her. "Thank you—again. Seems like I'm saying that every five minutes," she said.

"You are very welcome," Lucas answered. "It's quite a treat having someone in the bunkhouse with me. I've always had lots of guys around in the past, and this old place can get really lonely and empty feeling. So, I'm glad to have you and Theron here, but the thanks should go to you for making dinner and supper for us. I can do a fairly good job of breakfast, but I'm not much of a cook with the other two meals." He took the platter from Theron and helped his own plate. "And FYI, I can't bake at all, so the cake you made the first day, the pie the second, and the cookies that seem to magically appear in the jar are very welcome."

"It's the least I can do since you won't let us pay for staying here." Vada bit the end from a piece of crispy bacon—cooked just the way she and Theron liked it.

"If Mama cooked every day and made cakes and pies, do you think we could stay here a little longer than a week?" Theron asked.

Vada sucked in air and almost choked on a sip of coffee. She opened her mouth to tell Theron that wasn't polite, but she locked eyes with Lucas, who just barely shook his head.

"I reckon that Buttercup would be glad to have someone to talk to for a while longer," Lucas said, "and I do like your mama's cookin'. Have you put up a Christmas tree at your house in town?"

"No," Theron said.

"What would you think of me and you going out in the woods and cutting down a tree? I bet my mama has some extra decorations. We could set it over there by the fireplace, and put our presents under it," Lucas said between bites.

"I would like that," Theron said.

"Then if it's all right with your mama, maybe you could stay until after Christmas—just so I wouldn't be lonely," Lucas said.

"I suppose that would be all right," Vada said, "but if you change your mind, we can go home at any time."

"Yes, ma'am," Theron said with a smile.

* * *

"Well, partner," Lucas said when they'd finished cleaning up after breakfast, "are you ready to go tell Buttercup that you're sticking around for a while?"

Theron nodded. "I just need to get my coat and hat on. It's very cold from here to the barn."

"This is a miracle," Vada whispered.

"No, it's a horse that likes kids," Lucas said out of the side of his mouth.

"Thank you for taking so much time with him." Tears welled up in Vada's eyes.

"Hey, he's making me feel like I'm doing something special," Lucas told her. "See you at noon, or before if he gets tired or hungry. We keep bottled water and snacks in the tack room, so we should be good until then." He lowered his voice. "And thank you for letting him stay longer. He's made such good progress that I'd hate to see y'all leave now."

"And it has nothing to do with my cooking?" she teased.

"I wouldn't say that." Lucas winked.

"I am ready," Theron said when he had changed from pajamas into jeans and a blue sweatshirt. His brown cap was pulled down over his ears, and his gloves were sticking out of the pockets of his coat.

"Do you think you should put those gloves on your hands?" Vada asked.

"I'll put them on if my hands get cold. I like to feel Buttercup's hair when I pet her," Theron replied.

"Okay, then," Vada said. "Are you sure you don't want me to go with you?"

"I have decided that if I am going to get better, I need to do some things on my own. That's what my research says," Theron answered in his most serious tone. He headed outside with a wave over his shoulder. "I have my phone. I will call you if I need to, but Lucas will be there, so I think I'll be fine."

"That is amazing," Vada whispered.

Lucas patted her on the shoulder. "I'll watch his every movement, and if he gets out that toy, I'll call you."

There it was again—Mia called it vibes, but to Lucas it was more like electricity between him and Vada. He wondered if she felt it, too, and if she did, would she even consider a date with him.

He hadn't made it twenty feet from the bunkhouse when the niggling voice in his head reminded him that he hadn't been out with a woman whom he could get serious with in years. "No time like the present," he muttered.

"Are you thinking about presents for you for Christmas?" Theron asked.

"I sure am," Lucas stammered and tried to cover his tracks without lying to the boy. "I'm hoping your mama makes some more of those peanut butter cookies and gives them to me for Christmas."

"I'll tell her," Theron said and then ran on ahead of Lucas toward the barn.

This was exactly why he wanted to work with disabled children—no matter what the problems—and help them to attain some level of self-confidence. His success story with Theron might turn out to be the best one he had ever had.

Lucas was feeling pretty good, right up until Theron came running hell-bent for leather out of the barn. The way he was going, it looked like he wasn't going to stop until he reached the bunkhouse.

"So much for feeling good," he muttered.

If the pathway had been paved and Theron's shoes had had rubber soles, he would have come to a screeching halt right in front of Lucas. As it was, Lucas reached out a hand to steady the kid when he stopped and bent forward to grab his knees.

"Are you sick, son?" Lucas asked.

"No," Theron panted. "Out. Of. Breath," he managed to get out. "Someone in the barn."

Lucas glanced that way and saw his father's pickup truck. "That would be *my* mama and daddy. They said they were bringing alpacas up to the barn today because there's a possibility of freezing weather tonight. I didn't think they would be out this early. Are you up to meeting them, or should we go back to the house?"

Theron rose slowly, whipped his hat off, and scratched his head. "Will you stay right there with me?"

"Yes, I will," Lucas promised.

"Do I have to talk?" he asked.

"Not if you don't want to, but I have to tell you, the alpacas, especially Dixie, are real friendly and they love attention," Lucas answered. "She would probably love for you to play chase with her."

"How do I do that?" Theron asked. "I haven't researched that game."

Lucas removed his hand and took a step toward the barn. "You chase after her, and then she whips around and chases you. After a couple of times around the corral, she will flop down and want you to pet her. That's the game that she and Mia play all the time. They make a sweet little noise when they are happy, and Dixie listens as well as Buttercup and Tex. But if you don't want to play, you can just spend some time in the stall with Buttercup."

Theron pulled his fidget toy from his pocket and started playing with it. "I will try. I researched cowboys, and you are one? I think the man in the barn might be one, too."

"No, but I'm not surprised," Lucas said with a smile. "You are really good at researching and learning new things."

"I love to learn," Theron said with a sigh, "but that makes me kind of a weirdo, doesn't it?"

"I don't think of you as a weirdo at all," Lucas assured him. "You are an awesome person that I'm glad to get to know, but I don't want you to be uncomfortable around my folks. Should I call your mom to go with us?" Lucas asked.

Theron shook his head and put the toy back in his pocket. He started back to the barn, one slow step at a time.

When they arrived at the doors, he took a deep breath and put his hand in Lucas's. "I can do this if you will hold my hand."

Lucas took his hand and gave it a gentle squeeze. "I believe in you. Just remember, these two people already like you."

"Yes, but according to my reading, it's not unusual for kids like me to have difficulty in social situations," Theron said. "Buttercup helps me, and so does Tex. How do you know those people in the barn like me?"

"And you help Buttercup." Lucas led him into the barn and toward where he could hear his mother's and father's voices. "She would be very lonely if you didn't come see her and talk to Winnie, too. And the way I know about those people is because they are my mom and dad. They must already like you because they told me that they wanted to meet you. They love kids."

"Do they even like kids who are different?" Theron asked.

"Yes, they do. I was a different little kid when they adopted me," Lucas said.

"Really?" Theron cocked his head to one side.

"Really. They had already adopted Jesse, but then my brother Cody and I needed a home, and they took us in, too, and made us all a family," Lucas explained as they walked toward the back of the barn. "I was kind of shy, but they helped me and loved me so much that I got over it."

"I'm glad to know that," Theron said. "That makes me feel like there is hope for me."

"Always, son," Lucas said. "There is always hope."

As if he had settled something in his mind, Theron let go of Lucas's hand. "Winnie is almost as good a listener as Buttercup is. Sometimes I just talk to both of them at the same time since their stalls are so close together. Today I will tell them that I met more people than just you and Mama."

Lucas remembered the first day he had gone to school. If it hadn't been for Cody and Jesse, he would have hidden in the back of the bus until the day ended. *Socially challenged* were the words he heard his teacher tell his mother when she came for parent-teacher conference that year. He didn't know what that meant and wasn't as smart as Theron, so for years, he worried about whether it meant he had a horrible disease that would kill him.

Finally, he looked it up and agreed with what the teacher had said, and like Theron, he worked hard to overcome it. Having to stay in a bunkhouse with other guys—complete strangers at first—was his first test, and it took him weeks to be even semi-comfortable. He still had trouble opening up to people he had just met, and he liked his "alone time."

So, what's different about Vada and Theron? asked the voice in his head.

"I understand them both," he muttered and then wondered if he'd said that out loud.

Sonny came into the barn from the corral and leaned on his cane while Pearl closed the door and hurried over to drag a lawn chair across the floor and set it beside him. Sonny eased down into it and said, "Well, hello, son."

"How are you feeling today, Dad?" Lucas asked.

"Better, and I see you brought someone with you," Sonny answered.

Theron slipped his hand back into Lucas's. "Hello, I am Theron. I am here to get better at being social. Buttercup is helping me."

"I'm glad," Sonny said.

Pearl brought over another chair and sat down beside Sonny. "I hear you are very smart."

"Yes, I am. You are Mrs. Ryan and"—he turned to face Sonny—"you are Mr. Ryan. Is it all right if I don't shake hands with you?"

"That's fine," Sonny answered. "Dixie and some of the baby alpacas are out in the corral. We thought we'd let them romp and play for an hour and then put them in stalls. They'll have to stay inside for a couple of days if the weatherman is right."

"Would you like to go out and see them?" Pearl asked.

"Yes, ma'am," Theron answered, barely above a whisper.

"Lucas, you could go introduce him to Dixie and the others," Sonny said.

Lucas started around them, and Theron's grip got even tighter. "Will you still be here when we get back?"

"Probably not, but y'all feel free to come see us anytime you want. I've been making Christmas cookies this week," Pearl answered. "If y'all are going to be out here awhile, would you mind bringing Dixie and the babies all inside to the stalls?"

"Sure thing," Lucas agreed.

"Did I do all right?" Theron's hand relaxed once they were outside, and after just a few seconds, he pulled it free.

"You did just fine. I was proud of you," Lucas answered. "Now, that bigger alpaca over there is Dixie. Stevie, that's my sister-in-law who is a veterinarian, rescued her last year. We've all babied her, so she's a big pet."

Dixie came across the corral in a run and stopped in front of Lucas. He reached into his pocket, pulled out a banana, and offered it to Theron. "She likes bananas. Do you want to feed her?"

"Do I peel it?" Theron took it from Lucas, and Dixie came right to him.

"Yes, and then just hold it out to her. She'll bite chunks off until she's finished the whole thing," Lucas answered.

"When she is done, will she want to play chase?" Theron removed the skin and held out the banana toward the alpaca.

She made a noise in her throat and took the first bite.

Lucas backed up to the rail and leaned against it. "I imagine that she will."

Within minutes Dixie had finished her banana and nudged Theron on the leg.

"Does that mean she wants me to run?" Theron asked.

"Yes, but not as fast as you did a while ago," Lucas answered.

Theron stayed close to the fence when he started running laps around the corral. Lucas slipped his phone from his back pocket and videoed about three minutes of the little boy and the alpaca. Theron's laughter echoed through the air as Dixie and the four baby alpacas chased after him.

When Theron got tired, Lucas sent the video to Vada with a message: *I feel like a king sitting on top of the world.*

Theron was already in the barn, telling Buttercup and Winnie all about his day, when Lucas got a text from Vada: *Have tears in my eyes. I've never seen him play like a child or laugh that much. I will treasure this video forever. Thank you, Lucas.*

Lucas pretended to need something from the tack room so that Theron wouldn't see his emotional state. He wiped his wet cheeks, gathered up two bottles of water and a couple of protein bars, and carried them out to where Theron was sitting facing Winnie and Buttercup. He handed a bottle and a bar to Theron and then headed out to bring in the alpacas. He wanted more than just nine more days with Vada and Theron. Falling in love with Vada would be so easy.

"This is crazy. I've only really known her a few days," he muttered. "I've never been a guy who drew women to him like my two brothers do."

Be yourself, the voice in his head said.

"What if she doesn't like who I am?" Lucas whispered.

You've got nine days to see if she likes you for more than a horse therapist, the voice in his head told him. *Make the most of it.*

CHAPTER SIX

Vada waited until she was sure Theron was sound asleep before she crawled out of her bunk and tiptoed across the cold floor. She pulled a warm blanket from the back of the sofa, sat down and covered her feet with it, then opened the video on her phone and watched it a half dozen times.

"Having trouble sleeping?" Lucas asked as he came out of the bedroom. "Beer?"

"Love one," she answered, "and yes, I couldn't sleep, so I got up to look at the video you sent and to think about what's next."

"What do you mean by next?" Lucas asked.

"I've never seen my son act like kids his age," she answered. "He loves it here, and he is opening up in ways I never thought possible. He actually wants to go outside, and before we went to sleep, he said that he wanted to walk out to the barn by himself tomorrow to talk to the animals."

"Do I hear a 'but'?" Lucas sat down on the end of the sofa and pulled her feet over into his lap.

"You do," she said with a nod. "I like you, Lucas, and

Theron thinks you are a superhero, but what happens when we go home? What happens when...?"

"What if that never had to happen?" he asked.

"We can't stay here forever," Vada said.

"Why? I like having company, and you're a fantastic cook. I could hire you, and Theron could be my sidekick," he said. "Why don't we leave the end date open. You can stay as long as you and Theron want."

"That's very generous of you." Vada smiled. "I just keep thinking that if he's come so far in less than a week, what could happen if he has more time."

Lucas reached under the blanket and began to massage Vada's feet. "We can give him all the time he needs."

"Thank you for that," Vada said. "Can you imagine being in college when you were only twelve years old?"

"No, I couldn't imagine being in college when I was eighteen. That's why I went to work on a ranch," Lucas said. "I wasn't book smart like my brothers, but I loved ranchin'. Still do. I was serious, Vada, about you staying on. You can do your work here. I'll find a desk somewhere on the ranch for you, and you can cook for me and Theron to pay your way."

She groaned and then clamped a hand over her mouth.

"Does that mean you hate the idea?" he asked.

See there, you didn't do it right, the niggling voice in his head said. *You should have been more romantic—told her that you wanted her to stay because you have feelings for her, not because you like her fried chicken.*

"No, it means that I've never had a foot massage before. That is downright glorious," she muttered.

"Never?" he asked. "Have all the men you've dated been idiots?"

"I haven't dated in years. Theron has...well, you know," she said.

Lucas slowly shook his head from side to side. "A man would be lucky to get to know that boy. He's so smart and has such a big heart. He just wants someone to accept him just like he is."

"Yep, but there aren't many men like you out there," she said.

"Don't I know it," he said with a sigh.

Vada pulled her feet back and scooted over next to Lucas. She laid her head on his shoulder and said, "Lucas Ryan, I have never met anyone like you—and I like you a lot."

Lucas slipped an arm around Vada's shoulders and kissed her on the forehead. It felt oh, so right to sit there in a simple bunkhouse with her in the semi-darkness with a ten-year-old boy sleeping soundly across the room in a top bunk. If this was what having a family of his own felt like, then he wanted to hold on to Vada and Theron forever.

* * *

The air was so crisp that it looked like smoke came out when Vada exhaled. Her face was chilled by the time they'd gone a hundred yards from the truck, but she could still feel the warmth of Lucas's kiss on her forehead from the night before. She hadn't known what to expect when she awoke that morning, but he had acted like nothing had happened the night before.

Enjoy the day and stop trying to analyze everything. Her grandmother's voice seemed to float on the cold wind.

"Yes, ma'am," she muttered.

"I'm not a ma'am," Theron said. "Who are you talking to?"

"I was thinking about something my grandmother said," Vada answered. No way was she telling Theron that occasionally her granny popped into her head. He would be researching the issue of hearing voices and what it meant.

"What did she say?" Theron asked as he eyed a cedar tree.

"She said for me to enjoy the time I have with you and Lucas while we're picking out a Christmas tree," Vada said.

Theron eyed her carefully, "How did she know we were picking out a tree today?"

"She didn't, but I just figured since she used to tell me to enjoy the day, that she would want me to have a good time today," she answered. "Are you having a good time?"

"Yes, I am," Theron answered. "I think this tree would be just right. It's about four feet tall and not too big around."

"How do you know how tall it is?" Lucas asked.

"The sun is right there"—Theron pointed—"and the tree is throwing a shadow over there"—he moved his finger—"so if you do the math, then the tree is four feet tall and about two and a half feet across. That's unusual for a cedar because they are most usually kind of round."

Lucas set his tool bag down and removed a small chain saw. "This will get noisy, but it won't take long."

"You should leave as much trunk on as you can, and then we have to put it in a container that will hold water," Theron said.

Vada still had trouble believing that this child was her son.

Lucas fired up the chain saw and cut down the tree in a matter of minutes. When it had fallen away from Theron and Vada, he put the saw back into the bag. "You want to help me take this to the truck, Theron?" he asked. "You grab the end, and I'll take the trunk."

"I can do that," Theron said. "I've never decorated a tree before, and I forgot to do research last night before we went to bed."

"You didn't help your mama trim the tree?" Lucas asked as they started back toward the vehicle.

"No, sir, I did not," Theron answered. "I'm not really religious, and I don't believe in Santa Claus. It's hard to believe in something I can't see."

"What changed this year?" Lucas asked.

"Buttercup did," he answered. "I talked to her and figured out that this can just be a holiday where families get together. It doesn't have to have a lot of meaning, and Buttercup and you and Tex and now the alpacas, especially Dixie, are like family to me. I want to share this holiday with all of them. Can we put a tree in the barn?"

Without a moment's hesitation, Lucas pointed toward a small cedar only a few feet from the truck and asked, "Is that one big enough?"

"I think so," Theron answered. "They will like having a tree of their own, and I will tell them all the stories about Christmas, from Jesus to Santa Claus."

"That's a good reason, and I'm sure they'll like having a tree of their own in the barn," Lucas said as he dropped his tool bag and took out the saw.

Vada's eyes filled with tears, but she blinked them back.

When both trees were in the back of the truck, Theron hopped into the back seat, fastened his seat belt, and began to hum. Vada cocked her head to one side and tried to pick up the tune. She'd never heard him hum or sing, either one. His first therapist suggested having soft classical music playing in the house, but that seemed to agitate him even more than normal. Vada loved country music, so she listened to it with her earphones as she worked most days.

"What song you got going in your head?" Lucas asked.

Theron stopped humming and said, "That will be 'Everything's Gonna be Alright,' by David Lee Murphy. When we drove to the barn it was on the radio, so I looked it up and found out that I like country music, so I've been listening to it on my phone. I let Buttercup listen to a couple of songs, and she seems to like it, too."

"So do I," Lucas said.

"And me, too," Vada chimed in.

"That's interesting," Theron said. "Three people in a car, and we all like the same kind of music. Very unusual."

Lucas glanced over at Vada and winked. A surge of happiness filled her breast. These feelings were crazy, she thought. Sure, she'd known Lucas in high school, and she had felt some chemistry last night when he kissed her on the forehead, but she had been around him only a week this time around. Was it even possible to feel the way she did in such a short time?

She remembered a plaque she'd seen several years ago that said, "The heart knows. Listen to it."

"Penny for your thoughts," Lucas whispered.

She told him about the plaque and what was written on it.

"Amen!" Lucas said. "If we paid attention to what our heart tells us, we wouldn't make nearly as many mistakes."

"What is your heart telling you right now?" Vada asked.

"That's a silly question," Theron piped up from the back seat. "A heart pumps blood. It doesn't talk."

Lucas winked again, and Vada smiled. Just having someone who understood and accepted her child was beyond any miracle the universe could boast about.

CHAPTER SEVEN

There's a tree stand in the storage room, so we can set up the tree, but I'll have to go to Mama's to get some decorations," Lucas said as he hauled the bigger tree into the bunkhouse and laid it on the floor.

Theron took a deep breath and blurted out, "May I go with you?"

Vada almost hyperventilated. "Are you sure about this?"

Theron nodded. "I'm not ready for a big crowd with lots of people around me, but I'd like to talk some more to Sonny and Pearl. They were nice to me." His hands trembled, but he didn't shove them into his pockets or get out one of the fidget toys that calmed him. "I researched the idea of going around people, and from what I read, if I try just a couple at a time, it's better."

"Baby steps," Vada said.

"I'm not a baby, Mama," Theron protested. "I'm ten years old and very smart."

"Yes, you are," Lucas agreed as he brought out the tree stand that had been red at one time, but now the paint was chipped, "but baby steps just mean that you take one little step at a time in this journey to get better."

"I see." Theron nodded again. "I agree that it has to be a slow process so as not to overwhelm the patient—that's me in this journey. So, are we going now, or are we going to put the tree up first?"

"Let's set the tree up and water it real good so it doesn't dry out," Lucas said. "This is the first Christmas tree I've ever put up."

"You didn't have one when you were a boy like me?" Theron asked.

"Yes, but that was for our family," Lucas explained as he worked. "We helped decorate it, and we all loved Christmas, but this is the first one I'm putting up that's kind of like for my own little family."

"I like that," Theron said.

"You reckon you could hold the tree real steady for me while I get the screws into the bark to hold it upright?" Lucas asked.

"Yes, sir, I can do that." Theron reached into the limbs and grasped the tree firmly. "I am glad that I'm wearing gloves. These things are kind of prickly."

When they finished getting the tree in position, Lucas and Theron waved goodbye to Vada and disappeared outside. She grabbed her phone and called Stevie.

Stevie answered the phone with, "Hey, girl, how are things going? I've been dying to get over to the bunkhouse for a visit, but I didn't want to spook Theron."

"I'm in total shock," Vada said and then told Stevie about all the progress Theron was making. "I'm so proud of him, but I can't help but be afraid he will revert back to his hermit lifestyle. I don't want to ever leave the ranch for any reason for fear that the magic lies right here. What if I take him home and...?" She paused for a breath.

"The difference in the way things were and the way they are is that he wants to be helped," Stevie reminded her. "I don't think that will change one bit. How about you, Vada? How are you doing living out here in the boonies?"

"After living in the small house and seldom getting outside, I feel like a bird let out of a cage," she answered. "When Theron and Lucas go to the barn, I have time to myself. I'm getting my work done in a shorter time because I'm not constantly worried about my son. I love cooking for three. Theron is eating more, and Lucas is so sweet. He compliments me and thanks me for every meal."

"That's a Ryan thing for sure," Stevie said. "Cody does the same thing, and I love it. I understand you've agreed to stay until after Christmas, right?"

"I'd stay forever, but..." Vada said and then clamped a hand over her mouth.

"I bet it could be arranged," Stevie told her.

"Do you think the family would sell me an acre of ground to put a double-wide trailer on?" Vada asked, but in her dreams, she and Theron and Lucas lived right there in the bunkhouse.

"One never knows," Stevie said with a giggle.

"They're back with the decorations. Give us a couple of hours and then come see our tree," Vada said.

"Do you think Theron is ready to be introduced to another person?" Stevie asked.

"He went with Lucas to get the decorations, so he's getting acquainted with Sonny and Pearl," Vada replied. "And if he gets nervous, Lucas can take him out to the barn and let him talk to Buttercup or the alpacas."

"What about bringing Cody?" Stevie asked.

"Let's give it a try," Vada said. "Theron is into all things cowboy right now, so maybe…"

"If you think it's too much for him, just give me a signal, and we'll leave," Stevie said.

Vada cocked an ear toward the door. "I will, and, Stevie, he's laughing, so I guess things went well at Sonny and Pearl's house."

"Good sign. See you later," Stevie said, and the screen went dark.

Who was this child coming in out of the cold with a cardboard box in his arms? He looked a little like her son, Theron, with his blond hair that needed cutting, but his blue eyes sparkled with joy. How could a horse cause such a fast turnaround in a kid?

It wasn't the horse, her granny answered her questions. *It was the fact that he decided he wanted to get better.*

Lucas carried three boxes into the bunkhouse right behind Theron. "There should be enough stuff here for our tree and the one out in the barn. This kid says that he wants to do both trees tonight, so we'd better get busy."

Theron set his box on the kitchen table. "This one has cookies, some fudge, and part of a chocolate cake. Pearl says I'm supposed to call her Granny and Sonny is Poppa. Is that all right with you, Mama? It's not disrespecting my real granny, is it?"

"Your real granny would be glad that you have found a new granny and poppa," Vada assured him. "I can almost feel her smiling."

Theron frowned as he opened the box and took out a sugar cookie. "How do you *feel* a smile, Mama?"

"How does it make you feel to brush Buttercup after you walk her around the corral?" Lucas asked.

"All warm inside," Theron answered without hesitation.

"That's what a smile feels like," Lucas explained.

"Thank you. Now I understand. All of this is really new to me, but I like it so far," Theron said and bit off a chunk of the cookie.

Vada felt as if her feet were floating six inches off the floor. "A tree needs presents under it. Do you still want boots and a hat?"

"Yes, I do, and gloves like Lucas has," he replied. "I want to ride Buttercup after Christmas, and I need a new external hard drive to keep all my pictures of the ranch, and the horses, and the bunkhouse on."

"If there was a Santa Claus, what would you ask him for?" Lucas asked.

"I would ask for enough money to buy this ranch, so I never had to leave it," he said. "Now can we put the stuff on this tree? I can't wait to see what Buttercup and Winnie think of the one in the barn. And, Mama, tomorrow I'm going to meet the twins and Mia. I think I'm ready."

"Stevie and Cody might drop in for a few minutes tonight to see our tree," Vada said.

"Could they come to the barn and see that one, too?" Theron asked with a long sigh. "Lucas says I can fix it up all by myself."

Vada wouldn't have cared if he wanted to decorate forty trees. To hear him excited and asking for boots and a hat even before something for his computer put a big smile on her face.

"I think Stevie and Cody would love to see your barn tree. I'll call her and tell her to meet us out there."

"Is Cody a cowboy?" Theron asked.

"Yes, he is," Lucas answered as he opened the first box and took out a strand of lights. "This is a two-person job. I'll feed them to you, Vada, if you'll get them situated."

Theron plopped down on the sofa and frowned. "Why would you feed lights to my mama? They are made of glass. Humans do not digest glass."

Lucas bit back a chuckle. "That's just cowboy talk that means I will put the lights around my arms and let your mama pick them off, one at a time, to put on the tree branches. We won't do lights on the barn tree because it might spook the horses. We'll just put garland and unbreakable ornaments on that one."

"Unbreakable?" Vada asked as she began helping get the lights on the tree.

* * *

"When we were just little kids, Dad made Mama some ornaments out of wood. Three boys romping around in a house can be rough on things that break," Lucas answered.

Every single time, without fail, that Vada reached for another stretch of lights, her hand brushed against his, and her touch jacked up his pulse a notch or two. His mama always said that whatever you do on New Year's Day would be what you did all year. With that in mind, he hoped he could convince Vada to stay on the ranch until after that day. Then there would be the possibility that the three of them would be together for the whole year—if his mama's superstition was right.

When the lights were finally on the tree, Lucas opened another box and brought out a long rope with bandannas tied to it about every six inches. "This is the garland that Mama used when we were kids."

"A cowboy Christmas tree!" Theron whispered.

"Yep, complete with one of my dad's old hats to put on the top instead of an angel or a star," Lucas told him.

"Can we make the one in the barn just like this?" Theron's eyes were as big as silver dollars.

"We can, but we've only got one hat," Lucas said.

"Why don't you guys use the hat for the barn tree and let me create a topper with whatever I can find?" Vada suggested.

Theron looked so happy that Lucas was glad Vada had come up with the idea. He planned to go into town the next day and buy Theron boots and a hat as near to the ones he wore as he could find. Maybe he would need a work coat, too, to go with his gloves.

"What are you thinking about?" Vada asked.

"Christmas presents," he answered. "What do you want?"

"I've got everything right here that I could possibly want," she replied.

Lucas raised an eyebrow. "Oh, really."

She raised her head and looked him right in the eyes. "Yes, Lucas Ryan, I really do."

She blinked, picked up the rope garland and began to drape it around the tree and then started hanging ornaments—small wooden boots, steer horns, birdhouses, angel wings, and more than a dozen other shapes. Theron stood to the side and told her where each piece should go, and when she was finished, he crossed his arms over his chest and walked around three sides of the tree.

"This is a good tree," he declared. "I like it better than the ones I saw on the Internet when I researched how to decorate one."

"That's great," Lucas said with a grin. "You ready to go set up the barn tree?"

"Yes, I am." Theron headed across the room to the sofa where he'd tossed his coat.

"I'm buying him boots and a hat," Lucas whispered to Vada. "Want me to pick up a work coat like mine?"

"You don't have to do that," Vada argued.

"Nope, I don't, but I want to," Lucas said. "He's made such good progress, and he's a wonderful kid. A little too smart. Sometimes when he's done his 'research'"—he air-quoted the words—"he tells me things that are even above my head, but I love spending time with him."

"Then, yes, I'd like for him to have a work coat," Vada said with a nod.

The whole room lit up brighter than the Christmas tree when she smiled up at him. He wanted so badly to take her in his arms and kiss her, but there was no way when Theron was right there staring at them.

A knock on the door startled all three of them.

Theron stood perfectly still and locked eyes with his mother. Lucas hurried to open the door and let Pearl into the bunkhouse.

"Come on in, Mama," he said. "Is something wrong?"

"No, I wanted to see your tree," she answered. "It's just like I remembered it. I'm so glad you could use all those ornaments. And I wanted to ask Theron if it would be all right if Sonny and I watch him decorate the one in the barn. You can say no and we won't be offended, but Sonny wanted to get out a little while this evening. If that big winter storm hits us, he'll be in the house for a while."

"Yes, you may," Theron said. "I liked your cookies, Granny Pearl."

"I'm so glad," Pearl said. "When you eat all of what I sent, you come on down to my house and I'll give you some more. Poppa and I will go on down to the barn and be ready when you get there," Pearl said with a smile and closed the door behind her as she left.

"Are you coming, Mama?" Theron asked.

Vada picked up her coat. "You bet I am. I want to see how you fix up your barn tree. I just know that Buttercup and Winnie, and even Dixie, are going to love it."

Lucas's hand brushed against hers as they followed Theron outside to the truck, and he locked his pinkie finger with hers. Even though it was a brief walk across the porch and to the vehicle, he enjoyed every moment of being united with her in that small way. He felt like a teenager on a first date—or in his case, a twenty-year-old. He hadn't dated anyone in high school, and his first experience with a girlfriend had been when he was with the daughter of the rancher where he worked. He gave Vada's hand a gentle squeeze before he let go to open the door for her, and she responded by patting him on the arm.

"I wish Lucas was my daddy," Theron piped up from the back seat.

"Oh, my!" Vada muttered. "I'm sorry."

"Why?" Lucas asked.

"Why?" Theron must have thought Lucas was talking to him, because he unfastened his seat belt and leaned up so that his head was between Vada and Lucas. "Because you understand kids like me, and because I like you, and Sonny and Pearl like me, and they would be my real grandparents if you were my daddy."

"We understand each other very well, son," Lucas said, "and it's okay for you to wish that. I'm honored that you like me that much."

Lucas had to swallow hard to get the lump in his throat to go down. He would love to have Theron for a son—he'd even adopt him if that was possible—but what he'd like most was to deck the man that was privileged to have such a smart little boy and yet made him feel ashamed and unwanted.

CHAPTER EIGHT

Lucas and Theron came in after doing the feeding chores that Tuesday evening. The aromas of fresh bread baking and savory soup filled the bunkhouse. Theron followed Lucas's lead and hung his coat on the rack inside the door, then kicked off his shoes and set them beside Lucas's boots.

Vada gave the pot of soup bubbling on the stovetop a stir, then turned to face them. Her brown hair hung over her shoulders in two thick braids. She wore a pair of faded skinny jeans and an oatmeal-colored thermal knit shirt that hugged her curves.

Lucas's mouth went dry, and his pulse went into overtime—again. The light from the kitchen window created a halo around her head, and had she sprouted big, fluffy wings in that instant, he would not have been surprised.

"Something smells good," Theron said as he headed toward the bathroom. "Is it all right if I take a bath before supper?"

"Of course. The bread won't be done for about twenty minutes," Vada replied. "Did you have a good time?"

"I learned that cattle need feed in the winter as well as hay."

Theron closed the door behind him and then opened it back up. "And I'm going to research and learn more about cattle. I'm going to study agriculture in my spare time this semester." The door eased shut, and then Lucas heard the water running.

He crossed the room in a few long strides, wrapped his arms around Vada, and hugged her tightly. "You are so beautiful." He buried his face in her hair.

"Good grief," she said with a laugh, "what brought all this on?"

"I'm just happy that you and Theron are staying on the ranch for a while." Lucas took half a step back, tipped up her chin with his knuckles, looked deep into her aqua-colored eyes, and kissed her.

The kiss started off slow and sweet, but then her arms snaked up around his neck, and she pressed her body close to his. He deepened the kiss, and a jolt of pure, fiery desire shot through his body. He'd kissed women, dated women, slept with women, and even had a couple of fairly serious relationships, but nothing had ever prepared him for the way he felt right then.

"Oh! My!" Vada gasped when the kiss ended.

"Sparks?" Lucas's voice sounded hoarse even in his own ears.

"No," Vada said breathlessly, "white-hot fire like I've never felt before."

"Me, too," Lucas said. "I've wanted to kiss you for days now, but..."

"But we've got a little boy underfoot," Vada said with a smile.

"I love that kid," Lucas said, "and I really like his mama."

"His mama thinks a lot of you, too," Vada said.

Lucas drew her back into his arms and brushed a soft kiss across her lips. "Is it too soon to say that I could so easily fall in love with you?"

"Probably, but the feeling is mutual," Vada told him. "And as much as I hate to ruin this romantic moment, if I don't take that bread out of the oven, it's going to be burned." She rose onto her tiptoes and kissed Lucas on the chin. "And if that happens, I'm going to let you explain why it's ruined to Theron."

"Go, good woman, go!" Lucas teased.

Vada crossed over to the stove, grabbed an oven mitt, and removed a pan of hot rolls from the oven. She set them on the counter and buttered the tops. Lucas slipped his arms around her waist from the back and kissed her on the neck.

"This is a cowboy's dream," he said.

"What's that?" Vada asked.

"Coming home after a day on the ranch to a hot meal and even hotter kisses from a beautiful woman," Lucas said.

Vada turned around and slipped her arms around his neck. "I always thought you were the shy Ryan brother."

"I am, but you bring out the romantic in me," he told her. "Never even thought I had that side, but I'm kind of liking it."

"Mama!" Theron called out. "I forgot to bring in my pajama bottoms."

"And the romance ends," Vada said with a chuckle.

"No, honey, the romance is just beginning," Lucas told her.

* * *

Vada had thought she would need to buy a *Flirting for Dummies* book if she ever had the opportunity to date again, but it was coming naturally with Lucas. For the past couple of days, she could see the same longing in his eyes that she felt in her heart. The kisses and brief romantic time had proved she wasn't wrong.

Now what do I do? she asked herself. *I've got to think of Theron, not just myself. How would he react to sharing me with someone else?*

Don't rush, but don't slam the door to the opportunity, either, her grandmother's voice answered. *He's already said that he wishes Lucas was his daddy, so that's a good start.*

"Good advice," she muttered as she found Theron's pajama bottoms in his perfectly organized suitcase and carried them to the bathroom.

When she knocked on the door, he opened it just a crack, stuck out a hand, and took them from her. "Thank you. Is supper ready?"

"It will be on the table when you get there," she answered.

When Theron came out of the bathroom, he was dressed in his superhero pajamas and a pair of socks. His blond hair, usually parted on the side, had been combed straight back like Lucas's. "I'm hungry," he said. "I will have to talk to Buttercup about it, but I think the ranch is giving me a big appetite."

Vada led the way to the kitchen area, where Lucas was busy bringing out supper. "I bet all that fresh air and walking Buttercup around in the corral has made you need more food for fuel," she said.

Lucas had just finished setting the table and serving up three bowls of soup. Vada's ex-husband had never helped her get food on the table, not even after Theron was born and things got hectic. That simple gesture was almost as romantic as his kisses had been.

Oh, really. Her grandmother's giggles were so real that she stopped and glanced over her shoulder to see if she was there.

"Well, almost," Vada muttered.

"Almost what?" Theron asked as he pulled out his chair and sat down.

Vada noticed that his pajamas were tight on him, and his face had filled out some. His eyes didn't have black circles around them, and he wasn't pale anymore. If he had changed this much in less than two weeks, then she couldn't imagine what six months or a year on the ranch would do for him.

"Did I do something wrong?" he asked.

"Of course not," Vada said. "I like your hair fixed that way, and I was just thinking that you have more color in your face than usual."

"That would be vitamin D from the sunshine," Theron told her. "A person needs time in the sun every single day. I knew that, but I used to not like going outside. I like it here because Buttercup and Dixie and Tex are here. And Cody and Stevie and Granny and Poppa. Today I met Mia out in the field. She can drive a tractor, and she said when my legs get long enough to reach the pedals, she will teach me how to operate one."

Lucas seated Vada before he took his place. "You'll have to eat good, run and play with the alpacas, and sleep good at night to grow tall enough to drive a tractor. Mia started off driving a hay truck when she was just a kid. She's really good help on the ranch, plus she is learning to be a vet tech from Stevie."

"I don't want to be a vet anything," Theron said. "It would make me sad to see an animal die. Please pass the rolls and butter. This soup is wonderful, Mama. I don't remember you making it at our town home."

Vada handed the basket of rolls across to her son. "If you

will remember, you were on a grilled cheese kick before we came out here."

Theron looked up and sighed. "That's before I did the horse research. I'm glad I did."

Lucas tried a spoonful of soup. "You are right. This is very good."

"Thank you both. My grandmother taught me to make it, and it's always good on a cold day like this." Vada couldn't remember a time when Theron had complimented her on her cooking. He ate. He thanked her politely for the meal—sometimes. He went back to his room. She might just go out to the barn after supper and kiss Buttercup right between her pretty brown eyes for the change she had brought about in him.

And then kiss Lucas right on his sexy lips? the pesky voice in her head asked.

"Yep," she said under her breath.

CHAPTER NINE

One year later

Vada awoke before daylight that morning, eased out of bed, and went to the kitchen. When she reached into the cabinet for the coffee, she noticed that there was a big red circle around the date on the calendar. She smiled and let her mind wander back to what had happened one year ago— the day that she and Theron had come to the ranch for the first time.

A lot had changed in that year, and every single bit of it for the better. She and Lucas had gotten married in June. They'd thought about building a new house, but Theron loved the bunkhouse, so they had just built on to it—a bedroom and bathroom for Theron and an office for Vada. They'd removed the bunk beds and put in a couple of recliners, and she'd added a few feminine touches to the kitchen to make the place homier.

Vada's pride and joy was a simple little sign hanging from chains that squeaked every time the wind blew. Sonny had helped Theron make it to give to her and Lucas as a wedding gift. The lettering for "Buttercup Farms" wasn't perfect, but every time she looked up at it, a new rush of love filled her heart. Buttercup Farms was the name that Theron had given the bunkhouse, and Lucas had adopted it for his therapy business as well. Now it was home—all three of them had finally found a place to belong and a family to belong to.

As usual, she felt Lucas's presence long before he slipped his arms around her waist and kissed her on the neck. "Good morning, darlin'."

She turned around and wrapped her arms around his neck. "Happy anniversary."

"But we haven't been married but six months." He frowned and then flashed a brilliant smile. "It's been a year since y'all came to the ranch the first time. That was the best day of my life."

"You said our wedding was the best day." She tiptoed and kissed him on the cheek.

"Every day since a year ago today has been the best." He pulled her in tighter to his chest. "And every day from now on will be even better."

"Mornin'." Theron yawned as he came out of his bedroom. "Are we going to put up our tree today? Buttercup is excited that she gets another one this year."

"Yes, we are, right after you take your final exam for the semester," Lucas said.

"I got up an hour ago and finished it." Theron went to the refrigerator and brought out the orange juice. He poured himself a glass and downed half of it. "I've decided to major in agribusiness for my bachelor's degree when I start taking college classes next fall."

"We could always use that kind of brain power right here on the ranch," Lucas said.

"I hope I'm a real Ryan by the time I start my college courses." Theron sighed.

Lucas locked gazes with Vada, who gave him a brief nod.

"We were saving this for Christmas, but you'll have lots of presents that day." Lucas headed off toward the bedroom and returned with an unwrapped box. "This is for you, son."

Theron took the box and sighed again. "It feels kind of light, so it can't be new boots. Mine are getting too small, so I thought that might be what you and Mama got me."

Vada was so excited that her hands shook. "You are right. It's not boots. Go ahead and open it."

Theron gently removed the lid and picked up a new leather belt. "But I didn't ask for this."

"Turn it over and look at the back," Vada said.

"Oh. Oh. Oh!" Theron gasped when he saw the name "Ryan" engraved across the back of the new belt. "Does this mean...?"

"Your copy of the adoption papers is right there in the box," Lucas said. "You are officially my son now and..."

Theron jumped up and hugged Lucas for the first time. "Now you are my daddy. This is the best Christmas ever. My high school diploma will have the name Ryan on it, and so will all my degrees."

Vada's eyes filled with tears, and she didn't even try to stop them from flowing down her cheeks. She had been worried that Travis would refuse to sign the papers and let Lucas adopt Theron, but he had sent them back with his signature on them within a week.

"Why are you crying, Mama?" Theron asked.

"These are happy tears," Vada said.

"Then I should be crying, too, but I'm too happy to cry. Can I go tell Granny and Poppa and the rest of the family after breakfast?" Theron asked.

"Yes, you can." Lucas swiped away a tear. "Mama has a plaque in her house that says *Home is where the heart is.*"

"Is your heart here?" Vada asked.

"I've always thought that home is where I hang my hat," Lucas said, "but I agree with her now. This is home, and my heart is right here."

"Yep, it is." Theron put his new belt on over his pajamas. "It fits me, and I love my new name. Theron Ryan. We are all Ryans on this ranch now."

"Yes, we are," Lucas said.

"I'll be back in a minute." Theron rushed into his bedroom.

"What's that all about?" Lucas asked.

Vada put her arms around his waist and laid her head on his chest. "He's got to go look at himself in the mirror to see if he's different than he was ten minutes ago."

"He's sure enough different than he was a year ago. He may never be like other kids his age, but that's okay, too. We have a special kid, and now he's mine as well as yours," Lucas said.

"Yes, he is, and, honey, my heart is right here, and it always will be," Vada whispered. "I love you, Lucas Ryan."

"And I love you, Mrs. Lucas Ryan." He smiled.

Don't miss the other Ryan brothers in

SECOND CHANCE AT
SUNFLOWER RANCH
and
TEXAS HOMECOMING.

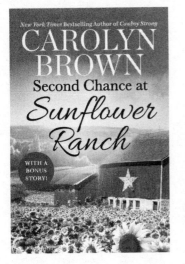
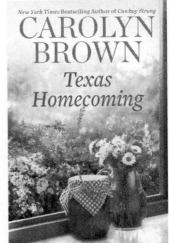

About the Author

Carolyn Brown is a *New York Times* and *USA Today* bestselling romance author and RITA finalist who has sold more than eight million books. She presently writes both women's fiction and cowboy romance. She has written historical and contemporary romance, both stand-alone titles and series. She lives in southern Oklahoma with her husband, a former English teacher who is not allowed to read her books until they are published. They have three children and enough grandchildren to keep them young.

For a complete listing of her books (series in order) and to sign up for her newsletter, check out her website at carolynbrownbooks.com or catch her on Facebook/Carolyn BrownBooks.